A/P
August 2019

Pre-Cat

When Glory Met Jerry

D1605852

GERRY BARTLETT

Dedication

This book is dedicated to Gloria McDowell Ray.
Gloria died at the age of 94 the week I finished the
final draft of WHEN GLORY MET JERRY.
She led a full and interesting life and was always
convinced I named Gloriana after her.
Who knows? Maybe I did.

Gerry Bartlett
http://gerrybartlett.com

ONE

London, 1604

How do you like it here, Gloriana?" The voice was barely a whisper.

I woke up with tears on my cheeks. That dream again. Or was it a memory? Michael St. Clair had found me lying in the gutter. He'd fought the boys who'd stolen the jewel holding my strange costume together and beat them off with his cane. Then he'd wrapped me in his cloak and carried me to his rooms. He'd saved me that night. Why? I'd never know. I was just grateful he'd loved me and never cared that I had no memories except for that name, a whisper in the dark.

"Gloriana! Hurry, Becks is looking for you. He's got a ripped sleeve and he'll be on stage in moments." Sire Goodall, the stage manager, nudged me with his boot and I surged to my feet. I was living here on borrowed time. If Master Shakespeare found out I was sleeping in the dressing area, he'd send me packing. Not that he was harsh, it was just that he had rules. And if one of us lived here at the Globe Theater, there'd soon be a dozen making the area behind the stage home.

I hurried to find Becks, one of the actors, and quickly began the repair. My clumsy but decent enough way with a needle was really the only reason the company had let me stay on after Michael was killed in a nasty accident. I'd take their pity. What choice did I have?

I also put up with the crude remarks and sly touches by the men when I wore a costume cut low in the bosom. Shakespeare encouraged the women who served his actors to stroll around the audience in the interval and jolly them when the night's play wasn't going well. He'd been trying out a new comedy this week, changing lines so often the actors were complaining.

"I'll be twizzled. If I don't get a laugh this night, I may just split my hose and show me bum. That always gets 'em going." Becks complained to one of the other players. "I can't remember from one night to the next what I'm to say. Ow!" He stayed my hand and studied me closely. "Girl, when did you last break your fast? Your hand is shaking and you look as pale as the drapery the ghost wears in the second act."

"Oh, did you think that prick was an accident? Mind your own hands, sirrah." I looked to where he'd managed to rest his fingers on my breast before I'd stabbed him with my needle. He was right though. I was near to starving. "I will eat when you lose your lines and stand with your hands in the air looking for help from the gods. Then they'll be throwing rotten fruit like they always do. There's usually a good apple or two that rolls back stage."

"Cheeky wench." He swatted my bottom, not afraid of my needle at all. "How long has Michael been gone now?"

"Almost a year." I looked around. "Please. Don't say anything to the master. I think he's forgotten that I'm not one of the wives who belong here."

"He's not forgotten, Gloriana."

I winced and turned slowly. It was the master himself. I curtsied, giving him a good look down my bodice. Master Shakespeare did like a woman with a nice pair of titties or so my Michael had always claimed. I hoped that would soften him. But I'd fasted too often and had lost too much flesh.

Either that or my dingy shift put him off.

He frowned as he studied me in my loose gray gown. It was the same one I'd slept in and I'd not bothered to do much more than shove my hair under a cap.

"I've given you plenty of time to mourn, I believe."

"You've been very generous, sir." I took a steadying breath and almost choked. Becks thought bathing unhealthy and he reeked of sweat and the cologne he doused himself with each night. I prayed he didn't burst the seam on his hose. I surely didn't want to stitch *those* noisome things.

"Make yourself presentable then see if you can find a protector. It's high time you moved on." Shakespeare eyed the bunched fabric where I'd tried to repair Becks' sleeve. "Your needlework isn't exactly earning your keep."

"But, master..." I wilted under his stern look.

"If I could, I would put you in this play. Certainly a comely wench would be better than what I have to work with." Shakespeare shook his head. "You think I don't know you helped Michael learn his lines? You have a good memory, Gloriana, and are well spoken. Someday, mayhap the laws will change and women will be allowed on the stage. Come see me then and I will write a part for you. Until then, your best notion will be to find a man who can afford to keep you in style."

"Thank you, master. You have been very generous to let me stay this long. I know that." So there it was. My time was up here. I would not shed bitter tears. The mending could be taken over by the wives of the actors easily enough though they'd complain about it.

Becks raised an eyebrow, took my hand, and bent over it. "Surely Gloriana can have another day or two, Will. There might be someone close at hand who could arrange a place for her." He turned over my hand and kissed my palm.

I could barely control my shudders. His codpiece jumped and Shakespeare nodded, seemingly appeased for the moment.

"I hope you spend as much time learning your lines as

you do tending to your bedmates, Timothy Beckham. Perhaps Gloriana can help you with the lines at least." Shakespeare strode off to speak to his star, Richard Burbage.

"What say you? Come with me to my rooms tonight, Gloriana, and I'll show you what you've been missing since poor Michael departed this mortal coil." Becks patted that dreadful codpiece, overacting even in his effort to seduce me.

"And what would your lady wife have to say to the matter, I wonder?" I knew he had two children and another on the way.

"Packed her off to her mum in the country for her lying in just yestereve." He licked his full lips. Some would call him handsome with his dark beard and wicked smile. He certainly had no trouble finding mistresses when his wife was not about to keep an eye on him. "I am known to be a lusty bedmate. Ask the other women here. You will not be disappointed, my lady." He gave me one of his exaggerated bows.

"Oh, yes. I've heard you have sampled many here. Your poor wife. Or mayhap she encourages you to swive elsewhere to spare her your attentions." I looked him over. I doubted he had much care for any but his own pleasure.

"Come now, Gloriana. I've had no complaints." He strutted like he was cock of the walk as he circled me, taking my measure. I was not too thin or too dirty for him. "Why, I've a mind to buy you a meat pie on the way to my lodgings as well. What say you?"

"A meat pie? You do know how to tempt a woman, Becks. But I'd have to be knocked senseless before I'd ever lie with you, sir." I flounced away, sure I'd probably doomed myself to working in a bawdy house. God, the man reeked! Mayhap I did, too, since there was no bathing here, just a jug of water and a rag when I got lucky. I had often confounded Michael with my need for cleanliness. He had joked that wherever I came from, it had obviously been a place with none of the superstitions that many of the theater folks had about immersing themselves in water. I yearned for a thorough cleansing but had no idea why.

My grand exit was ruined when I ran smack into one of the other women lurking about. Maggie claimed she was married to the short plump actor who filled the women's roles in Shakespeare's plays. Their marriage was a sham that we all pretended to believe since her man clearly preferred male lovers. We held the secret because he was a decent actor and we had no wish to see him hang for his sins. She grabbed my arm and dragged me to a dark corner.

"Gloriana, you cannot afford to be so choosy. Becks may smell like a cess pit but he's well paid. Jenny says he has fine rooms and is quick to find his satisfaction. After, he sleeps like the dead." Maggie shook my arm. "You could do worse."

"I suppose. But for how long?" I heard my stomach moan for want of food. How long could I continue like this? Hoping for a stray piece of fruit or the kindness of one of the company? "Becks' wife will be back and show me the door soon enough. Am I brought so low, Maggie, that I'd lie with him for a meat pie?" I sniffed. "I'd sooner sell myself on the corner." I looked down and tugged at my shapeless dress. "What am I saying? Who'd pay more than ha'pence for *this*?"

"Michael would be angry to hear ye speak so." Maggie dug in a pile of cloth and pulled out a piece of emerald green velvet. "I've been saving this. It won't fit me now as I'm too fond of meat pies meself. There's a full house tonight with many of the men in the King's court from Scotland come to see the new play." She grinned and gave me a nudge. "Lusty men in kilts? There are fine pickings."

"I reek, Maggie, almost as much as Becks does." I couldn't deny it.

"I saw this coming, dearie, and fetched some water for you to freshen up. You can put on that dress and stroll out between acts. There's bound to be a man who's looking to set up a handsome woman while he's in town to serve the king. Why shouldn't it be you?" Maggie shook my arm in case I thought to be stubborn about this.

"I hate…" Starving. Because that was the hard truth I had to face. And the velvet was beautiful even if the hem was a bit dusty. I saw in Maggie's face that it was a dress that held special memories for her and I pressed it carefully against my breasts. "It's beautiful, Maggie, and just the color I would choose if I had coin for such a fine piece." I blinked back tears. So I'd come to this. I'd parade my wares and hope that whatever man thought to sample them would treat me kindly.

"Come now. There's a sliver of soap and a cloth next to the pail in the corner. I have a chemise too, that will fit you. Fine lawn. The play is set to start. By the time the first act is over, you should be ready to take a turn and see whose eyes you can catch." Maggie led me to her corner and handed me her own comb. "Mind now, look for kindness. Hard eyes will not serve. You must find a man who will be gentle with you."

"I may not have a choice in the matter." I glanced around and realized no one was watching us. I threw off my filthy dress and stood in my worn shift. I had sold everything I had worth anything months ago, even my petticoats. I scrubbed myself all over, inhaling the sweet scent of roses from that bit of soap. I smiled at Maggie.

"Lovely, isn't it? I found it in one of the dressing rooms. One of Will's doxies left it. Use it all if ye need to." Maggie leaned against the wall as I tugged on the pretty clean shift. It was fine, sheer and hid nothing. "Ye are too thin, Gloriana. I'm sorry I don't have anything to feed ye."

"So am I." I sighed as I pulled the velvet over my head next. The dress laced up the front and was tight, showing most of my breasts. Well, that was probably for the best. Michael had always said they were my best bits.

"Ye look a treat, Gloriana," Maggie said after we'd fussed with my hair, finally leaving it tumbling down my back for lack of hairpins. Michael had always praised my golden locks anyway. Too bad they were dull from lack of a good wash. "Here, see if these fit." She handed me a pair of worn slippers.

I hugged her. "They're a bit loose but we can stuff a rag in each toe. I'll not forget this, Mag. When I'm mistress of a rich man, I'll come and find you. Bring you meat pies aplenty."

She laughed and patted her wide hips. "You do that. I won't turn them down." She cocked her head. "Ah, there's Horace's giggle. This is where he's playing the lady to Beck's foolish lover. That means they're almost to the end of the act. Are ye ready to show yourself to the men?" She adjusted my bodice, pushing up my breasts until I could almost see the pink of my nipples. "Flaunt those bubbies, dearie. Most men are silly about such things."

"Don't I know it." I took a breath and wished for a handkerchief or bit of lace to hide them. "All right, there's the curtain. Wish me luck."

"Luck." She kissed me on one cheek then pinched both of them. "Rosy cheeks don't hurt. Bite your lips too." She shoved me toward the stage door. "Outside. The toffs like to take the air."

I stumbled outside, holding up my skirt so it didn't slide through the mud or hit the stream of waste running down the middle of the alley. I could feel the stones through my thin slippers and it was cold. No shawl of course. Even if I had one that wasn't soiled and tattered, how would the more than dozen men gathered in the alley have been able to see what I had to offer if it covered my beautiful scandalous dress?

They would be able to see, thanks to the many lanterns strung across the alley, lighting the area. A blind beggar coaxed a merry tune from his whistle, earning a few pennies for his efforts, and it was a party atmosphere outside the Globe. I gathered my courage and found a smile. It wouldn't do to look as terrified as I felt, now would it? I lifted my chin and took a step forward, nodding to the vendors as I eyed a cluster of men drinking wine. What would I say? Was it too late to turn back and beg Master Shakespeare for more time?

Of course I wasn't the only woman to venture here. Other ladybirds, better prepared than I, strolled through the crowd, plying their fans and laughing up at the men who talked and drank in groups near the theater doors. Wine sellers were doing a brisk business and so were other vendors. The smell of one of those delicious meat pies made my stomach groan loudly.

"Lass, is that an empty stomach I'm hearing?" A man appeared next to me. He'd been so quiet that he startled me and I squeaked in surprise.

"Oh, I didn't see you, sir." I kept my hand over my chest. Surely my stomach hadn't been *that* loud. A glance and I was reassured that no one else seemed to have noticed my blasted pains.

"And your answer?" He was tall and clearly one of the Scots. He wore a kilt of blue and green plaid and a black waistcoat embroidered with fine silver thread. There was a fall of beautiful lace at his neck and wrists. His jacket was a rich dark green velvet and his sword proclaimed him one of the nobility. A toff indeed. Only a lord could carry a sword in London.

"Hunger." I managed a laugh, sure my cheeks were very rosy now. "I fear I forgot to break my fast this eve."

"Then let me remedy that." He waved at the vendor who hurried over to us. "A meat pie for the lady." He flipped a coin at the woman and then selected a plump pie wrapped in a cloth.

"Oh, you shouldn't--" I couldn't say the rest. My mouth watered as the smell of meat and pastry wafted up to me. He simply thrust the pie into my hand.

"Eat. Now. You look almost ill." His smile was gentle. "Women shouldn't deny themselves meals to stay small. I like a woman with generous curves." He slid a warm hand around my waist, as if to prop me up. I didn't mind. My legs were unsteady with hunger and my thoughts were all on that pie.

"Oh. I didn't, that is--" I lifted the food to my lips. To my shame I bit quickly, almost forgetting to chew before I took another bite. Before I could stop myself I had devoured the entire thing before I remembered to delicately, I hoped, dab my face with the cloth and brush away any errant crumbs. "Thank you, sir. You were right. It was foolish of me to try to avoid a meal."

"I enjoy watching a woman with a lusty appetite." He gestured and the woman handed him another pie. "Take this for later. I wouldn't like to think you went to bed hungry."

"Oh, you are too kind. That's not necessary." Now my pride stung. He must think me desperate. It might be true but… I lifted my chin and really looked at him. Oh, but he was handsome. His eyes were as dark as was his hair. He wore it unpowdered and long, tied back with a ribbon. Were his eyes kind? I decided they were. He'd fed me after all. I couldn't afford pride, truth be told.

"Are you going to spout nonsense about pride?" He smiled, showing straight white teeth. He'd obviously seen my struggle. Either that or he was reading my mind. What a foolish thought!

"I won't listen to it," he continued. "Now tell me your name, beauty."

Beauty. That certainly softened me. "It's Gloriana. Gloriana St. Clair. And yours?"

"Jeremiah Campbell. I serve the king here."

"King James." I took a step back when his lace sleeve brushed my arm. Too close. "So you are far from home."

"Aye, I am that. From the Highlands in Scotland. And you? You don't speak as if you are London born." He moved close again. This time his wool kilt touched my skirt. He was so tall and masculine. His broad shoulders spoke of a warrior, a man with real strength, not like the actors I knew who pretended to play a soldier on stage, as my Michael had done many times. Michael had used false armor and broad gestures to show his might. This man looked as if he could crush an opponent with his bare hands.

I shivered. What had he asked? "Of course I'm from London. I speak as I do because my late husband was an actor. Anyone who stays in or near the Globe soon learns to speak with care or risk Master Shakespeare's displeasure." I saw people going into the theater. "The play is about to start again. You won't want to miss it."

"Perhaps I don't care if I see it or not. Men dressed as women pretending to be lovers?" His gaze lingered on my bodice, making my breath come faster. The dress was laced so tight across my breasts they were like to pop free. "I'd much prefer to look at a real woman." His smile made me think he'd much rather be doing, not looking. The word "lovers" hung in the air between us.

"But I'm sure you will enjoy the next act, sir." I glanced at the theater. I was losing my nerve. Perhaps another night . . . "'Tis most amusing."

He gestured toward the stage door. "Of course you wish to go in. You're shivering. Do you have a cloak inside? May I get it for you, lass?"

"No, I don't have one." I hated to admit that. "Just a shawl. I'd rather not…"

"Ah, say no more. It doesn't match your gown. I have sisters. I understand." He took off his own short cloak and set it on my shoulders. "There. Is that better?"

"Yes, and I thank you." It smelled like him. Like man and wool and a hint of something dark and mysterious. Silly of me. What could be mysterious about a simple man in a kilt?

"Will you walk with me?" He held out his arm.

I glanced around. We were alone in the alley except for a few vendors counting their coins. Maiden Lane was just steps away. His smile coaxed me and his eyes… Yes, they softened as they swept over my body, lingering again on my bodice. I left the cloak open, reminding myself of why I'd come. What harm could a walk do? And there might not *be* another night when an interested man singled me out so quickly. I could not afford to hesitate.

"Yes, I will." I still held the second meat pie, a firm reminder of what this man had done and could still do for me. I took his arm. We strolled to the end of the alley until we reached the entry to the wider lane. I took a breath of the cold night air. The smells were a little better here--some foul, most better not identified. I turned to him, my smile dying when I saw him reach for his sword.

"Don't move, Gloriana. I'll return in a moment." With a move so fast I could have sworn he leaped an impossible distance, Jeremiah Campbell faced a pair of armed men who had jumped out of a dark doorway and into our path. Metal clanged and sparks flew as his sword hit a knife, knocking it to the ground.

I gasped, falling back against the stone wall, as a man screamed and clutched his belly, desperately trying to hold himself together as blood pooled around him. I stuffed a fist in my mouth, trying not to retch when the man died in front of me. The other man swung his sword, the ring of metal on metal loud in the air.

"Help! Someone help!" I screamed. Would no one come to aid the Scotsman? But it seemed the lane was suddenly deserted as the two men circled each other, lunging, their swords clashing. They tried to stab each other in the way I'd seen on stage, only this was deadly, not play acting at all. They struggled, pushing against each other until a sword flew across the stones and a dagger appeared in the stranger's hand.

"He has a knife!" I shrieked.

I needn't have bothered. The Scot's fist closed around the other man's wrist and I heard a sharp crack, then a curse, before the attacker stumbled and fled down the street. I fell back, propped against that wall. My heart thundered and I realized I had crushed the meat pie in my fist. I gagged, trying desperately not to lose the first decent thing I'd had to eat in more than a month.

"It's over, Gloriana. Are you all right?" Jeremiah drew

me against him and pulled me back toward the alley. Of course none of the tradesmen there had ventured out to help. They knew better than to interfere with a fight or to show one of the king's men that they might carry their own weapons.

"All right?" I staggered, not sure I wasn't going to swoon, then shook my head. "You just killed a man."

"I had no choice." He leaned me against the wall and ran his hands over my shoulders. "Let me get you some wine."

"I—no!" I breathed through the urge to cast up my accounts and finally looked up into his face. "Are you hurt?"

"No, not at all. Sorry you had to see that. I am sure you took a bad fright. 'Tis not the first time I've been attacked since I've been in London. It seems some people don't like the Scots here with King Jamie. A more prudent man would put off his plaid, but I am proud of my clan colors." He had obviously called for the vendor and now put a goblet of wine to my lips. "Drink. It will settle your stomach."

I did as he asked, sipping carefully. The wine was sweet, which was almost more than I could stand, but it did warm my insides. I took the goblet from his hand and drank it down.

"Would you like some more?" He drew his thumb across my lips where I must have spilled a drop of wine.

That intimate touch made me shiver and sway toward him. Was it the strong spirits? Or the gleam in his dark eyes? He was clearly excited after routing his foes. Men! Yes, he'd want to celebrate his victory with a lusty romp in his bed. Michael had been randy too, after a successful night trodding the boards.

This was what I'd come out here for, wasn't it? I should give him a seductive smile now, throw back my shoulders and offer him a good look at the swells of my breasts. Instead, I pulled his cloak tight around me.

"More wine?" He took the empty goblet from my hand and set it on the stones at our feet.

"No, but thank you. Were those the king's enemies who attacked you?" I wanted to keep him talking. Blood ran down the middle of the alley. Not far away were the feet of the man he'd killed without a second thought. I shuddered. I wasn't used to such violence.

Then again, I had to admire the way he'd vanquished his foes. He'd been so strong and fearless. And had protected me as well as himself. Was that reason enough to lie with a stranger? *Don't be a fool. You have many more reasons than that to allow him to seduce you.*

"The king's enemies or mine. There's a neighboring clan from home that my family has been warring with for years. But those men tonight weren't Scots. They could have been hired to ambush me I suppose but 'tis not a Scot's way to send others to do our killing." He shook his head. "No matter. Obviously they should have sent more than two for that job." He grinned and put his hands on my shoulders. "I'm that sorry you were frightened, lass. There was no need. Louts like that are easily dealt with as you saw."

I blinked. Impossible. His smile. I'd admired his straight white teeth before. But now? I took a breath, the blood of that dead assassin fresh in the air. Blinked then looked again. His eyes narrowed and he stopped smiling. But it was too late. There was only one lantern here but I'd seen what he was hiding. Jeremiah Campbell no longer had the perfect teeth from before that fight in Maiden Lane. Now he had two enormous fangs sprouting from his upper jaw, pressing against his upper lip and changing its shape.

I reached up, as if touching them would make them go away. He jerked back his head, proof enough for me that those terrible, frightening things were not going to disappear.

Oh, God. The alley grew dim and the meat pie slipped from my fingers. I'd just spent the last few minutes trying to seduce a monster.

TWO

"You will not go into a swoon." He commanded me.

I steadied myself. "What are you?" I shoved off his hands. There were people near enough that a scream would bring them running. Though they certainly hadn't stirred themselves when a sword fight had gone on just steps away. God's blood, a dead body still lay nearby and there was little interest in it except to a young boy who crept close, hoping to steal the hat and boots that could sell for good money in the stalls.

"Stay here." He turned, ignoring my question. "You there, lad!" He tossed a coin at the boy who had managed to snatch the cap off the dead man's head. "Take what you want from the body but bring any scrap of parchment you find to me."

"Aye, sir." The ruffian got busy, stripping off the boots first, a real prize, then going through the cloak and waistcoat pockets. He seemed not a bit put off by the blood soaking the man's shirt and pantaloons. He grunted, his grimy face alight when he pocketed several coins then pulled out a scrap of paper and brought it to the Scot. "Here ye be, sir. Nothing else but the clothes on 'is back and a sticker." He nodded toward a dagger he'd left by the man's bare foot.

"Keep the knife." Jeremiah frowned. "Mayhap it will come in handy for you." He flipped the boy another coin then studied the paper.

I was shaking, trying to come to terms with what I had seen. This man, whatever he was, didn't plan to let me go. He kept a hand on the wall beside my head, between me and the vendors who were setting up for the next interval and gossiping among themselves. If they had any curiosity about what had happened at the end of the alley, they'd learned early on to keep it well hidden.

I knew from theater gossip that many things had happened out here—murder, rape, even a baby born to one of the trollops unlucky enough to ply her trade in the street nearby. The wine and pie sellers fought hard for a place here where there was good coin to be made. They held their places by keeping their mouths shut and their goods fresh.

Jeremiah was studying the scrap of paper and frowning. "Can you read?"

I shook my head. I wanted to know, though it was common enough for women not to have the skill. Michael had started teaching me but had spent little time on it. He claimed I must have lost my memory of schooling along with my other memories since I was so eager to learn. I had no recollection of parents or birthplace. So we made up a background to satisfy the curiosity of the theater folk. Even a birthday, choosing the day he'd found me in that gutter. It had amused Michael. He claimed it was as if he'd given birth to me. I'd tried to remember my past but the effort always gave me an aching head.

"I doubt the ruffians who attacked me could either. There is one word and a drawing. Not sure what it means." He showed me a crude symbol. "Do you recognize it, Gloriana?"

"What? Do you think I am part of a plot against you? You approached *me* this night." I tried to duck under his arm. It was as I thought--he grabbed my waist and kept me from darting away toward the stage door.

"I didn't accuse you, did I?" He smiled and his teeth were now as even as my own.

I looked up into his dark eyes. Had I imagined those enormous things in his mouth? Mayhap I'd been dizzy from lack of food and then there had been the wine. My head had never been quite right since the night Michael had rescued me. He'd always thought I had hit it on the rough stones in the alley where he'd found me. It was easy enough to blame my memory loss on that. There were simpletons wandering the streets begging for pennies who had taken hard blows on their noggins. Thank the gods Michael had taken me in and spared me that.

Now I tried to get free but Jeremiah still held me firmly. "Am I your prisoner?"

"Nay, Gloriana. But I had hoped our evening was not over." He shoved the paper into the leather pouch tied onto his belt at his waist then turned his hold into a soothing touch. "You are very lovely."

I took a steadying breath. He had bought me food and tossed coins at the boy as if they were nothing. Those coins could have bought me a room for a night, maybe more than one night. If I could ignore the stench of death in the air, Jeremiah himself seemed clean and fresh. When he had fought off his attackers I'd seen how strong, how brave he was. Now he moved closer, pushing aside the cloak so he could gaze upon my breasts. He just looked, and my nipples tightened, stirred by the lust in his eyes.

"I have never done this before." I braced my hands on his jacket. Oh, it was the finest velvet, the richness worn by a lord. "I don't know you."

"Done what? Have I told you what I want yet, Gloriana?" He teased me, his grin charming. "Perhaps it is just a stroll down Maiden Lane. Have you not walked there before?"

I dropped my hands to place one on his arm when he offered it as any gentleman would to a lady. I appreciated the courtesy. I was nothing but a strumpet from the theater yet he was making an effort to give me my dignity. I found myself warming to him. It made me bold. "And why do I think a stroll down the lane is likely to end at your rooms, my lord?"

"You elevate me, madam. I am merely Jeremiah to you. My father is the laird of my clan. I am his heir but do not expect to inherit for a verra long time." He covered my hand with his then carefully steered me around that body and the boy who'd decided the pantaloons were not too soiled to sell and was struggling to pull them off the dead man.

I held my skirt out of harm's way and looked away. No dignity in death here.

"Laird. That is a fine title. Is there a castle then, in Scotland?" I heard myself making conversation until we were safely past the stench of death. He answered, telling me about his family's fine estate in the Highlands. He seemed determined to charm me. To get me into his bed? It was bound to be more comfortable than my pallet on the hard boards behind the stage. If I said no this night would he turn to someone else? The doxy with the flame red hair who'd watched us in the alley would be eager to take my place.

I could not afford to play the coy maiden. I must be sensible. Most would say giving my body to him would be a fair exchange for a warm bed and food. I could close my eyes and pretend he was Michael if my nerve began to fail me. If my luck held, he would be kind and gentle. If not? I shivered and clung to his arm. No, I would not allow that terrifying thought to send me scampering away like a scared rabbit. While he'd been a fierce fighter, ready enough with his sword when facing his enemies, thus far he'd shown me nothing but care and concern for my welfare. Surely that tender handling would continue whilst I was in his bed.

I walked beside him the length of the lane until he stopped.

"Well, Gloriana. We are at the moment when you must decide. Will you come to my rooms with me? Make me a happy man?" His clasp on my hand tightened. "I will aim to give you pleasure as well."

I couldn't breathe, my heart pounding with such alarm I feared I would swoon after all. I couldn't speak, just stared at him, trying to form the words that would see to my future.

"The choice is yours, Gloriana." He seemed to be reading my mind again. "I willna force you. Say me nay and I will return you to Master Shakespeare and the Globe. But before you decide, let me see if I can help you make up your mind." He pulled me into a dark doorway. No one could see us as his hands went around my waist and he pulled me close, so close my breasts pressed against his chest.

"This is difficult for me, Jeremiah. I am not a doxy, taking coin for what should be…" I couldn't say more, struggling to find my courage and to see him and what he was thinking with his face in shadow. "I can't--"

He leaned down and kissed me, taking my mouth with his. Cool lips, skilled as well. His tongue slipped inside, finding mine and playing with it until I gasped and had to hold onto his shoulders to keep from falling. I struggled to breathe as he seemed to drink me in. On and on he kissed me. Had I ever found this much pleasure before with just this? Michael hadn't been one for kissing, wanting to "get on with it."

Jeremiah finally dragged his mouth from mine to trace a path across my cheeks to my neck, behind my ear and down to the swell of my bosom. I shivered with feelings that had nothing to do with the cold everything to do with a rising need. He didn't talk, just kissed his way up to my mouth again. Gods, but the man was wicked with his tongue and his lips. I held onto his hair, knocking his hat askew as I stood on my toes to get ever closer to him. What a wondrous thing, this kissing.

"Gloriana." He groaned and lifted me to fit my body even more perfectly against his. One hand held my bottom and the other stayed around my waist. I could feel that he wanted me, his need hard against my stomach. He wasn't rushing me, just letting me get used to the taste of him as we kissed and kissed and heat rose between us.

Finally he leaned back and looked at me. His mouth was damp, his eyes half closed. "What say you?"

I knew there was something I should remember. Some warning. The fight. After the fight… But my body ached and my mouth was full of his taste. The pleasure he'd given me pushed everything else out of my mind. I took a breath and my breasts, tender and swollen, pressed even more firmly against his waistcoat. All I could think about was being naked with him, letting him inside to satisfy this yearning that made me forget I'd ever been afraid of him.

"Take me home with you, Jeremiah. Not for coin. Never for that. I will lie with you for pleasure." I took his hand and laid it on my breast.

He grinned, gently thumbing my nipple before he closed the cloak I wore, his cloak. A quick kiss then he took my hand, pulling me along until we reached another alley. He unlocked a door and led me inside, picking up a torch and lighting it with a flint he pulled from that pouch at his waist. He led the way down a rough stair lined with stone until we came to a passageway. We walked along for several minutes, his torch casting shadows that made me wonder why he'd choose to live in such a place. Defense against those enemies perhaps? They would certainly never think to look for him here, under the ground.

Finally we came to a massive wooden door covered with iron brackets that made it seem suitable for a dungeon. Jeremiah lifted a heavy knocker and banged it, three times then two. A signal?

A huge man with a plaid thrown over his shoulders answered the door. He was dressed simply other than that. A servant perhaps. "Jeremiah, you're late."

"Gloriana, this is Fergus. My father sent him with me from home. To watch over me." Jeremiah's laugh was not amused. "I believe you can safely leave me alone with this woman, Fergus. Unless you think she looks too dangerous."

"Mistress Gloriana." Fergus bowed. "Laugh if you

GERRY BARTLETT

wish, Jeremiah." He frowned when Jeremiah tossed him his sword. "What's this? Blood?"

"A minor annoyance. I took care of it." He handed him the paper. "One carried this. Mean anything to you?"

Fergus studied it with a frown. "Nay." He put it in his pocket then picked up a cloth and kept the sword with him. "I'll see what I can find out and leave you to your sport." He stepped outside and I heard the door shut and lock.

"Did he lock us in?" I was tempted to try the handle.

"His idea of protection." Jeremiah slid his cloak off my shoulders and dropped it on a table. "Don't let it concern you." He pulled me deeper into a room made comfortable with beautiful rugs on the stone floor and furniture facing a huge fireplace. "Come close to the fire."

"Where are we? Under the ground, I know. Why?" I looked around. No windows of course. But this was no dungeon. There were fine pieces everywhere. Jeremiah was obviously wealthy. But where did the air come from? I could see several doorways. I had to stop feeling closed in. The room was large and there was more than one. No reason to think I was trapped. I inhaled and realized there was fresh air coming from somewhere. God knew it was better than the rank odors of the place where I'd been forced to sleep for the past twelve months.

Of course the worst or best was yet to come. I couldn't look at the man who'd brought me here. Instead, I walked around the room, pretending to examine books I could not read, touching a glass jug here, a fine piece of cloth there.

"Fergus thinks we are safer here. It is easier to protect us with only one way in and out." Jeremiah had filled a goblet with wine and brought it to me. "Drink. It will help put you at ease."

"Won't you drink with me?" I sipped the wine. It was very fine and did make the knot in my stomach untangle a bit.

"I am used to being here." He smiled. "Come, sit in front of the fire." He pulled me to the velvet couch facing

26

the fire and sat beside me. "Where were we?" He slid his arm around me and kissed my bare shoulder. "Ah. Lovely."

"You are very determined to get on with it, aren't you?" I set the wine glass on a nearby table. Would this be Michael's way after all? A quick tumble? Perhaps that would be best. Then a fine sleep for the first time in a year. I was sure there was a bed somewhere nearby. But that thought brought only dread. I realized the excitement from those kisses in the alley had vanished and I was nervous again. He was very big, masculine. I had to handle this carefully or risk angering him. "Would you be disappointed if I asked you to go slowly?"

"Very disappointed." He leaned in and kissed my neck then inhaled deeply. "You smell like roses and woman. Pleasing."

"Thank you. That's the scent of my soap." I leaned back against the cushions as he kissed me again. A seducer then. And so very, very good at it. Why was I resisting? I tried to relax. When he slipped his hand inside my bodice, palming my breast, I found the pleasure again, my breath catching.

"So very beautiful." He pushed the velvet down so he could use his tongue then his lips to pull my nipple into his mouth.

"Jeremiah." I ran my fingers through his hair, pulling the satin ribbon out of it and casting it aside. He'd tossed his hat on the table when we'd come inside. He moved to my other breast and I landed on my back, my head on a pillow at the end of that couch. He lay on top of me, one hand pulling me up so he could bring my breast to his mouth and devour it. My body arched and I was on fire for him.

"Let me see all of you." He unlaced my bodice, pulling it open. "This must go." He reached as if to tear the shift.

"No!" I stayed his hand. "Have a care. This is a borrowed shift."

"Then you must take it off yourself." He grinned and sat up. "Be my guest." He helped me until I stood before him.

I looked down to where my dress gaped open to the waist. A simple shrug and the dress fell to the floor. I stepped out of it and carefully laid it across a nearby chair, then toed off my shoes and left them there as well. No stockings of course. Mine had been mended until they were the rags I'd stuffed into the toes of those borrowed shoes. When I looked back over my shoulder, I saw him staring at me. Yes, that shift was very sheer. When I turned around again, I would be as good as naked for him. And he sat there wearing every bit of his clothing except for his cloak.

I moved the dress and sat in the chair, my hands crossed over my breasts. "Mayhap I would be ready to take off my shift if you were more comfortable yourself, Jeremiah."

"Really?" He stood and took off his jacket. "Does that help?"

"The waistcoat as well, if you please." I made an airy gesture with one hand. I couldn't believe he'd dropped that rich jacket on the floor. I waited while he opened his buttons and discarded the waistcoat in the same careless manner.

"And then there is the shirt and collar. Such fine lace but it would be a shame to tear it in my ardor." I fanned my face with my hand, almost laughing at his haste to pull his shirt off over his head. Oh, but he had a fine broad chest. He'd obviously seen battle as scars marred the golden skin of his shoulder and low on his stomach as he strode toward me. He stopped mere inches from my chair.

"Look your fill, love." He still wore his plaid belted at the waist though he pulled the pouch from it and tossed it on a nearby table. I heard the clink of gold coins as it hit. I noticed he'd stripped off his stockings and shoes while I'd been losing my dress.

"I see you believe in saving the best for last." He grinned as he held out his hands.

"And have you as well? Saved the best for last?" I could see the bulge in his kilt. My God, if it wasn't the best, it was certainly the biggest.

"You will see, Gloriana, you will see." He lifted me to my feet and took my shift's hem, pulling it up carefully when I raised my hands over my head. Then it was off and I stood naked in front of him.

I started to cover my breasts with my hands again. No chance. He pulled me flush against him. Ah. Skin touching skin. He moaned. It felt wonderful that I could pull that sound of wanting from him. His hardness pressed between my legs and I needed the rough wool plaid to hit the floor, too. How did it fasten? I reached for it at his waist but didn't have time to find out. He swung me into his arms and carried me toward one of those dark doorways.

THREE

There was no fireplace in this room but it was obviously a bedchamber. A massive bed claimed pride of place against one wall. Only the firelight from the doorway allowed me to see shapes in the dark. Jeremiah stopped beside the bed then tossed me into the middle of it.

"Oh!" I lay there, stroking soft furs as he moved around the room. A candle bloomed to life next to the bed and I drew in my breath in surprise. He'd removed his belt, the plaid along with it, and was gloriously naked.

"You are a bonny lass." He stared down at me. "Should I light more candles?" He held a flint in one hand.

"No, please." I licked my lips. Though I liked seeing him, I felt shy as he studied my body. I thought to pull one of those furs over me.

"Don't cover yourself." He dropped to one knee on the bed. "I want to see all of you." He slid a hand over my shoulder and down one arm. He spread my hands wide so I was open to his gaze. "Don't move." He shook his head when I started to cover my breasts. "You are perfect. Though I think you could do with more meat pies. Fergus will bring in food when he returns. But that won't be for hours." He leaned down and kissed one of my nipples, making me gasp. "Will you mind waiting?"

"I think you can keep me well occupied until then." I couldn't believe I spoke so boldly. But he was making me feel flutters low in my belly when he stroked my stomach. He had a swordsman's hands with callouses on his fingers and palms. The roughness did delicious things to my skin as he touched me even lower.

"Aye, I will make sure of it." One of those fingers brushed my nether curls then eased inside me.

I writhed beneath his touch, grasping his soft hair when he kissed a path down my stomach. "Jesu, but you cannot mean to--" I had heard the women in the theater whisper of such but hadn't believed them. Now Jeremiah pulled my legs apart, draping them over his shoulders to kiss me deeply there.

"Gods!" I shrieked at the stroke of his tongue, my grip on his hair no doubt painful. Keeping him there or wrenching him away?

Of course I didn't want him to stop. I fell back, lost to rising desire that moved my hips. He held me firmly, using me as if as pleased by this as I.

"Stop! I cannot--" I arched off the bed, gripping the furs when something inside me crested and broke. He finally, finally pulled back and slid up my body. That smile, that satisfied look on his face. I turned away from it, my body shaking. When he gripped my hips to push inside firmly, possessing me, the pleasure pain was almost unbearable.

"Bastard!" I hit his shoulders with my fists but the way he filled me ... I closed my eyes when my body betrayed me, thrusting upward to meet him eagerly. My hands opened and I grabbed his shoulders, holding on. Now I was shameless in my craving to take and take while he used me. But wasn't I using him as well? I didn't care. Suddenly I was desperate to see his face. I prayed he would look down and see me, Gloriana, not a nameless slut to be used then cast aside.

To my shock, he stopped moving and gazed into my

eyes before he gently brushed my tangled hair back from my forehead.

"Ach, I do see you, lass. Gloriana, you are beautiful." He leaned down to kiss me, then nuzzled my neck before he began to move again.

I held on, my legs wrapped around his narrow hips. Joy filled my heart while pleasure swept over my body. Perhaps this would be all right. I could lie with this stranger and we would ease each other. It was a fair bargain. I had been lonely and scared. He thought me beautiful. I knew I was not, but I could at least give him as much pleasure as he'd given me. I touched his face, pulled his lips to mine and kissed *him* this time. When I ventured to use my tongue, I pricked it on his sharp teeth. What was this? Oh, no matter. His mouth went to my neck again and he thrust into me until I could barely gasp out his name.

"My lovely. I must taste you." He murmured just before he stroked my neck with his tongue. A sharp pain then a hard pull when he pressed his lips to my skin. I'd never felt such a thing. Was he trying to bite me? Surely not. He wrapped me in his strong arms as he took his pleasure, pounding into me until he found his release with a final groan of satisfaction.

I couldn't move, his weight crushing me. "Please, release me. I cannot breathe." That was the least of it. I fought tears at the throbbing in my neck. "Jeremiah!" I pushed at his head. The room darkened and I feared I might faint. "Let me go! I feel unwell."

He finally heard me. His lips brushed my neck then he sighed and pulled back. He leaned on his elbows, so masculine, so very handsome as he studied me. The scent of our joining and something sharp that I recognized but could not place, lingered in the air.

"You are pale. I'm sorry, Gloriana. I lost myself in the pleasure of tasting you." His own cheeks were flushed as he wiped his mouth, then reached for a goblet of wine he'd left beside the bed. "Here, drink." He threw a fur over me then helped me sit up. "It will help. Strong red wine."

"Help? What happened?" His words made little sense but I drank deeply then touched my neck. It was sore and torn. Then I noticed the back of his hand was streaked with blood. "Did you bite your lip?" I reached for him but he moved away.

"Nay." He took the goblet from me then lay beside me. "Here, let me take care of you." He leaned closer and stroked my neck with his tongue. Miraculously, all pain vanished.

I touched it and the wounds were gone as well. Had I imagined them? No, of course not. Yet they had disappeared as if by magic. "Jeremiah, what is happening here?"

"We enjoyed bedsport, Gloriana." He smiled and stared into my eyes.

I had that feeling again, as if I were falling under a spell. What nonsense. I tossed my hair and smiled, all my foolish worries had vanished. "Yes, indeed. You are a skillful lover."

He looked under the fur and ran his fingers down my side. "You are too thin. I hope Fergus brings back roast beef and fruit tarts. Perhaps some hot chocolate? Would you like that?"

"It sounds delicious." I would eat every bite and be glad of it. A quick romp in his bed and Jeremiah could well send me on my way after he fed me. Michael had taught me that was the way men treated such things. Get the deed done then off you go, there's a good girl. Dear God, what would I do if Jeremiah felt the same?

I sighed and ran a hand along his shoulder. My knee rested against his hip and his cock stirred. Bedsport was clearly still on his mind. I ached from the unaccustomed use of my body but it was a pleasant ache and I could certainly accommodate him again. I wondered if I should say or do something to encourage another go.

How long would he have me stay? Would I be back on the lane soon? What future did a trollop like me have? I determined to make this last as long as I could. I would not ask for coin. That would make me a whore. But I would do my best to please this man who'd saved me from walking the streets and landing with someone who might have given me rough treatment. I turned to him and smiled, tracing a path across that fine, broad chest.

"Bedsport. Yes, we had a fine time, didn't we?" I leaned over him to kiss his firm stomach. "You taught me something new this night. I wonder. Would it please you to have me kiss you as you kissed me?" I looked down to where he was already aroused.

"It most certainly would." He laughed and pulled me on top of him. "But first, my girl, I think we could both use a bath. What say you?"

I closed my eyes, wondering if I was dreaming. Not since I'd waked up on the stones of that alley and seen Michael fighting off thieves had I met anyone who *wanted* to bathe. Now here was a man who had suggested it? I opened my eyes and saw him smiling at me.

"There is a hip bath in the next room. Will you help me fill it? Or we could wait for Fergus to return." He said no more when I kissed him full on the mouth.

"Show me where to get water." I hopped off the bed and dragged his plaid around my shoulders. I staggered, the room spinning and my knees weak. Not surprising since the exercise I'd just enjoyed in Jeremiah's bed was more than I'd done in ages and with no more than a meat pie and wine in my belly. I gave him a flirtatious look, well aware that I was bare from the thighs down. Perhaps it would please him to see me half naked, dragging pails as we filled the bath. I laughed as I watched him carry the tub to the front of the fireplace. He handed me a kettle so I could heat water on the hob. I threw off the plaid when the tub was half full and sank into it with a sigh.

"Ah, this is heaven. I've not had more than a rag and a pail for bathing in an age." I took the cloth he handed me and the bar of plain soap and went to work. My hair! I slid under the water and gave it a good wash. It shamed me that the water was soon gray with my dirt. There was no chance Jeremiah would use this water on his own body after I was done. I scrubbed and scrubbed some more. Between my toes, My elbows. La, there was no part of me that didn't need to be rubbed raw.

"Gloriana, spare yourself." He stepped up to the side of the bath. "Let me dump this water and put in fresh." He frowned. "You have been ill-treated. I can see that." He held out his hand. "Come. I swear, you will have another clean bath and can just sit and soak in it."

"Truly?" I gazed up at him. He was being so kind, tears filled my eyes. No, that would never do. Men hated such displays. I took his hand and stepped out of the tub and into a cloth he had warmed next to the fire. If I could lose my heart over a simple kindness, mine had just dropped into the hands of this Scotsman.

He didn't answer me, just walked away with the heavy tub as if it weighed nothing, dumping water into a corner where it went down a hole in the floor. Then he quickly brought it back in front of the fire and filled it again while I just stood there, watching the play of firelight on his strong body. I couldn't look away from the strain of muscles in his arms and shoulders as he poured bucket after bucket of water into the tub. Jesu help me, I admired the way his fine buttocks and thighs moved as he bent over. He was a lovely figure of a man and seemed not to care that I gazed at his body as if he were a meat pie and I'd not eaten for days.

"There, 'tis ready for you." He turned and held out his hand.

"Only if you'll join me." I dropped the cloth on a chair then walked toward him. Oh, yes, his eyes darkened as he watched the sway of my hips. When my breasts brushed his chest as I took his hand and stepped into the water, his smile widened.

"It will be a snug fit." He studied my pose as I waited for him, one hand on my hip, the other held out in invitation.

"I'm sure we can manage." I leaned down and scooped up water, letting it stream down my body. He'd added a good bit of the hot water and the temperature was perfect. "Come, I will wash you." I picked up the cloth and soap from the hearth, aware that I was giving him a good look at my backside. "Front first? Or back?" My smile was as saucy as I could make it. God knew I'd never done anything like this before.

"As you wish." He stepped carefully into the water then sat, pulling me into his lap. Of course his cock was standing at the ready. Should I ignore it? Wash it? I settled astride, moving the cloth over his chest and shoulders. He leaned back and closed his eyes. "You are being very helpful."

"Not really. But I do like to be clean. And I like a clean man as well." I put more soap on the cloth and slipped it down his stomach. His eyes popped open.

"What's this now?" He grinned. "Are you playing with me?"

"Nay, sir. I think to make you comfortable." I rinsed the soap from the cloth and began again, at his shoulders, his chest, drawing circles around his brown nipples. Then I let that cloth travel below the water again. When I felt his cock jerk I dropped the cloth and took him in hand.

"Ah. Do you know what you are about?" He eyed me, smiling.

"Nay, but perhaps you could show me what pleases you." I placed one of his hands over mine. "Should I be firm? Or gentle?" I let him guide me as I ran my hand up and down his length.

"Firm but not--Christ!--like you're squeezing water from the cloth, Gloriana." He peeled away my fingers and showed me how he liked to be held. "Think of the rhythm we enjoyed before. Do you remember?"

"How could I forget?" I grinned, leaning forward to brush my nipples against his chest. He took the bait, lifting his head to kiss the slope of my breast. I moved my hand, quickening the pace. His groan of pleasure meant I was learning. When he released my hand to find the seam between my legs, I widened my stance.

He explored me with a clever finger, grinning when I squeaked my surprise that he'd found a spot that gave me instant excitement. "You are very lusty, Gloriana. That pleases me." He lifted me, until he was almost inside. "Ride me, lass. Bring us both pleasure."

"As *you* wish." I grabbed his shoulders and eased down, the novelty of the warm water, the hard man and this ride making me feel like a wanton. When I was fully seated, I looked into Jeremiah's eyes. He was studying me, as if trying to see into my soul. What would he read there? That I needed to be held? Told that this was not a sin, but a harmless way to see to my future? He pulled me close and kissed my lips, then murmured my name. It made me feel cherished.

Foolish. He hardly knew me. No, he didn't know me at all. But I took the false feeling and the comfort with it. Then I rode him, taking and giving pleasure until water splashed the stone floor and we both fell sated against each other. He finally rose from the tepid water and carried me to his bed, laying me down and covering me with furs before blowing out the candle.

It may have been hours or minutes later that I heard the rattle of the key in the lock and Fergus talking in a deep voice to Jeremiah. They were arguing. But that didn't bring me out of the warm cocoon of furs. What did was the smell of roast beef and hot chocolate. I couldn't lie abed when I was starving. I wrapped the length of plaid around me, still trying to look decent in the shadow of the doorway when I heard Fergus speak.

"You canna keep her here. I know you need blood, but for God's sake, Jeremiah, this is unwise."

"She will not betray us. She is staying. You may take her shopping during the day. Buy her clothes and trinkets. Then she and I will spend the night hours together. It is none of your concern." Jeremiah was obviously not taking orders from his servant.

"How do you know she is not sent here by the MacDonalds? She could be a spy and could very well sneak into your room and kill you while you sleep like the dead."

"You think I canna see into her mind? What do you take me for, Fergus? I am not so besotted by a fine pair of tits that I forget to be cautious." Jeremiah lowered his voice and I had to strain to hear him. "Now wait outside. She is stirring. I heard her move around the bedchamber and I'm sure she smelled her dinner."

"That's another thing. Am I to be her servant then? Fetch her meals?" There was more grumbling then a door slammed.

"Was that Fergus?" I decided it was best to walk into the main room as if I'd heard nothing. Indeed, some of what they'd said made no sense and my stomach was grumbling again. If Jeremiah thought he could read a woman's mind, he was beyond foolish. I'd let him believe what he wished if it gave me meals like the one set out on the table in front of the fire. "Something smells delicious."

"Come, break your fast." Jeremiah was dressed in pantaloons and a loose white shirt. "Sit and eat." He waved toward that table set for one.

"Won't you dine with me?" I sat in the chair he held for me.

"I ate while you slept." He smiled. "I'm sorry if Fergus woke you. He's not happy at our arrangement but I do not have to please him. He is supposed to do as I ask in service to my family."

"He does not act like a servant." I couldn't wait and sipped from the steaming cup of chocolate. Oh, I had never tasted anything so sweet and delicious. "This is wonderful."

"He gets it from a shop nearby. Please ignore his attitude. He has earned the right by his loyalty to speak his mind. But I know he will come around. Give him time." Jeremiah sat across from me. "Which is what I hope to speak to you about. Will you stay with me for a few days, maybe longer? I have been lonely in London. You have pleased me very much this night, Gloriana."

"Thank you, Jeremiah, I would like to stay. You have certainly pleased *me*." I reached for his hand. What a relief to have a few days without worrying about a place to lay my head at night. I looked around the room before picking up a knife and spearing a piece of beef. "I can help tidy your rooms if that will make Fergus feel better about my staying here. I wouldn't mind."

"Thank you. I couldn't ask you to become a housemaid, Gloriana. We will be fine." Jeremiah reached across and guided my hand to my mouth. "Eat. I swear I could count your ribs when we lay together."

"I have been having a difficult time since my husband died." I chewed the tender beef and swallowed. It was all I could do to keep from hastily stuffing the food into my mouth with both hands. It would shock him and perhaps make him change his mind about keeping me. So I took a breath then daintily speared a second bite. "You are saving my life, coming along when you did. I won't forget it. I don't know how to repay your kindness."

Jeremiah sat back. "Just eat, get your strength and health back. Fergus will take you shopping during the day while I am busy with court business. You can buy some pretty things then I will take you with me to meet some friends tomorrow night. We might even go to court and greet the king. Would you like that?"

"Are you sure? You want to introduce me to King James?" I dropped my knife. Was Jeremiah forgetting who and what I was? Or perhaps in Scotland taking one's mistress into society didn't matter. He must not be married. Unless…

"Do you have a wife back home? How will you introduce me?" I had no reason to complain, I just wanted to know my place.

"No wife, no child." He looked away and I could see there was more to tell that he chose not to share. He nodded and faced me again. "I will introduce you as a special friend. It is no one's business what we are to each other." He smiled, his eyes on my shoulder where the plaid had fallen, exposing the curve of my breast. "I will not mind appearing with a beautiful woman on my arm. How we met will not be mentioned. Is that clear?" He lost his smile. "If you want to help me, you will keep your eyes and ears open for any court gossip concerning my family, the clan Campbell or a clan called MacDonald."

"Of course. I will be happy to help you. Are the MacDonalds the clan that could have attacked you?" I picked up my knife again and began eating in earnest.

"Aye. We have feuded for years. But I doubt they would hire English thugs to do their dirty work for them. So we will listen for threats from other quarters as well. Hatred for a Scot. 'Tis not uncommon but that was a daring attack, next to the Globe. I would think they were common cutpurses except for the quality of their weapons." Jeremiah got up from the table and walked over to look through some documents.

How I wished I could read. God above, I had no doubt I could find gossip aplenty in notes at court and I'd not be able to tell an important one from a bit of nonsense. It was maddening. Would Jeremiah consider teaching me? It was too soon to ask. But I would strive to make him want to keep me around. It started with putting on flesh. So I cleaned my plate, sopping up beef juices with a hunk of bread then draining my chocolate. I leaned back, my stomach aching at the unaccustomed fullness. And I was drowsy. It was a delightful feeling. After living too long on the edge of starvation, I wanted to thank Jeremiah properly.

I strolled over to where he frowned at a piece of paper. "Hmm. I think I shall go back to bed. Will you join me?" I slid in front of him and ran a hand down his neck to where his shirt lay open.

He turned the paper over so I couldn't see what was on it. "Are you sure you canna read?"

"I told you so, didn't I?" I leaned up to kiss him behind his ear and let my plaid fall to the floor. "But I would dearly love to learn. When you have time, please teach me. But not now. Not when I am feeling so pleasantly full and eager to show you how much I like being here." I pulled him toward his bedchamber. "Come, Jeremiah." I looked over my shoulder and laughed. "I believe you have other things to teach me besides reading, do you not?"

He swatted my bottom. "Aye, I believe I do. You have no idea how long I have spent learning how to please a woman, Gloriana. No idea at all." And with that he drew off his shirt and tossed it aside. In moments he was naked and eager to start my education.

By the time I drifted off to sleep, I had indeed learned something new. The man was a bloody genius at pleasuring a woman. A bloody genius.

FOUR

I woke alone. Or so I thought. Until my feet hit something solid. A large black cat stood and stretched then stared at me with malevolent yellow eyes. It hissed before leaping off the bed and hurrying from the room.

"Jeremiah!" I looked around for the plaid I'd taken as my own but it was gone. Instead, that green dress and my chemise were lying on a chair next to the bed. While I wondered if I should just put them on, Fergus walked into the bedchamber, rubbing his dark hair and looking ill-used.

"Jeremiah is gone for the day, mistress. He asked me to take you around to the shops." He frowned. "Cover yourself."

As if I hadn't done that as soon as I saw his sour face. I held the furs to my chin. "I didn't hear him leave."

"No. He didna wish to disturb ye. Now get dressed while I go fetch ye something to eat." He glanced at the dress on the chair. "Where's your cloak?"

"I don't have one. Jeremiah let me wear his last night." I was ashamed I'd brought so little to this arrangement. I could see how disapproving Fergus was as well.

"Jeremiah seems to have taken to you so we'll buy one

while we're out. Is there something you need from the theater? He did say that's where he found you," Fergus said as if I'd been a stray dog his master had brought home.

"No, there's nothing, though I wouldn't mind leaving word there that I am fine and with a kind man. A friend might be worried when I didn't come back after the play." I looked away from the judgment I was sure to see in his eyes.

"Aye, we can go by there. I'll be back soon with your food. Be dressed when I see you next. There's water for a wash, though clearly someone had a fine time in the bath yester eve." He nodded at a pitcher and bowl on a table, then turned and left. I heard a key turn in the lock after the door closed to the passage outside.

My face burned. We had left the tub out, with water on the floor and wet cloths in front of the fire before we'd gone to bed. I should have gotten up and tidied things. Fergus would never be happy with my place here if I didn't strive to make less work for him. I climbed out of bed, washed quickly, and donned my clothes. I looked around for the black cat, but didn't see him. Of course the tub and our mess had been cleared away. A fire was going in the fireplace and I had a few minutes to explore what proved to be several rooms besides the two I'd already seen.

I found the retiring room with the hip bath, a chamber pot and the source of our water—a pipe coming out of the wall. I had seen such things before on a street lined with expensive houses. A spigot turned to fill a pail or bowl. Such luxury! There was a small room next to it with a bed that must belong to Fergus judging by the size of the clothes hanging from pegs in the stone walls. There was another room with a door that proved to be locked. Did Jeremiah keep his own clothes and gold there? I had no interest in stealing, of course, and turned away just as Fergus burst through the outer door carrying a laden basket that smelled like heaven to me.

"Stay away from that door, girl." He frowned and set the basket on the table where I'd dined the night before.

"That is not for you."

"I was looking for the cat. It slept on my feet." I stepped over to the basket and lifted the cloth. Fresh rolls and a pot of tea. Berries too. I couldn't believe I would be treated to such luxuries.

"He hides in nooks and crannies. Don't worry about him. He's been fed." Fergus set out a feast. "Eat. Jeremiah seems to think you were starving at that theater."

"Near enough." I sat and let him wait on me. He poured tea into a fine porcelain cup he pulled out of a cupboard then handed to me.

"I didna think of sugar or milk. I can go back." He frowned as he dug into the basket and pulled out honey. "Here. This might do."

"You are being very kind. I know you don't want me here." I stayed his hand when he started to add the honey to my tea. "This is fine. I thank you."

"You don't understand. Jeremiah is too trusting. He told me you saw him attacked by two armed men. There are more who will come after him, who would see him dead." Fergus studied me, his dark brows furrowed. "I see no harm in you, but there was no guarantee, ye ken, that you are not sent by someone to kill him in his bed. I promised his da I'd see to his safety. I've known the lad since he was a boy. I'll no let some doxy be his downfall here."

Now I couldn't look at him. Some doxy. Yes, that was where I stood.

"Lass, look at me. He didna call you that. And I am that sorry if I offended you." Fergus sat across from me and took a roll out of the basket. "Jeremiah wants what he wants. It will do no good for you and me to be cross with each other. We will be together all day, every day, as long as he fancies you. When I'm not about, you will be locked in here alone for your own safety. I'm sorry but that's how it will be if you wish to stay here."

"Locked in? Like I am a prisoner?" I swallowed.

"A precaution. You'll be marked as having his favor

once he takes you to court. The same enemies who want Jeremiah dead could well decide to use you as a lure to set a trap for him. I won't allow it." He tore the roll in half.

"Are you trying to send me running, Fergus?" I stared into his unusual eyes, more gold than brown. "You wouldn't be wrong to call me a doxy. I have fallen on hard times. Made desperate enough to trade my body for a… a meal." I lifted my chin. "I cannot afford to leave here. I have no place else to go." Oh, it hurt my pride to say so. But I didn't look away. "I promise I mean Jeremiah no harm. And will help you if you are here to protect him."

Fergus grinned. "You do have spirit. And, how, may I ask, will you help me? Do you know how to wield a knife? Shoot?" He laughed. "I know. You will distract the enemy with a look down your bodice." He shook his head. "A woman has brought down more than one man, I vow. Which is why I was worried when he brought you home, clearly besotted." He stuffed the roll in his mouth, washing it down with tea. "Eat, lass. We must find you a court dress. Jeremiah intends to take you to meet the king this night."

"He's mad." With that I took the honey and poured a generous dollop into my tea then drank. It warmed me as did Fergus's smile. Winning him over helped my cause. Because I needed to stay here as long as possible.

Fergus stopped chewing and his eyes narrowed. "Lass, take this one day at a time. Jeremiah has taken a fancy to you for now. Be glad and enjoy his generosity. But have a care. His heart is not yours to take." He shook his head. "You've no idea what pain he has endured in the past. What losses. He will tumble you and enjoy your company. But when we go home to his family's castle, he'll give you a fat purse and say farewell. You can plan on it."

"Did I say anything?" I wondered if I was the one who was mad. First Jeremiah, now Fergus seemed to read my thoughts as easily as if I had said them out loud. It was infuriating. "I just met the man and we had a fine time in his bed. That is all. What happens next is up to him."

My face burned at such plain speaking so I looked inside the basket and found a crock of butter. I covered the roll with it to keep from meeting Fergus's keen gaze. It was clear to me that I had no right to claim delicate feelings now that I had given myself so cheaply.

"It does not take a mind reader to see you've set your sights on him. No mistake about that." He set a bowl of strawberries on the table and twisted off the stem before he popped one in his mouth. "Survival. I've no quarrel with your motive. But have a care. It won't be him who will be hurt at the end of things. Mark my words." He pushed back from the table. "Jeremiah says you've a cravin' to learn to read. I can teach you, if your certain you want to work at it. 'Tis not easy."

"Seriously?" I stopped with a berry halfway to my mouth. "It is my fondest wish."

"Even before shopping for a pretty dress?" Fergus laughed and pulled out a bag of coins. The jingle and bulk of it meant Jeremiah had been extremely generous.

"A dress is important. I would not shame Jeremiah in front of the king." I bit into the strawberry, savoring the burst of flavor. I had never tasted anything so sweet! "But I could help him if I could read as well. Don't you think? I may see things in court. Be able to read a note." I shook my head. What did I know of such fancy doings?

"I can see you mean it. After shopping we'll begin." He sat in front of the fire and pulled out a knife to trim his nails. "Eat your fill, then more than that. Jeremiah is right, you look half-starved and it makes me want to knock someone's teeth out. How did it happen that you got in such a state?"

So I told him about Michael and my loss of memory as I ate sweet buns with currants, drank more tea with honey and finished the strawberries. My stomach ached from the unaccustomed fullness by the time I pushed back from the table. Why was I being so honest with this man when no one in the theater had earned my trust? I had no idea. But there was something in Fergus's eyes, the way he listened… I felt like I could tell him the truth and he wouldn't judge me or call me simpleminded.

"Killed by a falling chamberpot!" Fergus shook his head. "Not a pretty way to die."

"It was horrid. People should look out the window when they throw things. There was a fight between a woman and a man. We found out later that the wife had caught her husband dallying with the upstairs maid. She threw the pot at his head and it sailed through the window. Michael just happened to be walking down below. He never knew what hit him."

"I'm that sorry for your loss, girl. And this was a year ago?" Fergus got up and fetched the same short cloak that Jeremiah had put over my shoulders the night before. "How have you survived since?"

"Master Shakespeare let me stay in the theater, sewing and earning a bit of coin helping with the costumes. But his patience ran out yester eve and I was told to leave." I shuddered, thinking of the offer from Becks.

"You landed on your feet, lass. You couldn't find a kinder man than Jeremiah, though…" Fergus got a thoughtful look. "There are things you don't know. But it's not my place to tell you." He unlocked the door to the outside. "You will find that he has a use for you. Just as you are getting a safe place to stay, clothes and a lusty bedmate on your part. Mayhap it is not such a bad bargain." He turned and locked the door behind us after we were in the passage.

"That's what I keep telling myself, Fergus. I have never done something like this before. Or at least not that I can remember." I put my hand on his sleeve. He wasn't dressed richly but not as a servant either. More like a prosperous shopkeeper or a secretary to a lord. His velvet coat was unadorned, but wherever we went, we would be served promptly--if for no other reason than he was big and fierce looking. No one with good sense would ignore him.

"No memories of a family. That would be hard. In the

Highlands, family, clan, is everything to us. Loyalties run deep." He took my elbow and escorted me toward the outer door.

I breathed deeply when we finally emerged. Yes, it was damp and cold and cloudy. But I was glad to be where I could see the weak sunlight and know that the air was fresh. I was afraid living underground would become hard after a while. And locked in? I tried not to dwell on it. There were benefits to this arrangement that would more than make up for the strange quarters.

We walked until we came to the Globe Theater but no one was about. It was too early for theater folk. Fergus promised to send someone round later with a message that I was fine and well-situated.

Then it was on to a fashionable street where the rich traded. I must not be the first woman Jeremiah had dressed because Fergus knew right where to take me. The dressmaker greeted him warmly and quickly found a dress that would suit the king's court. It was a rich red silk trimmed in gold that swished when I moved. I felt like a princess in it. I wished Maggie could see me and wondered how to manage that. When lace cuffs, heeled shoes, and a cloak of black velvet were added, I felt as if I had fallen on the stones again and was dreaming.

"No ruff." Fergus was firm in his orders. "Jeremiah likes to see a woman's neck. Perhaps he will buy you jewels for it, Gloriana. That would be much better than a ruff, I'd say." If the man's face was red, I didn't wonder at it. He'd sat through my trying on dress after dress. He was surely tired of the shopkeeper and me discussing stockings, chemises and petticoats. He wouldn't allow things to be delivered either, whispering to me that he never gave out Jeremiah's direction to tradesmen. Instead, he ordered this night's dress and accessories put in a large package for him to carry. He would pick up the half dozen other dresses on the morrow.

We were outside again when Fergus mentioned yet another shop for hats.

"Oh, no. It is too much. What if Jeremiah—" I couldn't say it. If he tired of me quickly?

"Let him spend his gold, lass. He can well afford it." Fergus stopped suddenly. "Go back inside, Gloriana."

"Ho, cousin, do you think to hide Campbell's new fancy piece from me?" A large man who looked very like Fergus stepped into our path.

"Mind yer tongue, Bran." Fergus glowered at him.

"I'm sure my master will be happy to know Campbell has a new ladybird." The man winked at me. "Comely as well. No wonder you carry such a large package."

I kept my mouth shut, staying behind Fergus when he pushed into his "cousin.'"

"You'd do well to keep this meeting to yourself, Bran. The lady has no part in the quarrel between our masters." Fergus's voice was low and hard.

"Aye, 'tis true. But she could very well end up the spoils of war. Like most Scots, my master does enjoy variety in his bed." Bran did back up a pace when Fergus growled. "But take up with Campbell's leavings? I doubt you have reason to worry about the lass, cousin." With that the man quickly turned and strode away.

Fergus looked like he wanted nothing more than to chase the man down and pound him with the fists that clutched my package.

"Fergus?" I put a hand on his arm.

"I'm that sorry, Gloriana. My cousin was ill-mannered. Which was not like him. It must come from listening to his master speak ill of mine. Pray ignore him and his loose tongue. It is unfortunate that we serve men who hate each other. Were it not so we would be happy to see each other." He kept frowning in the direction where the man had disappeared into the crowd. "Jeremiah will be in no hurry to let you go. You will look a treat tonight when he shows you to the king and that will make him happy. He certainly seemed well-served when I last saw him as well." Fergus hurried me along until we were back at the door of the underground lodgings and he escorted me inside.

Well-served. The words haunted me as I unwrapped the beautiful dress. How had I been brought so low? I bowed my head to hide my tears. Fergus obviously noticed.

"I will go get us food. Then perhaps you would like another bath. Jeremiah told me you are greedy for such things. Another reason you please him. He is fond of his baths as well." His beefy hand landed on my back, like a quick pat of reassurance. "Lay out your things so they won't get creased. I'll be back soon."

"I thank you. I couldn't put on that beautiful dress tonight without a bath." I flushed. Where would Fergus be while I took one?

"I'll fill the tub in front of the fire then wait outside. You can call me when you're done." He winked. "I know better than to gaze on Jeremiah's ladybirds."

"Have there been many?" I couldn't help it. That word again. If I was one in a long line of his women, I didn't know what to think. It made me feel cheap, used, no matter what sweet things Jeremiah said to me. He had been "well-served." The words kept playing in my head, putting me in my place right enough.

"Not as many as there could have been." Fergus frowned. "We will eat first. I say too much and it is not my story to tell. Just know that Jeremiah has needs. Special needs. If ye keep pleasing him and make no unreasonable demands, he'll have no cause to replace you. But--" He shook his head. "I canna say more. His hunger…" He stalked to the door then turned to look me over. "Lass, it might be best for you to take the new clothes when they come and a bag of gold and run for your life." With that he left, locking the door behind him.

Now what did that mean? Run? And what kind of hunger? Yes, Jeremiah was lusty. Hunger for a woman, no doubt. I'd heard some men liked more than one woman at a time in their bed. Would he want that at some point? I couldn't imagine it. If I refused would Jeremiah call me unreasonable?

The idea made me shudder. Then wonder how that would work. What would we do? Blast. Now I was thinking too hard about it. With these men around me who seemed to read my mind, I would have to stop those thoughts or the next thing I knew there would be a comely lass as Fergus called her, showing up beside the bed eager to please both me and Jeremiah.

I wandered over to the pile of documents on a table and tried to puzzle out words. Fergus had said he would teach me. So I would do what I could to stay here long enough to learn as much as possible. There was a map among the parchments. I traced the lines with a fingertip. Borders between lands. Was that why Jeremiah had enemies? Did this MacDonald clan think to lay claim to his property? Such things seemed important to men. Master Shakespeare had written plays about disputes of that sort. They always included violent clashes and war.

I knew my letters, thanks to Michael, but not much more than that. I hated to be so ignorant. Certainly the actors were all men of intelligence and learning or they'd never be able to memorize the lines the master wrote. Michael had declaimed long and complicated speeches with passion. I could have listened to his deep voice for hours as he practiced his parts. I had even managed to memorize some of them.

I still missed my husband. He'd been a kind man, though not always attentive. The stage was his mistress, he'd told me more than once. He came alive there. He'd certainly never taken the time to give me the kind of pleasure Jeremiah had last night.

Oh, but I was disloyal! What did I really know of men? If only I could remember my life before falling on the stones… Michael had been afraid to let the actors know I had no memory. So we'd made up parents in Cheapside who had cast me out when I took up with an actor. It had been a common enough tale that was readily accepted by the people in the troupe.

Our marriage was also a story, an act made believable by the cheap ring Michael had bought me in a shop one day. No priest had spoken words over us. He'd insisted I take his last name since I had none of my own. Because he'd seen the way other men had watched me and grown jealous. It had been a sad day when I'd been desperate enough to sell that ring. Everything else I'd had of value had gone long ago.

"Here you be." Fergus was back with a full basket again. "Jeremiah told me you are partial to meat pies. So we'll dine on them this night."

"Should we wait for him?" I walked over and lifted the cloth. The smell made my stomach rumble.

"He will eat before you see him again." Fergus pulled out two plates. "Sit. I have ale. Will you join me?"

"Of course. Thank you." I sat and smiled at him. "You are being very kind, Fergus. I have made my choice to stay here and will keep my eyes open. You have warned me and I appreciate it. I have food, fine clothes and a comfortable place to stay." I took the brimming cup he poured for me. "Surely I can count those as blessings." I looked down when my cheeks grew hot. "Jeremiah is handsome and kind. I may be sorry to see him tire of me, but I am not so foolish as to think this is anything more than a temporary arrangement." My stomach clenched and it wasn't from hunger this time. "If there is any real danger, I hope I can make the decision to seek a safer situation." Though the idea of trying to find someone else made the cup in my hand drop to the table.

"Very sensible, lass." He sat across from me and pulled a pie from the basket. "Now I think Jeremiah would agree it is all right for me to tell you about the MacDonalds. They are bitter enemies though their lands lie side by side with those of Clan Campbell."

"I was looking at the map on the table. If they are neighbors, it is too bad they cannot get along." I took a bite of the fragrant pie. I was finally able to eat without gobbling it down like I'd never get another meal. It was a good feeling.

"The two clans have accused each other of stealing for centuries—cattle, sheep, even crofters. But things went bad a while back. Verra bad. People were killed. I canna say more. But it was unforgivable. Now Jeremiah and Robert MacDonald are set against each other." Fergus drank and wiped his mouth with the back of his hand. "I hope it doesn't end in murder. Their fathers would never get over it."

"Is it Robert MacDonald who your cousin Bran works for?" I sipped my ale. It was rich and tasty. I was careful to drink slowly. I would need my wits about me if I was to meet the king.

"Unfortunately. The MacDonalds also have the ear of the king. Naturally they sent their son and heir as well. It is politics, ye ken."

"I suppose." I kept eating as Fergus fussed and fumed while he polished off two meat pies. I could barely finish one. Nerves. Meeting the king. Worrying about dangers at court.

"No one will make a move in front of the king. And Jamie will demand they cry peace. It is one reason he wants them at court. He canna have the clans at war. He wants them to support him and be reasonable with each other. Show the English that he has level heads in Scotland, not wild clansmen he canna control." Fergus pulled out a block of cheese and cut a wedge. He waved it in the air.

"But Highlanders answer to no man, not even a king. Be careful, lass. Watch and listen. Robert MacDonald likes the ladies and the ladies like him. Bran is wrong. MacDonald will want you, if only to rile Jeremiah."

"I am not so foolish as to get in the middle of a war between clans." I pushed my plate away, the strong smell of the cheese making my stomach roll. "Surely the men will hold their tempers at court."

Fergus merely laughed and ate his cheese.

I had seen Jeremiah fight. And he insisted on wearing his plaid even though he admitted it made him a target for some who disapproved of it. "I've only just met Jeremiah but he seems to have a mind of his own. Will he make peace with the MacDonalds as the king demands?"

"If he does not, he risks the future of his clan." Fergus finished his ale and rose from the table. "He does have a temper when goaded. It is a worry, make no mistake about that. If there's one thing you can do, lass, it is to keep him in a jolly mood. He hates Robert MacDonald and may well lose control if he comes face to face with him at court. Throw yourself between the men if it looks like they're about to take out their swords. Distract them even if you have to drop your bodice to do it. Do you understand me?"

"Fergus! I couldn't do that." I laughed, sure he was jesting. But one look at his fierce visage and I knew he wasn't. He wanted me to keep Jeremiah from making a dangerous play. I gripped the cup of ale and felt that meat pie sit like a stone in my gullet. If Jeremiah fell into disfavor with the king, where would that leave me? Mayhap I'd fallen from the pan into the fire.

FIVE

I had bathed and retired to the bedchamber to get dressed when I heard the key in the lock again. I quickly shut the door when I heard him move the hip bath then water going down the drain. Fergus then. I had no idea if it was dark outside or not. When would Jeremiah come? I fussed with the strings of the many petticoats before slipping the red silk over my head. I needed a mirror but could find none. How would I do something with my hair?

I heard another door open and close, then voices. Jeremiah was home at last. A knock on the door before he stuck his head inside.

"Ah, you are getting ready." He smiled. "I must bathe and won't ask you to wash my back in that gown. Your shopping went well, I see. You look beautiful." He studied me. "What's amiss?"

"I need a looking glass and a brush for my hair." I hated to complain. Fergus had spent a small fortune on the dress I wore. But how would I look without the fancy hairstyle ladies were sure to wear with their gowns at court?

"Of course." He nodded then left, shouting for Fergus and issuing orders. He was back in moments. "He will find what you need. A mirror and comb if nothing else. I am that sorry you had to ask." He moved closer and dropped a kiss on my lips. "You smell good."

"Fergus bought some special soap for me. Scented with roses, like I used in the theater. You said you liked it." I brushed a hand over his chest, then unbuttoned his waistcoat, eager to please him. "You did say you needed a bath. Is it ready for you? You don't want the water to cool."

"Are you trying to undress me?" His grin said he didn't mind it. "Here. Let me help." He threw off the coat then made quick work of his shirt, drawing it off over his head.

Oh, but he had a fine chest. I ran my hands over it. "You have scars. Were you in battle?"

"Aye, I was a warrior. Long ago. Before…" He pulled my hands to his lips and kissed them. "I wish we had time for love play now, Gloriana. But I must get ready for court. The king does not like to be kept waiting." He looked down to where my breasts were almost fully displayed in the low neckline. "I promise we will have ample time for it later." He leaned forward and kissed the top of each mound that I feared would burst free from the tight bodice. The dressmaker had insisted it was the latest fashion. I dared not take a deep breath.

"I will hold you to that promise, sir." I followed him into the main room where his bath waited. He sat to take off his shoes and stockings then got up to remove his pantaloons, winking at me when he strolled over to the bath as naked as the day he was born. Of course he saw me admiring his muscular buttocks. Oh my!

The key turned in the lock and Fergus arrived as Jeremiah settled into the bath with a sigh.

"I've got what she needs here." His hands were full. "Gloriana, the goodwife wants her mirror back, 'tis a family piece. The rest you can keep. I paid heavily for it." Fergus ignored Jeremiah as he strode past him and handed me a bag and a silver hand mirror. "There are several patches if you want to put one on your cheek. Powder as well. Do not ask me to act ladies maid for you. I've no hand for hair dressing."

"Now, Fergus, don't be modest." Jeremiah laughed as he picked up a cake of plain soap from the hearth. "I'm sure you could do a credible job with Gloriana's hair."

Fergus muttered something in a language I didn't understand and stalked out of the room. He returned with the fancy clothes Jeremiah would wear to court. There was another plaid, this one of the finest wool. The doublet to go with it had slashed sleeves that showed red and gold to match my dress. There was golden lace for the cuffs and the entire look would make it clear that Jeremiah was rich and belonged in a king's company.

"Do the ladies at court use powder and patches, Jeremiah?" I didn't want to seem too plain, though the dress alone would surely make me look acceptable.

"Aye, some of them do. But I don't much care for the powder. It can make a mess in close quarters. Add a patch if you like." He grinned at me. "Next to your mouth, I think. And a little paint on your lips if there is some in that bag Fergus brought for you."

I hurried into the bedchamber and closed the door. Jeremiah seemed to know a good bit about women. Not that it should surprise me. Clearly he was a lusty man with needs. I sighed and set about making sure I wouldn't shame him in front of the king.

It wasn't easy, dressing my hair without help. I managed to prop the hand mirror against the pillows and worked the brush through my hair. Finally I had it pinned it into something resembling a fashionable style I'd seen on some of the fancier ladies who'd come into the alley looking for protectors.

Fergus had done well, bringing me many hairpins, some gold netting and a small pot of paint for my lips. I took Jeremiah's advice and placed a tiny round patch beside my now rosy lips. The Gloriana in the mirror was transformed when she smiled back at me and I knew my lover would be pleased.

"You make me sorry we have to leave now." Jeremiah

had entered so quietly I hadn't heard him come up behind me. I wanted to see us reflected together but he took the mirror away from me in a firm grip and carefully laid it face down on the table beside the bed. "I see I'll have to keep my sword close at hand. You are very tempting, Gloriana. You will have your choice of protectors this night." He slid a hand around my neck where my heart beat fast.

"If you tire of me, I will know where to look then." I gave him a saucy grin.

"No chance of my letting you go any time soon. I have barely tasted you. I cannot imagine tiring of this." He pulled me roughly to him and claimed my mouth. I clung to his broad shoulders, just as hungry for him as he was for me.

He ended the kiss too soon with a laugh then moved my patch back beside my mouth from my cheek, where it had slid out of place. "You are a dangerous distraction, lass. I cannot afford to be late to attend the king. Not with my enemies whispering in Jamie's ear. Fergus told me you saw his cousin today. So you know he attends Robert MacDonald. That cur will no doubt be at court as well." His smile was strained as he turned to pick up my velvet cape. He settled it over my shoulders then pulled me back against him. "Put more paint on your lips. I kissed it off and it did make you very pretty."

A flush heated my cheeks as I picked up the pot of paint and dabbed it on again. "Thank you, Jeremiah. I am honored that you are taking me with you. I will do my best not to disgrace you before the king."

"Hah! The disgrace will be mine if I start a fight with someone trying to steal you away." He kissed my neck, lingering there to inhale my scent. "Roses. I do like it. Now come." He took my hand and pulled me toward the door.

"You are certainly looking like the fine lord tonight. I will help you if I can, Jeremiah. No one will steal me from your side." I couldn't take my eyes off of him. Tall, strong, and masculine, no matter that he wore what some ignorant folk would call a skirt. His stockings were silk shoved into shoes with diamond buckles. His plaid had the vibrant green and blue that made me think of grass and sky, though there was little enough of that in the London I knew. Some lost memory pushed at my brain but would not come.

"Come now, what's that frown?" He tugged me closer. "I think you will be the most beautiful woman there. You aren't afraid, are you?"

"Do you think the king will notice me?" I sighed. "I've heard he is a man of letters. Master Shakespeare admires his writings. I know King James will scorn me when he learns I cannot even read."

"I doubt he'll do more than acknowledge you if I have the chance to introduce you. Jamie has his favorites and his mind on things other than the women with his courtiers. He has just ended the war with Spain. It is all he can talk about, this treaty of his. It is a great accomplishment." Jeremiah lightly kissed my lips. "But there will be other men there who may try to take what's mine. That's why I will keep my sword at the ready. And to prick MacDonald should he cross my path." He pulled me out into the passageway.

Fergus, looking fine in a plaid thrown over a velvet jacket said something in that language I didn't understand.

"Aye, Fergus, I know to mind my manners in front of our king." Jeremiah gave the man a hard look. "And I certainly would not do anything foolhardy with Gloriana by my side."

"I thank you for that. I have enough to worry about with court manners and such. At least I learned a proper curtsy watching the actor who plays the women in Master Shakespeare's plays. I think I can manage that credibly enough." I smoothed my skirt with trembling hands. I couldn't imagine how I would act with these nobles. It would be best to watch and listen as Jeremiah had asked me to do. I would be an ornament on his arm, saying little.

"Then you will be fine." Jeremiah kept me by his side as Fergus locked the door behind us then led the way. We walked down the block until we came to a street where, to my surprise, there was a coach waiting for us. Silly of me not to expect it. Did I think we would walk to court in all our finery?

"There will be a crowd, Gloriana." Jeremiah and I were alone in the carriage. Fergus had climbed on top with the driver. "Whitehall Palace is vast but there are many who curry favor with the king. I will do my best to stay by your side but may be called away to discuss some matters concerning my clan. If that happens, you should just do as we discussed."

"I will listen and try to remember anything that might interest you, Jeremiah. Master Shakespeare himself praised my memory." I hid my shaking hands in the folds of my skirts.

"Excellent. Remember the symbol I showed you when I was attacked in the alley? Look for that. I still have no idea what it meant or why I was ambushed." He picked up my hand and soothed it, calming me. "I was not lying when I said there will be other men who would be happy to become your protector, Gloriana. I hope you will not be swayed by their flattery." His eyes were dark and intent.

"And why would I be tempted when I am very well pleased with my situation as it is, sir?" I smiled and leaned toward him. How had I gotten so lucky? I smoothed a line between his dark brows. "Is there something I should know? Some matter that concerns you that I should listen for mention of?" I could see he was worried about the coming meeting.

"You are perceptive. Yes, if the MacDonald heir is there, it will be difficult for me not to kill him on the spot. If you see me reach for my sword, stop me. The king would not approve of our discord in front of his new English friends. Jamie pretends that all the clans are one big happy family, supporting his reign of England and Scotland." He leaned back against the seat. "Damn MacDonald. Why did he have to come to London now?"

"So you must hold your temper in check, Jeremiah.

Even in the theater we heard that the king is all powerful. Upset him and you could wind up in chains or," I swallowed, "hanged." I knew nothing about politics but anyone could see that ruining the king's victory celebration would be seen as unforgivable.

"You're right. I must not let another man goad me into doing something foolhardy. Especially when that could very well be his intention." He kept gripping the hilt of his sword though. "That's why Fergus is with us. He will also be keeping me in check. I have a deep and bitter reason for hating Robert MacDonald. It is not easily discarded in the name of polite behavior." He turned to look at me in the dim light from the carriage lamp. "But I would be risking you as well if I lost my temper and caused a scene. I would do well to remember that." He finally released his sword and took my hand. "Stay by my side as much as you can. Feel free to lay a calming hand on me if I seem about to go after the man."

"What does he look like?" I held on tight. Clearly this was a grudge that meant the world to Jeremiah.

"He'll be in his damned plaid of course. And he looks like a Northman. Light hair, light eyes. They say his ancestors crossed the North Sea and were marauders, raping and pillaging their way across Scotland. I believe it. They are still a bloodthirsty lot." He looked like he wanted to bite the head off of something or someone.

I shuddered. "Such hatred is like a festering wound, Jeremiah. I hope that you can rid yourself of this. Surely whatever is between you will eventually become a distant memory."

"Never!" Jeremiah stiffened and jerked his hand from mine. His glare made it clear he would hear no argument for reason. "I should never have spoken of this without explaining the cause and I do not feel that I am ready to share something so personal with a woman I barely know." He looked away. "We are here. Forget it, Gloriana. Put on a smile and see if you can act as well as your late husband could. Pretend we are lovers of long standing. Can you do that?"

I took a breath. Dear God. His outburst had startled me. A temper. Yes, he had one. At least he'd never had cause to turn it against me. He was right. He barely knew me and I barely knew him. It was wise to remember that. I nodded, words stalled in my throat. The coach door opened, the steps lowered. Jeremiah was out first and he extended his hand to me.

"Smile, if you please. You are not going to a funeral." He had on his own smile, though I could see it was strained.

"Am I not? If you cannot use restraint, I might very well be weeping over your body before the night is over." I swept down the steps with my hand in his. His hold tightened and I looked up to see him nod.

"Very well, Gloriana. I am going to try, that's all I can promise. Come." He escorted me inside, through two rows of guards.

The noise hit me at once. There were richly dressed people everywhere, laughing and talking loudly. The colors were brilliant. But then there were the smells. This was the London I knew from the theater. These people were not as eager to wash as Jeremiah and I were. Still, they did love their perfumes. The air was redolent with them and the odors they were supposed to mask. I was glad I had a lace handkerchief to put to my nose as we made our way inside the massive doorway and Jeremiah handed a servant our cloaks.

There was music as we worked our way into the hall. It was almost impossible to pick out the tune but a quartet valiantly played in an alcove balcony above the crowd. No one was dancing, there were too many people to manage that. The dais at the end of the large space held an elaborate throne occupied by a man who laughed up at the men standing on either side of him. Clearly our king was in good spirits. He held a bejeweled goblet in his hand. But it was nothing compared to the heavy ornamentation around his own neck.

King James was bedecked in glittering gold and emeralds this night. It made me sigh to see such beautiful stones. A fortune was on display. Not just on the king either. Solemn soldiers stood at attention around the room, their hands on their weapons, to make sure no one tried to snatch any of the dazzling jewels. And there were plenty for the taking. I realized that my dress and hair were perfectly fine. What I was missing were the lavish displays of glittering stones the other women wore in their ears, on their hands, and around their necks. Was Jeremiah noticing? Of course not.

He focused on a tall man across the room. This one wore a plaid, somewhat like Jeremiah's green and blue. But his had red as well as the blue and green of the Campbell plaid. Of course this must be MacDonald, Jeremiah's hated enemy. The light hair and pale eyes gave him away. I dropped my hand on Jeremiah's sword arm where I could feel the muscles tense before I glanced at his face. His jaw was tight, as if he had bit hard into a peach pit.

"Jeremiah, shouldn't you greet the king first?" I wanted to steer him to the other end of the room, away from that man who now stared at us.

"Aye." He made an abrupt turn, pulling me with him. "I should buy you jewels, Gloriana. It is a way to secure your future. After I leave here and return home, you can sell them. It is better than just handing you coin, don't you think? Or so I've been told." He glanced down at my hand on his arm. "Relax, my dear. I am not going to disgrace us, yet."

I was speechless. Reading my mind again? And now he was talking about leaving. And my future without him. So mistresses sold the jewels their protectors gave them after they were abandoned. If this was the way my life was going to be, I wondered if it would be better to just cast myself off a bridge into the Thames. I could already see how some of the women around me looked hard, ill-used and desperate. I did not want to become like them, worried that I'd lose my looks and be unable to find a new man when the one I was with tired of me.

"Gloriana, don't fash yourself. I am not leaving right away. Did I not tell you I am happy with our arrangement?" He smiled down at me and squeezed my hand. "You please me very well."

I forced a smile though my stomach twisted as we neared the king and his favorites. The smells were so strong and the air so close, it was little wonder that I felt faint. And then there were all the thoughts swirling through my head. The future, the past or lack of it. I was suddenly directly in front of the king and had the presence of mind to sink into the deep curtsy I'd learned at the theater. Jeremiah introduced me to King James.

"Well now, you've found yourself a pretty one, Campbell." The king gestured and I rose to stand beside Jeremiah. "Where are you from, Gloriana?"

"Here in London, your majesty. My late husband was an actor in Master Shakespeare's company." I managed to get that out without stammering but I felt heat in my face.

"Ah, an actor. Did you know we are having a new play here in a week or so? Othello, I believe he called it. Burbage in the lead. Do you know it, Gloriana?" The king kept his hand on the arm of one of his favorites. "Another goblet of wine, if you please. Mine is empty." The man beside him snapped his fingers.

"Oh, yes. The master is very proud of it. There have been many rehearsals. You will be very pleased, I think, your majesty." I glanced at Jeremiah. Was I talking too much? Did he wish for me to be quiet?

"Excellent. Campbell, you must bring Mistress Gloriana with you to our production. I will make sure you get good seats up front. Not a comedy, is it?" The king frowned.

"Oh, no! You may well need a handkerchief, your majesty. It is quite dramatic." I was glad I had watched the players work on the production. It was one of Shakespeare's most complicated and he'd made them go through it again and again. The performance at Whitehall before the king had been on everyone's minds. Now I would get to sit in the audience and they could see that I had found a fine protector, known to the king.

I suppose I should be embarrassed. No marriage or ring on my finger. But I wasn't starving, was I? Jeremiah bowed and I curtsied again. Obviously our audience was over as the king greeted yet another Scot, this one in a different plaid. It seemed there were several variations of colors to show a man's clan. Jeremiah was obviously happy to see this man as they smiled and nodded in passing, speaking in that language Fergus had used earlier.

"You did well, Gloriana." Jeremiah smiled down at me.

"Gloriana is her name? Unusual. Very pretty." A man had come up silently behind us. "Are you going to introduce us?"

"No." Jeremiah kept his hand around my waist. "Come, Gloriana. Let us see if there are refreshments. Would you like some wine, my dear?"

"Robert MacDonald, at your service." It was the man with the light blond hair and goatee and pale blue eyes. He moved in front of me and bowed over my hand before Jeremiah could stop him. "The king seemed quite taken with you. Did I hear you say you were married to an actor? Did Campbell kill him for you?"

"What? No! He died in an accident a year ago. Long before I met Jeremiah." I snatched my hand from the man's cool grip. "Pray excuse us, sir. We were on our way to the refreshments."

"I will not be goaded into a scene, MacDonald." Jeremiah kept his hand around my waist. "Move out of our way."

"A scene? Here? That would not serve and you know it." MacDonald smiled. "I heard you were attacked recently. By footpads. Unfortunate. That they failed to kill you."

"By God!" Jeremiah reached for his sword.

"No!" I threw myself on him, trapping his arm against his body. "You will not let him do this." I turned to MacDonald. "I don't know who tried to teach you manners, sir, but obviously they failed in the attempt." I glanced toward the throne. "Step away or I shall rip my own bodice, cry rape, and point at you. Are you understanding me, sir?" I gripped the front of my pretty red dress to prove my intention.

"My, you chose one with spirit, didn't you, Campbell?" MacDonald nodded and backed up a few paces. "You win this match, madam, but I am intrigued." His smile had a glint of teeth that made me shudder. "When Campbell hurries back to his parents' castle, you will need a man to satisfy you. I can do that better than this whelp. And I am very generous. You would have jewels for your pretty neck." He lifted his chin, then said something in that strange language that made Jeremiah snarl. Without another word he turned on his heel and disappeared into the crowd.

"Ignore him. Did you suggest wine?" I took my hand off my bodice and leaned closer to Jeremiah. "You have no idea what I am like after a few glasses of wine." I whispered a naughty suggestion in his ear. "Would you like that?"

"Minx. What man wouldn't?" He finally let go of his sword hilt. "You routed the bastard. Would you have really ripped your bodice and cried out in this crowd?"

"Of course. I told you I would help you. I am loyal to those who deserve my loyalty, Jeremiah." I took his hand and saw a servant balancing goblets on a tray across the room. "Now about that wine…"

He laughed and tugged me toward the servant. "I will make sure you are rewarded for that loyalty, Gloriana. Would you like sapphires? To match your eyes. Yes, a necklace, I think, and matching earrings." He handed me a brimming goblet. "And drink up. I am looking forward to your promise of entertainment after this hellish evening is over." His eyes roamed the room. Obviously he was watching for

Robert MacDonald.

I might have stopped Jeremiah from fighting the man this time, but their feud was far from over. And what about Robert's offer to take me on when Jeremiah left? Even I had to admit the man was very handsome indeed. A Viking of sorts. And in that plaid with broad shoulders and a swagger that had women watching him as he made his way through the crowd? He did have a way about him.

Jeremiah touched my neck and growled. Yes, growled.

"Robert MacDonald is not for you, Gloriana. I saw the way you looked him over. Aye, he has a way with the ladies. But he would use you then toss you aside."

"And you will not?" I drank deeply though the wine was nasty tasting. The truth of that was enough to make me want to drown my thoughts in spirits. This was the path I'd chosen. I didn't look at the man by my side. I couldn't read minds like he seemed to, but the truth was inescapable. I was a mistress who would be useful for the short term. I'd never be considered for marriage again. I would be wise to accept that and make the most of my situation. I turned to him.

"Sapphires. Yes, that would be lovely." I leaned into Jeremiah's side and smiled up at him, regretting my churlish comment already. I couldn't afford to show any resentment toward my protector. Instead, I had to hope he gave me many jewels and that I could save for my future. Because that was the only security I'd have now.

A family? I had to forget that dream. I needed to see one of the women in the theater to find out how to make sure an accident didn't make me a harlot with a child to raise on my own. That would be the saddest tale of all. Perhaps Master Shakespeare could write a play about it. I drained my cup and held it out to be filled again.

Luckily Jeremiah didn't seem to be interested in my bitter thoughts. He was too focused on his enemy who was making his bow before the king. So I sipped my wine and did my best to keep despair at bay. I had one of the most handsome men at court next to me. And I was clean, well-fed and dressed in the finest dress I had ever owned. I pasted on a brilliant smile when Jeremiah finally remembered to turn to me. When he announced we could leave, I was happy to see Fergus with our cloaks.

As we climbed into the waiting carriage, I wasn't surprised when Jeremiah turned to me, hungry for my body. Yes, that was my role here. I put aside my worries and went into his arms gladly. When he tossed my skirts up to my waist and took me right there as we drove through the streets, I wondered if he was trying to prove something. That he owned me? That MacDonald could never have me? No matter. He was rough and yet he gave me pleasure, swallowing my scream of completion with his mouth on mine.

He pulled down my skirt and straightened my bodice before he sat across from me, his kilt smooth as he moved his sporran, what he called the fancy leather pouch he'd worn to court, back from his hip to the center.

"Are you all right, Gloriana?"

"Of course." I reached up to push back an errant curl. "Are you? I see why you hate MacDonald. He taunts you."

"I will tell you the full story someday." He looked away. "I am sorry if I made you feel ill-used."

"There is no need to apologize, Jeremiah. I am new to this, but I will learn my place." I reached out to touch his knee covered by that fine wool. "Please be patient with me if I make demands that are not right for someone of my station. I have never been a mistress before."

"I like that you are passionate and speak your mind. Don't turn into one of those simpering women with no thoughts but how to wheedle another dress or jewels from me." He pulled me across the coach to sit in his lap. "We will figure out this relationship together, shall we?"

"Thank you." I kissed his chin, then his lips. I was so lucky. I had seen many of the men at Whitehall treat their women like ornaments. Cold-eyed men. And some of the women had looked fearful. I prayed I would never have to settle for such a protector. But who knew what the future would hold for me? I needed to quit thinking about anything but the present or I would go mad. I must enjoy what I had. So I slid my hand under that fine wool kilt. Oh, yes, Jeremiah liked my touch. And I'd made that naughty promise at the king's court.

So, as the coach bumped along, I dropped to my knees and did something I'd never done before. Did I please my man? If his groans meant anything, I believe I did.

SIX

When the coach finally shuddered to a stop, Jeremiah grinned at me. He had certainly had a fine time and seemed almost reluctant to leave it, but held out his hand for me get down when Fergus opened the door.

"What's this?" Jeremiah glanced around as I carefully took the step with his help then held my cape together against the chill night air. "You didn't take us close to our door." It was dark, torches from the corner casting little light as the coach rumbled away.

"We canna go home yet. We've been followed from Whitehall." Fergus stood nearby, his hand on a cudgel as if prepared for footpads. "We have more to walk once we've dealt with these brigands." He nodded at a pair of men coming toward us. "Look."

"Gloriana, step into that doorway." Jeremiah pulled out his sword.

I hurried to do his bidding. What was this? Why was he constantly beset by men trying to harm him? Then I heard him call a name and recognized the light haired man who now pulled his own sword.

"Are we really going to fight with such puny instruments?" Robert MacDonald laughed and tossed his sword to the man beside him. "Come, Campbell. Meet me man to man as we are meant to fight."

Jeremiah threw his sword to Fergus who caught it with a curse.

"You're mad, both of you. Remember where you are." Fergus glanced at me. "And who you're with."

"You've not told the lass yet? Such a lovely blood whore. I will enjoy her once I've ripped out your throat." Robert leaped with a snarl. He was met by Jeremiah in what seemed to be midair.

I couldn't believe my eyes. Fangs. The men had suddenly grown long, enormous teeth that made their faces change into masks of hatred. They clashed with snarls and murderous intent, determined to tear each other apart. Curses filled the air as they fell to the stones, ripping clothes and pounding each other with their fists. They rolled in the filth of the street and blood splashed the ground.

It was Bran, cousin to Fergus, who had arrived with MacDonald. He now stared at Fergus and they seemed to come to some silent agreement not to interfere.

"Make them stop! They will kill each other." I pulled at Fergus's sleeve.

"Nay, lass. 'Tis an old quarrel between them. They won't thank us for pulling them apart." Fergus pushed me behind him. He made it clear a mere woman had no say in it.

But when MacDonald ripped a hole in Jeremiah's shoulder with those ungodly teeth and blood streamed from what surely would be a mortal wound, I couldn't be still and rushed forward. "He will surely bleed to death! Fergus, please!"

Fergus clamped his arms around me. "No, lass, it's not as grave as it looks. This is something they must do. I hope to God I don't have to carry Jeremiah's body home to the Laird when they are done."

"Then stop this, please." I was sobbing. Their teeth were so horrifying and dangerous. Robert's neck was bleeding and one eye had been torn and was swollen shut.

How did he see to keep going? Then Jeremiah… One arm hung limply at his side, the bone obviously broken. But still he fought, landing a vicious kick that made Robert scream with rage and double over.

"I cannot interfere. Nor can Bran." Fergus pushed me back when the men fell close to us.

"They're killing each other!" It seemed like a river of blood pooled under them and I stuffed a fist in my mouth to keep from distracting Jeremiah with my cries. Robert had ripped away that lovely jacket and had his fangs locked on my lover's shoulder, shaking him as Jeremiah held onto Robert's hair and banged his head against the stones.

"Horses are coming! Stop this. We will be found out." Fergus gestured and Bran moved in to help him tear the men apart. It wasn't easy.

I gagged when I saw Robert's mouth dripping blood, his fangs wet with it. He panted, his one open eye wild with hatred.

"Let me finish him!" He screamed and desperately tried to wrest free from Bran's grip. But he was clearly weakened by blood loss from a dozen wounds.

"As if you could." Jeremiah staggered, still straining against Fergus who held him, both arms around him.

"Look you, a coach is coming. Change and be gone. Or are you too weak for it, MacDonald?" Fergus taunted him though I didn't understand it.

Robert's answer was a screech and then he disappeared. In his place a falcon fluttered, then flew off into the night. Bran soon followed. Or what had been Bran. He'd become a bird as well, a hawk. I rubbed my eyes, wondering if I'd gone mad. How much wine had I drunk at the king's castle? Was I now in bed, dreaming?

"Gloriana, your cloak." Fergus held out his hand.

I hurried from where I'd stood staring at what I couldn't believe and pulled off my cape. Fergus wrapped it around Jeremiah and pushed us together, out of the way of the coach-and-four rumbling toward us. The driver pulled up just in time to keep from running us down.

"What's this?" A man I recognized as a lord we'd spoken to at Whitehall leaned out of the coach window. "Is aught amiss here?"

"Footpads, my lord." Fergus nodded in a semblance of a bow. "Master Campbell drove them off but he took a hard hit to the head. Nothing to worry about. We're just steps from home."

"I can take you up. I will send for my physician." The lord frowned at the way Jeremiah leaned against the wall, propped up by his servant. Jeremiah never spoke nor raised his head. "He may need to be bled."

"Not necessary, but thank ye, sire." Fergus bobbed again. "Aye, here we are at our door. All he needs is his bed. Isn't that so, mistress?" He looked at me to say something.

I sensed his desperation and couldn't ignore it. I stepped up to the coach. "Yes, yes. Of course. Lord Summers, you are too kind." I leaned closer, letting my low bodice do what words could not. "Truth be told, the footpads had not reckoned with Jeremiah's skills with a sword and ran away quickly, bleeding and afraid for their lives." I touched the lord's hand. "Oh, one of them may have landed a lucky blow, but I think what my man is feeling now are the effects of too much wine." I laughed.

"I don't recall seeing him touch the wine." The lord frowned.

"You were much too busy with the king, I'm sure, to pay attention to a simple Scotsman and his mistress." Oh, no, this man wasn't as unobservant as I'd hoped. He frowned at the stain on the stones but it was dark and impossible to tell whether it was blood or merely some household's night soil. I took the kind of deep breath that I hadn't dared before in the low cut dress. As I'd feared, my breasts lost the struggle and popped free. It was enough to distract the lord from the sight of Jeremiah clearly about to fall to the ground. I let my hands flutter over them in my "distress" and that got his eyes where I wanted them.

"Oh, I certainly noticed you, my dear. Who would not? Campbell's mistress. Gloria, was it?" He smiled.

"Gloriana."

I bit back a gasp when he boldly reached for my breast and ran his cold and clammy hand over it. Dear God.

"His majesty is always bragging about how a Scot can drink any man under the table. I will have to tell him I saw one of his own the worse for wine this night."

"Oh, please, sir. Do not tell anyone that he came away from the castle tipsy. It was my fault. I made Jeremiah stay too long at the palace, so eager was I to see all the courtiers in their finery. It was not his choice to stay so he drank to ease his boredom." I glanced back at Jeremiah, as if to make sure he wasn't watching us, then covered the lord's hand with mine. "I am new at this, still learning how to please my protector." I sighed, then looked up at Summers through my lashes. "I don't want to make Jeremiah angry."

"I suppose I could stay quiet." He roughly pinched one of my nipples, watching my face to see if I liked it. "As a favor to a pretty lady."

I bit my lip to keep from screaming when he moved to the other breast, giving my nipple a brutal twist. "My lord!" I gasped. "You are too kind."

"Not at all. But I can be generous. This neck should be adorned with jewels, I think. Remember that when Campbell tires of you." He held a cane in one hand, the top of it a silver ram's head. He ran it over my chest then up to my throat, smiling when I swallowed nervously against the chill metal. "Yes, you would suit me, I think."

"You flatter me, my lord." I forced myself to stay still when I wanted to run away screaming.

"Mistress Gloriana, the master needs to find his bed." Fergus dared speak up.

"I know it. One moment." I carefully pushed the lord's hand from my breast and his cane from my face. The thought of what else he might do with that ebony stick made me sick to my stomach. Oh, yes, I had heard tales at the theater of cruelty in the bedchamber by those of his tastes.

"Thank you, my lord. And I will stay quiet as well. These Scotsmen have unsteady tempers and the ear of King Jamie. It would not do to let one know that another man had handled his property carelessly. Jeremiah Campbell *is* a master swordsman, even when the worse for wine." I backed away from the coach. It was all I could do not to wipe his filthy touch from my chest with my lace handkerchief. To my relief the lord just smiled and hit the roof of his coach with that cane. It lurched into motion down the lane.

"Well played, Gloriana." Fergus hefted Jeremiah into his arms.

"At least he's moved on." I doubted he could have seen exactly what I'd let the lord do to me in the coach window as I stuffed my breasts back into my bodice. Or perhaps he had and didn't care as long as I'd successfully distracted the man so that his master was left alone.

"He's fallen into a faint. I don't like it. We still have a ways to walk. Straight ahead, if you will." Fergus nodded and I started out.

I was cold in my beautiful dress without my cloak. I looked back at that dark pool of blood on the stones. Would Jeremiah die from his wounds? I hurried, rubbing my arms and following Fergus's directions until we were at our door. He had me pull his key from the pouch at his waist while he held Jeremiah in his arms like a babe. It was remarkable that he could carry such a weight.

But then I was learning that there were many things about these men I didn't understand. They had strength that was unnatural and could do things that made me doubt my sanity. Birds. Surely I had imagined… No, I'd seen what I had seen. But how could that happen? And then there were those horrible fangs—lethal, appearing and disappearing at will it seemed.

"Stand back, Gloriana." Fergus laid Jeremiah on his bed then efficiently stripped him and examined his wounds.

"I can heat some water and bring you clean cloths to

GERRY BARTLETT

bathe the wounds." I hurried out of the room and put the
kettle over the fire. I wouldn't risk this fine dress and
grabbed one of Jeremiah's shirts left next to the bathtub. I
pulled off my petticoats and that dress with its tight bodice
before finally slipping the shirt over my head. I didn't care if
Fergus saw me like this. He seemed to be immune to my
allure, if you could call it that. And he certainly had more on
his mind right now than staring at my legs showing from the
knees down under that cotton shirt.

"Here." I took a bowl of hot water and a pile of cloths
to him.

Fergus frowned down at several very bad tears in
Jeremiah's skin that still oozed blood. The one on his
shoulder was the worst. You could see the bone beneath a
gaping hole where MacDonald's enormous teeth had torn
away the skin. The arm that had been broken looked straight
again, so Fergus must have already snapped it back into
place. I couldn't imagine the pain that would have caused. It
was a good thing that Jeremiah had slept through it.

I swallowed and dipped a cloth in the water, crawling
on the bed to wipe away blood from Jeremiah's face. He
didn't move or seem to breathe. How could that be? I
gathered my courage and wiped his lips, peeking at his teeth.
Where were his fangs now, those horrid sharp things that
had done such damage during the fight? But his teeth were
as ordinary as my own.

"He needs your help, Gloriana." Fergus's voice was
rough.

I looked at him and, if I didn't know better, I'd think he
was near tears. "There is much I don't understand here,
Fergus. How can Jeremiah be a man one moment and a
monster the next?"

"There's no time to explain things now. I wish…"
Fergus cleared his throat. "He's been kind to you, Gloriana.
Please trust me when I say he needs you this night."

I took a shaky breath. Trust? After what I'd seen? But
I'd come to no harm in spite of the violence mere feet away

from me. There was no denying that Jeremiah seemed on the verge of death. I couldn't bear it.

"I'm trying to help. Is there something else I can do? I'll watch him while you fetch a doctor. Or I'm not a great hand at it but I can see these wounds will need stitching. Do you have thread and a needle? I can try…" I certainly hated the idea of putting a needle through Jeremiah's skin. And that one huge hole in his shoulder… there wasn't enough skin left to pull taut no matter how much thread I used. Oh, God, but I was going to be sick.

I wrung out the cloth, the water turning pink, and washed blood from his forehead. The men had pounded each other against the stones. I ran my hands through his hair and felt a lump the size of an egg on the back of his head. No wonder he didn't wake.

"He needs your blood, Gloriana." Fergus whispered the words, as if he didn't want Jeremiah to hear them.

"What?" I remembered then what Robert MacDonald had called me. Jeremiah's blood whore. What did that mean? "A physician would bleed him, cup him or use a leech. I never like to see that. And he has lost so much blood already. Look how pale he is, Fergus." I touched Jeremiah's cheek, rough with the beginning of an evening beard, then ran my fingers over his soft dark eyebrows and his closed eyes with their long eyelashes. Tears pricked my own eyes and I had to blink them back. Falling on his chest sobbing wouldn't help matters. But, oh, I wanted to do that very thing. I barely knew this man but I didn't want him to die. He'd saved me from starving and shown me more caring than anyone else had in more than a year.

"You don't understand. It is not my place to tell you why or how, but he needs more blood. Human blood. He has been taking yours from you when you are unaware. This time you need to offer to let him drink from you. It's the only way to save him." Fergus sighed and sat on the foot of the bed. He'd tossed a sheet over Jeremiah's hips since there were no wounds below them. Now he stared into my eyes.

"I don't have the knack to make you forget things like Jeremiah does. But know this. If you will lie next to him and offer your wrist, where your blood flows through your veins, he will smell it. It will make him wake, or at least hunger for it. His instinct to drink will take over. Or at least I hope it will." He rubbed his face with his hands.

"Drink? My blood?" I swallowed and eased away from Jeremiah. I knew now what Fergus was asking. My stomach lurched. I couldn't…

"Please. Listen to me." Fergus started to reach for me but I held up my hands to stop him. "You saw his fangs. This is how he survives, Gloriana. It will heal him. Let him take your blood from your vein if he can and he will be all right, I know it. Can you do that for him?"

I jumped from the bed and scampered to stand in the doorway. Fergus's words ran through my mind. *Taking it from you unaware. He will hunger for it.* "Instinct to drink." My blood. Dear God in Heaven. And finally? *The knack to make you forget things.* My heart raced and I wanted to do the same. I would run and keep going until I was far away from this madness. Yes, I'd seen those fangs. They were long, lethal things that could rip through skin. The men had certainly done it to each other. I saw the evidence lying on the bed, Jeremiah was so still.

"What is he?" I wrapped my arms around myself, shivering. I couldn't stop.

Fergus stared at me, his eyes bleak. "He is one of the undead, a blood drinker."

"No, you cannot mean it." I had heard of such things but they were always associated with evil, demons. Jeremiah wasn't like that. He had seemed vital, warm, alive! I couldn't understand… "I know that since I've been here I've seen things that I don't understand, Fergus. Also, I've heard stories about such monsters. The people in the theater love to sit around with their drinks and tell such tales. Make you have nightmares." I looked away. This was impossible.

And yet I'd seen more things tonight that I couldn't

explain with what Master Shakespeare had called the logical mind. Oh, how he loved to play with fantastical images. Dreams, he called them. This was no dream. Or even a nightmare. I was standing here, the floor cold under my bare feet. The man lying on the bed nearby was so still. I watched closely but his chest wasn't moving, not with even a breath. I could swear he was already dead. Fergus was giving me a look that dared me to be brave enough to save a man who'd been kind to me. A man who had rescued me from starvation or worse--whoring in alleys for pennies.

Fergus was solemn, his gaze seeming to probe my mind. "You *were* starving when Jeremiah brought you here. He was gentle with you. Others, like Lord Summers, wouldn't be so thoughtful of your feelings. They would use you cruelly." So he had seen what had gone on in the coach window after all.

"Jeremiah got something from me in return, you know." I was sick of these mind readers. I turned my back on him, my face hot. I'd given my body to Jeremiah freely, of course. *Whore.* No, *blood whore.*

"You may leave if you wish, Gloriana. I can go out on the street and find a stranger to give him blood. It won't be pretty. I'll probably have to knock someone in the head first." Fergus stood and walked past me. "Put on your clothes. I'll give you some gold since I won't see you starve."

"You'd let me go?" I glanced back at Jeremiah. Could I really leave him like that? He was going to die. Or maybe some stranger would be sacrificed to save him. "Wait. You say he's been taking my blood and I didn't know it. So it doesn't hurt or kill me if I give him my blood?"

"I'm sure it hurts when it happens." Fergus picked up my fine silk dress, discarded on the floor, and began to fold it. "But he can make you forget things. It's a skill his kind has. He has made you forget many things, Gloriana. It's not something I admire in him."

"You aren't one of them then. What are *you*?" I watched him pick up my petticoats and fold them as well.

Was he planning to pack them for me? Or throw them in the fire if I refused to help his master?

"A shape-shifter. I can turn into many different animals at will. You saw my cousin Bran turn into a hawk. I can do that. Or—"

"A black cat!" I knew he'd done that. The cat I couldn't find. "It was you, wasn't it?"

"Yes, that was me. I am tasked with protecting Jeremiah during the day while he sleeps. His kind dies at sunrise, wakes at sunset. They are vulnerable to attack during the daylight hours. So they hire shifters like me and my cousin to protect them. If someone came in to harm him I could become something much more deadly than a house cat in an instant. Believe me."

Oh, I did. Hadn't Bran changed in a moment and flown away? I still had trouble believing it. I sat on a hard chair, overwhelmed and yet seeing all the things I hadn't understood falling into place. "Robert MacDonald is one of those blood drinkers as well."

"Aye. The Campbells and MacDonalds are neighboring clans and both are the same. It is why they are so pitted against each other. They live forever and have bitter histories. Things have happened between them that they cannot and will not forget." Fergus stopped his housekeeping and stared at me. "While we are talking, Jeremiah is lying there, perhaps finally coming to the end of his long life. I have to do something for him. It is my duty. And he has become my friend. I *want* to help him. If you will not go to his aid, get out of my way and let me find someone who can." He frowned. "But these are our secrets, Gloriana. You cannot tell anyone what we are."

"Who would believe me? I would be treated as a madwoman if I started raving about men who change into birds and monsters who dance attendance on our king." I gasped. "Does he know? Is he one as well?"

"King James? Nay." Fergus shook his head. "Enough talk, Gloriana. Jeremiah needs help now. We cannot delay another moment."

I walked back into the bedchamber and stared down at Jeremiah. Was he breathing? I didn't think so. Perhaps he was already gone. I bit back a sob. He'd certainly saved *me* but saving him meant allowing him to sink those horrible fangs into my skin, perhaps tear it open as I'd seen him do MacDonald's during that horrid fight. Fergus was at my back and he laid a steadying hand on my shoulder. I was shaking and nothing would calm me.

"We're running out of time, Gloriana. Stay and do what needs doing or get you gone. I must act quickly now." Fergus squeezed my shoulder, clearly urging me to choose Jeremiah's well-being no matter my qualms.

I staggered then ran from the room to throw up, heaving over a bucket next to the fire until my stomach was empty. With Fergus's eyes on me, I wiped my mouth with a clean cloth then picked up a jug of wine and drank deeply. False courage. But I couldn't do this with a clear head and I knew it.

"Stop. If your blood is full of wine, it will not heal him as well as he needs with such serious wounds." Fergus wrested the jug away from me. "Does this mean you will help him?"

"Aye." I used his own word, the Scottish one for yes, then stumbled toward the bedchamber again. I wasn't drunk, only wished I were. I couldn't let a man die, not even one who was obviously not human. A monster. Yes, he must be. But a kind one. And one who could make my body feel things it had never felt before. I shook my head. Foolish to think of pleasure now when I had pain ahead of me.

"Lie close to him. He must smell your blood. I must cut you so he can sense your fresh human blood. He says your blood is special. No reason why, but he fancies it." Fergus held a dagger and stayed close to me. To stop me if I changed my mind? I didn't doubt it.

"Hand me the knife. *You* will not cut me." I glared at the shape-shifter. Impossible that such a thing even existed.

But it certainly explained the black cat. I had seen his cousin change with my own eyes. Obviously the undead could change shapes as well since MacDonald had flown away into the night. Oh, God, why hadn't I run and never looked back? Then I stared down at Jeremiah, so still, so pale and yet so handsome. He looked like a man, not a monster, as he lay there. My hand trembled but I was not giving up on this.

"Give me the knife!" I climbed up on the bed when Fergus slapped it into my palm. Whatever Fergus saw or didn't see as I tried to get where Jeremiah could put his mouth on my wrist, didn't matter. I wanted this over and done. I might be wasting my time. With one hand on Jeremiah's chest, I could tell his heart had slowed and perhaps stopped. I was lying on a dead man. I sniffled but stayed the course.

"Slash your wrist and rub some of your blood on his upper lip. That should make him stir. Then put your vein against his mouth. His instincts should do the rest. Unless…" Fergus cleared his throat. "Unless we're too late."

"You said his kind live forever." I had certainly heard that. "So he must have unusual strength. Say a prayer, Fergus." There was no movement under me as I sliced my wrist and blood welled. It hurt but I ignored the pain. I handed the knife back to Fergus then ran my wrist across Jeremiah's upper lip, just under his nose. It seemed almost disrespectful to wipe my blood on him this way until I saw his nostrils flare.

"There. Do you see it? He smells it. Lean in, Gloriana. Offer him your vein. Do it now!" Fergus shoved me forward until I fell on Jeremiah, my arm hitting his shoulder.

I'm sure the shifter heard the same growl I did. To my horror large fangs grew in Jeremiah's mouth while his arms wrapped tight around me. I was trapped against him.

"Fergus!" I couldn't help it, I struggled. But one of Jeremiah's hands tangled in my hair, keeping me still. I was unable to move as he grabbed my bloody wrist. His eyes stayed closed but his mouth opened and his nose quivered.

He inhaled deeply before he angled his head to take my vein. I closed my eyes when he suddenly struck. Pain, sharp and undeniable, made me gasp. I couldn't help it as I tried to wrench my arm away. It wasn't to be. I was well and truly captured as he pierced my skin and drew blood. I heard him groan in what must be satisfaction before he swallowed.

My stomach clenched. How could he do this? Drink from a human? It was a sin, an abomination. I wasn't a religious person and couldn't remember ever setting foot in a church, but it seemed that only a creature from hell would take another's blood like this. I pushed against him with my free arm, desperate to get away from him. He held me even tighter and kept drinking, pulling on my vein and swallowing, over and over again. The room darkened. Was I the one bound to die this night?

"Jeremiah, stop!" Fergus shouted. He pried his master's hands off of me then shook him, squeezing Jeremiah's jaw with his fingers. "Let her go before you kill her, damn you."

I realized I might be able to crawl away if he would just take those bloody fangs from my wrist. Bloody. Laughter burst out of me. Was I mad indeed?

I found myself suddenly free.

"Get away from him while you can, Gloriana." Fergus gestured and I hurried to do as he bid, pulling my hair from Jeremiah's grip until my eyes watered. I crawled off the bed. Gods, but I was weak. The room dipped and swayed when I tried to stand. I fell to the floor.

"Fergus!" I wanted to get up but there was no help for it. Spots danced in front of my eyes then the world disappeared.

SEVEN

I woke with the same empty feeling I'd had in the theater. But I wasn't backstage at the Globe, I was in Jeremiah's bed. Thank God there was no sign of that monster. I thought to run but even moving the furs seemed beyond me. Little wonder. The creature, whatever he was, had sucked out most of my blood. Dear God. Why hadn't I run when I had the chance?

Because you have nowhere to go. That stark truth couldn't be denied. I had nothing, was nothing. I wanted to bury my face in the pillow and weep. But what good would that do? No, I needed strength and I smelled roast beef, the aroma making my mouth water. If only I could get to it.

"I thought the smell might bring you 'round." Fergus stood next to the bed, a plate in his hand. "Can you come to the table? Or will you eat here in the bed?"

"I want out of this bed. Let me see how I manage." I took a breath then threw back the furs. I still wore only Jeremiah's shirt. There was nothing for it but to pretend this shape-shifter was no gentleman but merely a servant, trained to ignore the bad behavior of his employer. He did avert his eyes as the shirt slid up to my thighs.

"I'll put this on the table. Call for me if you want my help. There's the chamber pot if you need it." He hurried out

REAL VAMPIRES: WHEN GLORY MET JERRY

the door.

I managed to stand then swayed with the room. Damn Jeremiah Campbell. I'd thought him so kind, so gentle, feeding me and seeing to my pleasure. His pleasure as well of course. Oh, yes. All so he could take my blood. Dear God, sucking it from my vein like a damned leech. Yes, that was what he was. Preying on innocent victims. I wouldn't have believed it if I hadn't felt the pull at my own wrist. My legs shook, threatening to collapse under me.

But I was determined to leave that bed where Jeremiah had used me. I made it to the doorway and grasped the frame, the smell of food drawing me closer. When Fergus saw me there, he hurried to my side and helped me to a chair. The plate he placed in front of me held rare roast beef, potatoes and bread. There was a mug of ale as well. I picked up a knife and cut a piece of meat with a shaking hand. I hesitated, needing to ask a question before I could take a bite.

"Where is he?"

"It's daylight outside. He's locked in his room, dead to the world." Fergus pushed the mug of ale closer when I stuffed the bite into my mouth and chewed. "Careful, lass. I know you need food, but eat too fast and you'll sicken."

I swallowed, furious that he could think to give me advice when he'd pushed me to sacrifice myself mere hours ago. "I am already sick. From what that man did to me." I tried to swallow another bite but couldn't. Instead I turned and lost what little I'd managed to get down. Of course clever Fergus had placed a bucket there, just in case.

He got up and brought me a clean cloth he'd dipped in fresh water. "I'm that sorry, lass. It's a vampire's way. He must have blood to live, you see. You are clean and pretty. He was drawn to you right away, he told me."

"Vampire. That's what you call his kind." I wiped my face and hands then sipped the ale cautiously. "Am I to be flattered that he wanted me? I suppose my blood is to his taste as well."

"Yes, he says it is something special. Unlike any he has had before." Fergus looked away at that, staring into the fire.

I slammed my mug onto the table. "Is that so?" I would have run from the room but doubted I could even stand. "By all that is holy, I am a high treat then." And just like that my anger turned to despair. What was to become of me? I was as trapped as a rabbit in a snare. Weak, my stomach heaving at the smell of the food in front of me now, I had no hope of escaping.

"Perhaps you should go back to bed." Fergus stared down at me then handed me a handkerchief.

I realized I was crying. My silence turned into sobs as he helped me to my feet. When my legs wouldn't hold me, big strong Fergus picked me up and carried me back to bed. He laid me down gently, drawing the furs up to my chin.

I turned my face into the pillow, grateful that it no longer smelled like the man who'd wooed me for his own use. What was I to do? The shape-shifter's hand landed on my back then there was a quiet sound. A purr? I rolled over and saw what I suspected. Dear God, but he'd changed into that black cat so quickly. There was no denying I'd fallen into a strange world here. I took a shuddery breath.

"May I..?" I reached out tentatively as he stared at me with those golden eyes that saw and knew too much. I stroked his soft black fur until he pushed his head against my face. It was comforting. I wiped my wet cheeks with his handkerchief and closed my eyes. His warm body curled against me, his tail brushing softly across my chin, I sighed and finally relaxed.

What would happen when I woke and it was dark again? I couldn't imagine it and didn't want to think past this moment. For now I would rest and try to regain my strength. Because I was not going to be Jeremiah's victim. Oh, no. We would have to come to terms if he thought to take my blood again. I swore to that. He would pay and pay dearly for using me.

"What will happen now, Jeremiah?" Fergus sounded angry.

I kept my eyes closed, desperate to hear the answer.

"Did she eat? Stir at all?" Jeremiah's deep voice at least sounded concerned. Pretense or did he care if he killed me with his thirst?

"She woke but could not eat. You were greedy and took too much. It's a wonder you didn't kill her." Fergus must be next to the bed. To keep me safe? I didn't doubt that his loyalty lay with Jeremiah. If the master demanded more blood from me now, what would Fergus do?

"I was out of my head because of my wounds. It won't happen again. Move out of the way." Jeremiah was clearly issuing orders.

I opened my eyes. Jeremiah stood next to the bed, Fergus behind him. Of course the master looked as if all was right with his world. He wore one of his white shirts and pantaloons with high boots. His dark hair was clubbed back and he'd shaved. I'd expected him to still show the effects of that fight from the night before but all his cuts and bruises had disappeared. Magic? Or the healing power of my blood? That thought made me shudder.

"You don't have to be afraid of me, Gloriana." Jeremiah sat on the edge of the mattress.

"Don't I?" I grabbed a heavy candlestick next to the bed and heaved it at his head. It hit him with a satisfying thump and opened a wound on his forehead.

He held up his hands when I followed with slaps and a pillow. "I deserve that and worse. I know it."

I fell back, the brief burst of energy draining me. "Much worse. You could have killed me."

"I know. I'm sorry." He took a cloth from Fergus and wiped away a trickle of blood. "I wasn't myself. The blow to my head last night robbed me of my senses."

"Hah! Are you saying that was the first time you'd taken blood from me?" I was as far away from him as I could get, hugging the edge of the mattress.

"No, I admit I've been taking your blood since the night we met. It's what my kind does." He tossed the cloth back to Fergus and I gasped. The cut made by the candlestick was healing before my eyes. "I see you are shocked. At this?" He pointed to the wound that was now almost gone. "That's what your blood does for me, Gloriana. It makes me strong, keeps me--"

"I don't want to hear it!" I heaved the pillow at him but he caught it easily. "How is it I don't remember the other times when you took my blood? How do you erase my memory?" This was something I could not and would not forgive. What few memories I had were new and precious to me. I couldn't stand the idea that he could make any of them vanish at will.

"It's how I survive, Gloriana. I can look into a mortal's eyes, your eyes, and make you forget what has happened between us. It is for your own protection." He tossed the pillow aside.

"Liar!" Oh, but I wanted to hurt him as he'd hurt me. I could hardly breathe with my rage. I slammed a fist on the mattress. "You protect yourself, Jeremiah. I could bring soldiers here, witch hunters, and it would be the end of you." I couldn't meet his gaze. I stared at my hands clenched in my lap. What did I care if he was burned at the stake? Handsome or not, he was an abomination.

"Gloriana, if you left here shouting of blood drinking and vampires, it is very likely you would end up treated as insane and thrown into Bedlam in chains. Remember, I am from an old Scottish clan with deep ties to King James and well known at court. Who would believe you over me?"

I knew better than to look at him. Would he be smiling at the truth of that?

He stood. "Now be reasonable. I told you I enjoy your company. And, yes, your blood. I promise when next I take it, I will restrain myself. You will not be left frail as you were this time. Have you ever been weak before after you woke up?"

I did not bother to answer. I knew he was reaching for me but I ignored him. I would sooner let a viper touch me with *its* fangs. I shuddered.

"Come now. I would like for us to cry peace and make this work. The decision is yours. Will you look at me?" He used such a deep and seductive voice to woo me.

I steeled myself against it. There was one thing I would not forgive or forget. He'd robbed me of my memories. It must have been when he'd looked into my eyes. I'd had that funny feeling and...

"Only if you swear on your mother's grave that you will not make me lose my memories, ever again." He was right about my circumstances. My choices were limited. Fangs or not, he was better than many protectors I could have. I remembered being rapped by a cane and groped cruelly. To my shock, Jeremiah laughed.

"My mother will live forever. She has no grave." He was suddenly on my side of the bed and close, very close. He picked up my wounded wrist and unwound the cloth Fergus had used as a bandage for it. "Ma is a vampire as well, both my parents are. See how I trust you with my family secrets?" He frowned at my wrist. "I'm sorry I was such a beast last night. There is no excuse for this." He pulled it toward his mouth.

"No! You will not drink from me again now. I am weak from your last swill." I struggled, desperate to pull away from him. God, but he was strong.

"Relax, Gloriana. I am only going to heal this hurt. There is magic in my tongue. Watch." He slowly licked the ragged edges of the wound and they sealed together, the skin turning pink then quickly becoming unblemished. It was as if he'd never torn it open in his hunger. "Do you see?" He laid my wrist in my lap.

I couldn't believe my eyes. Turning my wrist this way and that, I looked for any sign that it had been ripped open by his fangs. But he was right. He had healed me. Magic? Or the work of the Devil?

"I don't understand." I peeked at him. He was smiling, quite proud of himself, I was sure. "I still don't trust you."

"I will give you my word that I won't attack you again like I did last night. Or erase your memory of it. But you must give me your word as well. That our secret stays with you. No one, not even your best friend at the theater, will hear from you what I am, or what Fergus is." He stared at me, his handsome face serious. "I can read your mind, Gloriana, so can Fergus. If you cannot swear this in good faith, then you will not leave these rooms until I have cleared your mind of our time together. It will be as if we are strangers, that you never knew me, never slept in my bed. You will end up in the alley where I met you, richer and better dressed than you were before but with no idea how that came about." He said it with such conviction that I had no doubt he would hold my head in his strong hands until he made sure I had no choice but to bend to his will.

I could well imagine it. Fergus would leave me there with a bag of gold and a bundle of clothes. But then what? Wait for a man with crude tastes like Lord Sommers to come by and become his victim? Or worse, mayhap the MacDonald vampire would see his chance to take a woman who had served his enemy. I wouldn't recognize him and would go along with a handsome man, having no idea he'd be attracted by my fine blood as well until it was too late. I plucked at the furs, more confused than ever.

"Well, what say you?" Jeremiah was clearly impatient. Because he could read my mind, of course, and knew I was uncertain when faced with so many horrid choices.

I glared at him. "Bastard. I knew you were in my mind. It, it is horrid. My every thought? Have I no privacy?" I clenched my fists, wanting to hurt him as he'd hurt me. But what good would it do? He would see my intent before I could even lift my hand. One glance and I read that in his face. Damn him.

"It is not something I do every moment, Gloriana. You can have your privacy. But this is important. I must be sure you won't betray me." He watched me, waiting to see how we would go on. "I can promise you this—as we proceed, now that you know I am vampire, I can make taking your blood part of our pleasure together." He grinned and actually ran a finger down my arm. I jerked it away.

"You're mad!" I glanced at Fergus, who was heading for the door. "No, don't leave. I know you are his man but I'm not ready to be alone with him just yet. Perhaps never." I leaned back when Fergus did turn and stand just inside the room at Jeremiah's nod.

"Blast! This is not how I thought being a man's mistress would go." My mind was too full of one bad choice after another. Did I leave only to face an uncertain fate? I had just learned that my judgement couldn't be trusted. A handsome face could hide something I could never have imagined. At least here I knew I'd have a warm bed, beautiful clothing and lovemaking so satisfying…

I gripped the bedding. "You bit me like a rabid dog last night. I would have died if Fergus hadn't pulled you off."

"That will not happen again. I can take blood from you and make it painless, I swear it. When you are stronger, of course." Jeremiah reached for my hand but I wouldn't let go of the covers.

"How can I believe you?" I looked away so he couldn't see my tears. "You have betrayed my trust since the moment we met. You will never have it again." Why had I ignored all the signs that I was dealing with someone not as he should be? I looked at Fergus. "Your shape-shifter has shown more concern for my welfare than you have."

"Is that so?" Jeremiah frowned. "I suppose I should be grateful that you are happy with his care." He stared into my eyes as if deciding that erasing my memories might be best after all.

"Stop!" I covered my face with my hands. "If you are planning to make me forget all that has happened, stop it now!" I pressed my face into the mattress. "Leave me. Please. I have had enough torture for now. I need time to think." I waited, praying they would heed my request. Surely with the lock on the outer door, they knew I wasn't going anywhere. The idea that I could lose more memories was unbearable. Fergus knew that had happened to me once. Had he told Jeremiah my story? Would that persuade him to leave my thoughts alone? Was the man even capable of pity?

I heard footsteps and the bedroom door close. I rolled over and looked around the room. Alone. But for how long? I had to decide on my future. And think how I could persuade these two men that I could be trusted with their secrets. My stomach rumbled. Then I noticed a bowl on the table next to the bed. Someone, and it had to be Fergus, had left broth there. I scooted closer and the smell hit me. Fragrant, delicious. I lifted it carefully and took a cautious sip.

Mindful of how my last effort to eat had ended, I took my time drinking the broth. It was still warm and settled into my stomach like a comforting friend. I immediately began to feel stronger. God bless Fergus. He might be something strange, but he had a good heart.

Was it possible that Jeremiah could also be more than a monster who drank blood? I tried to think of all the good things he'd done for me. But then he'd chosen me for my delicious blood, hadn't he? And my body, of course. He'd certainly enjoyed that. He was a lusty man with two appetites. A rich man as well. I should be wise about this.

I wondered how often he needed blood if he wasn't injured. I had many questions as I drained the bowl and set it back on the table. Drowsy and sated, I lay back and stared at the rough stone ceiling above my head. I hoped they would give me time to think. To weigh my choices. Because my entire future rested on my next move.

I was struggling into that same green velvet dress Fergus must have left out for me when there was a thundering sound and yelling. I finally realized it was someone knocking on the outer door. Who could it be? This was the first visitor Jeremiah had had since I'd been here. That I remembered.

Oh, but I'd go mad if I started down that path with my thoughts, so I hurriedly pulled the laces tight and grabbed a shawl that had been left next to the dress. Then I carefully opened the bedchamber door. At least I hadn't been locked in. A man was standing in front of Jeremiah. He was in tears.

"They took her a few hours ago, just after sunset. She didn't have time to shift and escape or didn't bother. I wouldn't know about this but our man who serves her came to me as soon as he knew where they took her. I tell you, it is true. Marin is in the Tower. I saw her through the bars." The man was dressed in fine clothes but they were in disarray and, as I watched, he tore at his long blond hair then fell into a chair. "*Mon Dieu!*"

"This makes no sense, Jean-Claude. Marin Marchand is the oldest vampire I know. How could she let herself be taken?" Jeremiah pulled up a chair and faced him. He glanced at Fergus who quickly moved to my side as if to force me back into the bedchamber.

"Who is this?" The man, Jean-Claude obviously, pointed at me. His nostrils flared. "Mortal. Your blood slave. Can you trust her? I think Marin drank from someone who betrayed her. Yes, she's old, ancient. And has talked of having lived too long. This careless behavior of late is part of it." He sighed deeply. "Well? Answer me, Jeremiah. Is this mortal going to be a problem?"

"Gloriana, come here." Jeremiah stood and held out his hand. "We have nothing to fear from this woman. You know me. I am very careful. She will not mention this meeting or you to anyone." He gave me a look that dared me to defy him.

I realized I was outnumbered and that disobeying even this simple command would be foolish. I walked closer and took Jeremiah's hand, dropping into a curtsy. "Gloriana St. Clair."

"French?" He broke into a spate of that language.

"No, sorry. My husband took that name. He was an actor. I don't speak French. Not a word of it." I saw his face crumple in disappointment.

"Of course. It is common enough. These English admire us, so they pretend…" He pulled a handkerchief out of his waistcoat and wiped his eyes. "My Marin. She became a true Frenchwoman after we met. So cultured, elegant. And now doomed!" He wept into the fine linen.

"Now, Jean-Claude, surely we can think of a way to rescue her. Who is guarding her?" Jeremiah must have noticed how pale and weak I was as I tugged at his hand. I still hadn't eaten a meal. "Gloriana, sit. Break your fast while we talk." He released me so I could step away from him.

"I brought you some berries and cream." Fergus pulled me across the room to the table and gestured at a basket. "I remember you liked the strawberries. Perhaps you wish to go back to bed."

"No, I will eat at the table." I was not about to miss learning more about these men and their plans. "Is Jean-Claude..?"

"A vampire?" Fergus set a bowl in front of me then brought over a cup and saucer, carefully fixing tea for me with cream and sugar this time. "Yes. Marin is his mate. They have been together for centuries."

Centuries! I didn't say what I was thinking. Why bother? Fergus stared at me and nodded, reading my mind of course.

"Jeremiah told you his kind lives forever. Unless someone kills them. And that isn't easy." He shook his head as he poured cream over fresh berries. "I won't tell you how 'tis done. I'm not that foolish."

I began spooning food into my mouth, too interested in the nearby conversation and filling my empty stomach to argue.

"How could they possibly capture her?" Jeremiah had waited until Jean-Claude stopped crying to ask that but I could tell he was impatient.

"She let them. *Elle ne veut plus vivre.*" The man looked about to burst into tears again.

"Suicide? That's madness." Jeremiah gripped the other man's arm. "I know you tried to talk her out of it."

"*Mais bien sûr.* I begged her to stop and think. But she is so tired of living." He turned toward the fire. "Did you know she has over three thousand years? When I met her in Paris, she was already ancient. She was Egyptian in the beginning of her life, when she was turned."

"I had no idea." Jeremiah got up. "Perhaps we should let her go. It is her decision if she wants to end her life."

"True. But not like this! When they carry her out in the sunlight *du matin* while she is still in her death sleep, you know what will happen."

"She will burst into flames as soon as the sun hits her. Not even a cloudy day can save her." Jeremiah frowned at me when I gasped.

"Yes, she will turn into ashes in front of everyone who is waiting to see her tried as a witch." Jean-Claude stared at me. "Oh, yes, that's what happens when we are exposed to the sun. He didn't tell you that, did he?" He laughed bitterly. "There have been rumors about what we are forever. But recently someone is carrying tales anew, hoping to expose our secrets." He pulled a paper from his pocket. "Have you seen this symbol?" He showed it to Jeremiah.

I recognized it as the same as the one the man he'd killed in the alley next to the Globe had carried. "Jeremiah!"

"Yes, I have seen it. What does it mean?" He frowned at the sign.

"Vampire hunters and Catholics carry it. I have no idea how they find out who to target. The Catholics don't care about vampires except that they think they are aligned with the Devil, if they do exist. Most don't believe they do. But the hunters have heard rumors that there are vampires among the Scots with the king." Jean-Claude eyed me. "Are you sure you trust this woman?"

"More than I trust yours." Jeremiah paced the floor in

front of the fire. "Could Marin herself have done that? Passed on our names?"

"No! She could never endanger me or her friends." Jean-Claude grabbed Jeremiah's arm.

"Nor would Gloriana. I was attacked before I had even shown my mistress what I was, so no more talk of her betraying us. We need to find the real traitor. Stop these rumors." Jeremiah glanced at me. "This is why I erase the memories from anyone whose blood I take, Gloriana."

I had nothing to say to that.

"Marin and I do as well." Jean-Claude shook his head. "You must not think otherwise. But then she grew careless and was caught taking blood from a man in an alley by the night watch. Already there are whispers about what she is. Witch? Or something even more evil to those who know no better? Do we wish to show the world that vampires exist?"

"No, of course not." Jeremiah studied me.

I held my spoon suspended above the bowl. My imagination drew a picture of a dead woman going up in flames. The smell of burnt flesh, the screams from the crowd of witnesses would make it into a nightmare scene. I shuddered. And of course those who had heard the whispers about these blood suckers would know then that the rumors were true.

"What happened to the man she was using for blood?" Of course I had to ask. Had she left him dead drained of his blood? Like I'd almost been when Jeremiah had been out of control?

Jean-Claude shook his head. "I wish it were so. Instead he is hale and hearty, serving as a witness for those who plan to burn my Marin at the stake. He is telling everyone who will listen that she looked into his eyes and made him lose his senses. Then she put her fangs into his neck and drank his blood. That is enough for any judge to pronounce her guilty of witchcraft." He jumped up and walked toward the door.

"They've had the trial already? In the middle of the

night?" Jeremiah was close on his heels.

"Who knows if they bothered? All I know is that they are already building a pyre around the post in the courtyard next to the Tower. Runners have been sent out, calling for a large crowd to witness what will surely be the execution of a witch caught casting a spell on a sober citizen." Jean-Claude leaned against the door. "Did I tell you she selected a priest to dine upon?" He banged his head against the wood. "Oh, yes, this couldn't be worse."

"Some say King James has gone soft on witchcraft lately. This will prove he will not tolerate such creatures in the kingdom." Jeremiah exchanged a look with Fergus. "It is almost as if it is planned." He walked over to drop his hand on his friend's shoulder. "I'm sorry, Jean-Claude. What can we do?"

"Just stand as my friend. I am afraid there is nothing…" He buried his face in his hands, his shoulders shaking in silent sobs.

"Is there any chance she will change her mind and escape on her own?" Jeremiah kept his hand on his shoulder. "She is very powerful. I've seen her shift in an instant or make men unable to move with just a glance. Marin could never be kept in a cell if she chooses to leave there."

He took a breath and straightened. "*Non.* She is too weak for her usual powers. The priest lived because she took very little of his life force. Of course he claims it is because he pulled out his crucifix and she fell away from him. You know a cross has no power over us. Marin has been starving herself as she prepared to die." He bowed his head again, lost in his grief. "I thought she would live for me, but clearly I am not enough for her."

Jeremiah had nothing to say to that. "Where are you going now?"

"I have to see her again. Alain, our shifter, is keeping vigil, but I want to watch her as well. In case she changes her mind. I will be a bird sitting between the bars of her cell. It is all I can do." He reached for the door handle.

"Wait!" Jeremiah stepped in front of the door. "Whatever Marin intended, this public execution will harm us all. We must rescue her from the Tower whether she wants us to do it or not. Stay and tell me more."

"I'm afraid rescue will be almost impossible." But Jean-Claude did come back inside to stand next to the fire. "The guards are wearing full armor. Since hearing that she drinks blood, they became determined to protect themselves. And someone has been talking. They are armed with bows and arrows." He looked at me, then at Jeremiah. "Arrows made of olive wood, my friend. I could smell it from the window."

"By God! Who could have told them about that?" Jeremiah paced the floor. "That is something only a few know. Our one vulnerability." He gave me a hard look. "And I won't hear a peep out of you, my girl, if I choose to erase this from your benighted memory."

I shoveled food into my mouth. I'd need my strength for whatever was coming because I'd be damned if I submitted meekly to any plundering of my thoughts by this blood sucking scoundrel. Or be locked in this room while they went off to do whatever they planned.

Jean-Claude barked a bitter laugh. "Who is calling the tune here? You or your blood slave?" He shook his head. "No matter. You see how impossible this will be. Marin is lost to me. She is too weak to shift out of there, even if we could get her to try."

"I won't accept that. And I'll thank you not to use that term for Gloriana. We prefer mistress, if you please." Jeremiah walked over to gather his sword and belt. He strapped them on. "I want to see this arrangement for myself. We have hours before dawn. Fergus, stay here with Gloriana. Surely there will be something we can do for Marin before then."

I laid down my spoon. The idea of any woman going up in flames had killed my appetite. Even if she was one of these cursed vampires, I realized I wanted to help her. I knew something about losing the will to live. I'd come very close to it when my belly had been empty and I'd despaired of finding food. Oh, but then I was the food this creature, Marin, would be needing to survive. I swallowed, wondering if the madness around me had affected me as well.

"Perhaps Fergus and I should go with you. I could distract a guard if that could help." I threw aside my shawl and showed Jean-Claude what I had that could provide a distraction.

"Yes, most men would be diverted by your charms." Jean-Claude took my hand. "Madame, I am sorry if I have offended you. I am not myself. I hope you understand."

"Of course." I flushed when he bowed and kissed the back of my hand. He was handsome and now charming. No wonder the missing Marin had been with him for hundreds of years. "No one should be carried out to burn in the sun. No matter who or what they are. If I can help Marin, I will. Women should help each other."

"Marin would like you, I think." He straightened and headed for the door. "But it is too dangerous. Stay. Eat and gain your strength. I'm sure Jeremiah agrees with me. You are no good to him until your blood is strong again."

Well, that certainly put me in my place. Jeremiah studied me then glanced at Fergus. Some of their silent communication, no doubt. Oh, how I hated their mind reading.

"As soon as she has finished her meal, bring her to the Tower of London. If we find a way to release Marin, we will need blood for her right away. Gloriana's is special and very potent. It will be just what Marin will need to put life back in her." And with that Jeremiah followed Jean-Claude out the door.

I sat back, my mouth open but not so I could eat another bite. I needed no other confirmation that I was nothing more than the blood slave the Frenchman had called me. Or perhaps MacDonald had been even more accurate. I was Jeremiah's blood whore. I threw down my spoon, daring Fergus to force me to eat.

I had volunteered to distract a guard or two, not serve another ravenous vampire. The woman would tear into me in her thirst. Just as Jeremiah had. Fergus stared at me, but I ignored him. Really, what could he say? He would drag me to the Tower if necessary, the master had spoken.

Did Jeremiah really think I would serve another vampire by opening my vein? He would have a fight on his hands before that happened. I finished eating, determined to be strong. I was getting ready to fight.

EIGHT

My wishes didn't matter. I huddled in my cloak at the foot of the Tower of London in the middle of the night. Two hawks landed on the stones nearby then turned into men I recognized. I jumped and held onto Fergus when I almost fell. I would never get used to such a thing. How men fully dressed and wearing swords could be birds one moment and men the next was beyond my understanding. Yet here they were. No wonder sane folks thought they should be burned at the stake. I shuddered, still unnerved by witnessing it.

"What did you find?" Fergus pushed me down so I was sitting on a stone wall next to the river. It was cold and damp but I welcomed the seat. Blasted mind reader.

"Two guards, both in full body armor. They are well-covered and hold bows and arrows. Olive wood as Jean-Claude told us." Jeremiah fingered his sword. "Despite that, I like the odds."

"What about Marin? How is she?" I tried to understand this woman who was a vampire. I had no idea how it would feel to never see the sun, drink human blood or even live so long. Would it make you despair after a while? Even during my worst times, I had always been determined to do whatever it took to keep living. Why, look at me now. Gloriana St. Clair, blood whore. I had a ridiculous urge to laugh wildly. Was I going mad? It was possible. Jeremiah frowned at me and I breathed through my panic. No one was going to hurt me. He had promised. But then what did I know of a vampire's promises?

"Marin still lives. Barely." Jean-Claude paced around us. "We must hurry. I think we can take them, Jeremiah. Alain will help us. Three against two, I will carry Marin out of there."

Jeremiah fingered his sword. "What are we waiting for?"

"There will be guards at the entrance to the Tower. The place is full of cells with more guards in the corridors as well. You cannot just carry a prisoner out of there and not expect to be stopped." Fergus was being the voice of reason.

"I've heard tales of how prisoner are treated here. There's been talk in the theater. I'm sure the guards are open to bribes. You have gold. I know you do." I knew gold was the only way to get prisoners decent food, medicine or even a blanket against the chill of a winter's night.

"Gloriana's right. Bribes would work. But I am known to be in the king's favor. I cannot ask about an accused witch. Word would get back to King James and my entire clan would be at risk." Jeremiah frowned. "Marin would not want you at risk either, Jean-Claude."

"What if Fergus and I approach the guards with some gold? I can claim I wish to visit someone else. A brother or father in gaol. I'm sure the guards won't care who I visit as long as they get coin. Fergus has brought along a basket of food. We can use it to make my role seem real. Surely we can distract them long enough for one of you to carry Marin to safety once you get rid of the guards in her cell." I almost fell off my perch when Jean-Claude lunged at me, pulling me into a hug.

"Gloriana, you are *tres sage*. That is exactly what we should do." He pulled me to my feet. "Open your cloak, *comme ça*, and all those guards will remember are your beautiful *poitrines*."

I looked down. Obviously that last French word meant breasts because with a move that made both Jeremiah and Fergus growl, Jean-Claude had plumped them up to almost burst out of my dress. Yes, the guards would certainly notice them and, if not for a glowering Fergus, try to do more than look.

"Gloriana's right. I brought a basket of foodstuffs for Gloriana." Fergus glanced at me. "For after she gives blood. We'll not need it if we don't get Marin out." He turned to me. But, lass, there's no need to risk yourself. I will approach the guards. Stay here and wait for them to bring Marin to you." Fergus frowned and pulled my cloak closed.

"Gloriana, this is too dangerous. I'm not sure you are even strong enough to do what is necessary. Wait here for us. No one is nearby to bother you." Jeremiah was showing actual concern for me. Or was it only for the blood in my veins?

Suddenly I was tired of being nothing but a vessel to them. "I'm fine. I forced myself to eat some cheese and drink wine before we came. And I doubt Fergus will be enough to distract a guard. They will gladly take his gold, but send him on his way with threats, waving weapons in his face."

I threw my cloak open again. "I think I can use my powers of persuasion to get us inside those walls. All I need to know is when to distract the guards on the stairs." Was I mad? Perhaps. Terrified? Definitely. I linked arms with Fergus. His bulk was reassuring but trying to fool armed guards at the Tower of London could well end with me in a cell alongside Marin. I swallowed, that wine and cheese sitting uneasily in my stomach. But I was tired of being nothing but a blood giver. I needed to prove my worth and not just in the bedchamber.

Jeremiah stared at me, reading my mind of course. He finally nodded. "One of us will fly down the stairs. The guards won't notice a bird or a bat. That will be your signal to do whatever you can to move them out of the main stairway so we can bring Marin down. We will take out the guards in her cell as quietly as we can." Jeremiah turned to Jean-Claude but he had already changed and was flying back up to the Tower window where Marin was kept.

"He is impatient and I don't blame him. She looked very weak. I'm not sure we can save her." He grabbed my shoulders and looked deep into my eyes. "Go quickly and have a care." He pulled me to him, giving me a hungry kiss that shocked me to my toes. "Fergus, if the guards prove difficult, take no chances. Get Gloriana to safety." And with that he stepped back and did his own change, a blur of man and then feathers that made me slightly sick to my stomach.

I watched him go. Would I ever understand him? I could still taste him on my tongue. Smell the wool and masculine scent of man that had made me want to cling to him. He'd used me. I shouldn't want him. Yet, there was something about him …

"Settle, lass. The men will handle the guards easily." Fergus led me around the stone building.

"You think I'm worried about Jeremiah?" I shook my head to try to clear it. It might be best if one of those guards shot him with a deadly arrow. Then I'd be free of whatever spell he'd cast over me. Olive wood. Oh, yes, I'd made note of the fear in the vampires' eyes of that particular wood. So they could be killed by it. Not that I knew where one would get a piece of such a rare wood. You'd not see an olive tree in London, not to my knowledge.

"I see you're still angry at the master. Not that I blame ye." Fergus pulled out some coin, ready to approach the gate. We walked a good ways around a forbidding stone wall to the courtyard. While we watched, a man came out with a weeping woman clinging to his arm. Money changed hands before they hurried away.

So I'd been right. Bribes were taken. The guard didn't bother to lock the heavy iron gate as he waited for us to approach him, eyeing us suspiciously. I threw back my cloak, letting my low cut bodice lead the way. The night air was chill and I shivered as I walked up to the burly guard who smiled at me.

"Please, sir. My father is in a cell in the Tower. Innocent, I swear it. He was taken off the street by mistake. Could I see him for a minute or two and take him some bread and cheese? My servant carries a basket." I lifted the cloth and showed him that we only carried food inside.

"To hear prisoners and visitors alike tell it, there's not a man or woman here who is anything but a saint." He laughed and leaned closer, his breath reeking of garlic and ale. "Tell me this, my girl. Why would I be wanting to do you any favors?"

"Mayhap a coin would persuade ye." Fergus slipped one into the guard's hand.

"Mayhap a favor from the girl here and two coins would make me happy to walk you inside." The guard pulled me close with a hand around my waist.

"Three coins and no favor until I see that my father is all right." I poked the man in the middle of his doublet. "Jenkins. My pa is Alfie Jenkins." It was such a common name that I was sure there had to be someone in there with it.

The guard frowned. "Don't rightly know…"

"Two coins now and another when we come out if we've found him." Fergus shoved me past the guard. "There's another man inside who keeps a list, no doubt."

"There may be. But that'll cost you as well." He tried to grab me as we went past. "Guards up and down are keeping watch o'er the prisoners. Best have plenty of coin. Or favors." He winked.

"Here. Squeeze this until I get back, handsome." I grinned and wiggled my bum as I tossed him a hunk of bread from the basket. "I'll save my favors for you." I winked back.

"Left him right besotted, lass." Fergus led the way.

"Careful or I'll have to kill the man."

"I thought you could just make him lose his memory."

"That's not my trick, 'tis the master's. Careful now." Fergus nodded toward a pair of guards ahead.

The place was certainly a prison. I heard moans from the people locked up in the cells that lined the narrow hall, then one long scream that made me stop in my tracks. Fergus nudged me to keep going. The smell made me gag and I pulled a handkerchief from my bodice to cover my nose. That act did double duty, filtering the stench and drawing the eyes of the two men who stared at us as we approached.

"Who let you in here? State your business." A tall man with a padded waistcoat and a helm with the royal badge on it moved forward and blocked our path with his lance.

"Please, sir." I moved the handkerchief to my eyes, feigning tears. "My dear papa is said to be in a cell here. We brought him food. Would you be so kind as to let us slip him a bit of bread and cheese?" I leaned forward, my breasts about to tumble into this guard's hands. He noticed, of course.

"If your Pa is here, it's because he broke the king's laws. He's probably set to hang. Best you forget him, missy." The guard looked Fergus up and down. "Get you gone, man, before I hurry you along with the end of my lance."

A big black bird flew overhead with a squawk. "Blast!" The other guard threw his own lance at it. "What's afoot? That's the second pass by the creature. The witch must be casting a spell up there. The sooner we see her burned at the stake, the better, I say." He stalked over to retrieve his lance.

"Ooo. A witch? Have you seen her? What does she look like? Tell me all about her." I pulled both men into an alcove when I saw shadows coming down the stairs. "My servant here doesn't believe in such things. Have you seen her do magic, cast those spells?" I leaned in so they could both take a good look down my bodice. Fergus was at my back, his bulk blocking their sight of the stairs, as a man silently went past with a bundle in his arms.

"I stay well away from such evil." One of the guards pulled out a cross and kissed it.

"Of course. Do you think she turned a man into that raven? I heard witches can pull such tricks." I clutched each guard by the arm holding his lance. "You will protect me, won't you?" I shook and pressed my breasts against a burly arm.

"Now, missy, you know we will. Right, Billy?" One of them grabbed me with his free hand, thinking to steal a kiss. "You'll be grateful, I'm sure."

I gasped when Fergus suddenly pushed in between us. "Mistress, your father would skin me alive if he knew I let the likes of these varlets put their hands on you." He thrust the basket at them. "This was a mad idea. We'll be going now. If you have a heart, you will see that the man Jenkins gets the food. But I hold no hope of that." He grabbed my arm and hurried me down the walkway toward the gate.

"Hold! There's no Jenkins here that I know of, not alive anyways. What's your business? You, girl. Come back!" The men were close, and one of them grabbed my cloak, stopping me in my tracks.

Suddenly there was a roar, one so loud I swear the stones beneath my feet trembled. Next to me a giant bear stood on its hind legs and raised paws with long lethal claws that swiped at the two armed men. They fell back, shouting of witchcraft and waving their lances before drawing dirks and stabbing at the beast.

A black bird flew in behind them and, in an instant, became a man armed with a sword. Jeremiah. His surprise helped him make quick work of one guard who fell bleeding to the ground. But more guards were coming, we heard their boots hitting the stones.

"Quickly, follow me. This way!" Jeremiah left Fergus the bear to handle the other guard, who realized he stood no chance against such a giant creature and ran away down a corridor. We hurried in the opposite direction, toward a door that led to a warren of twisting passages that ended at the river. I sensed someone behind me and glanced back. Fergus, in his human form again, stayed with us but kept watching for pursuit. I hoped we had lost the guards but I still heard their shouts.

Jeremiah dragged me by my hand as we ran. When I stumbled, he tossed me over his shoulder. That knocked the breath right out of me but he kept going. The way I bounced as he ran, he was lucky I didn't lose what little I'd eaten. Soon he stopped at a set of stone steps leading down to the riverbank and put me down. I dragged in air ripe with smells I didn't want to name. Before I could catch my breath, he snatched me up again and dropped me into a boat with a man inside.

"Hurry!" When he threw back his hood I realized it was Jean-Claude who whispered. He held a bundle in his lap. Surely it was too small to be a woman. "She can't last much longer."

Jeremiah leaped into the boat too then helped Fergus cast off lines. Both men grabbed oars, pushing off quickly. They were silent as they rowed, getting as much water between the boat and the quay as they could. We were in such total darkness I didn't know how they could see to steer us safely across the river.

I gasped when lights showed on the bank we'd just left, men shouting as they searched for us. I could only pray that we were far enough out that they couldn't see us.

"Get down, Gloriana." Jeremiah pushed my head between my knees and we all lay in the damp bottom of the boat. It drifted along silently until Fergus whispered that the lights had moved on.

The men had just started rowing quietly again when a barge appeared, moving toward us in the middle of the river. A man with a lantern stood in the bow. Jeremiah managed to steer to the far side of it. Just in time. The men were back on the river bank next to the Tower, clearly convinced we must have used a boat for our escape. There was much shouting and many lanterns this time. We could hear them clearly, calling for their own boats to search the river.

"Gloriana, come here. Marin is in desperate need of your help." Jean-Claude whispered.

I knew sound carried well across the water. I could certainly hear the frustrated guards on shore. Did I want us to be discovered? I could call for help. And be recognized as part of the group that had rescued a witch? I'd made my choice and now I had to do my part to save this female vampire. Jeremiah's eyes were on me as I carefully scooted closer to where Jean-Claude bent over Marin who was wrapped in his cloak.

"Please. You must let her drink your blood." He moved aside the dark cloth and I saw her face for the first time in the dim moonlight.

She was pale, so very pale, with long black hair. He'd claimed she'd originally come from Egypt and she did have an exotic look. She was a beauty with a slant to her large eyes and thick lashes. But it seemed as if all the moisture had been drawn from her body. I studied her full lips. Inside would be those horrible fangs that would pierce my skin. I didn't know this woman but clearly Jean-Claude adored her. He brushed back her hair and picked up her lifeless hand.

"Feel how cold she is. She may be beyond saving but I beg you to try, Gloriana. If you don't..?" He hissed, his own fangs startling in his handsome face. "By all that is holy I will kill you and throw your body in this stinking river." He said more in his native language but stopped when the boat rocked and Jeremiah was on him, his hands at his throat.

"You forget yourself. The woman is mine." Jeremiah's grip was unyielding until Jean-Claude nodded once, his fangs disappearing.

"Pardon, *madame*, I am *dérangé*. If I lose my Marin, I won't want to live either." He bent his head and kissed Marin's lips. "Please, please, help her."

"Will you, Gloriana?" Jeremiah spared a glance for the Tower and the disturbance there. Boats were being launched, filled with armed men. But Fergus was rowing with incredible speed.

Our distance from them was increasing as we approached a crowded dock. I hoped we could hide among the many boats there. Fergus caught my eyes and nodded, steering toward them. But I had to answer these men. I pressed a hand to my roiling stomach then nodded. She might not be human now, but she had been once. She'd certainly earned Jean-Claude's devotion. And spared the priest who'd given her blood recently. She didn't *look* like a monster.

"Ah, *merci*! *Merci beaucoup.* You are an angel." Jean-Claude produced a little knife. "I will be gentle. Let me make this painless for you." He picked up my hand before I had a chance to change my mind and pulled it to his lips. "*Comme ça.*" He ran his tongue along the inside of my wrist then used the knife to make a cut across my vein. It didn't hurt as he had promised.

"Lovely blood. Smell it, my heart." He pulled my bleeding wrist to Marin's face, waving it under her nose.

I waited. This was what we'd done for Jeremiah when he'd been unconscious. I braced myself, afraid she would suddenly wake and attack me.

"Watch her carefully, Jean-Claude. Gloriana's blood is very potent. Marin may harm her in her eagerness to drink it. Don't let her take too much." Jeremiah had gone back to rowing. We were among fishing boats now and he and Fergus whispered, searching for a hiding place while Marin fed.

Fed. I couldn't take my eyes off her. I waited. Had her nose twitched? Jean-Claude and I both peered down at her. He was certainly desperate for a sign of life. He squeezed my wrist, causing more blood to well and trickle onto her lips.

"*Mon amour*, you must drink. I can smell this woman's delicious *du sang*. It is for you." He reached down and smeared it across her lips, slipping a finger inside her mouth. "Yes, that's it. Your fangs are coming down. I feel them!"

He turned to me. "Press your wrist against her lips, Gloriana. Please, *mon ami*. I know her thirst will take over any moment now."

Mon ami. I knew that meant friend. I wanted to shake my head. As if I considered myself a friend to any vampire! Blood slave. That was all I was here. But I did as I was told, easing closer and laying my wrist against Marin's cool mouth. I braced myself for what would surely come next. When her thirst took over she would strike, just as Jeremiah had and become the same kind of ravening beast.

Would Jean-Claude really pull her away before I was drained of all my life force? I knew who he would choose to save if it came down to a choice. At least Jeremiah kept watching us when he could take his eyes off getting the boat settled in a safe place to dock. He'd shown a protective instinct toward me that I would have appreciated if I hadn't realized it was his own greed for my blood behind it.

I felt the stir against my wrist even before Jean-Claude's glad cry echoed through the air.

"Hush! Remember we are being hunted." But Jeremiah watched as we all did when Marin's eyes fluttered open and she suddenly grasped my arm. "Careful now, Jean-Claude. I will not stand for Gloriana to be sacrificed for your mate."

"I understand."

I barely registered the man's soft reply as long nails dug into my forearm and sharp fangs pierced my wrist. Whatever magic had dulled the pain at first had worn off and there was no relief as Marin drew deeply. I bit my lip to keep from crying out at the pain. Abruptly she released me, her eyes opening wide.

"Who are you?" She had black eyes, fathomless as they searched my face. "*Mon Dieu*, I've not tasted such divine blood since the pharaohs walked the streets of Thebes."

"I am Gloriana, Jeremiah Campbell's, um, mistress." I jerked my arm back into my lap and covered it with my cloak. "We must be quiet. The guards from the Tower are still looking for us."

"If we dock here, I think we can make it safely to your place, Jean-Claude." Jeremiah nodded toward the crowded area where many boats were tied to pilings. "It's not far."

"Marin, darling, you must drink more." Jean-Claude reached for my arm, impatiently pulling my cloak aside. "What does it matter who this woman is? She has fresh, clean blood. I'm sure it is to your liking. Take more, *mon chéri.*"

Marin licked her lips clean of the blood her mate had smeared there. "Yes, it is to my liking. But I had hoped to end my life, not start a new one." She held out her hand to me. "This is a mystery, though. I can see into your mind, *ma petite femme.* You have no memory of where you came from, who you are." She smiled, the effect ruined by a pair of the longest, sharpest fangs I'd ever seen, longer than Jeremiah's. "I will not force her, *cheri.*" She waited, staring into my eyes. "Please?"

I couldn't look away and finally reluctantly gave her my hand. Why? Oh, of course she was casting a spell and I had no control. Vampires. Witches. What was the difference?

"Ah, thank you. I promise I will be gentle. But I must have another taste." She glanced at Jeremiah. "Yes, we will all go to our home. I need to rest, restore. This woman has what I need. I must shift there or any guards searching will recognize me. So I must feed a bit more first." She inhaled when she had my wrist next to her mouth. "By all the gods, but this is what I have been missing for most of my long lifetime." Then she delicately licked the vein before she struck and took a deep draw.

It didn't hurt but I struggled despite my best intentions. The pull was so strong, it felt as if she wanted more of me than just my blood. The boat bumped against others then steadied as it was tied to the dock. Marin held me with a hand on my shoulder, drawing me even closer. I couldn't have moved if I wanted to. It was as if I was powerless. Could she indeed be a witch as well as a vampire? I had no idea and wasn't sure I wanted to know the answer.

"Surely that is enough," Jeremiah said it firmly and moved closer.

She finally released me, smiling and daintily licking my wrist again. As I'd seen before, the wound where the knife had cut me healed almost instantly. Magic indeed.

"Time to go. How are you feeling, Marin?" Jean-Claude stood, ready to pick her up.

"I am fine, don't fuss so." She waved him away before she stood. I could see in the light from nearby street lamps that her cheeks were now flushed. "But I should feed once more before we send Jeremiah and Gloriana on their way. I hope that is all right."

Jeremiah glanced at me. "Once more. After she has had a chance to recover. Gloriana?" He helped me out of the boat. "Are you able to walk? I doubt we could find a hack this late. And the fewer witnesses to our being abroad near the river this night, the better."

"No, I can walk if it's not too far." I *was* feeling weak and wished I had some of that bread and cheese we'd left in the Tower.

"Thank you, Jeremiah. Our home is not far from here, Gloriana. Where is Alain?" Marin looked around.

"The shifter flew above us, ever watchful. As soon as he saw you sit up, I'm sure he headed home." Jean-Claude smiled. "You cannot know how happy I am to see you looking so well, *chéri*."

"Yes, I am on the mend. He can prepare something for Gloriana to eat and drink." Marin leaned against Jean-Claude. "I feel well enough to shift and will meet everyone there."

Jean-Claude took my hand. "Thank you, Gloriana." He turned to Jeremiah. "Will you escort her to our home? Your shifter is welcome but he could be recognized in his human form. It is best he shift there."

"I know where it is. I will meet you there. The guards could well recognize Gloriana, too." Fergus was on the dock, looking around as if to see if our pursuers had found us yet.

"Is that what she wore?" Marin had flicked aside my cloak. "Was she your distraction in my escape plan?"

"Yes. I approached the guard at the gate and those in the corridor, claiming I brought food for a prisoner in the Tower." I pulled the cloak closed against the chill in the damp air.

"Believe me. The men didn't look at your face." Marin chuckled. "And your cloak is ordinary enough to be unrecognizable. Can you bend over, as if you are an old woman? If you walk with her, Jeremiah, call her Grandmother, and help her as if she is ancient, no one will look at her twice. Just keep your hair and your breasts covered, Gloriana, and all will be well." Marin wrapped Jean-Claude's cloak around her and kissed her lover. "You took a foolish risk, *mon amour*. I am glad you were not harmed."

"How could I not save you? I am going to make sure we have many things to live for from now on. Just tell me what you want and I will see to it." He held her for a moment, clearly overjoyed.

Marin looked back at us then stepped away from Jean-Claude. "We will talk later. I cannot believe I feel so restored. Your blood, Gloriana. I will need more of it as soon as you have had time to rest and eat." She gave me a brilliant smile then turned into a bat that flew into the night sky.

"Oh! That was quite a recovery." I stared after her. Jean-Claude had shifted as well, following her in the same form. "Bats. Not birds."

"They seem to prefer it." Fergus looked me over. "Are you all right, lass? She drank a good bit."

"She wasn't greedy." I turned to Jeremiah. "Not like some."

"Yes, yes, I know. And have apologized. I will do so again if it will get me back in your good graces." He made me an elegant bow. "You helped save Marin, Gloriana. I won't forget it." He took my hand and kissed the back of it, reminding me of how he could charm me and make me want him.

"I couldn't imagine letting a woman burn to ashes in the sun." I didn't resist when he pulled me close to his side.

"You were very brave. Now, Grandmother, Marin gave us excellent advice." He turned. "Fergus? Are you cat or bird?"

"Or bear? I admit you had me terrified at first. Certainly the guards thought the witch had worked a spell on them." I shivered as I fastened my cloak and pulled up the hood, making sure my blond hair and my breasts were well out of sight.

"You know what I like." Fergus gave us a rare grin then became a black cat, racing off into the night.

"We'd best be on our way, Grandmother." Jeremiah tucked my hand into the crook of his arm and began to walk. "Remember, you are old and infirm."

"Easy to do when I am light-headed from lack of blood." I wasn't lying. Clutching his arm, I took a moment to steady myself. Being a blood slave wasn't a high calling. It seemed more like the human version of a milk cow. I started off with a slow, shuffling gait that I was sure maddened the soldier in Jeremiah.

"Wait until you see their home, Gloriana. My place is temporary for my stay here. They have been in London for years and Marin has created a fine…" He laughed. "Well, I will enjoy seeing your face once we arrive."

"Is it underground? Do all vampires live that way? To avoid the sunlight?" I might as well learn as much as I could since I was clearly throwing in my lot with them.

"I--" He turned as if he had heard something. Soon I did as well, the tramp of a dozen boots on the stones making it clear we had company. It was a group of the king's men wearing those helms with an emblem I recognized.

"You there! Halt. State your business. What are you doing abroad this time of night?" The leader of the group pulled his sword and approached Jeremiah. "Captain Arnold of the Tower Guard."

I clung to Jeremiah, so bent over all I could see were the stones beneath our feet.

"My grandmother doesn't sleep well. She insisted we visit the apothecary. To see if he has something to help her rest."

"Now? I know of none who would be open." The man leaned down as if to peer into my face.

I slapped at him. "He'll open for me, young man. I have gold enough to see to that." I used the old lady voice I'd heard from the stage. It had a crack in it. I added a wheezing cough. "This night air ain't good for me old bones. Can we get on with it, Sonny? Or must I give this lad a gold coin? King's man? Or robber?"

Jeremiah squeezed my hand. "Sorry, sir. She's got a mind of her own and says whatever comes into it." He sketched a bow. "No insult intended."

The captain laughed. "'Minds me of my own granny. But we're looking for a witch, escaped from the Tower. And a comely wench and her man who helped her."

"Witch!" I trembled and held onto Jeremiah. "Sonny, get me off these lanes now! I heard tell they can turn people into wild beasts. Make sane folks crazy with their spells."

"It's true, madam. The guards claim they saw it with their own eyes. Mayhap the woman distracting them was a witch as well." The captain patted my bent back.

"We've seen no one this night but the usual riffraff looking to take our gold. I sent them on their way with my sticker." Jeremiah pulled out a knife. "Got to protect my granny."

"Right you are. Go on, then. Good luck to you." The captain signaled his men and they kept going, checking alleys and then turning down the lane that we'd just come up, the one that ran to the river.

"You are quite the actress. It's too bad women aren't allowed on the stage," Jeremiah said as soon as they were well out of sight. He squeezed my hand. "Now we are almost there but I want to make sure the soldiers are long gone before we knock on their door."

"Living with an actor helped me learn a few things." I longed to straighten my back which ached from the unnatural position. As soon as Jeremiah gave the signal, I stood tall, sighing at the relief.

"You look exhausted." Fergus had been waiting for us in front of a plain building. He looked me over, frowning while Jeremiah knocked several times in what seemed to be a code.

"I am. It's been a long night." I started when a heavy door creaked open and Alain, the shapeshifter who worked for Marin and Jean-Claude, greeted us.

"Jeremiah, we should have taken Gloriana straight home with us." Fergus barely acknowledged Alain.

"We are here now. She can eat and gain some strength, even rest awhile." Jeremiah took my arm so we could follow Marin's shape-shifter.

Alain held a brace of candles and guided us down steps until we were underground. Then we walked down a long corridor, Alain pausing to unlock two more doors before we were at a wooden door painted the color of blood. I shuddered, thinking the color choice was a symbol of what the two vampires loved most.

"Welcome to our home." Marin stood just inside, Jean-Claude's arm around her. She looked freshly bathed, her hair sleek and shining. She wore a silk dressing gown of deep blue and held out her hands to me. "Come, I have had Alain fix you something to eat and drink. Jean-Claude, take Gloriana's cloak. It is warm in here."

She was right. It was very warm with a fire blazing in an enormous stone hearth. I was happy to be out of my damp cloak as well. But it made me very aware of my bare throat and low bodice. Marin actually licked her lips and stared at the vein in my neck, making me swallow nervously before I was distracted by the beauty around me.

Jeremiah lived in a comfortable place but it was plain and masculine. This home was like something out of a fairy tale. There were colorful rugs, silks and pillows everywhere. I could have been inside a palace. Gilt framed paintings hung on the walls with tapestries behind them. And jewel-toned velvet covered the cushioned chairs and sofas. If I had dreamed of a place to live were I to suddenly come into a fortune, this might be it.

"Gloriana, Marin asked you a question." Jeremiah was clearly amused.

"Sorry. What was it?" I stopped gawking like a milkmaid fresh from the country and faced Marin.

"Would you like wine?" She held out a glass of red liquid. The color looked too much like blood to me and I shook my head.

"No, thank you. Perhaps just water for now." I smelled something delicious and realized I was hungry. Of course I had to eat. Marin kept staring at the places where blood pumped through my veins. I was certainly on the menu for her.

"Relax, Gloriana, I will fix you a plate. Your blood did me much good. I am thinking about living again. Obviously there are still things, secrets, to be learned. I haven't felt such curiosity in many, many years." Marin nodded to Alain and he brought a fine china plate to the table. It was filled with roasted chicken, tiny vegetables and a savory cheese tart.

"It looks delicious. Thank you." I settled into the armchair he held out for me and sipped a goblet of cool water. With Marin's avid gaze on my throat, I was losing my appetite even though the food did look and smell wonderful.

Fergus stared at Marin disapprovingly. I smiled at him and got a small smile in return. He had been in a dark mood ever since we'd arrived at the door. I remembered that he had advised me to leave after Jeremiah had taken so much blood before. He had become a friend to me. Jeremiah watched me, too. Not as a friend, though. Something… else.

Marin hovered over me and handed me a fork. "Eat, relax. I can wait a while for another drink from you."

"I hope so, Marin. Remember, we helped save you. I

don't owe you a continuing supply of blood from Gloriana."
Jeremiah moved closer to the table. "I will say it again. She is
mine. This was a favor. Because, if you'd been taken out of
the Tower in the morning, your destruction in the sunlight
would have raised questions about our kind that could have
harmed all of us."

"Of course. I understand. You were very generous.
And I appreciate the risks you took. The risks to your shifter
and to Gloriana as well. She was especially brave." Marin was
clearly in charge here, waving a hand when Jean-Claude
started to speak. "*Non, C'est mon problème, je vais le résoudre.*"

"The way to solve this problem, as you call it, Marin, is
to have one last drink from Gloriana before we leave."
Jeremiah dropped his hand onto my shoulder.

"What if I pay you for her? I want her, Jeremiah. I must
have her." Marin moved closer to him, her face intent. They
were making serious eye contact. I had no doubt there was
mind reading going on that I would never understand.

"I am not an object to be bought and sold." I tried to
stand but Jeremiah's hand was firm and I couldn't move. All
eyes were suddenly on me. "I don't *belong* to you, Jeremiah."

"You are wanted by the Tower guards. You aided a
witch to escape from the Tower. And you know I can erase
your memories of vampires and our ways. It's best if you let
me decide your future now. I can protect you. I promise to
do it with my life." His hand tightened on my shoulder.

I inhaled, shocked by the intensity of that promise. But
to act as if he *owned* me? I bit back all the angry words I
wanted to fling at both of them.

"Listen to me, Gloriana. If you left here on your own?
Well, I wouldn't give you five minutes before you landed in a
cell, waiting for your own stake in the courtyard and a fiery
death." Jeremiah pinned me with a fierce gaze, a silent
warning to stay quiet, before turning to our hostess again.
"Now, Marin, where were we?"

"I believe you were about to name your price." She
smiled and ran a fingertip across my throat before he could

stop her. "I will pay anything, Jeremiah. Anything to have her."

NINE

"Exactly why is her blood so important to you, Marin? I have my own reasons for wanting to keep her." Jeremiah gave me a smoldering look that made me shift in my seat. "But worth a fortune?"

Marin's long fingernails slid across the vein pulsing in my neck, making me shiver.

"Listen and you might understand why I want her." She sighed and glanced back at Jean-Claude. He quickly brought a chair for her. "*Merci*. I am still very tired from my ordeal." She sat but never took her hand off my bare neck.

"This can wait, *mon amour*. You should rest." Jean-Claude hovered close, frowning at Jeremiah who took a chair across from me.

"Gloriana is tired as well. I am taking her home with me. You have fed once. Surely that is enough." Jeremiah frowned and stood.

"*Non*, I need more. You asked. Now I want to explain why I'm willing to pay a high price to have Gloriana." Marin gripped Jean-Claude's hand when he stood on her other side. "Listen to me!" She waited until Jeremiah nodded and sat again. "You see, when I was a young vampire in the royal household of Nefertiti in Thebes, I was exposed to many wonderful things. The Pharaohs were treated as gods and I do believe they were more than mere mortals. They had amazing powers!"

I wanted to fling her hand away when she kept stroking my neck. To shriek at them to stop this haggling over me as if I was something that had caught Marin's eye in the market. But I was struck dumb. My will was gone and I couldn't even move. Oh, but I hated these powerful vampires!

"Go on." Jeremiah met my gaze. "Gloriana, trust me. Eat, regain your strength." He looked deep into my eyes and I picked up a fork to stuff a bite of chicken into my mouth.

I tasted nothing, eating as he watched. There was silence in the room except for the crackle of the fire in the hearth and a sudden movement behind me.

Jeremiah frowned. "Fergus! You and Alain may step outside to settle your differences if you cannot be civil."

Jean-Claude laughed. "It seems our shifters are territorial and very protective." He kept his hand on Marin's shoulder. "By all means, go outside if this conversation disturbs you two. I'll not have brawling in my home. Alain can defend our honor quite nicely."

"Gloriana deserves better, Jeremiah." Fergus moved to the end of the table so I could see him. The shifter Alain followed him and attempted to shove him back.

"This is their business, not ours. Outside. Or I will show you the point of my knife." Alain reached for it at his belt.

"Ha! It won't be knives we'll be using if it comes down to a fight." Fergus shimmered and seemed to grow in size, as if about to change.

I wished I could beg him to be careful, but all I could do was keep stuffing food in my mouth, under Jeremiah's command. Stab and chew--carrots, potatoes and chicken. I had no appetite for it but couldn't stop.

"Enough! I will ask you to trust me as well, Fergus. Gloriana is under my protection. Now go outside." Jeremiah's frown worked. Jean-Claude nodded to Alain. The two men grumbled, broad shoulders bumping against each other as they left the room, the door slamming behind them. "Continue, Marin."

"Of course. I was telling you about Nefertiti's court." She glanced at my plate which was almost empty, then slid it out of reach and took my fork. "That is enough, Gloriana. We don't want you to become sick."

I sagged in my chair. My hand twitched, wanting to take the fork again, but she squeezed my shoulder and I finally relaxed.

"She is right, Gloriana. Drink some water while we listen to Marin's tale." Jeremiah pushed the goblet into my hand. "It had better be a good one."

"Oh, it is." Marin watched my every move, especially my throat as I drank until the goblet was empty. "Nefertiti was beautiful and surely a goddess. She could read minds as easily as you or I can, Jeremiah, and it pleased her to have vampires in her court. I was one of her favorites. My love bites gave her pleasure while we were in bed together and she allowed me to drink her blood." She closed her eyes with a smile, obviously remembering.

"Her divine blood was so potent it made the finest wine seem like rank river water. And the power! I would feel strong, invincible, for weeks after just one feeding. Believe me, to serve such beauty… " Her eyes opened and she studied me. "Gloriana's blood holds the same thrill for me. That same *je ne sais pas* that reminds me…Well, it was a wonderful time in my long life."

"I am sure." Jeremiah's look at Jean-Claude was as sharp as a knife cut. "No wonder you lost your will to live, Marin. An ordinary vampire's blood must be a disappointment to you."

Marin glanced over her shoulder. "Don't let him tease you, Jean-Claude. You have *never* disappointed me and well you know it, *chéri*. I have always liked variety. Even then."

"Yes, *mon coeur*, you keep our *faire l'amour* very entertaining." He settled a hand on my back. "Gloriana, if you join our household, you can look forward to exciting times with us. Scotsmen are not known for their imagination in the boudoir. "

Jeremiah leaned forward. "Take your hand off her. I won't tell you again."

"Ah, you are jealous, Jeremiah. Jealousy is something we have learned is a waste of our time, have we not, Jean-Claude? We share our love. Variety keeps our bed interesting for both of us." Marin smiled at her lover. "*Chérie*, step away for now. Jeremiah and I are still coming to terms."

And I was still taking in her story. Lover to a goddess? What did she mean? I had heard that women could be lovers. The theater folks were nothing if not adventurous, even the wives of the actors. But this was the first I'd heard that there could be gods and goddesses who walked the Earth. Marin didn't remove *her* hand from my shoulder, instead sliding a bold fingertip across the edge of my bodice as if daring Jeremiah to object. It was driving me mad that I still couldn't move when I wanted to push it away. She looked me over and licked her lips.

"Have you had a woman make love to you, Gloriana? It can be thrilling." She laughed. "I see you are shocked and intrigued. Come live with us and you will learn many things that will give you pleasure."

If she didn't get greedy for my blood and kill me. I could see the thirst in her eyes, the desperation there.

"This has gone on long enough. There are no terms." Jeremiah threw back his chair. "You are clearly ready to go on living, Marin. Send Jean-Claude or Alain out to find another blood whore for your purposes. I am taking Gloriana home with me. She is not for sale and never will be. I don't barter for human lives. When we part ways, she will be free to do as she pleases."

"But you promised! You said I could have one more drink from her!" Marin jumped up, her eyes wild. "And surely we can and will come to terms. She is a mere mortal. Why would you ever let her go free? She is much too valuable." She grabbed his arm as he helped me up. At his steely look, she dropped it.

"*Je vous demande pardon.*" She looked down at her hands. "Perhaps my recent ordeal has overset my nerves. I am weak. I admit it. I let old memories and my weakness make too much of her."

"Don't try to stop me again, Marin." Jeremiah warned Jean-Claude away with another look.

Marin followed us to the door. "Jeremiah, please don't take her away yet. I must feed one more time. Even you admitted her blood is very potent. I need it."

Jeremiah grabbed our cloaks and faced her. "Yes, it is. But not so extraordinary that I would liken it to the blood of a goddess from ancient Egypt. I think you are right. You clearly need rest and are still light-headed from starving yourself." He glared at Jean-Claude when he suddenly stepped between us and the door. "Do you really want to fight about this? Now? When your woman needs you?" He stared into the man's eyes. "Feed her yourself. I'm sure your own ancient blood will be just the thing to make her stronger."

"Marin, he is right about that. Whatever you saw in this human, it can't be as good for you as my own ancient blood, *mon amour.*" Jean-Claude threw open the door, startling the two shape-shifters who stood nose to nose in the corridor. "Alain, step aside. Our guests are leaving."

"About time." Fergus had a bruise on his cheek and blood on his knuckles. "We've done enough for these people, Jeremiah. Best be on our way. Sunrise can't be too far off."

"I know, I feel it." Jeremiah glanced at Alain, who had a bloody nose and swelling around his eye, then turned back to Fergus. "Can you find a horse for us? We need to get back in a hurry."

"Aye, I saw a stable close by when we arrived. I'll meet you outside." Fergus took off at a run.

I was feeling surprisingly strong, the benefits of my

forced feeding. I took a breath and finally found my voice. "Do we have time to beat the sunrise? Perhaps you should go back without me. You know I'll just slow you down. Fergus and I can come after you."

"I can make it if we ride. I want to see you safely to our door myself. You and Fergus shouldn't be seen together on the streets again so soon after Marin's escape. There may still be Tower guards looking for you. He is too recognizable and they will take up anyone caught with him, whether they think she is a grandmother or not." Jeremiah nodded to Jean-Claude. "We are done. Marin is safe for now. It would be best if you both left the city as soon as possible."

"I agree." Jean-Claude bowed. "Thank you for helping with the rescue. I am in your debt." He glanced back into their rooms. "My pardon, Gloriana, for Marin's demands. She is usually not so particular about her blood sources." He smiled and reached for my hand but I kept it tucked inside my cloak which Jeremiah had thought to lay over my shoulders.

"Jeremiah's right. Leave town before she's caught. I won't help try to rescue her again. It was foolish of me to do it the first time." I didn't resist when Jeremiah pushed me down the corridor. "We'd better hurry."

"Yes, go. Be well. And safe!" Jean-Claude followed Alain inside then shut their door. We heard it lock.

Jeremiah picked me up and ran. He was so fast the stone walls went past us in a blur. Soon we were outside and there stood Fergus with a horse wearing only a bridle, no saddle. That didn't seem to concern Jeremiah who handed me to Fergus, leaped on the animal, then took me in his arms again. Before I could do much more than hold onto him, we were off.

I had never been on a horse before that I could remember. But I felt secure in Jeremiah's arms as we rode through deserted streets. I prayed we wouldn't run into search parties of Tower guards and our luck held. The only people abroad in the hours before dawn were tradesmen setting up stalls and people like us, scurrying about doing things that were best not done in broad daylight. Fergus must have shifted because he was waiting for us when Jeremiah pulled up in front of the building where he made his home deep underground. Somewhere nearby a clock tower chimed five bells.

"You've only minutes to spare." Fergus took the horse's reins. "I'll see this beast back to where he belongs. Go now. Gloriana, will you be all right if I leave you alone with him?" He nodded toward Jeremiah.

"I guess I'll have to be." I gave Fergus a smile. "Thank you for looking out for me. I know I'm only a lowly mortal to both of you."

"Hah! So was Jeremiah at one time. It would be wise for him to remember that." Fergus walked away leading the horse.

I thought about that as Jeremiah took my arm and led me inside the familiar doorway and down the steps to his lair. Yes, that was what I decided his home was. He had a place to hide during daylight hours, just like any nocturnal animal. But now I knew he'd been mortal once, just like me. Interesting.

"So you weren't born a vampire." I had to know about this.

Jeremiah escorted me inside after he'd unlocked the door. "No, I was turned vampire when I was eight and twenty."

"Turned." I took off my cloak and sat while he stirred up the fire. So much had happened it seemed an age since we'd left here. "How can you be 'turned'?"

"Another vampire does it. It's complicated. I made the choice at the time." He cast off the long black cape that had allowed him to hide his sword from the guards who'd stopped us earlier.

He took off that sword and examined it, then set it aside for Fergus to clean. I noticed it still had blood from the guards he'd killed or wounded in the Tower and wondered for a moment if those men had left families who'd mourn them. Too late to consider that. Now I could grab that sword and... What?

Jeremiah didn't seem concerned that he had left a weapon where I could reach it. Of course not. He would heal if I managed to hurt him. And where could I go if I did run from here? Straight into the arms of a Tower guard who would be happy to see me burned at the stake? I deliberately put my back to the sword and watched Jeremiah sit on a chair to pull off his boots. Getting ready to die at sunrise.

I picked up his boots and cape to carry them to the bedchamber. But then I remembered that he didn't die for the day there. No, there was a locked room. He had followed me and pulled off his shirt. As always, I couldn't look away from his broad and masculine chest. Was he thinking he had time for bedsport? How did I feel about that? I had yet to refuse him and wondered if I could. I did like the way he'd defended me against Marin's attempt to "buy" me.

I dropped his boots next to the bed. "Who did it? Turned you vampire?"

"My father." He sat on the bed but didn't remove his pantaloons. "I see that shocks you. I told you my parents are both vampires. We are a family of vampires. As we gain maturity, we are given a choice of becoming vampire or staying mortal. Most of us marry and have families before we choose immortality. That's how my parents had me and my brothers and sisters. Once we are vampire, our seed is no longer fertile."

"Do you? Have a wife and children?" I sat beside him. Mortal first. It was difficult to imagine. His face certainly gave nothing away about how he felt about his decision. He wouldn't look at me, just stared at the wall, as cold as he'd been when he'd stared down Marin in their rooms. Did he have regrets? I wanted to touch his hand but wondered if he would welcome it.

"No." He got up and walked into the other room. I followed close on his heels. "I'm feeling the sunrise. I know

Fergus told you we die when the sun comes up. I will be locked into my room as long as it is light outside, Gloriana. That is when we are vulnerable to attack. I cannot trust anyone near me then." He stared at me for a long moment. He didn't say it aloud but he might as well have added *even you.*

"Fergus has a key and he's the only one who should be allowed inside these rooms during the day. I know Marin and Jean-Claude still want you. I read it in their thoughts. They will die at sunrise too, but Alain may try to come for you with hired men to help him. Don't let anyone in. Do you hear me?"

"Of course." I followed him to that sturdy door and his special room. He didn't let me see inside though I wanted desperately to get a look at where he slept. Was it an ordinary bed? Or something else? He died at sunrise. Would it matter what he laid his head on?

"You could go to them if you wished, but I didn't see that desire in your mind." He pulled me to him. "I meant it when I said I would protect you. I cannot erase their thoughts of you. I would if I could. Marin it too strong for me to do that to her."

"I wondered..." It would have been a simple solution.

"Now that you have been seen in the Tower helping Marin, we have something of a problem. I doubt any of those guards would ever be near the King but if I could find the right ones..." He ran his hands over my back. "I'm afraid it will be impossible to take care of all the guards who might have seen you. I know you won't believe me in your present mood, but I don't enjoy killing. You were brave, foolishly so. I can only wonder why you would take such a risk for a vampire. I know you hate us."

"Because you treat me as if I am nothing but food!" I jerked away from him. "I am already regretting it. I suppose I was trying to prove to you and to myself that I have more value than just my blood." I couldn't look at him. I did sound foolish.

"You certainly impressed me. First in the Tower and then by my side as Grandmother." He turned me so I faced him. "I won't deny your blood is what first drew me to you, Gloriana. It is very fine indeed. Marin is right about that. But there is more to my fascination with you than that now."

"Oh, yes. I am comely enough to satisfy your lust." I was not going to shed a tear, but I felt the pressure behind my eyes and looked away from him. "Go to your death sleep, vampire. I have nowhere to go now. You are right about that. I did this to myself." I forced a laugh that sounded hollow even to my own ears. "I might as well enjoy a nice long bath before I sleep. It is one of the few pleasures living here has given me."

"One of the few, Gloriana?" He pulled me close and held my face still so he could kiss me breathless. "Deny that my kisses mean nothing, I dare you." He rested his hand on my rapidly beating heart. "You want me. You get pleasure from lying with me. Admit it."

"Yes, damn you. You are quite an accomplished lover, Jeremiah Campbell. I won't deny *that*." I slid his hand inside my bodice. "But then you are only good for it about half a day, more's the pity." I noticed his eyes drooping and knew his time was running out. I glanced down and saw that even the bulge in his pantaloons was losing the fight. "Die then and I'll see you when the sun goes down." I jerked his hand from my breast and shoved him into his room then pulled the handle toward me. I heard the key turn in the lock before I staggered to the sofa in front of the fire. Bold words. Too bad that's all they were, words. I was trapped and now in league with a vampire, for better or worse. What did the future hold for me now? I couldn't imagine.

***

Fergus had filled the bathtub for me then left so I could have a good long soak. He was off to fetch the rest of my new clothes from the tradesmen. I hoped the cap and cape he wore kept him from being recognized by any guards still searching for us, even though I don't think the Tower could hold him if he was caught. His talent for shape-shifting could surely help him escape.

I was out of the bath and in a velvet dressing gown when I heard his key in the lock again. He brought a basket that smelled of chocolate and warm bread as well as the bundle with the last of my new dresses.

"Here, lass. Eat a bit before you sleep." He poured hot chocolate from a crock into a cup and handed it to me as I sat in front of the fire.

"Thank you, Fergus. You must be exhausted." I sipped the fragrant brew and sighed. Delicious. I was already filling out, my ribs no longer visible when I'd washed. I wondered if my new dresses would even fit now. "Did you have any trouble while you were out? See any guards looking for the witch?"

"Nay." He handed me a warm bun stuffed with candied fruit. "I get the idea that the Tower guards would like to forget the witch's escape. I am sure they are afraid what will happen if they catch her. Stories are being told of men turning into giant bears." He chuckled. "Can you imagine?"

"But they have to make the attempt." I was afraid to leave this place though it still seemed too much like a prison to me as I was locked in every time Fergus left.

"Aye. We will stay inside for a few days and let things settle. There is talk on the street of a new plot against the King. That will no doubt keep the guards busy as well." He sat with his own bun and a mug of ale. "Dress you in some of your fine new clothes and no one will have any reason to think you had anything to do with the Tower and the witch."

"You are right. I want to go to the theater soon and visit my friend Maggie. The one who gave me her velvet dress." I bit into the bun. Delicious. I had to admit that Jeremiah and Fergus had seen to it that I was well-fed. Of course that insured my blood would be hearty. I deliberately forced that thought from my mind. "You know I won't tell her what I have really been up to, just that I have found a wealthy protector."

"Aye. You understand how to go on." Fergus brought us both another bun and refilled my chocolate.

"Do you think Marin and Jean-Claude will come after me again? Jeremiah seems to think so." I sipped the chocolate. It was easy to get used to such luxuries and hard to believe I'd been starving mere days ago. "I don't want to become their latest plaything."

"Of course not, lass. But Jeremiah's right. I could tell this was very important to Marin. And what Marin wants, Jean-Claude will move Heaven and Earth to provide." Fergus looked me over when I yawned. "I think you should seek your bed, lass. Might as well get used to sleeping all day and staying up all night. We live by Jeremiah's clock here."

I set down my empty cup and took his hand so he could pull me to my feet. "You're right. I can hardly keep my eyes open." I smiled at him. "Will you shift and sleep on the bed again? Keep me safe?"

"It's my job, lass." He didn't smile back. "But it's best if you put on a sturdy night rail and climb under the covers before I join you on the bed." He turned his back and stared into the fire.

I realized he was giving me privacy to leave the room. But I had no sturdy night rail and he knew it. Hadn't he paid for my clothes himself? I laid my hand on his back.

"Fergus?"

"Just keep your covers up to your chin, Gloriana." He turned and looked at me, his amber eyes solemn. "I am a man, ye ken. While I know my place and keep to it, I am still and all a man. I can be tempted. So go now. Get into yer warm bed and go to sleep. There'll be no close sleeping, even in my cat form. I'll be at yer feet. Betwixt you and harm." He nodded then turned back to face the fire.

I was speechless. And touched by the way he had made it clear he would guard me, no matter his own feelings. He was loyal to Jeremiah and that was his first priority. I hurried into the bedchamber. My night rail was sheer, of course, and hid nothing. I was a bought and paid for mistress after all. I climbed into bed and stared at the rough ceiling. Fergus was a huge man but a gentle giant. And he was handsome if you liked a man with dark red hair, unusual amber eyes and the kind of strength that made a woman feel small and protected. If he hadn't been constantly in the presence of Jeremiah Campbell, he would have been drawing his own admiring women to him, I didn't doubt it.

I turned and punched the pillow. But that dark-haired vampire with eyes that could see into my soul had something that made me lose what little sense I had. He was not as tall or as broad as Fergus, but he was strong as well. He had a way with a sword and a knife that was almost elegant. And then he could woo me with his clever hands… I sighed and closed my eyes. I didn't love Jeremiah, I couldn't. Not when he'd used me so. But I couldn't deny that I was drawn to him like I'd never been drawn to another man, not even my husband.

I'd been grateful to Michael. Had even loved him in a way. But he'd been all about his own pleasure, not mine. There had been times when I'd been left lying with him on top of me, wanting more. And he'd been snoring, done for the night. I couldn't imagine Jeremiah behaving in that fashion. Every time he'd taken me, he had spent long minutes making sure I was mindless with wanting before he'd pushed inside me. It had been a revelation. And yet…

Michael had called me a temptress. It was one of Will Shakespeare's words. Michael loved to bandy them about. But one night, in his cups, he had sworn that he'd taken me home when he'd found me because he hadn't been able to help himself.

I rubbed my forehead, remembering that. Yes, it had been during an argument between us. He'd been angry. The money had been gone, wasted, he'd said, on a frippery for me. He'd claimed that he had been "spelled" that night. Drawn in to save me against his will.

What nonsense! I'd tossed his wine in his face, telling him he'd drunk too much and that the money he'd spent at the tavern was why he didn't have the rent for our room. We'd argued and then ended up in bed. But after he'd discovered his rod was useless, he'd said it again. That I'd pulled him into that alley, casting a spell on him that forced him to attack those thieves with his cane when he'd never before or since done such a heroic or foolish thing. And he'd certainly never thought to chain himself to a wife, now had he?

Once done with that ridiculous claim he'd fallen over and started snoring. We'd both never mentioned it the next morning. But now Marin said I had blood like a goddess. Ridiculous. As if such a thing even existed. She just had a craving for my blood. So did Jeremiah. She was just greedy. Anyone could see that. I doubted she'd even known an Egyptian Pharaoh or his wife.

Made up stories. I was certainly used to them in the theater. Every actor could trot out one that featured himself as the hero along with a famous person he'd saved or bedded. Maggie's Horace claimed he'd even shared a bed with the King. How we'd laughed at that tale.

I felt the bed move. It was Fergus in his cat form jumping on the foot of the bed. He didn't touch me but I knew he was there. I wanted to reach out and stroke his soft fur, hear him purr. But I knew better than to encourage him. Nothing could happen between us. He knew it and I wouldn't cause strife between the shifter and his master. The best thing I could do now was sleep. I had to clear my mind of Fergus and anything more than friendship between us. Because, damn him, Jeremiah might say he'd stay out of my mind, but I knew better. He'd see every stray thought and pounce on it.

I let my mind go blank. The exhaustion of a full night should take me right to sleep. At least here I felt safe. It was only when there was pounding on the door that I woke. Not again!

TEN

Fergus answered the door and I heard male voices.
At least they didn't sound angry. I found my dressing gown
and got up, wrapping it around me. I wasn't about to stay in
bed when clearly Fergus had allowed someone inside the
rooms.

"I tell you I was almost tossed into gaol, cousin. We
look too much alike. Luckily there was a roomful of people
in the tavern who could swear I had been there most of that
night, not helping a witch escape from the Tower.
MacDonald had a woman in his bed and had ordered me
out." His cousin Bran paced in front of the fire then stopped
and grabbed Fergus by the arm. "Are ye mad, having truck
with a witch? This is Campbell's doing, I'm sure of it."

"The less you know, the better, cousin. MacDonald will
read your mind and he'd have something to hold over
Jeremiah's head if he knew the truth of it." Fergus glanced at
the doorway where I stood. "Now look what you've done,
waked up the lady."

"Sorry, mistress." Bran doffed his cap. "I wasn't
thinking, raisin' my voice like that. Had a bit of a scare and
came over as soon as I could. It wasn't wise to do it right

away, ye ken."

"Yes, I heard what you said. You were lucky you had witnesses." I knew I should probably leave them alone, but I felt well-rested and wanted to get out of this place for a while. We'd been staying in since the raid on the Tower. It seemed like forever since I'd seen the sun but probably little more than a week. "What time is it?"

"A bit after noon." Fergus handed his cousin a tankard of ale. "I can fetch you a meal if you're hungry, Gloriana."

"Thank you, but you've stuffed me like a Christmas goose since I've been here. What I'd really like is to go for a walk. Mayhap I can get dressed and see a bit of the outside. Breathe fresh air. If you think it's safe." I saw Bran frown. "You said you were almost arrested. When was this?"

"A few days ago. The search for those who helped with the Tower escape has finally been called off. At least for now. All the troops are surrounding the palace and looking for traitors who have plotted against the king. Word is the Catholics are causing trouble again." Bran drained his tankard. "The king has asked for his Scottish noblemen to stand with him. That makes the English worried about their future. As soon as our masters wake, they'll need to go to court and show support."

"I'll let Jeremiah know." Fergus nodded toward me. "Aye, we can go out now. Dress in your finery, Gloriana. We can go to the theater and you can invite your friend to come with us to dine. You'll eat, of course. Hungry or no. Those are Jeremiah's wishes." He ignored my pout. "To be safe, I'll darken my red hair with ash then cover it with a cap. I doubt anyone will give us a second look."

"Even if a meal is part of it, I thank you, Fergus." I rushed into the bedchamber and closed the door. Maggie had been so kind to me and I couldn't wait to see her. We could take her to a fine inn and order a meal she was sure to enjoy. Horace would no doubt be busy learning lines for the new play to be presented at court soon.

It took me a few minutes to decide what to wear and

then to fix my hair. The mirror had been returned to the neighbor so I had to do the best I could by touch. When I was satisfied that I was presentable, I opened the bedchamber door. There was no sign of Bran.

"You look fine as a new mint coin, Gloriana." Fergus had donned a plain jacket and waistcoat without a bit of plaid in sight. If the English were unhappy with the Scots, I guessed that was wise. His hair looked darker, dull from the ash, before he pulled on a cap. He laid my cape over my shoulders.

"Thank you, Fergus. I hope Bran was right and we won't be running a risk going out." I waited while he unlocked the door. "I miss your pretty red hair but it did help change your look." I smiled at him.

"Aye. And no one would think that the elegant lady you are now could be the same as the woman who spoke so saucily to the Tower guards the other night." Fergus escorted me into the corridor then locked the heavy door behind us.

"Is it safe to leave Jeremiah alone?" I suddenly thought about what Jeremiah had said. This was when a vampire was most at risk. He'd been protective of me since Marin's rescue, staying close to home and making love to me each night. He'd not taken blood from me, claiming I needed to recover from Marin's greed. I'd been relieved, yet foolishly a little disappointed. Madness. Perhaps I was under this vampire's spell.

"I wouldn't leave him if it wasn't safe. Don't worry. Bran certainly would never tell anyone about this place. He and I are like brothers, even though we can have our differences from time to time. Our family honor relies on our loyalty to our employers. Though it's a worry. MacDonald ordered him to find out where we live. Bran has held our secret so far, but it's only a matter of time before he lets a careless thought slip." Fergus offered his arm and escorted me down the long passage and into the sunlight.

It was a rare bright day in London and I stopped to

look around and just breathed. How I had missed being out during the day! I turned to Fergus.

"I'm sorry you and your cousin have been set against each other. That must be hard."

"Aye." He had nothing more to say about it.

"But it seems you were both hired for a job. How long have you served Jeremiah?" I took his arm as we walked toward the theater.

"Fifteen years." Fergus let me go ahead of him when we came close to the Globe. There were street vendors and more fashionable ladies about.

"Really." I couldn't imagine such a lengthy service.

"That's not unusual. Alain has been with Lily and Jean-Claude for well over a hundred years. He is an ancient shifter." Fergus frowned when I stopped and took his arm again. "Stay ahead of me, mistress. I am your servant now."

"Are shape-shifters immortal as well as vampires?" I kept my voice low while dropping his arm and nodding to a passing lady with a smile. Her own servant carried a laden basket and stayed a few steps behind her. We were playing a role and I would do well to remember that.

"No, we are not, though we live much longer than ordinary mortals. Alain is showing his age. He has trouble shifting now. It pains him if he does it too often. He did fine at the Tower but it takes a lot out of him." Fergus shook his head. "The vampires will replace him soon. I hope they are kind about it. Some vampires are careless, nay, cruel, with someone who outlives his usefulness."

"What would they do?" I stopped in front of a shop window and pretended to look at bonnets. But my mind was full of how bloodthirsty vampires would get rid of a man who couldn't serve them anymore. It wasn't a pretty picture.

"Don't fash yourself, Gloriana. Alain has surely made plans for that day. We all do. He probably has a wee cottage in France somewhere and a lass in mind to keep his cot warm. It's my plan for when my shifts become painful. Of course we do know the vampires' secrets. Some of their kind don't trust one of us to keep them." Fergus nodded toward the Globe which was in sight at the end of the street.

I stopped. So I'd been right. Alain or some other devoted shape-shifter could well die at the end of his lengthy service. I could imagine selfish Marin deciding that ending Alain would be best for her own safety.

"You are imagining the worst, Gloriana. If word got out that those we serve could not be trusted, none of our kind would be persuaded to take a place in a vampire household, no matter how much gold was offered." Fergus patted my hand then let go quickly. "Now we'd best be on our way. Dark comes early and I want to be home long before the sun goes down."

"Of course." I moved on. Soon we came to the alley where I had met Jeremiah. It had rained recently and all signs of his bloody struggle were gone. This time of day the place was deserted. I led the way to the stage door and smiled at the old man who guarded it. Master Shakespeare did not like anyone spying on his productions before they were ready for an audience.

"Matthew Wiggins, will you let me in? Or can you call Maggie for me?" I smiled wider when I realized he didn't recognize me with a fuller figure and wearing my new finery. "'Tis I, Gloriana St. Clair."

"No, it can't be. Why last I saw you, you were about to drop from hunger and so thin you could have slipped right under the door without me unlocking it." He laughed, then reached out and pinched my cheek. "Look at you in such a fancy cape and with some meat on your bones." Then he frowned at Fergus behind me. "Is this your protector?"

"Nay, I am merely her servant. My master treats her very well and insists she be guarded like a precious jewel." Fergus tipped his cap. After he put it back on, he slipped a coin into the old man's hand. "Could you see to granting the lady's request to step inside?"

"She *is* a lady and don't you forget it." Matthew frowned and bit the coin. "Gold. Yes, it will buy you through

this door, Gloriana, but not this varlet. He can wait here."
He opened the door and I stepped inside.

"I'll be out in a few moments." I patted Matthew on
the back. "I hope to bring Maggie with me. Fergus, Matthew
here likes his drink if you happen to have something on you
that you'd be willing to share."

"I just might." Fergus brought out a flask and
Matthew's eyes lit up. "Seems there's a chill in the air. This
will warm you up. Good Scot's whiskey."

The doorkeeper frowned. "Their whiskey is the only
thing good about the Scots. But I won't turn it down." He
held out his hand.

I waited to be sure Fergus didn't take the comment ill.
He just handed over the flask and nodded. Of course. We
were acting. He hadn't even sounded like a Scot when he'd
spoken, now that I thought about it. So I left them sharing
the drink and walked inside, looking for Maggie.

A rehearsal was going on, the front of the stage a busy
place. Master Shakespeare was unhappy with the scene and
kept barking orders as different cast members ran about,
papers in their hands.

"Gloriana! My, but you look a treat. Clearly your
protector is a generous man." Maggie came out with a dress
in her hands and shook it out. "Horace's costume. He'd
better stay out of the tavern or nothing will fit him."

"Oh, Maggie, it is so good to see you!" I gave her a
hug. "Did you get my note?"

"Yes, thank you for letting me know you were all right.
I was that worried about you." She frowned. "Look out. See
who's coming."

"Gloriana!" Becks, of course. I had hoped to avoid
him. "My eyes are stunned by your beauty shining so
brightly." He grabbed me, trying to steal a kiss. "You are
radiant."

"Look but don't touch, Becks." I shoved him away.
"My new protector is very handy with his sword. I have seen
him kill two men already who came to close to this." I

opened my cloak and ran my hand over my bodice, unable to resist the taunt.

"Now you are just being cruel. Your charms are even harder to resist now that you are clearly eating well." He feigned a stab to his heart. Always overacting.

"I am eating very well. And treated like a queen." I closed my cloak. "I am very happy with my new situation."

"What brings you by then? Did you miss me?" His grin was playful as he reached for me again.

"Not at all. But I did miss Maggie." I turned to her. "Can you come out with me? I want to take you to an inn so we can dine together. My servant has gold and will pay for everything." I glanced back at Becks. He was frowning and obviously calculating how much my finery must have cost this new "protector."

"I would love to. Let me get my cloak." She threw Horace's dress at Becks. "Tell my husband that the rip is repaired. That's as big in the waist as I can make it. If it don't fit now, I will have to add more cloth." She laughed and hurried to the place where I knew she stored her things when she worked in the theater.

"Husband." Becks tossed the dress on a crate. "Like we believe that."

"Be nice, Becks. How is your lady wife? Has she had the babe yet?" I played with my gloves as I looked up at him.

"Another girl. That's the third. She sent a note round yester eve." He grabbed my hand. "What are you doing, Gloriana? Michael wouldn't want you to settle for being some toff's mistress."

"Really? What would he want for me? To be passed around here? To sleep with every actor at the Globe?" I jerked my hand from his. "I had no choice, Becks, but to take the first kind man who approached me and well you know it. Lucky for me he *is* kind." I looked away from Becks' keen study of my face. Kind? That depended on whether I was satisfied with being a blood whore, now wasn't it? I shoved such bleak thoughts aside. I knew I was lucky in Jeremiah. He had never forced me to do anything except when he'd been in pain and out of his mind.

"I'm sorry, Gloriana. If I had more to offer you…" He seemed sincere but then he was an excellent actor.

"But you don't, Timothy." I dodged his hand which, as usual, went where it had no business going. This time it was toward my backside. "You'd best go back to your rehearsal. I heard Master Shakespeare calling for you. It's not wise to keep him waiting. You have many mouths to feed and need this job."

"That's the truth." He shook his head. "I hope he truly *is* kind to you, Gloriana. Some men--"

"You don't have to tell me about some men. I had plenty of time to know them while I was sleeping back stage this past twelve months." I looked around at the rough surroundings. The smells, the sounds, it all came back and I knew I would do whatever I had to so I never faced such a sad situation again. "Some men have a passing acquaintance with soap and water. Some men even know how to make a woman scream with pleasure in the bedsheets." I poked him in his doublet when he moved too close one more time. As if he really cared how I was treated now. He only cared that he'd missed his turn at me. His poor wife! I hoped she stayed in the country a good long while and enjoyed a rest from his company.

"Off with you, Becks. The master is about to dock your pay." Maggie grinned and took my arm. "My, oh, my. Tell me about this man who takes baths and knows how to make a woman enjoy the bedding." She walked us to the door. "Sounds like you landed in the honeypot, dearie. Oh, yes, you did."

I wished I could tell her the truth. All I had to do for my finery, baths and pleasure was offer my vein. But I kept my complaints to myself, stepping out with her toward the nearest inn that I knew served good food. We enjoyed a fine meal and I watched Maggie flirt with Fergus who insisted upon sitting at a separate table. She looked well and I saw that he appreciated her fine wit and round figure. It would be a wonderful thing if Maggie could find a bit of romance in her life. As for Fergus...? Well, I had no idea what he did to satisfy himself. It had to be difficult to be around Jeremiah and his endless parade of lovers. Surely the shape-shifter was allowed time to find his own lady friends.

It was late afternoon by the time we left the Globe. A group of soldiers passed us and I froze, turning to stare at a shop window for fear my face might be familiar to one of them. Fergus kept his cap on and bent over as if to pick up something from the ground. Thank God the men moved past without giving us a second look.

"It's a good thing we are close to home." Fergus turned down an alley, pushing me gently ahead of him. "We will take a new way there. I want to make sure we aren't followed."

I looked up at a bird that flew overhead. "I don't see any soldiers, but what about..?" I nodded at the crow that had settled on a rooftop not far above our heads.

Fergus stopped and sniffed. I had no idea what he could smell besides the disgusting scents of garbage and offal. But he picked up a stone and threw it at the bird. Clearly my instincts had been right.

"Slimy bastard! Get you gone, Alain. You won't get near this woman. Tell your mistress that!" His stone hit close to the bird but missed its mark. The bird squawked and flew away.

"Alain?" I pulled my cloak around me, shivering. "Do you think he was planning to attack us?"

"Not now. Not without help. But he might have been making plans for another day. He can certainly hire a gang of thugs to snatch you off the street." He shook his fist at the sky. "Hide then, you coward." He sniffed the air again. "He's finally gone but I've made up my mind. We won't be going to the Globe again." Fergus firmed his lips and took my elbow. "Stay close to me, Gloriana. I liked your friend, but it's best if we keep our distance."

"But I promised Maggie--" I'd made plans to see her again. Staying inside every day while Jeremiah slept was driving me mad.

"Remember who is paying for your finery, Gloriana. And your meals. I'm sure Jeremiah will agree with me. You need to be safe. No more daytime strolls or visits to the Globe." Fergus almost dragged me to the doorway that led to what I was beginning to think of as my prison.

"Can she come here?" I wasn't giving up. We could keep each other company. Play a card game perhaps. Anything to make the time go past!

"Of course not! Bring another mortal into a vampire's lair? You're forgetting your place, madam." Fergus stopped in front of the door and pulled out the key. He sniffed the air and frowned. "Damn me but someone's been here." He studied the sturdy door, which had scratches around the key hole. "And tried to get in! We'll have to move. There's no way around that." He unlocked the door.

"Stand back. I have to check on Jeremiah. By God! If they got to him…" He ran inside.

I almost stumbled when he shoved me aside. I'd never seen him so upset, not even when we'd been watching Jeremiah fight MacDonald. Or when he'd had to persuade me to give my blood to save him. Obviously Fergus felt that he'd failed his master.

He pushed the door to the vampire's room. It held.

"Isn't it latched from the inside?" I stood behind him.

"Aye. It seems undisturbed." Fergus wiped his brow. "Start packing." He began dropping supplies into a basket.

"Do you know where we'll go?" I hesitated in the doorway to the bedchamber.

"Of course. I always have a second place ready. Jeremiah's safety is my responsibility." He glanced at the fireplace. "I'll build up the fire. If you want a bath, take it now. We won't have a pipe for water at the new place so it will be more difficult to arrange. It's not as nice as this one has been. But you'll see for yourself soon enough."

"You're sure we have to move?" I would certainly miss the baths.

"Don't question me, Gloriana. Do you want a bath now or no?" His Scot's accent was back.

"Yes, please." I hurried into the bedchamber and began laying my new dresses on the bed. He came into the room carrying a large trunk.

"Put all your things in here. I'll have your bath ready in a few minutes. Then I'm going out to give you privacy. I have to see to the new place and make it ready for us anyway. When I set it up I didn't really think we'd need it or that Jeremiah would have a steady mistress living with us. I'll have to purchase fresh bedding, tidy it up a bit. Jeremiah hates dirt." Fergus set the trunk down with a frown. "I'm that sorry I fussed at you, Gloriana. I guess I'm taking out my aggravation on you. If Jeremiah wakes before I get back, tell him we're moving. He'll know why."

"All right." I walked over and put my hand on his arm. "Please don't worry about my feelings. I know you just want us safe. I appreciate it."

"Aye, that's right. Now pack first. The bath will be ready when you're done." He patted my hand, stared down at our hands for a moment, then shook his head and left the room.

* * *

I leaned back with a sigh. If this was to be my last hot bath in a tub, I wanted to enjoy every moment. The fine soap smelled wonderful and I lifted my foot to run the cloth between my toes. I don't know why it was so important to me to be clean. Certainly the actors at the Globe had shown no love for soap and water. I shuddered thinking about the way the costumes had always smelled so rank. Even dear Maggie had rarely washed. At least I'd found a protector who shared my love of cleanliness.

"Now that's a sight I could wake up to every evening." Jeremiah stood beside the fireplace.

"I guess night must have fallen." I draped the cloth

over my breasts. Of course he'd seen them, but I was suddenly shy. I needed to tell him about the move. Would he just read it in my mind? But he was looking at my body, my mind not of interest at the moment.

"Somehow I just know when the sun goes down. It's one of the mysteries of being a vampire." He pulled his shirt up and off. Oh, but his chest was a treat to see. Then he began to unbutton his trews, those tight-fitting pants made of his plaid. When he stepped out of them, I could see he certainly liked the look of me in the bath.

"And is another mystery of being a vampire that you are always eager for loveplay, Jeremiah?" I scooted back in the tub when he stepped in with me, making it very crowded indeed. Water splashed the stone floor.

"Not sure if it's the vampire in me. I was just as randy before I was turned, my girl. And the sight of your bubbies makes me want to get closer, much closer." He grinned, tossed aside my washing cloth and pulled me against him. "Ah. Better."

I heard the cloth hit the stones. I had to admit the feel of his hard chest was better for me as well. Oh, yes. His hands ran up and down my back before he leaned down and kissed a path from my neck to my nipples.

"Ye Gods, woman! That tastes disgusting! Rinse, if you please." He leaned over and spit on the floor.

"You don't like my soap?" I laughed and splashed water on my chest. Of course I was eager for his mouth on me. He was very clever with his tongue and teeth. As long as he didn't use those fangs…

"Relax, Gloriana. I am not going to drink from you. Yet. But later I will. I have denied myself long enough." He smiled then leaned down again, taking a nipple into his mouth.

My head fell back and I moaned. Oh, but it felt good. My legs were around him, my bottom on his lap. His hard cock nudged my backside and I wiggled against it. Yes, I wanted him. He was a wonderful lover. The first one I'd ever had who had bothered to see to my pleasure. That I could remember anyway.

His head snapped up and he looked in my eyes. "Were you a virgin when you and your husband first were together?"

"What a question!" I slapped his arm. "I don't remember my past. I told you that. I may have been married before." I flushed. "When Michael and I made love the first time, there was no pain. So I suppose there might be a husband somewhere mourning me. I have no idea." It was something Michael and I had discussed. But what could we do? We had walked around town in case someone might have been looking for me, but no one had recognized me. So I had started a new life with that first name I remembered from a voice out of dreams. Michael had given me his own last name, one he'd made up when he'd become an actor.

"So you weren't a virgin." He slid his hands under my rump and lifted me until I settled on his hard cock. He pushed inside me and I was filled.

"No." I couldn't deny he felt wonderful, satisfying and distracting. I was glad. This was not a conversation we needed to continue. My eyes closed and I began to move. Virgin or not, I enjoyed loveplay as much as Jeremiah did. I wanted it, him, and didn't care about a murky past that no amount of struggle could help me remember. Had I been a virtuous wife or a whore? Wondering only made my head ache. I pushed such thoughts away and held onto his shoulders, my nails digging in as he gripped my thighs, urging me on. Oh, but he could make me feel things. I finally looked at him, need spiraling inside me until I felt compelled to see if he'd gone as wild as I had.

"Yes, Gloriana, you make me mad with lust as well." He stood suddenly, water sluicing off both of us, and stepped out of the tub. Before I knew what he was about he'd laid me on the table and pulled me to the edge. He pumped into me hard and fast, with such an intense look on his face I wondered he didn't hurt me. But, no, he had a care, one hand beneath my head to keep it from hitting the rough wood, the other reaching between us to touch me in a spot I'd had no idea even existed.

"Jeremiah! Gods!" I lost all sense of time or place and just fell apart. My knees locked around him while I raked his chest with my nails. I drew blood. But did I care? No. I leaned forward and licked it clean, quivering inside and desperate to show him how much he'd given me. Was I turning vampire as well? I didn't care about that either.

Suddenly I was cradled in his arms, his hands gentle as I sobbed, lost to all reason. Something inside me had broken open. Could I actually love this man? Impossible. He was a vampire, a blood drinker. And yet I couldn't deny he'd saved me, still protected me, and showed me care. He carried me to bed and almost stumbled over the open trunk.

"What the devil is going on here?" He dropped me on the bed, his eyes hard when he stared down at me. "You aren't thinking of leaving, are you?"

ELEVEN

"No, of course not. We have to move. I thought you'd read it in my mind." I pulled the sheet over my naked body. He still looked dangerous, but at least he wasn't aiming that anger at me now.

"What happened?" He ran a hand through his wet hair.

I told him, watching him pace the floor. Perhaps it was foolish of me not to be worried. Instead I just watched the play of candlelight on his hard body.

"Damn them! Of course this is all Marin's doing. She wants you, and Jean-Claude will do anything to please her. I don't like the idea of hiding from her, Fergus has to know that." He strode from the room.

I grabbed a dressing gown from the trunk, slipping it on as I followed him. I realized he'd gone into his room. I stopped at the threshold. I'd never been allowed inside. What did I expect to see? It was a plain room with a cot and large trunk to hold his things. There was a table with papers strewn over it. His leather belt and sporran—he'd told me that was what the pouch he carried was called--lay on top, along with a pair of knives. While I watched he plucked a plaid from the trunk and quickly wound it around his waist, securing it with the belt.

"We must move this very night. If whoever came during the day had managed to get to you, it would have been…" I couldn't say it.

"I know, Gloriana. 'Tis why Fergus is usually here, on guard. Of course if they are determined to end me, they could bring an army, and Fergus would be no match for them." Jeremiah sat on his cot and gestured for me to come to him. "I understand it's been hard for you to stay inside this past week, without any chance to see the sun. I don't usually keep a mistress for long for just that reason. Mortals don't adjust well to my hours."

He pulled me into his lap. "I should have tired of you by now. For some reason I don't want to send you on your way just yet. And now it wouldn't be safe to do so." He brushed my hair back from my face and kissed my forehead, then my lips. What started out as a gentle gesture quickly turned eager.

I held onto his shoulders and kissed him almost frantically. The idea that he could have been killed on this very bed terrified me. When had I come to care so much for him? I think it had started when he'd sought me out in that alley the first night. He'd seen my desperation but had spared my pride. And he always sensed my needs before I had to speak of them. *Mind reader.*

He pressed me down to the cot, his hand inside my gown and sliding over my breast. Oh, but he knew how to make me want him. Want. Was it only lust between us? And his thirst for my blood? My thoughts and feelings were in a whirl. Master Shakespeare said love and hate were two sides of the same coin. I could believe it.

A noise at the front door had Jeremiah springing to his feet, almost dumping me on the floor in his haste. He grabbed both knives and was out of the room in a moment.

"Fergus! Announce yourself next time. I could have thrown a knife through your heart before I'd known who was coming through the door." Jeremiah turned back to me.

"We need to finish packing. I don't like to run and hide, but for your sake we *will* move this very night. Then I'll make sure this problem with Marin and Jean-Claude is finished for good." He tossed his knives onto the table and pulled me to my feet, carefully closing my dressing gown.

"What will you do?" I handed him a shirt from a peg on the wall.

"Nothing so cowardly as arrange an ambush for them in their death sleep." He pulled the shirt over his head then aimed me out his door. "Go, ready yourself for our move. Dress in dark colors and wear a dark cloak. We don't want to draw attention."

"Jeremiah's right, Gloriana." Fergus stacked a basket next to the door. It held my soap and the cloths I used after my bath. "I've done what I can to make the new place to your liking but 'tis no palace, I'm sorry to say."

"I'm sure you've chosen well, Fergus." Jeremiah glanced at me. "Gloriana, it's necessary for us to put safety before comfort. I'm sure you understand."

"Of course." I couldn't forget those scratches on the outer door here. "You must be able to sleep during the day without worry."

"I'm dead during the day, sweetheart, with nary a thought in my head. No worries at all." He pulled shirts down from the pegs on the wall and dropped them in his trunk.

"Jeremiah, leave the packing to me." Fergus took the shirts and began to fold them neatly. "You have other business to think about. The king is calling for his supporters to come to court in a show of force this night. The Catholics are at it again. They have tried once more to bring him down because he refused to send an emissary to meet with the Pope. Apparently their plot was a serious threat this time and he wants his lords from Scotland around him. After we are settled, you should appear there, to do the pretty."

Jeremiah frowned. "More politics! I don't see the need for such plaid posturing. James has soldiers aplenty. But, you are right, I cannot let my clan be seen as disloyal." He picked up his knives and tucked them in his belt. "I'll not leave Gloriana unprotected while I go to court. You'll both come with me. I won't let Gloriana out of my sight while Marin and Jean-Claude still pose a threat to her."

I said nothing, secretly excited to go to court again. I always felt safe with Jeremiah. He was a fierce warrior no matter where he was, even in the midst of courtiers in fancy dress. It was his attitude, his stance. As if he dared anyone to challenge him. Of course no one did. Except that MacDonald. He'd be there again, I was sure. Hopefully they both knew better than to let their tempers override their good sense and continue their fight in front of the king.

We soon managed to pack all we would need. Fergus carried my trunk and the basket. Jeremiah shouldered his own trunk. We made slow progress through mostly deserted streets as we avoided areas near the theaters and bawdy houses where crowds gathered at this time of night. Both Jeremiah and Fergus stopped frequently, sniffing the air and taking narrow alleyways, until we finally stopped next to a place that looked like little more than a burned out shell of a building next to the river.

"Surely this isn't where we are going to live." I whispered this to Jeremiah.

"Trust Fergus. He's done this kind of thing many times." Jeremiah set down his trunk and gestured for me to sit on top of it while Fergus took his time strolling up and down the dock next to the building, his own burdens on the stones next to us. Finally Fergus seemed satisfied that we were unobserved and came back to gesture at a charred door at the bottom of some steps.

"This is it. I know it doesn't look like much but it was once storage for wine. The stones are thick and there are large rooms behind the casks down below." He pushed the door open then led the way. "I'll come back for your things, Gloriana. Follow me."

It wasn't easy to ignore the smell of burned timbers as I

lifted my skirts and picked my way through broken stones and glass. Of course Fergus hadn't swept the entrance since he wanted the place to still look deserted. Inside, we walked down a long hallway where a torch was mounted in a socket on the wall.

"I lit this when I came earlier. It won't be here every night. Not wise to show this place is in use." Fergus held out his hand when I tripped over a fallen board. "Careful now. We're almost to our door. It's got a strong lock on it. I have the key here." He pulled a large key, like a jailer would use, from his waistcoat. The lock seemed well oiled and didn't make a sound as he opened it and threw open the door.

"Oh!" The smell of spilled wine hit me first. It was a sour smell. Broken casks so large they were taller than my head had been rolled out of the way so I could see a fireplace in the middle of a room that could have held dozens of the enormous wine casks.

"Well done, Fergus. A smuggler's den?" Jeremiah set down his trunk. "There are other chambers, are there not?"

"Yes. One suitable for your bedchamber, Gloriana. And a place for your daily sleep, Jeremiah." Fergus gave us a tour. The bedchamber was merely an open area on the other side of the massive fireplace, the hearth open to it as well. There was little privacy. Jeremiah's space was a very tiny room, hardly bigger than the cot Fergus had placed there but it had a stout bolt on the inside of the door, obviously newly added. All our clothes would be kept in the so-called bedchamber.

It was obvious that there was no bathtub here or access to water. I hoped we wouldn't have to make do with water from the nearby river. I had seen strange things floating in it. And the smell! But there was a wide bed, made up with clean sheets and a fine coverlet, set up for me. And of course for the times when Jeremiah joined me there. I flushed thinking about that. The fact that Fergus would either have to wait outside or hear our every move made my face even hotter.

"We must dress for court now." Jeremiah opened his

trunk. "It's a damned nuisance but King James as ally is not a bad thing. I would never turn another vampire over to the king's men but the threat of it may help convince Marin to leave the country and forget her thirst for you, Gloriana."

"What good would speaking to the king do?" I knew he would never mention that he knew a vampire. "We have proved that no cell can hold her, Jeremiah." I was frankly afraid of Marin and her ire. She had proved she had powers well beyond my understanding.

Fergus set my trunk at the foot of the bed. "Let us hope it doesn't come to that."

"We know where she lives, Gloriana." Jeremiah looked grim. "If she does not leave you alone, I can let the king know where to send his men during the day. I will tell them to be sure to end her and her consort during their sleep."

"Jeremiah!" Fergus looked shocked. "You could betray one of your own kind?"

"Only as a last resort." Jeremiah touched my cheek. "Some things are worth such a high price."

"A high price indeed. If word got out to other vampires that you did such a thing …" Fergus shook his head. "I'd not give a farthing for your chances of convincing any of them that you wouldn't do it again." He glanced at me where I stood speechless. "I'll dress on the other side of the fireplace. I brought my own finery here earlier." He took off his cap and rubbed his head. His hair was still dull from our earlier walk. "It will be best if I wait outside the court, Jeremiah. If I wash the ash out of my hair, I'll be too easy to recognize from the Tower."

"You may be right but I can't allow it. We must take the chance so Gloriana is well guarded while I wait on the king. So wash out your hair or the other Scots may take note and wonder what we are about." Jeremiah pulled out his fanciest waistcoat and shoes with diamond buckles. "Bran will also be wary but Macdonald will insist he attend him regardless. Gloriana told me your cousin was almost arrested just for looking very like you."

"Aye. And the same guards may well be near the king now. We must hope the new threats from the religious fanatics will have put the witch's escape out of their minds." Fergus saw me gazing around my new bedchamber. "I'm sorry these are such poor lodgings, Gloriana. I'll figure out a way to get you baths in the future. Trust me on that."

I managed a smile. He was doing the best he could and right now our lodgings were the least of my worries. "This will be fine, Fergus. Go now and let me change my dress. You know I want to go to court. It will take my mind off of Marin and her obsession with me. In this lovely gown Jeremiah bought for me, no guard will ever think I was the doxy at the Tower." I pulled out a beautiful blue velvet dress. The gold trim on it matched my hair, or so Jeremiah claimed. Foolishness, but I did love the way the dress moved when I walked.

Unfortunately I had been eating too much, stuck underground for a week. Jeremiah laughed as he tugged free the laces on the dull brown dress I'd worn for our walk here and I gasped with relief.

"La, but that was the first easy breath I've taken since I put the thing on. I swear I will not take one bite until these new dresses fit again. You cannot keep insisting I eat so much, Jeremiah."

"If you were vampire, you wouldn't bother to breathe or eat, food that is." Jeremiah turned me to face him. "Look at you. Your beauty would steal my own breath if I had need of it." He drew me close. "I am sorry you are in danger because of my world. I pulled you into this and I will make sure you come to no harm. Do you believe me?" He'd lost his smile.

"Yes, I do. What is it you say? Don't fash yourself." I brushed his hair back from his brow then kissed his lips. "You have made me feel safe since the moment we met." I laughed. "Well after you fought off the two men who attacked us in that alley."

"I should have let you go then, Gloriana. My life is not

155

an easy one." He shook his head.

"And leave me to starve? Or fall prey to a man who likes to add pain, my pain, to his bedding?" I held his head and looked deep into his eyes. "Read my mind, lover. I am quite content being here. I have no regrets. Nay, not even with the blood drinking. I am sure when we come home, you will finally take my blood tonight. I want to remember it. Will you let me?" I tried to show him that I was ready for that. It was something we could share. Now that I knew how important it was, I would freely give him that part of me. Because it helped him live.

I'd never had the power to do something so vital for Michael. Our relationship had no deeper meaning than two people who fell into bed together. If he hadn't died, I wasn't sure he might not have tired of me. He had a wandering eye and most actors I'd met seemed to enjoy variety. Without the bonds of matrimony to tie us, it was very likely he might have someday passed me on to someone else or given me a few coins and sent me on my way.

"Gloriana! You value yourself too cheaply. No man with any sense would cast you off without a care." Jeremiah hugged me closer. "Or tire of you. You have a good heart. I see that in you daily. Believe me, I've lived long enough to have met many who take what they can and think of no one but themselves. You are rarer than you know." He rubbed my back as he held me against his chest.

I listened for his heart beat. There were times when I wondered if he had one. Yes, it was there but faint and slow, so slow. Not thundering like mine to hear his sweet words. I leaned back to look into his face.

"Thank you, Jeremiah. I hope you don't regret fighting for me. Marin and Jean-Claude seemed determined to bring you grief over me. I doubt I am worth it." I ran my hand over his jaw, so firm and very masculine. He should shave before going to court. Many men wore beards but he didn't favor them. With his rough new growth he merely looked careless of other's opinions and more dangerous than usual.

"We must get ready. It won't do to have his majesty upset with you."

"You are right." He kissed me then set me on my feet. "Fergus! Is there warm water to be had for a quick shave?"

Of course he'd read my mind and that concern. I was getting used to that, but still found it irritating. I sometimes wished I could have a stray thought that he didn't immediately read.

He grabbed my arm and looked into my eyes. "If it makes you feel any better, I must be in the same room with you to read your thoughts."

"You did it again." I hit his chest. "Truly? If I went into the next room with Fergus, you couldn't know what I was thinking?"

"Right. I need to see a person to read his or her thoughts. It's the way a vampire's powers work. And it's really easier if I'm touching the person. Then the thoughts are clear and strong." He ran his hands down to my bottom and held me close. "Ah, you are plotting already." He smiled. "No, holding something in front of you won't help. Though if it was as thick as a wall… are you that strong, lass?" He leaned down and kissed me hungrily before he leaned back. "Can you read my thoughts now?"

"That bulge between your legs doesn't make it necessary, sir." I was breathless and not above lifting my skirts for this man who made me want him desperately.

"Water's hot. Best hurry with that shave, Jeremiah." Fergus's voice came from the other side of the fireplace. It was proof enough for me that we would have no private moments as long as we were staying here. "Gloriana, if your decent, I'll bring in a pitcher and bowl."

I wrapped a shawl around my open bodice. "Come on, Fergus." I busied myself finding the gold slippers I would wear while Fergus came in with the steaming pitcher, soap and bowl for Jeremiah.

"I'll be outside as soon as I'm dressed." He nodded. "I'm that sorry that we're so crowded here, Gloriana.

Jeremiah and I are used to rough conditions." Fergus was careful to keep his eyes away from the bulge in Jeremiah's trews.

"Yes, we are and much worse than this." Jeremiah picked up a razor after soaping his face. "We will get used to this." He winked at me then started to shave.

I fumbled with my shawl to stay well covered, wincing to see him take the first swipe at his lean cheek. How he could do it without a mirror was beyond me.

Jeremiah smiled. "Vampires cannot see their reflection in a mirror, lass. Did you not notice how we avoid them?" He laughed. "Fergus has been very clever about bringing one in for you then whisking it away before you knew it was a vampire you lived with."

"So he has." I sighed. "If I could have one again, I won't test or tease you with it, Jeremiah, I swear it. Do you think it's possible to buy one for me, Fergus?" I was waiting for him to leave before I tried to fit into my court dress.

"Of course, Gloriana. I'll see to it tomorrow. If I think it's safe to leave for a while to shop for one. Now we must all get moving. The king does not like to be kept waiting." He stepped around the fireplace and out of sight.

I pulled off my dress and simple chemise. I could feel Jeremiah's eyes on me but just turned my back. We didn't have time for dalliance and that was what he usually had on his mind. By the time I was ready to pull the laces on my dress, he was in his finest plaid. I appreciated his help as we both worked to make the bodice meet over my newly round figure. The result was what I thought was a scandalous amount of breast pushing out above my tight bodice. He merely kissed the mounds and claimed there was no danger of any soldier recognizing me from the Tower. No man would be able to raise his eyes above such bounty.

"I can barely breathe." I wasn't joking as he settled my cape over my shoulders. "I meant what I said. No more hearty dinners for me."

Jeremiah's arms went around me. He pushed aside the

cape so his lips could trace the swells of my breasts above the straining bodice. "I love the way your body has filled out since you've been with me. Eat whatever you crave. You must tell Fergus what you want and he'll fetch it. It gives me joy to see your lusty appetite." His fangs were down and he ran them up to the pulse at my throat. "Later, I will enjoy *this* bounty. As you promised. Are you sure you're not afraid?"

"Mayhap I am, but I will allow you to take your pleasure and be glad to serve you. If that witch Marin proved one thing, it's that you can drink my blood without pain and without killing me." I held the back of his head, my hand shaking despite my best intentions. Of course I was terrified. But I was determined as well. I wanted to do this for him. If we weren't already late, I'd let him take my blood now, let those fangs sink into my neck and feel the pull as he took my life force. I shivered and realized that the very thought had me throbbing low in my belly, an almost sexual excitement making me damp.

"I am glad you trust me to restrain myself this time, Gloriana. I promise I won't hurt you or take too much. It is a fine thing, to give and receive blood. If you were vampire..?" He slid his fangs over my lips. "There's nothing more passionate than two vampires making love. Giving and receiving blood creates a deeper bond. Not that I would want you to be anything but what you are. Never think that."

"So you've had vampire lovers." I pulled his hair so he looked into my eyes. "Does vampire blood taste as fine as mine, Jeremiah?" I dared him to ruin this moment.

He smiled. "There is no comparison. You, my dear, are unique. Marin was not wrong about that. Vampire blood may have power--the older the vampire, the more power you can taste. But you," he nipped at my lip, drawing blood then enjoying it in his way. He groaned. "It is easy to understand why Marin is so determined to have you. There's something there, something ancient, but not like a vampire can be ancient." He kissed me deeply, his arms tight around me. When he finally pulled back, I felt dizzy, almost as if he'd sipped at my very soul while he'd claimed my mouth.

"Jeremiah?" I brushed my thumb across his lips and those impossibly long fangs. I should hate them, fear them. Instead they now fascinated me.

"I cannot explain. But I know I want it, you. The two are intertwined for me. Not for Marin. She will merely use you as a vessel, draining you nightly. She will not be cautious and you could well end up dead from her callous disregard of you." He frowned and set me away from him. "I will not allow it. Even if I have to raise an army of my own."

I arranged my bodice for what modesty it afforded me and straightened my skirt. How I loved that he was so protective of me. So fierce. What did it mean? Was it only because of my blood? Or could it go deeper? I had no more time to worry about it as Fergus called us to come along. It was past time to go to the court and he had arranged a carriage and horses to take us there again even though it was just a few blocks away. He wanted to confuse anyone looking for us.

We hurried along, Fergus watchful for ruffians looking for someone to rob in this rough area near the docks. I jumped at every noise and every furtive movement in the shadows. Thankfully no one accosted us and we were soon at the carriage. Jeremiah and I settled inside, his hand on mine as it lurched into motion. Fergus rode on top, his own hand on a gun as he remained alert for an attack. We took a long and winding route before we finally arrived at Whitehall.

My excitement had turned to fear. There were so many soldiers about. What would we do if one of them recognized me or Fergus? I didn't have time to do more than straighten my shoulders as a footman took my cloak and announced Jeremiah before we joined a milling crowd.

* * *

Crowd or mob? The court was even more packed with people than the last time we'd visited. The walls were lined with stern faced soldiers armed with pikes and swords. Talk was all about the religious radicals who had been causing trouble. The king seemed determined to speak to his Scottish nobles and Jeremiah left me next to Fergus while he danced attendance on his majesty. I kept my back to those soldiers who all looked alike to me, their hard faces partially hidden by their helms. Some could very well be the same who had fought us at the Tower. Fergus's cousin was with MacDonald and seemed to be avoiding the soldiers as well. Both shifters were surely safe with their plaid in plain view. I had a feeling the soldiers had been told to just show their strength, not to bother the glittering crowd unless an obviously threatening move was made toward the king.

"Looking quite lovely this evening, Gloriana."

I turned to face Robert MacDonald and curtsied, knowing better than to make a scene. "Thank you." I ignored Fergus who actually growled and tried to step between us. "Fergus, would you fetch me a glass of something to drink. My throat is dry." I smiled at the shape-shifter. "I'm sure I am quite safe here in the middle of a crowded room." I tapped MacDonald with the painted fan Jeremiah had gifted me with before we'd left our new home. "What say you, sir?"

"Of course she's safe with me. I'm not so foolish as to anger our king by doing anything remarkable here." He waved Bran away. "Quit hovering. You are making me question your loyalty with your glower. Find me a likely woman for tonight. You know what I like. Clean and pretty. Not one wearing that cloying perfume that covers the sin of slovenliness, if you please."

I almost laughed at Bran's expression. So he was to play the procurer. I didn't have to be a mind reader to know what he thought of that.

MacDonald smiled. "Yes, I know he's cursing me. But he has an eye for quality." He reached for my hand but I tucked it behind my back. "Of course so do I. You really are a treat to the eye." He inhaled. "Nay, to all the senses tonight, Gloriana. Aren't you tired of that Campbell buffoon yet?" He frowned toward the throne where Jeremiah still stood in a circle of men wearing kilts, listening to the king. Then he snatched my fan and ran it across my bare shoulder up to my neck.

"I see he still hasn't bothered to buy you jewels. Bad of him, I must say. I would give you sapphires first, to match your eyes. How would you like that?"

I tried to back away from him. Insolent man, to touch me so familiarly. Who wouldn't want jewels? Especially when I'd already found out it was the only way to secure my future. But he was forward, and intent on snatching much more than my fan, I could see it in his eyes. He moved in closer and I was trapped, a wall of people keeping me from moving an inch.

"You are so easy to read." He flipped the fan open with a practiced hand. "Let me steal a kiss and I'll buy you a trinket anyway. See how generous I can be?" He played as if to shield us from prying eyes. "There's a girl. What harm? One little kiss?" He leaned in as if to press his lips to mine.

"Your drink, Gloriana. Wine." Fergus thrust it between MacDonald and me, his frown so fierce I could tell he wanted to toss the contents of the goblet into the man's face.

"Here, give it to me. I can hardly swallow I am so dry." I grabbed it before harm could be done. I didn't doubt MacDonald wouldn't hesitate to pull a sword or a knife, even here. I gulped the strong red wine, determined not to gag when I could barely tolerate it. The king must not care what he served. I'd had better at the local tavern.

"Give the lady her fan, MacDonald. I see Bran coming over with a woman in tow. Looks to be young and fresh." Fergus scowled. "Try not to drain her dry this coming night."

"What I do is my business, shifter." MacDonald bowed and handed me my fan. "Lady Gloriana, we are not done. Remember my offer. Campbell cannot give you what I can."

"The pox?" Fergus made as if to push MacDonald away.

"I'll ignore that." MacDonald snaked an arm around my waist and bent his mouth close to my ear. "Vampires cannot get the pox, so rest easy on that score, my dear." He touched me with a flick of his tongue then walked away before Fergus could do more than growl again.

I shuddered. His tongue in my ear! I thrust the goblet of disgusting wine at Fergus and picked up my skirts. I needed air. Between the stench of too many unwashed bodies, strong perfumes and that wine sitting uneasily in my stomach, I was afraid I was going to be sick right there on the floor of the hall. I could not disgrace Jeremiah so.

I hurried toward a doorway I saw that led to the outside. When I got closer to it, I realized it led to the river. Many had arrived here by boat. Yes, the river had its own stink, but I would at least have room to breathe out there.

"Gloriana, wait!" Fergus tried to follow me but people kept getting in his way.

I couldn't stop, my stomach revolting even more with every step I took. A man pushed into me, his breath fetid and his hand groping my breasts. My elbow into his ribs got me free and I finally managed to get to where there were trees and bushes. I bent over and lost the contents of my stomach with great heaving retches then dragged a handkerchief out of my bodice to wipe my mouth. I was feeling little better and was very afraid I might be sick again. I sought a place to sit, glad to see a stone bench a few feet away.

I had just collapsed onto it when something stirred nearby. A rat in the bushes? I didn't care and was too miserable to even look. Then a man sat next to me.

"I am ill. Please go away before I soil everything near me." I pressed the handkerchief to my lips and swallowed.

"You will feel better once you are away from here." A hand clamped on my arm and dragged me to my feet.

I opened my mouth to scream when a cloth was jammed into it. Then a cloak dropped over my head and wrapped around me to bind my arms before I was lifted and tossed over someone's shoulder to land on my stomach. Desperate for air, I kicked and struggled, sure I would die in this dark and stifling cocoon. I was obviously being carried, jostled with each step taking me farther from hope and safety, from Jeremiah.

I tried to make some noise but my sounds through the gag were pathetic moans. Hopeless. I could only pray that someone had seen me being taken and would ask one of those dozens of soldiers for help. I couldn't leave here. Couldn't.

Because I'd seen the face of the man who'd grabbed me. Jean-Claude. I knew where he was taking me. Straight to Marin to be drained dry.

TWELVE

We had to be in a boat. Between the smell of the river and the rocking motion as I was laid on a hard surface, I knew I was being taken away from Whitehall by water. Had Fergus seen what happened? Was he even now following us? I prayed it was so. He could become a bird, fly overhead and look for a chance to save me. But he was probably outnumbered. I couldn't imagine that Jean-Claude had come alone. I felt his hands on me even now and someone would have to row the boat. No matter what, I couldn't wait for rescue. I had to do something or I would well end up a blood slave with no future. I struggled against the cloth wrapped around me, trying to get my arms free.

"Stay still, Gloriana. If you go into the water, you'll drown. Your death won't bother me, but I'm sick of Marin's bad mood." A boot landed on my backside, pinning me down when I tried to squirm into a sitting position.

The splash of oars hitting the water meant we were on the move. I tried again to make a noise through the gag in my mouth. Useless. Shoving it with my tongue did little good. I breathed through my nose, knowing if I got sick again I would surely choke.

"Look up, Alain. That damned shifter is tracking us.

Mon Dieu, can't you do something about him?" Jean-Claude took his boot off my back. "I don't dare shoot at him. Not this close to the palace. It would bring soldiers down on us."

"You want to take over the rowing while I shift? Then who will watch the woman?" Alain's voice sounded strained. "If I fly away now to give chase, I will be useless to you for anything else for hours."

"Never mind. Keep rowing. When we get to the landing, you can carry this woman and I will take care of that shifter myself. I hope this makes Marin happy. I am sick of hearing about Gloriana's blood and how special it is." Jean-Claude grabbed my ankle.

He pushed aside my skirt and I felt cold night air on my legs as his fingers explored higher, up to my knee. Oh, God, what was he doing?

"I am thinking it's about time I have a taste of this wench for myself. Before we take her to Marin. My mate is so greedy for this mortal, this may be my only chance for a sample." Jean-Claude's fingers clamped on my thigh, despite the fact that I was kicking as hard as I could.

I concentrated, sure he could read my mind. I sent him threats that I would tell his lover that he wanted me for himself. If she was already in a temper because she'd had to wait for me, how would she act if she thought he'd taken my blood and mayhap intended to use me for . . ? I shuddered, screaming inside my head as his hand slid closer to where Jeremiah had claimed me so lovingly. God, if Jean-Claude actually put his mouth there . . .

"She's a fighter, Alain. But only a mortal, easily managed." Jean-Claude chuckled. "Save your energy, Gloriana."

The weak sounds of frustration and anger I made drove me mad. My struggles seemed to merely amuse him when he clamped his hands on my legs, forcing them apart.

"I see you don't approve, shifter. Let me have my fun. There's been little enough of it lately. Marin has been in a hell of a mood." Jean-Claude's breath gusted against my thigh. He rubbed his short beard up and down my leg. "Lovely. You are clean and fresh. If I only had more time . . ."

I gasped when I suddenly felt a sharp pain a few inches from my mound. Oh, Gods save me!

"Let her read your mind, Gloriana. All she will see is that I used my knife to test your blood to see if it is still fresh and untainted. I doubt Jeremiah has been foolish enough to tell you that there are things, food or drink, that can make your blood disgusting to a vampire."

Tears ran down my face and I struggled to breathe against that noisome gag when he pressed his mouth to my inner thigh. He sucked the cut then hummed. Desperate to get him off of me, I kicked and bucked but he managed a deep drink before he smacked his lips then ran his tongue across the wound he'd made.

I held very still. If he decided to rape me... Oh, Gods, he was so very strong. Nothing I tried could free me from his iron grip. The breeze from the river blew my skirts and petticoats over my face but I could almost feel his eyes on my most private place. I heard a bird scream and dive close. The oar splashed and Alain cursed.

"Hurry, Jean-Claude, you are risking us both with your actions. Her shifter may well come at you with his claws." The oar splashed again.

I couldn't see anything but I silently hoped Fergus would have a care for his own safety. Two men against one? He would do better to go for help once he knew where Jean-Claude was taking me.

"I will shoot him out of the sky if he comes at us again." Jean-Claude sounded very confident. "I am glad we took this chance. Gloriana, you are comely, clean and delicious. A true prize, even if I think my darling is mad to liken you to an Egyptian goddess." He sighed, his hands painful as he held my legs apart. "I swear, Alain, if I didn't love Marin to distraction I would have you take this boat further down the river, to a place where I could take my time with this wench. By God, but this blood is something special. I cannot believe the power just that sample gave me, and the taste! Like the fine French wines I used to enjoy before I was turned." He let go of my legs then wrapped the cloak around both of them again, trapping me. "But that damned bird is being a nuisance. I will need both hands if I am going to have to shoot it."

"Marin would kill you, Jean-Claude, if you took this woman for yourself for more than a moment and you know it. She will smell her on you as it is." Alain chuckled. "Try it. I would like to see the battle between you two."

"Mind your business, shifter. You think I don't know my mate? Marin has both this mortal's scent and mine. She would hunt us down if I didn't bring this creature to her as promised." He turned me over and patted my bottom. "Ah, Gloriana, I will do what I can to restrain my lover from being too greedy with you. It would be a fine idea to keep you for a while and feed you enough to make you our pet. What fun we will have, the three of us. Such bedsport!"

I swallowed bile. There was no sport in being forced to lie with such creatures and give them my blood. A pet? I'd rather throw myself overboard and sink like a stone. Of course he read that in my mind and grabbed me. The boat bumped into something and I feared we had reached our destination.

"Oh, no, you don't. We *have* arrived." He picked me up. "Alain, tie up the boat then take her from me."

"You missed your chance to shoot the bird. It has flown back toward Whitehall." Alain's footsteps were on the dock. "Hand her to me."

"Then I'd best shift so I can catch that benighted bird before it can fly back to Jeremiah with news of our whereabouts."

I fought them as they attempted to pass me from one man to another. I wasn't about to let him hurt Fergus. I wasn't going to meekly let Jean-Claude pass me to Alain either. The cloak I was wrapped in and the rocking boat made the transfer awkward. This was my chance.

I twisted in mid-air, risking everything when I was being lifted toward the dock where Alain was standing. My effort paid off and the cloak unwrapped enough for me to throw it into Jean-Claude's face. I could finally see the water next to the boat. Alain had only tied the bow to the dock and my struggles had made the boat swing away from it.

"Hold still, bitch!" The vampire staggered, reaching for me and fighting the cloak out of his way.

I kicked at his hands then flung myself toward that noisome river. Jean-Claude was left holding the cloak as I flew through the air and landed with a splash in the icy water. It closed over my head and I stayed under, sure it was safer to remain out of sight.

It was cold, cold and dark. I pulled the gag from my mouth and it floated away. Something hit above my head. My fingers touched ...the boat. *Move away.* A splash as there was a hit on the water again. Too close. An oar. Jean-Claude wanted me to reach for it. I'd rather drown. I held my breath, my lungs in agony. *Kick.* Velvet skirts pulled at me. Down, to my death.

I bumped into something. A post? Slimy. Couldn't hold on. The dock. Must get under it. *Hide.* Kick, keep kicking. *Can't... breathe.* Legs fighting skirt. Freezing. Hard to see. Murky water suddenly darker. Under the dock. *Air. Must. Have. Air.*

I prayed and took a chance, flailing my arms and rising, my face finally finding air. I dragged it in then remembered. *Quiet.* I groped for anything to hold onto, about to sink again. A long nail stuck out of another slimy post. I hung on, breathing as quietly as I could. I heard Jean-Claude and Alain talking and the slap of that oar hitting the water again and again.

"She'll come up. Watch and see." Alain's boots stomped over my head. "Shift and fly over, Jean-Claude. Look for her in the river. I will see if she is between these boats here."

169

I held too tight to the nail and it cut my palm. Blood. I tried to change hands. If Jean-Claude smelled it, he would know I was alive and nearby. Damned vampire. I sank again, clumsy with the cold. Whatever instinct gave me the ability to swim kept me under the water and moving. When I couldn't hold my breath a moment longer, I reached out again and hit wood. Not slimy but clean. A boat? Was it the boat I'd just been in? I didn't care. I had to catch my breath again. I found a handhold and got my nose above water, barely.

"You are right. I'm shifting now for a better look," Jean-Claude shouted as I held onto a crude raft of some kind.

When a hawk flew overhead, I ducked under the water again. Jean-Claude was searching for me. What about Fergus? Had he really taken off to fetch Jeremiah? Or was he still flying nearby? Would he and Jean-Claude fight? What chance did a shifter have when a vampire attacks him? I didn't know. I couldn't stay where I was another moment without breathing. I used the raft's rope to go nearer the dock, then bobbed up when I was under it again. I held on and waited. My teeth chattered with cold and I bit my lips to keep the sound inside.

"Gloriana, if you are still in the water, say something. Jean-Claude flew away, chasing Fergus. I will help you, take you back to Jeremiah. Show yourself and I will make sure you are safe." Alain kept calling my name.

Mind readers. Was he even now searching for my thoughts? No, Jeremiah claimed he had to be within sight to read what someone was thinking. So my worry now was the noise, the harsh sound of my labored breathing, and the smell of my blood. I held onto the post next to me with the unwounded hand and stayed very still, trying not to slide under again with the weight of my dress dragging at me.

Did I trust Alain? Of course not. I knew where his loyalties lay. I hardly dared to breathe as Alain stomped back and forth overhead and called my name over and over again.

I have no idea how long I stayed under the dock but it seemed like hours. My arm shook with the strain but I dared not change to my other hand. I prayed that the stench of the river water masked my smell.

"Come down, Jean-Claude," Alain finally shouted. "She could not stay underwater without air for so long. Remember, she is mortal. She must have drowned. And Fergus got away. I see no sign of him. He has surely returned to Whitehall and will tell Jeremiah what we have done and where we took his woman." Alain sounded worried now. "We should go get Marin and move again. Campbell will seek retribution for this act against him. He was fond of the lady."

There was a thump and sounds above my head on the dock. "Fond of her blood, you mean. Wait. If she drowned, shouldn't we see her body floating here?" Jean-Claude had obviously shifted back into his human form. "Damn it, Alain, you are becoming useless and as scared as an old woman."

I fumbled under my skirt for the ties to my petticoats. The knots were hopelessly tangled. If I could send at least one floating away, surely that would convince them that I had met my death in this foul river. I sank below the water again, ripping the cloth in my haste before letting a petticoat go. I pulled apart my beautiful dress as well. Whatever I could give them to prove my death, I would. I kicked the bits of cloth away then moved back, as far away as I could under that dock. My lungs were fair to bursting before I carefully raised my face to take in air again.

"Look, over there. You see? There's your proof. Clearly she has drowned." Alain sounded excited and I heard the oar hit the water again. "And here's a piece of lace and a sleeve. The fish are feasting on her now."

I could have wept with relief and pain. That last effort had cost me every fingernail I had and I was so terribly, terribly cold. I leaned back and floated, staring at the boards above my head where I could see just a sliver of light from a street lamp or perhaps the moon. *Please, God, let them give up and leave.* I was so exhausted I didn't even wonder how I knew the skill that let me keep my head above water by just moving my hands a bit. Was I *swimming*?

"I still say we never would have lost the prize if you were not so old, Alain. Do not be surprised if Marin makes us both pay for this night when we return empty handed." Jean-Claude stomped his foot, he was so unhappy.

"I still provide valuable service, sir. How would you have moved the boat this night without me?" Alain wasn't accepting the criticism. "And someone has to pack all your things and move Marin's treasures. Not to mention guard you during the day. Would you really want to go to your death sleep with enemies about with no one to watch out for you?"

"There are other shifters. Ones that are younger and can do the work in twice the time." Jean-Claude was clearly frustrated.

"Not here and not now." Alain wasn't giving up.

"Hush. I must think. Now I have to tell Marin we failed. Why don't we see the woman's body?" More footsteps on the dock.

Pacing above my head. The light flickered when Jean-Claude walked right over me. I felt a cough coming on and fought it back. Dear God.

"She wore a heavy dress. I'm sure she sank. When velvet gets wet . . ." Alain cleared his throat. "Come, we must move now. I'll fetch a carriage. You bring Marin and let's get out of here before Jeremiah and Fergus come looking for Gloriana and for us. There is nothing to gain from confronting those two. The girl is lost. We should go to Paris. Marin is always happy there. I will find a cousin there to serve you. You do need a new, young shifter. I agree with you. My family is a large one and there are some very good shifters who you will enjoy having in your service. I can train one in the ways you like things done then retire. I have saved for it and won't be sorry to have an easy life for a change."

"I am sorry I was hard on you. I admit I will miss you, Alain. You have been very discreet and loyal and are very good in making a home for us. I promise to be generous…" Their voices faded as did their footsteps as they finally walked away.

I was shivering as I finally took an easy breath that turned into a cough. Why hadn't I sunk to the bottom of the river? My dress, my beautiful velvet dress, *was* very heavy and pulled at me. But I could kick and keep my head above water. I had finally let go of the rope ages ago, afraid my chills would make it shake and give me away. And yet I felt safe enough with my kicks and arm movements that I knew I wasn't going to drown. Except for the fact that I was so very cold. How long should I wait before I tried to crawl out and onto that flat raft? Could the sounds of the men walking away be a trap? I had to wait. To make sure.

A bird landed on the raft a few feet away. Suddenly it was no longer a bird but Fergus, crouched down and peering at me.

"Gloriana." He spoke quietly and kept glancing above me, at the dock. "Are you all right?"

Tears filled my eyes. "How, how did you know . . ?" I couldn't say more, coughing as emotion and that blasted river water choked me.

"Even over this noisome river, I caught your scent, sweet lady. Lucky for us, Jean-Claude and Alain aren't as familiar with it as I am." He lay flat and reached out. "Here, take my hand."

I tried, I really did, to move closer to him. But it was impossible. I was unable to move, frozen in place by my fear. What if he was wrong and Jean-Claude attacked as soon as he saw me? I was safely out of sight under that dock.

"Come now, you were so very brave. When I saw you leap into the river, I swear my heart stopped." He scooted even closer, so close to the edge of the raft I feared he'd fall in as well. "You would not meekly go with them. Not our

Gloriana. Now take my hand. There's a lass."

"Wait! It will do no good if two of us land in this slimy stink." I could do this. Fergus called me brave. Brave? Desperate more like. I knew I'd have rather die than go easily into the clutches of a woman who considered humans "pets." I finally kicked and moved a few inches toward him, straining to connect. Our fingers almost touched. With a prayer that I wouldn't be sorry, I lunged, his hand clasped mine and he hauled me up and onto the raft with him.

"There you are." He pulled me in, hugging me close.

"I'm getting you terribly wet." I laughed and cried, so relieved I kissed his cheek. "Thank you, Fergus, I'll never forget this."

He closed his eyes and just held me. "Neither will I, lass."

"Oh, Fergus." I looked around, uneasy both with the look on his face and the place. I still worried that Jean-Claude and Alain could decide to come back and look for me once more. Their fear of Marin might just make them do so. "We must return to Whitehall. Does Jeremiah know what happened?"

"I didn't have time to tell him. I followed you here right away. I would have tried to save you from that bastard Jean-Claude, but I couldn't take a chance that you would be hurt in the fight, even though I think I could take them." Fergus gently set me away from him. "Then I saw Jean-Claude had a gun. If he'd managed to shoot me that would have left you at their mercy."

"I'm glad you didn't try. He boasted he was a crack shot." I couldn't top shivering. "Two of them, one of them vampire, against you? Yes, you are be big and strong and can be many things, but it wouldn't have been a fair fight."

Fergus frowned. "When I saw Jean-Claude taste your blood . . ." He looked away. "He will die for what he did, Gloriana, I promise you that."

I put a hand on his knee. "Fergus, please take me away. Quickly. You did the right thing. We need to leave here."

This time I was the one to look away from his keen gaze. "I cannot bear it here. I am afraid every moment we tarry."

Fergus shimmered, the sign that he was on the verge of changing. "I am sorry, Gloriana. I failed you. They never should have been able to steal you away from Whitehall. Jeremiah would be right to send me home over this."

"No! I ran outside. You tried to follow..." I looked around frantically. "There is the boat they used. And the cloak they wrapped around me. We must go. Now. And no more talk of your guilt. I am to blame. I left your side. It was my actions that got me stolen away. If you start telling Jeremiah any of this nonsense, you will disappoint me." I tried to crawl from the raft to the dock, glad when he helped me with a firm hand on my waist.

"Very well." He picked up the discarded cloak and wrapped it around me. "You are distressed and rightly so. I'll row us back down the river." Fergus helped me into that small boat, untied it and picked up the oars. Soon we were on our way back to the palace. I knew I was not fit to be seen.

"Leave me where no one will see me. Fetch Jeremiah. We cannot let anyone in Whitehall see me like this." I pointed to a spot near the palace where he could dock the boat. "I will be safe enough there. The king's guards are everywhere. We can tell them I fell in while taking a stroll too close to the river."

"They will never believe that. I will arrange for our carriage to come here as soon as I find Jeremiah. Take this." Fergus handed me a knife. "Stick anyone who bothers you."

"I wish I'd had this earlier. Though I don't think it would have bothered Jean-Claude to have blood drawn. It would probably excite him." I hid it in the folds of my cloak, glad to have something to defend myself with.

"You are right. And he would take it away from you too easily. Mayhap I shouldn't leave it with you." Fergus really didn't want to leave me alone while he ran to get Jeremiah.

"No! I'm glad to have it. Go now and hurry. I stink like that river. You know how I like to be clean. I cannot stand my own reek." I forced tears and he finally hurried away, casting suspicious looks around him as I settled on a bench under a torch and huddled under my cloak. I still had a cough. Vile river water. It was all I could taste.

I had much to think about. Had Jean-Claude truly been convinced I was dead? Would he and Marin leave London now? And would Jeremiah simply let them go? Honestly, I didn't think I would ever feel safe again knowing Marin was out there, lusting for my blood.

Jeremiah was a man with a strong protective instinct. Tonight he'd failed to keep me safe. I could almost imagine his reaction even before he came to me, his face a mixture of fury and concern. If I could, I'd lie and say I fell into the river, nothing more. But I knew that would never work. Cursed mind reader. Of course he'd see the truth even if Fergus hadn't already told him everything.

"Gloriana!" He pulled me into his arms and just held me. "Thank God Marin never got you. But to jump into the river!" He looked into my eyes. "How is it you didn't drown?"

I had no answer for him. Was it part of my missing past that I could swim? If only I could remember. But clearly someone somewhere had taught me. It still surprised me that I could kick and keep my head above water. Floating as well! I could do it. But I had been terrified the entire time. Water was not something I loved, except in a bath. What I wouldn't give for a nice hot soak right now.

"Bless you, of course you want to wash the stench of that river off. We will find a way to make that happen." He turned to Fergus. "Get her a tub. The lass is desperate to be clean again."

"Aye." Fergus gestured. "The coach is waiting. Give me an hour and I'll have a tub for you." He stomped off down the alley, expecting us to follow.

"You scared him, Gloriana." Jeremiah picked me up in

his arms, insisting on carrying me. "You scared me, as well, once I knew what had happened."

"I would like to forget the entire incident." I ran a hand over his tight jaw. "I hope that you will forget it as well."

"You cannot think I will let this go. Jean-Claude will pay for this." He stopped next to the hired carriage, where Fergus held open the door. "There are few enough vampires. We try to help each other. Did we not go to Marin's aid at the Tower?" His fists were clenched and he hit his thighs. "By God! And this is how they repay us. I won't stand for it."

"You left the king's presence rather hurriedly, Campbell. The king sent me to inquire if there was an emergency." Robert MacDonald stepped out of the shadows. "Mistress Gloriana." He frowned. "My dear! Did someone dump you in the river?"

"This is none of your concern, MacDonald." Jeremiah turned to face him.

"It might be, Jeremiah, that we could use a bit of help if we are going to take vengeance on Marin and Jean-Claude." Fergus stared over MacDonald's shoulder, meeting his cousin Bran's worried gaze. "You were telling Gloriana that vampires help each other in times of trial."

"I would never ask a MacDonald for anything." Jeremiah rested his hand on his sword hilt. "We can handle Marin and her mate without help."

"Can we? Marin has powers we have yet to test. And she has a powerful thirst for Gloriana's blood. She will not meekly go away, despite what Alain advised at the dock." Fergus turned to me. "Tell him, Gloriana."

"Alain was all for them leaving immediately, to go to Paris." I rested my hand on Jeremiah's back. If there was going to be a battle, I would like for Jeremiah to take a proficient fighter with him. MacDonald had certainly proved he could hold his own against another vampire when they'd fought each other. And Bran was like Fergus, big and brawny and a fairly young shifter. Alain wouldn't stand a chance against them.

"I saw Jean-Claude taste Gloriana's blood, Jeremiah." Fergus said this quietly but of course MacDonald heard him and stepped closer.

"Did he now?" MacDonald's mouth thinned and his fangs came down. "You will kill him of course. She is your woman. Even I know enough to respect that boundary. Though I enjoy teasing you about it."

I stared at him. What had that play with my ear been? Oh, of course it didn't count. Not like a knife on my inner thigh. I tried to send that thought to Jeremiah and he stiffened.

"He cut you on your thigh?" He turned to look into my eyes. "And drank blood from you there?"

"Yes. I fought him, I really did. But--" The hatred blazing in his eyes stopped me.

"Say no more. He is a dead man. MacDonald is right about that." He turned back to the other vampire. "Yes, I will accept your help. And we cannot wait. If they think to move quickly, so must we." Jeremiah looked at Fergus. "Can you find out where they were last staying? I feel sure they have moved recently, just as we have."

"Must there be a fight? They think I drowned in the river. They might leave now." I resisted when Jeremiah started to help me into the carriage. His face was a mixture of anger and frustration. He hated to admit MacDonald had given him sound advice. "Can we not just let them go?"

Jeremiah refused to listen, his mind made up. "Gloriana, you will go to a safe place while we take care of this." He turned to Robert MacDonald. "Your man Bran can escort her if that suits you, MacDonald." They agreed with a look and a nod.

"You will not lock me away in some tiny room while you defend my so-called honor." I thumped Jeremiah on the back with my fist. "I need to be there. If for no other reason than as bait. My blood is what Marin wants. She will come for me if she thinks she can get me." I pushed my wet hair out of my eyes. "I won't be safe anywhere but at your side. I would be vulnerable without you."

"Gloriana is right about that." MacDonald had his hand on his own sword hilt. "My dear, please get into the carriage. You look done in." He nodded toward the open door. "Campbell, the shifters can find out where we are going while you take the lady home and let her rest and restore. I'm sure you are right that the vile pair will not slink away without one more try for the woman."

"My shifter can see her home." Jeremiah lifted me into the carriage and put a fur rug over my knees, then slammed the carriage door. "I doubt Marin will leave now if only to make a point that she has the power to do as she pleases. She will not admit defeat to anyone. If she does find out Gloriana yet lives, she will certainly make one more try. But, for now, she is probably mourning her loss. We can attack as soon as we find out where she is staying." He turned to MacDonald. "I need to let the king know why I left so abruptly. We can make up a story about a group of Catholics and a rumor that we had to confirm. He will readily believe we are only concerned for his welfare."

"Yes, we cannot have his majesty upset with either of our clans." MacDonald walked over to the carriage. "Gloriana, please let our shifters watch over you. We will make sure you are never at such risk again from that Egyptian witch." He took my hand through the open window and bowed over it.

"That's enough, MacDonald. You think I don't know you want her for yourself? You've made no secret of it." Jeremiah waved the driver on. "Fergus, don't leave her side. Let Bran find her the hip bath. I will be home soon."

I sat back in the coach, exhausted. Surely they didn't think to attack Marin and Jean-Claude tonight. It already felt as if it had been dark forever. Perhaps vampires had an endless supply of energy as long as the sun was down, but mortals did not. I felt as if I could sleep a week. As the coach rumbled through quiet London streets, I sagged in my seat.

But sleep wasn't coming, despite a desperate weariness.

I couldn't forget that water closing over my head and the pressure in my lungs as I couldn't breathe. No air. I never wanted to be in water that deep again. Or in a boat. Or even near a river. Land, that was where I belonged.

I vowed to avoid water in the future. It was not for me. My past was obviously full of secrets. I might never know what they were but being able to swim was one skill I would just as soon forget again.

THIRTEEN

I finally felt warm enough. It had taken a bath and a change of clothes, then time in front of a roaring fire before I could stop shivering. Gods, I never wanted to see that foul and freezing river again. Fergus had waited outside until I called him that I was dressed and ready to go.

Ready? Of course I wasn't eager to face Jean-Claude and Marin. But I knew we must end this obsession the woman had with me. How? I was terrified that it would be a bloody battle and no guarantee that it would go the way I prayed it would. My knees were weak as I sat before the fire and waited for Jeremiah and Robert MacDonald to return from court.

A noise from outside made us both turn toward the door. Fergus aimed his gun and seemed ready to shift into something huge if the weapon wasn't enough.

"Who's there?" he demanded.

"'Tis I, cousin. Unlock the door and let me in." Bran's voice, if I wasn't mistaken.

Fergus laid his pistol on the table and turned the key in the lock. He didn't fling the door open until he sniffed the air and asked if his cousin was alone. Then he said something in that language of the Highlands. The answer must have satisfied him because he finally opened the heavy door.

"Well met. What news do you have for us?" Fergus stepped into the passageway. "Are you sure you weren't followed?"

"Aye. No one could have tracked me." Bran walked to the fireplace and held his hands out toward the flames. "It's cold out there this night. But I do have news. I found the spot where you said they took Gloriana." He bowed toward me. "You look much better, mistress."

"I feel better but won't relax until this is settled and Marin on her way somewhere else. Did you find where she and Jean-Claude have been staying?" I walked over and poured Bran a mug of ale. "Drink. I'm sure you would like a bite to eat as well."

"I wouldn't turn it down." He smiled. "Thank you." He took a deep drink.

"You can eat when you've told us what you found." Fergus sat on a stool next to the fire. "Spit it out, man."

"Impatient, are you not?" Bran sat at the table and plucked an orange from a basket. He quickly peeled it and put a section in his mouth. "You eat well here."

"Gloriana eats well. Speak!" Fergus snatched the rest of the orange from him, a knife in his hand. "I expect the masters any time now. We need answers for them."

"I know that." Bran frowned at the knife. "No need for threats. We are on the same side for once."

"'Tis rare enough." Fergus pushed the orange back to him. "Now eat and talk at the same time."

I sat at the table with them and tore a chunk off a piece of bread. I had a feeling we would all need our strength. "He's right. Talk."

"They weren't far from the docks. Alain was loading a cart. He is certainly showing his age." Bran frowned then popped another orange segment into his mouth. "That will be us someday, cousin. He should have caught my scent, with me not ten yards from him, sitting atop a building. But, no, he didn't even sniff the air, so busy was he hefting rugs and such. It was clear to me they are moving for good."

"I am glad to hear it." I slathered butter on the bread and took a bite. I prayed they would be gone before Jeremiah could mount an attack. Yes, I knew my lover was strong and skilled with a sword. With his fangs as well. But Marin's powers were untested. How would Jeremiah fare against such a strong and ancient vampire? I didn't doubt that she was also a witch after she had frozen me in place. What could witch's do? I shuddered to think about it.

"You really want them to get away?" Fergus frowned at me. "I do not believe you will be truly safe until Marin is dead, Gloriana. This move of theirs might have been an act, designed to lull a watcher into thinking they were running away."

"I wondered about that. It could be Alain knew I was there all along." Bran smacked the table making his mug of ale tremble. "Of course. No shifter worth his hire would ignore another that close by. He probably sensed me and kept loading that cart, showing me that they were giving up on taking the mistress here. Ha! It was but a feint." He dropped his head into his hands. "I should have stayed to see more."

"You had to come back and report what you saw. If the masters get back soon, we can catch Marin and her crew at their old place." Fergus got up. "I think I hear the vampires coming now." He looked at me. "Gloriana, it would be best if you stayed here. Bran can show them where to go. You and I can wait."

I had listened to them. Yes, Alain might well have pretended to ignore Bran. And what would he have done next? Followed him here, of course, bringing his masters with him. I said as much. "So you see? It is not safe to leave me behind. With only you to guard me, Fergus? Yes, you would do your best. But against two vampires and a shifter? I don't like those odds, do you?"

"By God, she's right, cousin. So eager was I to share

my news, I may have very well missed a sign and been that careless." Bran jumped up just as a key turned in the lock.

"You said you were sure you weren't followed." Fergus stood beside him.

"Are we ever sure when it comes to our own kind? Alain is old, aye, but that could well mean he has honed his skills and can do what we cannot. Gloriana is right. He works for a witch. What if she gave him a cloaking spell? No one can see through one of those." Bran frowned as the door opened.

I didn't have time to ask him to explain that spell before Jeremiah, followed by Robert, strode into the room and walked straight to the fire. Bran hurriedly took MacDonald's cloak. Both vampires looked to Bran for news, though Jeremiah held out his arms to me. I rushed to his side.

"How are you, Gloriana? Have you recovered from nearly drowning in the river?" Jeremiah brushed back my hair, frowning when he realized it was still damp. "Fergus, bring her brush. She will catch her death if she sits around with wet hair."

Fergus ducked into the bedchamber and came out with my hairbrush. He didn't say a word just laid it in Jeremiah's hand.

"Are we really going to stand around while you brush your mistress's hair, Campbell?" Robert smirked. "Not that it isn't lovely." He gave Bran a searching look. "Oh, get on with it while my shifter reports what he found."

Jeremiah was ignoring him anyway. He gently steered me into a chair in front of the fire and began running the brush through my hair. He carefully pulled the knots out while I sat, very aware of the eyes on me.

"I can do that, Jeremiah." I tried to take the brush from him. This tender care was unlike him. Was it part of his claiming me in front of MacDonald? If so, I didn't mind it. I couldn't deny his touch was soothing. "Please give me the brush."

"Nay, I will do it. You must be exhausted." He patted my shoulder. "Speak, man. Did you find Marin's lair?" He never quit brushing but his hand on my shoulder tightened.

"Aye." Bran told them what he'd reported to Fergus and me. "Did you see any signs that I was followed here when you came in?"

Jeremiah and MacDonald exchanged worried looks. He finally handed me the brush. I laid it aside and twisted my hair into a knot, securing it with pins from my pocket.

"We were careful and shifted here from court. Did you see anything unusual, MacDonald?" Jeremiah frowned at him.

"How would I know what to expect here? You live in a blasted hovel, Campbell." MacDonald nodded at me. "I would never keep so fine a woman in such a dismal place."

"By God! Gloriana is well cared for." Jeremiah was reaching for his sword when a green mist suddenly filled the room, slipping in around the door. The men braced themselves, keeping their swords or guns in hand, while they waited for whatever would come next.

I began to cough, the strange fog clogging my throat.

"What is it?" I could hardly catch my breath enough to speak and my eyes watered so I had trouble seeing. The mist thickened. The vampires and shifters stood very still and seemed to have stopped breathing. Could they really do that? Or was I imagining it as the noxious smell almost overpowered me. I covered my face with my shawl though it did little good. I felt unsettled, dizzy, as if I was about to swoon.

"Gloriana, go to my room and lock yourself in. This is Marin's work. She thinks this trick will give her an advantage in a fight. We might not be able to see her clearly but she has no doubt forgotten that this could be the end of you." Jeremiah took my elbow and pushed me towards his room just as the main door blew open with a crash.

I stayed behind him as he turned to face Marin, Jean-Claude and Alain. They must have followed Bran or the vampires from court. It didn't matter how they'd found us, they had arrived and were ready to fight. I wasn't going to hide. Marin would have to stop the mist if she saw it was killing me. I coughed and staggered, showing her what she was doing to her prized blood source.

"Don't be a fool, Jeremiah!" Marin screeched. She seemed to swell in size, growing taller and more fierce before my stinging eyes. "Give her over and you can walk away. Is she worth dying for?" She waved her arms then flung fire from her fingertips, searing the lace from Jeremiah's sleeves.

"You must think so. But you're going to kill her with your tricks first. Can't you see that?" Jeremiah slashed at her with his sword. I was sure he had her but she vanished, only to appear in a new spot a moment later.

"I think she can survive until I've ended you." She laughed, a chilling sound, and flung more fire. Only my lover's quick footwork kept him from being consumed by her flames. I gasped, choking, and sank to my knees.

Marin's eyes narrowed. She needed me alive and with my blood good for drinking. "What a nuisance. The mortal has to breathe." Her murky haze disappeared as quickly as it had come. She crooked her finger. "Come, Gloriana. Do you really want your lover to die like this? I see you fear for his life. You can save him. Just let me take you away now and I will leave him unharmed, I swear it."

"You must think me an idiot. I may not be able to read minds like you do, but I know a lie when I hear one." I crawled to a chair, finally able to take a deep cleansing breath, then grabbed a cloak. I tossed it to Jeremiah so he could put out the fire on his burning sleeve. "I trust Jeremiah to kill you and send you to hell." She knew as well as I did that my man would never stand by while she took me away.

"Gloriana, come." Jeremiah gestured for me to get behind him again.

I clambered to my feet and hurried to do as he bid. I couldn't be the reason the witch bested him by getting in his way. Robert and Jean-Claude were fighting each other with swords. The noise of their blades striking each other sent chills down my spine. When Jean-Claude's blade flew out of his hand, Robert laughed and tossed his aside. He was enjoying this! They pulled knives and began to circle each other. Marin smiled at the show but I could see she was working up to something, her hands moving while she mumbled what must be a spell. I looked away from her to see Bran and Fergus suddenly put Alain on the ground and hold him at gunpoint.

"Alain! What are you playing at? Get up! Change and attack them!" Marin was clearly incensed that her shifter had failed to win against the younger men of his kind. "Are you so old that you cannot take those two? Get up, I say!" When Alain ignored her, staring up at Fergus and Bran as if telling them something, she whirled, said something I certainly couldn't understand, then tossed a lightning bolt at her servant. Alain shuddered and smoke curled from his body. He jerked once and then was still.

"Marin! What have you done?" Jean-Claude paused, gaping at her when it became clear she had killed Alain.

"He was useless, *cheri*. Now we will kill them all except the woman." She turned to Jeremiah who had been joined by Fergus. "Did you like my lightning? It's a shame I wasted it on Alain. Now I will have to gather more power. Believe me, I can in but moments. As you saw, no one, not even an ancient shape-shifter, can survive it. I learned how to use it from a crone in Nefertiti's court." She stared at the fire dancing in the fireplace, waving her arms and obviously gathering strength from the flames while she murmured a spell in that language she'd used before.

No one dared approach her as sparks circled her body like a whirlwind of fire. Jeremiah tried and flinched when his sword touched one of them. "She's mad," he murmured. "I felt that like a jolt through my whole body or I'd have run her through."

"I hope you are saying your prayers, Jeremiah, and telling your woman goodbye. My lightning is a lovely thing, so powerful, so deadly. Imagine what I will be able to do once I have Gloriana's god-like blood inside me." Marin raised her hands toward the ceiling, as if pulling elements from the sky beyond it.

I couldn't let her do this. I imagined her making the man I loved smoke and sizzle right before my eyes. I lunged toward her, but was brought up short by Fergus grabbing one arm and Jeremiah the other.

"Wait." Jeremiah was watching Jean-Claude, who had taken a stake from his doublet. Robert MacDonald pulled out a pistol and had it trained on the vampire, but he didn't fire. Because we could all see it wasn't one of the men Jean-Claude crept close to with that stake. I recognized the scent of that wood, even through the stench of the lingering haze. It had the same strong odor as the arrows in the Tower. Olive wood. Lethal to vampires. Surely Marin would recognize…

But she was in a trance, uttering her incantations and waving her arms. She was gathering power until she was sure it would be strong enough to take out every vampire and shape-shifter in the room, everyone except her beloved Jean-Claude and me. The whirlwind died down until all the energy became a wild light from her fingertips as she chanted. She'd thrown back her cape so we could see the thin black dress molded to her slim body. Her eyes glowed red while her ebony hair lifted high above her head.

I gasped when she lowered her arms, ready to take aim at Jeremiah. I couldn't believe that Jean-Claude had the nerve to move close to her at that moment. She was a terrifying sight, clearly filled with her murderous intent.

"With the memory of my dear Nefertiti, I use the flames of Tefnut and the power of Ra to send you to the afterlife, Jeremiah. May you burn for eternity." Before Marin could send a single lightning strike outward, she shrieked, then looked down at where the stake had pierced her chest. "What have you done, Jean-Claude?"

"Good-bye, *mon amour*. I am sorry I was not enough for

you." Tears ran down his cheeks as Jean-Claude pushed the stake in with such force it went through her body where her heart must have been. Suddenly where Marin had once stood there was a puff of gray soot, then scattered ashes atop a pile of clothes on the stone floor.

I shuddered and clasped Jeremiah's arm. "It cannot be. Is it a witch's trick? To vanish like that?" I could barely speak, so horrified at what I'd seen. I buried my face against Jeremiah's chest.

"That is how we die, Gloriana. A stake made of the proper wood run through the heart and we turn to ash." Jeremiah's voice was rough but he held his sword in front of me. "There is no trick Marin could do, witch or no, that could permit her to survive what Jean-Claude just served her." His arm tightened around me.

"She is truly gone." Jean-Claude's voice broke and I looked up in time to see him drop to the floor. He gathered Marin's cloak and dress into his hands. He sobbed, mourning the woman he'd just killed.

We gave him a few moments as the fire crackled in the hearth and we all looked away from his tears. Jeremiah settled me on a stool as far away from Jean-Claude and his grief as the room would allow. Robert MacDonald sat at the table, exchanging glances with Jeremiah. They both held knives, ready in case the battle wasn't over. Finally, my lover spoke.

"Jean-Claude, what will you do now?"

"I have no quarrel with you, Jeremiah, or taste for the woman, now that I have seen the cost to have her." Jean-Claude still held the stake. He got to his feet and walked over to throw it into the fireplace where it burned and hissed as we watched. "Marin is the one who told the king's men about the olive wood. She was that crazed in her wish to die. She also gave the Catholics names of some of the vampires here in London. She deserved to die for that if for no other reason. When she told me what she'd done, I got the stake but couldn't use it. I kept it, though. Because I realized how madness had claimed her."

Jeremiah stood, clearly very disturbed by these revelations. "Who else is on the list she gave out besides me?"

"MacDonald, a few others. I did what I could to erase the memories of the people with that list. You should both have a care." Jean-Claude walked over to where Alain's body lay. "This was the final blow, the thing I could not forgive. Alain served us well for a century. He was a friend, not just a hireling. And this is how she repaid him? She cared more for your woman's blood than she did for me or anyone but herself in the end." He stared down at Alain. "I will see that this man gets a decent burial if you let me leave here. I will tell his family that he was an honorable man."

"He was. He could have taken us both, sir." Fergus spoke up. "But he didn't believe Gloriana should go with Marin. He knew it would be the death of her. He told us that, in his mind." He glanced at Bran.

"I suspected as much. Alain was not comfortable with Marin's darker spells or her recent obsession with Gloriana. He also knew that she'd turned traitor to her own kind. It endangered even the shape-shifters who guarded their vampires. He wanted to warn you, but his loyalty to us wouldn't allow it." He glanced at Jeremiah. "I should have spoken up as well, but love can blind us and turn us into fools." He dragged his sleeve across his face.

Jeremiah and MacDonald stared at each other, clearly communicating in their minds. "Yes, you should have stopped her. But you were together a long time. I suppose she did things without your knowing." Jeremiah glanced at me. "Women like Marin can be headstrong. And a witch? I cannot imagine what you dealt with."

Robert MacDonald stood near the door. "Where were your balls, man? To let her betray our kind like that... He fingered his knife. "Well, I'll not soon forget it. Best you leave London, England itself, and stay well away or I'll forget you saved us all with your stake."

"I hope to never see this place again. There is nothing but bad memories here." He looked from Jeremiah to MacDonald. "With your permission, I will leave and take his body with me." Jean-Claude took the cloak Bran offered and gently wrapped Alain in it so he could carry him through the streets. When he was done, he looked at Jeremiah, then MacDonald. "Are we indeed finished here, gentlemen? I will leave for France if you are satisfied that I am no longer a threat to you."

"There is something you are forgetting." Jeremiah kept his hand on his sword. "You tasted my woman." He pointed that blade over Jean-Claude's heart. "Do you think I can just let that go?"

"Jeremiah, please." I took a chance and stepped between them, the sharp blade mere inches from my throat. "I have seen enough violence this night. Jean-Claude is a man. And he was curious after hearing Marin rave about my blood. Are you telling me you wouldn't have wanted to know what was so special about it if you hadn't already tasted it?"

"You are certainly making me thirst for a sip." Robert MacDonald couldn't keep quiet. "Oh, you know she's right, Campbell. The man has just lost his mate and by his own hand. That took courage, by God. Even though he was late in finding it. I'd say he's suffered enough."

"I doubt you would think so if it was your woman he had put his fangs to." Jeremiah had a new target for his rage and he was ready to fight.

"Stop it!" I really couldn't bear to see more bloodshed. "I am sick and tired. Will you let Jean-Claude go as a boon to me, Jeremiah?" I didn't like the narrow look I was getting. "Oh, come now. Read my mind. Do you really think I enjoyed the way he pawed me? I would as soon lie with a river rat." I sniffed in Jean-Claude's direction.

Robert laughed and even Bran and Fergus grinned. Jeremiah finally put his sword away but he did look into my eyes. Yes, he wanted to see my thoughts. Did he trust no one?

"Go, Jean-Claude. MacDonald is right. We hope never to lay eyes on you again." Jeremiah threw open the door. "I am sorry about your shifter Alain. I know how valuable the men who watch over us can be."

Jean-Claude gave a sad smile, then winked at me, determined it seemed to leave Jeremiah with a bit of jealousy. "You are a lucky man, Jeremiah. Marin was obsessed with Gloriana and it killed her. She was right, though, that your woman has exceptional blood, the like of which I had never tasted before. I will always regret that we couldn't come to terms." With that he picked up Alain's body and walked through the door, disappearing into the darkness.

"Slimy bastard. I swear he will find a stake in his heart from me if I ever see him again." Jeremiah turned to Robert. "MacDonald? I think our temporary truce has run its course. Thank you for your assistance. Now leave." He gestured toward the open door.

"I cannot say it has been a pleasure. But at least we won the night." Robert bowed in my direction. "Mistress Gloriana, I renew my offer. If you tire of this lowly Campbell or if he goes mad and tires of you, please come see me. I am generous and my women leave me well-satisfied." He tried to take my hand but Jeremiah stepped between us.

"That's enough." Jeremiah all but shoved MacDonald out the door.

Robert ignored him as he donned his cape. "Bran, I am for home. No mortal woman tonight. Mistress Gloriana has spoiled me for the ordinary." With that he stalked out the door, Bran right behind him. The two no doubt changed into some kind of bird as soon as they were free of the building.

"Good riddance." Jeremiah slammed the door, then turned to me. "You look exhausted, Gloriana. Shall I help you to bed?"

"Yes, I would like to lie down." I glanced at Fergus. "Could you give us some privacy, Fergus? I need to be alone with Jeremiah for a while."

"Certainly, Gloriana. I need to find us a new place to live anyway. I might as well start now. Too many people have seen this one. And my pride chafed at MacDonald's remarks about these quarters. I will look for something more fitting for such a mistress." Fergus picked up his cloak. "What do you think, Jeremiah?"

"You are right. More room and more privacy for the lady. I don't like MacDonald knowing where I live. Or where Gloriana lives. See to it, Fergus." Jeremiah picked me up and carried me around the fireplace to the bedchamber.

I heard the door open and close then the key turn in the lock. "He's gone." I smiled up at Jeremiah. "Will you help me out of this dress?" Of course it laced up the front. I had got into it without help, but I was inviting him to do more than undress me and he knew it.

"Are you sure, Gloriana? You have had a rough night. Near drowning and then breathing that fog Marin sent in here. I told you that vampires don't need to breathe but seeing it is different. Shifters and my kind can go a while without taking in air. I hope it didn't upset you." Jeremiah made quick work of my laces so that the dress dropped to the ground. Then he helped me pull it over my head and toss it onto a chair.

"It was a surprise and did look strange. I just wished I had the same skill when I was choking on that green mist." I untied my petticoats and held onto his arms so I could step out of them. Then I was clad only in my sheer chemise. "Marin terrified me. I am glad she is dead. Does that make me a terrible person?" I unbuttoned Jeremiah's waistcoat and drew it off of him.

"No, of course not. She was evil." Jeremiah pulled his shirt off over his head.

"I heard Jean-Claude talk about making me their pet. Do vampires really do that? Make mortals into pets? Like a cat or a dog?" I ran my hands over his chest. I would like to stroke him like a pet. Make him purr. I dipped my hand between his belt and his firm stomach and found that he wore nothing under that kilt of his. Now I was the one purring.

"Some do. There are mortals who want to serve vampires. They like giving their blood. It is our life force." He ran his thumbs over my nipples. "Before you were stolen from me this night, we were planning for me to take your blood. But I won't ask that of you now." He hooked his fingers under the straps of the chemise and sent it the floor next.

I unbuckled his belt. He caught his sporran, laid it aside, then unwrapped his kilt and tossed it on top of my dress. He kicked aside his shoes and so did I. We were both naked now, face to face. He pulled me close and I reveled in the feel of his solid strength against me. He was bigger, stronger, tougher. His hands on my buttocks held me so that I was free to reach for his face and kiss him as deeply as I wanted.

"I am recovered, lover. So take me to bed, make love to me and, yes, show me how you will drink from me, as vampire lovers do." I felt his cock pulsing against my thighs. He was so eager, so much a man. Vampire. I'd felt the prick of his fangs when I kissed him but he hadn't hurt me. He was careful, very careful. Because he wanted me to find pleasure with him.

"Gloriana, you are so rare, so beautiful. Most mortals who had almost drowned would need days to recover from what you went through tonight. It makes me think that your rare blood gives you a special strength. I don't know how that is possible but I only know that I am amazed by you." He kissed me this time, holding me against him as if he'd never let me go.

"I think you are beautiful too." I ran my hands over his sturdy and very masculine body. I loved every inch of it.

"Now you are being foolish. This warrior's body is anything but beautiful. But it can give you pleasure." He pulled me down to the bed. "Come and I will show you."

I was happy to let him. Why was my blood so special? Was the answer in the secrets from my past that I couldn't remember? I had been lucky in never falling ill, that was true. No matter. Jeremiah laid me on the bed and took his time. He kissed me from my breasts to my thighs. I explored him, pulling a groan from him when I took his cock in my mouth. I crawled all over him, finding what pleased him.

Of course he wasn't satisfied with lying there. He wanted me to be mad for him. He pulled a nipple into his mouth while he rubbed the other one between his fingers. He pushed into me with his hard cock, swallowing my gasp of pleasure as I wrapped my legs around him. He smiled into my eyes and began to move.

"Jeremiah!" I tugged at his hair. "Please, I need…" I couldn't say it. There was this greedy craving for something too intense to name. I gasped and bucked as I bowed off the bed, pulling him even deeper inside me. I held onto him, my eyes closed as sensations shivered through me.

I opened my eyes and gazed up at him. He was staring down at me. Those fangs were down, long, lethal, and shining in the candlelight. I knew then what he wanted. What would make this complete for him.

"Yes. Take my blood. Do it now." I arched my neck so he could reach the vein I knew was pounding with my excitement. He kissed me often there. It was a pleasure point for him. And for me.

He growled, then licked the spot before sinking his fangs into it. I could feel him taking me. There was some pain and yet nothing I couldn't bear. We were becoming one in a new and very intimate way. I felt pressure and a pull, as he drew my blood into his mouth and swallowed. I held his head, my fingers twined in his soft hair. My life force. And his. Yes, that's what he had called it. I was giving him life.

The act made him crave my body as well and I clutched his shoulders as he began to drive into me, harder and faster. I had been reaching for something, now I knew what it was. I clenched around him even before I screamed his name.

The pleasure was almost too intense to be borne. I held on, keening with it, my eyes shut as his seed filled me. Gods. I lay under him, my body trembling, until he finally eased his fangs from my neck and licked the wounds closed.

"Gloriana." He breathed my name against my lips, then kissed me as if he'd never stop. When he drew back he rested his cheek against mine before he looked into my eyes, searching for signs of distress. "You are a wonder. Are you all right?"

I thought about it. Was I? Did I feel weak like I had when he'd taken too much before? No. He had stopped much sooner. I didn't tingle except between my thighs in the most pleasant way possible. I certainly didn't feel like I was going to swoon. Instead I wanted to kiss this man forever. Tell him... No, he wouldn't want to hear those words. I was a mistress. Nothing more.

"I am fine." I stretched beneath him but it wasn't easy. "Except you are like to crush me." I laughed. "No, don't move. It is a wonderful way to die."

He rolled until I was lying on top of him. "I have never had a woman like you. You are so generous, so giving."

"You were careful this time." I reached down and ran a hand over his cheek. Stubble. What a masculine man! "It didn't hurt and I found the way you took my blood very, um, exciting." I kissed his firm lips. The fangs were gone now. I didn't like what they did to the shape of his mouth. I had to admit that. He was much more handsome without them. "I can see why some mortals choose to become vampire pets."

"I would never make you a pet. That sounds too much like a mindless creature, trained to do nothing but please its master." He ran a hand over my bottom and squeezed. "You have a fine mind and challenge me as well as keep me entertained."

"Like a dog does tricks? Michael took me to a circus once. Dogs can jump through hoops--"

He slapped my bottom. "Stop it. You are not a trained dog. Fergus says he's teaching you to read. No dog could do that. And tomorrow night we will be going to court to see Shakespeare's new play. Would I take a pet there?"

"You might. On a jeweled leash." I laughed and reached back to rub my bottom. "Watch out. Hit me like that again and I am off to see Robert MacDonald."

"I'm sorry. I meant it for a love tap." He set me aside, face down on the bed, then proceeded to kiss the spot. "I will have to make it up to you." Which he did in fine fashion.

But I had that word in my head now. Love. A love tap. If only I thought he loved me. Because I was hopelessly in love with him. Jeremiah Campbell, vampire, had somehow stolen my heart. Was I mad? I must be. Because the idea of becoming his blood slave, pet, whatever he wanted to call me, didn't make me run screaming into the night. Oh, no. I was actually thinking it would be a fine way to live.

I had to face reality. No matter how extraordinary the lovemaking, how beautiful the clothes and good the food, this was a temporary arrangement. A man like Jeremiah, from a fine family in the Highlands, would never marry the likes of me. When he tired of me and my blood, and he would, I would be on my own to find a new protector. Yes, mayhap Robert MacDonald would take me on, but again that would be temporary. I could see my future a little too clearly: going from one man to another until I grew hard eyed and desperate like those women I'd seen at court. The idea of another man using my body sickened me. No, I'd rather starve than endure intimacies at anyone else's hand.

I hoped Jeremiah was too busy giving us both pleasure in this bed to read my dreary thoughts. Because my brush with drowning this night had made me think. Being a man's mistress was fine for the short term, but what about later? Did I really want to take a chance on my looks holding a man for longer than a few romps in the bedchamber?

Jeremiah did something very clever with his tongue and I forgot everything but him and his wicked ways. I'd been lucky so far. If I was wise, I would enjoy what I had while I had it. The future would surely take care of itself. Michael

197

had shown me that even marriage was no guarantee of a secure life. Jeremiah sat up and stared at me.

"Gloriana, tomorrow I will have Fergus take you shopping for jewels. I am sorry you are worried about your future. Will that make you feel better?" He pulled me into his lap and kissed me tenderly.

"I'm sorry. I am not going to be one of those grasping sluts--" I hoped he would stop looking into my mind. What would he think if he knew none of that mattered if I died of a broken heart if he abandoned me? Easy to think practical thoughts, but the reality was, I wanted no man but this one. I wanted his love, not his jewels.

"No, I apologize. I shouldn't be reading your thoughts when we are making love." He grinned. "Though it can make things very interesting." He set me on the bed next to him. "You can send me a message, without saying a word, to tell me what pleases you."

"Hmm. Now that intrigues me." I lay back and crossed my ankles. It was a good reminder that he could see my thoughts. I wanted him as happy as I was that we were together. "No more gloomy thoughts, I swear it." I smiled up at him. He was so charming when he was in a playful mood. "I'm sending you a message now. Can you read it?"

His eyebrows rose and he carefully pulled my legs apart. "Are you sure? I had not thought you ready for this."

"It seems there is a vein there. Certainly Jean-Claude thought so." I dipped a finger between my legs. "But if it doesn't please you to show me…"

"By God, I'll not only show you, I'll make you scream with pleasure, my girl." His fangs were down and he ran them along one of my legs from knee to thigh. He looked up and grinned at me. "And there will be a necklace, earrings and a bracelet for you tomorrow. Would you like that?"

I stared at the ceiling, refusing to let him see the tears that filled my eyes. Was I no more than a bought and paid for whore?

"Stop it." He was up in a moment, grasping my face in

his hands. "I didn't mean to cheapen you, Gloriana. I will buy you trinkets because I think you are wonderful. You are not a whore. Never think that again."

"How can I not?" I tried to turn my face away from his dark and probing gaze. He wouldn't let me.

"Damn it, Gloriana. I love you. Do you not see that? I was willing to die for you this night." He leaned down and took my mouth fiercely.

I sobbed into his mouth, almost afraid to believe what he'd just spoken. He loved me? Were those words easy for him to say? I didn't believe they were. It had taken him long enough to speak them to me. I kissed him back with all the love in my heart. When he finally lifted his head, he ran a fingertip across my damp cheeks.

"I hope those are happy tears. It is not easy being loved by a vampire. We are jealous as hell." He kissed my cheeks.

"I have seen that even when you weren't declaring your love, but I thought you merely possessive." I was smiling so wide my cheeks ached. I loved the feel of him between my thighs.

"Aye, I am that." He grinned down at me. "The idea of you with any other man makes me want to do murder."

"I have no desire for anyone but you." I kissed him again, eagerly, then leaned back with a sigh. "You have made me very happy, sir." I ran my fingers through his hair. "Now I believe you were going to show me a new vein and what I think must be a new pleasure."

"Gloriana." Jeremiah kissed his way down my body. "I will never let you go. I hope you are satisfied with that promise for now. No more worries?"

"Nay, no more worries." I sighed when he again showed me how his fangs could arouse me. He could be so very clever when he made love. Worries. He had certainly done his best to make me forget them. I decided to let pleasure rule the night. If pain was in my future, what good would it do to dwell on it? I touched his dark hair as he did things so intimate I had to wonder if I'd taken leave of my senses. No, I had just lost my heart.

When he looked up at me and smiled, I had a thought so insane, I immediately dismissed it. No, I could never … but once I let the idea in, I couldn't seem to let it go. Vampire. To live forever with this man.

Jeremiah left the bedchamber to fetch me a goblet of red wine. To help me renew my strength. Would he still want me if I was no longer mortal? I didn't dare ask him. Instead I took the glass and drank deeply then yawned, feigning an exhaustion I didn't feel. He tucked me in and began to dress, saying something about looking for Fergus as I closed my eyes. I relaxed slightly when I heard the heavy outside door close and the key turn in the lock.

Madness. Surely I didn't truly wish to become a vampire. Was it even possible? But then I knew Jeremiah himself had once been mortal. So if he could be turned, as he called it, then surely so could I. How was it done? Was I prepared for the difference? To never see the sun again? But the power and the strength. Would I be given those along with the fangs? I had many questions and wasn't sure Jeremiah would answer them. He liked me as I was. As his blood whore.

Oh, how I hated that term. But surely my blood would be even more to his liking if I was vampire. Didn't he say vampires drank from each other? Jean-Claude had claimed Marin would benefit from his ancient blood when she had been so weak.

I turned over in bed and stared at the fire. First things first. We would go to court tomorrow. Fergus and I would be alone during the day and he might be able to answer some of my questions. In fact, he might tell me enough to make me forget the entire idea. Once the glow of Jeremiah's incredible lovemaking wore off, I might wake up and forget it myself. Gloriana St. Clair, vampire. Surely I wasn't serious.

FOURTEEN

"It's beautiful, but too much, surely." I couldn't stop admiring myself in the mirror. The necklace was lovely and lay against my skin as if made for me. I imagined how it would look with the dark blue velvet dress we had picked up from the dressmaker before we arrived at the jeweler. It would be what I wore to court this coming night. I was almost giddy with excitement. A beautiful dress and now fine jewels. What would the people from the Globe think of me, sitting in the audience next to Jeremiah? Whore, or lucky to have found a rich protector?

"Mistress, only see how the stones complement your eyes." The shop owner brought out a matching bracelet. "You must try this on as well." He reached for my hand but Fergus gave him a hard look and he merely laid it on the cloth next to my fingers.

"The master insists. You are to have the very best." Fergus picked up the bracelet and examined the stones. "Do you have earrings to go with this?" He set a pouch, heavy with coin, on the counter.

"Certainly, sir." The jeweler hurried to pull out a tray. "Several to choose from."

I saw the perfect pair and reached for them before I could stop myself. Was I being greedy? No, it had not been my idea to come here and spend a fortune. Jeremiah wanted me to be a credit to him and to show off his wealth. He had chafed under Robert MacDonald's offer to me and seemed determined to let his enemy know that he could also be generous. I tried on all the matching pieces of fine sapphires set in a white metal the shop keeper claimed was gold. Then I turned to show Fergus.

"What do you think?"

"I think you look like a goddess, Gloriana. I hope Jeremiah doesn't have to use his sword to fight the men who will want you." Fergus smiled and leaned over the counter to start bargaining. When he had settled on what he considered a fair price and what I thought an outrageous sum, he asked the shopkeeper for a velvet bag for the jewels and one more thing. To my delight he bought a silver backed hand mirror. "So you can see to do your hair, lass. I know how you like to fix it in those fancy styles for court."

"Thank you, Fergus." I hugged him before we stepped out into the street. He kept the jewels with him and his eyes sharp. He'd whispered to me that it wasn't unheard of for men such as our jeweler to tip off thieves after a big sale. I would be surprised if any would be foolish enough to approach big, bulky Fergus, who was well-armed and looked ready to take apart any who dared approach us.

"Could we stop once more? I would like to buy a gift for Maggie. I know we will see her tonight, at the play." I saw a shop with some pretty shawls in the window. It was just the kind of thing Maggie loved and Jeremiah had made sure I had some coin of my own. For trinkets, he'd said.

"Of course." Fergus steered me inside. "I liked your friend. It is too bad she is tied to that buffoon by marriage."

I peeked at him. "I didn't know you had met Horace."

"Aye. He came out to relieve himself while I drank with the doorkeeper at the Globe. It was clear to me what manner of man he was." Fergus frowned. "Your friend is a fine figure of a woman and obviously lonely. If things were different…" He pointed to a blue and gold fringed shawl. "That one would look fine on her. Let me buy it."

"No, I'll pay. But she isn't really married to him. It, it is a sham." I took a closer look at the piece Fergus had picked. He was right. The gold was bright enough to suit my friend with bold tastes. And her blue eyes, which obviously Fergus had noticed, would look very pretty with this fabric wrapped around her shoulders. "You should court her, Fergus. She has no easy life at the Globe. You are right, she is lonely."

"And when would I have time to court any woman, Gloriana?" Fergus looked away, out the window and at the busy street. "Jeremiah demands my nights and my days."

"With a new place to live and sturdy locks, I don't see why you couldn't have time off to pursue a lady." I gathered the shawl and walked over to where the shop girl was talking to a woman trying to sell a shawl. In moments I had paid and the shawl for Maggie was wrapped. Because I was dressed finely, I had been helped first, the other woman pushed aside.

It was a lesson I wouldn't soon forget. When I had been near starving, I would have never been served in a shop like this, even when I was trying to sell a nice piece. No, I'd been told to wait at the back door, sometimes for hours, and then given very little even for something of great value.

I turned to the woman who was still clutching her shawl. She was too thin and her dress had obviously been patched many times. The shawl was lovely if a bit worn. "Excuse me. Are you thinking to sell that?" I saw her flush but, at her nod, I merely picked up the edge and examined it. I had no need of another shawl but knew she'd get little for it here. I dug in my purse and pulled out a coin I knew would last her a long time. "Would this be enough for it?"

She gasped and thanked me, handing me the shawl and giving the shop girl a sniff. "You are very kind."

"Not at all. I thank you. This is very nice. Good luck to you." I turned to Fergus. "Shall we go?" I heard the shop girl muttering behind me. She was not happy that I had interfered in her negotiations. Well, I could afford to be generous. I had found a man I could love and who loved me. I really wished I could give the shawl back to the woman, who shivered as she stepped outside. But her back was straight with pride and I knew she would not appreciate my charity.

Once we were outside, Fergus took my arm. "You shouldn't be throwing away your coin like that, Gloriana. Who knows what the future will bring?"

"Thank you for the warning." I jerked my arm from his hold. "It wasn't so long ago that I was going around to the shops and selling all I owned. I could not stand there and watch that poor woman beg for a few pennies. For all I know she has babies at home, waiting for something to eat."

"You have a soft heart. Be careful that it doesn't bring you to ruin." He looked almost angry.

"Aren't you a ray of sunshine? Really, Fergus, I am not worried. Jeremiah loves me. He told me so last night. Does that sound like I must be concerned about my future?" I gasped when he jerked me to a stop beside him.

"Is that why you are glowing with such happiness? Because of Jeremiah Campbell's love words?" Fergus looked like he wanted to shake me. "I can read your addled thoughts. Is it becoming a vampire now that you're thinking?" He sounded like he'd just come down from the Highlands, his accent thickening. "Lass, lass, I know how he can charm a woman. Ah, yes, he made you think you are everything to him." Fergus showed his teeth in a snarl.

"Fergus, stop it!" I had never seen him like this. As if he hated Jeremiah.

"Nay, let me have my say. Do you think you are the first woman to fall in love with the man?" He looked up into the sky, where clouds obscured the sun and a cold breeze ruffled his red hair where it hung down below his cap. "God damn him."

"He is your master and, I thought, your friend. Are you

calling him a liar?" I blinked back tears. Of disappointment. I thought Fergus would champion Jeremiah and understand that I was happy because I believed in this love.

"Oh, I am sure he is besotted. For now." He patted his waistcoat where he'd stowed the pouch with my jewels. "Here's proof of that." He shook his head. "Remember what he is, Gloriana. He will live forever. You will not."

I grasped his sleeve then looked around us. We were not alone and I had to be careful what I said. "That is why I want to know about becoming like him. Won't you--"

"Not here." He pulled me along, toward home. "I cannot believe you are even thinking about such a thing. You are mad to do so. Look up. See the sky. Yes, it's cold today and the sun is hiding behind the clouds, but to never see it again? Do you have any idea what that would be like?" He shook his head, hurrying so I had to skip to keep up. "Damned vampires. No one can resist them when they use their mind control." He muttered this under his breath but I heard him right enough.

This time I was the one who stopped suddenly. "Are you saying I was spelled? That Jeremiah has made me think this way? That I don't really love him?"

Fergus sighed and patted my hand. "Calm down, lass. I don't begin to understand women. You may truly love him, though he has certainly taken advantage of you, taking your blood from the first night you met." He looked around, finally realizing that we had been noticed by several people on the street. We had spoken quietly enough not to be overheard, but a servant and his mistress didn't quarrel. He stepped back and sketched a bow. "Hush, now. We will talk when we are safely inside."

"Yes, we will. I want to know about his kind. And about those other women. I mean it, Fergus." I wanted to pinch his arm, though it would do no good. His body was hard, impervious to my feeble efforts, just as his will was strong. He would do as he wished, like any man.

Of course we did not go straight home. Fergus insisted

we stop at his favorite food shop for a fine beef stew and crusty bread, fresh from the oven. Once we were safely locked in our place, he settled at the table and insisted I eat, even pouring me a goblet of fine red wine.

"You will have a long night at court and will need your strength." He tore into the bread and fixed himself a bowl of the still steaming stew.

I had to admit it smelled delicious and spooned a bite into my mouth. After I had eaten half of it and drank most of the wine, I leaned forward. "I have not forgotten my questions, Fergus. Tell me about vampire life. And their powers. I have gleaned some of them from watching Jeremiah, but I want to know more. And about the other women who have come and gone from his bed."

"Eat more stew. Isn't it delicious? And how do you like this wine? It is a very good one from France. I hesitated to buy it, thinking of Jean-Claude and his French ways, but I have to admit they make a fine wine." He drank and smacked his lips. "Have you noticed that Jeremiah never touches food or drink?" He smiled at me across the table. "What I have learned about you so far is that you are very fond of your suppers, aren't you, Gloriana?"

What could I say? I had been starving for too long before I'd met Jeremiah. Now it seemed I couldn't get enough to eat. I was particularly partial to all manner of sweets. Then there was the roast beef that Fergus seemed to enjoy as much as I did. He was right. I had never seen Jeremiah touch food or drink. I set down my fork.

"Vampires truly cannot eat food such as this? Or drink even a glass of wine?" I inhaled the aroma of that well-seasoned stew. I was almost full yet tempted to clean my bowl anyway. I thought of that woman in the shop, so thin and desperate. It had been mere weeks ago that I was that woman. I still could not leave even a bite of food to be tossed away and scraped the last of the stew into my spoon and ate it.

"No. They dine only on blood, Gloriana. From a

mortal such as yourself, or from another vampire." He grinned and pulled a wrapped package from the bottom of the basket. "Here. I bought it just for you. I know how you love a good lemon tart." He opened the cloth and set it in front of me.

"You are the devil, Fergus." I picked it up, the crust so flaky it fell apart in my hand. One bite and I moaned. It was the best tart I had ever tasted.

"The goodwife is quite the baker, is she not?" He grinned and finished his bowl of stew, then buttered a piece of bread. "There are fruit buns for in the morning. Unless you wish one now."

I swallowed the last bite of tart and patted my mouth with the cloth it had been wrapped in. My stomach ached I had eaten so much and my dress was so tight in the bodice I wanted to slip into the bedchamber and ease open the laces. "Stop it. I see you are making a point." I sighed and pushed back from the table. "Do vampires feel hunger, even though they cannot satisfy it as I just did?"

"They hunger, of course they do. It is a blood lust. Sometimes the thirst makes them wild. You saw and felt what happens when that hunger gets out of control." Fergus frowned. "Jeremiah almost killed you the night he fought with MacDonald."

"Yes, you had to pull him off of me when he took too much of my blood." I got up and walked to the fire. "But that has not happened again. He seems to know when he must stop drinking to keep me safe."

Fergus looked down at the table. "Do not do this, Gloriana. I beg you. It will change you. Forever."

"How? Besides the drinking and sleeping all day." I moved to sit beside him but he jumped up, obviously uncomfortable being that close to me. "I said it before and I'll say it again. You act as if you almost hate vampires."

He stood facing me but was careful to keep his distance. "Listen to me and listen well. Vampires have a strange and difficult life. They do sleep like the dead during the day and, if they aren't careful, anyone can stake them and end their lives while they sleep."

"That does sound terrifying. But a vampire with funds can hire someone like you, Fergus, to stand guard." Funds. I had just spent too much time without them. If I had been vampire, how would I have survived? Knowing that sunlight could kill me, I would have had to find a dark place, so dark there would be no chance that… "What happens if just a little sunlight touches a vampire, Fergus? While he or she is sleeping?"

"It will be the death of him or her. You saw Marin turn to ash. That is what happens if a vampire is touched by the sun. It is a horrifying sight and one I hope to never witness again." He began to pace. "God, Gloriana, I cannot believe you are seriously thinking about this. I remember times when Jeremiah was caught with no safe place to sleep. He had to dig a shallow grave and bury himself in the dirt during the day. Can you imagine that?"

I shuddered. Bury myself alive? But then a vampire wasn't alive, was he? "I saw all of you stop breathing when Marin's green fog came in here. Jeremiah had told me you could do that, shifters and vampires alike. Seeing it was," I swallowed, "a little strange. How is that possible? How can anyone stop breathing?"

"A shifter doesn't really stop breathing. We hold our breaths and can do it for a long, long time. As if we have changed." He ran a hand over his face. "I cannot explain it. Vampires? They are undead. Their hearts work very slowly. It is almost as if it is a phantom beat, a memory of when they were alive. The breathing is the same. The blood they drink makes the heart still pump, so that they can be strong. But during the day they rest, so there is no breathing and no heartbeat. They call it their death sleep and it is truly a death. They never age once they are turned. Jeremiah looks the same today as he did when he was made vampire over a hundred years ago. Impossible as it seems." He looked away from me, probably realizing that a woman would see that last as a reason to want to become vampire when she was still young and beautiful.

"He's never changed." I couldn't imagine that. Life was hard and I had seen the people at the Globe grow older right before my eyes. Or so it seemed. Hair grayed, eyes dulled. The list was long.

"Gloriana, think of what they are! Vampires are constantly on the hunt for mortals to drink from. That can make them into a kind of animal. At least that's what I think." He frowned. "They become users. Some think nothing of killing their blood source. Jeremiah isn't like that. But some vampires go mad because they miss the sun, miss their mortal life. Look at what happened to Marin. Many become killers and feel nothing when they take the life of a blood donor. It's the same to them as it would be to you, if you were forced to kill a chicken for your supper. You do what you must to feed yourself."

I sat again and poured more wine into my goblet then took a gulp. This was more disturbing than I wanted to admit. And I hadn't heard about the women yet.

"No, I won't tell you about his women. That is not my place. Just know that his usual way is to send them off with jewels and no memory of knowing him. That blasted trick vampires have of stealing your memories is certainly one of their powers." Fergus sat across from me and filled his own goblet. "Then there's the mind reading. Yes, a vampire can do it but try to read their thoughts? It is usually impossible. He or she can block *their* thoughts. Shifters can do it as well." He took a drink. "I will certainly make sure Jeremiah doesn't learn of our conversation from me. But he is going to see your thoughts on this as soon as he wakes."

"What do you think? If I asked him, would he turn me vampire, Fergus?" I finished my wine and felt the warmth of it in my cheeks.

"No way in hell." The voice behind me made me jump. I stood and faced him. "It must be sunset."

"Yes. It must. Now explain yourselves, both of you.

What is this nonsense about becoming a vampire?" Jeremiah looked ready to knock our heads together.

"A notion she had, Jeremiah." Fergus jumped to his feet. "I'll ready your bath. I have been trying to talk her out of it since she spoke of it."

"A bath. Yes." I smiled at him. "We can talk about this later." I walked up to Jeremiah and tried to kiss his firm lips which weren't smiling.

"There is nothing to talk about, Gloriana." He rested his hands on my shoulders. "I like you the way you are— warm, mortal and perfect."

"And growing older by the day." I had the sudden urge to look into my new mirror. "How long will it take before you cast me aside for someone younger and fresh?"

"I believe I said we were not going to discuss this." He turned away when Fergus lugged in the small tub he'd procured for me after my dip in the river. "We'll not both fit in there. You may go first. Is there water heating, Fergus? Or have you been too busy discussing Gloriana's future to tend to your duties for me?"

"Kettle is on the hob." Fergus set about filling the tub. I hadn't noticed that he had a barrel of water in the corner now, ready for our baths.

"Jeremiah, Fergus bought me beautiful jewels today, as you requested. If you are unhappy with me, perhaps he should take them back." I picked up the velvet bag that we'd left on the table.

"Let me see them." He took the bag and spilled the jewels into his palm. "Good color. I approve. I want to see them on you." He glanced at the tub which was almost full. "Leave us, Fergus. I'll let you know when you can come back in."

"Aye." Fergus said no more, just glanced at me then grabbed his cloak and left, locking the door behind him.

"Don't be angry with him. He was trying to talk me out of it." I backed up when Jeremiah reached for the laces on my dress. "What are you doing?"

"Getting you ready for your bath. Not becoming shy are you?" He made quick work of the ties and soon had my dress on the floor. The chemise went as well. "Now let me see this necklace." He fastened it around my neck. "Yes, it looks very nice." He handed me the earrings. "Put them on." He stood back while I fastened them in my ears. "Very pretty." Then he clasped the bracelet on my wrist. He walked around me. "If the court could see you like this, I think I would have to run through every man and some women there."

I flushed from my cheeks to my toes. I wore nothing but those jewels. "You were very generous."

He reached for my breasts and handled them carefully. "You are so very warm." He picked up my hand and lifted it to his chest, under his shirt. "Feel me. Can you tell the difference?"

"You are not as warm as I am." I realized that his skin was in fact almost cool. Why had I never made note of that before? Perhaps it was because we were usually so passionate in our touches. He would be pressed against me and my body would give his some of my warmth.

"Yes, I would miss your mortal warmth if you were to become vampire, Gloriana. Only mortals have the heat that their mortal blood gives them." He leaned in and inhaled next to the vein in my neck. His eyes closed and I believed he was listening to my heart pound. I knew it when he laid his hand on my chest, where my heart must be. "There. I feel it. That's what I would hate to have stop. It is your heartbeat. Mine is but a paltry thing, barely beating. You can make it gain some speed when we are together. And taking your blood also makes it go faster."

"But vampires take blood from each other, I heard you tell Marin to take from Jean-Claude and Fergus said..." I covered his hand with mine. I wasn't cold standing here, so close to the fire, but I felt exposed. He wore his shirt and a kilt. I wore nothing but those fancy jewels. It seemed like a symbol of our relationship. He held all the power. I was merely the vessel who served him.

"Yes, vampires can drink from each other. And it can be very enjoyable." He stepped back. "I have never made a mortal into a vampire, Gloriana. It is stealing their humanity. I won't do it."

"But then we could be together forever!" I reached for him but he wouldn't let me touch him, holding up his hands.

"You are a fool if you think anything lasts forever." He turned his back on me. "Get in the bath and get ready to go to court. I will not discuss this further." He stalked over to his room and slammed the door.

I carefully removed those jewels and dropped them into the velvet pouch. Did he really think we were done with this topic? I would not give up that easily. Someone had hurt Jeremiah in the past. He wasn't going to tell me about it and I knew Fergus wouldn't. Would Robert MacDonald? It might be worth a try.

I stepped into the small tub and scrubbed, determined to look as fine as I could this night. My own power was in my looks and my ability to seduce Jeremiah. If I could please him well, mayhap I could try to persuade him again on this subject. Because I did believe in our love. And that it could last forever. If not? Well, then I was the fool he thought I was.

FIFTEEN

I had to admit I felt like a princess in my velvet dress and jewels. Jeremiah stayed close by my side, making sure everyone knew I was his. I didn't mind. His arm under my hand and his proprietary air meant I belonged here as much as any of the women did. Of course it was a man's world. The king surrounded himself with his courtiers. And there were soldiers everywhere. Discord from the English Catholics was the gossip of the night.

When Jeremiah was called to make his bow before the king, I was finally free to find my way to the area behind the stage where there was the usual melee going on before a performance. Fergus stayed close under orders from Jeremiah. I was to be guarded at all times. The shifter had the package for Maggie tucked inside his waistcoat and we both smiled when we spied her working on a costume, stitching a tear in the sleeve.

"That used to be my job." I walked up behind her.

"Gloriana!" Her face lit with joy when she saw us. "And Master Fergus." A flush tinted her cheeks. "It is so good to see you." Her eyes widened as she noticed the sparkle of my jewels in the light from the few backstage candles. "My, don't you look fine. Are those yours to keep, Gloriana?" She reached out to touch the largest stone that hung between my breasts. The dress was cut scandalously low.

I nodded, suddenly embarrassed. Bought and paid for and all I'd had to do was warm Jeremiah's bed and satisfy his thirst.

"Aye. The master is right besotted with our Gloriana. Nothing but the finest will do for her." Fergus pulled out the package. "She brought you a little something, Mistress Margaret." He sketched a bow.

"Fergus picked it out, Maggie." I couldn't resist giving the pair a nudge toward each other. "He noticed that it might match your eyes."

Maggie looked up at Fergus in wonder. "I cannot believe it. I swear to this day Horace has no idea if they are brown or--"

"They are blue, Mistress." Fergus ripped open the package and placed the shawl carefully around Maggie's plump shoulders. "As blue as the sky on a summer's day in the Highlands."

Maggie's eyes filled with tears as she stroked the fine cloth. "It is the most beautiful piece I have ever owned." She looked around then grabbed Fergus's hand. "You are a true gentleman. Certainly the likes of which I've never met in *this* company."

"He is kind as well. He's been wonderful to me." I backed away when I saw Becks had spied me and was walking my way. "I had best be going. We will be sitting near the front, Maggie. I had hoped we could save you a seat, but Jeremiah says it is not for him to say."

"If you are free to leave the stage area once the play begins, I will find you a place, Mistress." Fergus still held her hand.

"I will get away." She smiled into his eyes. Finally she looked at me. "You are happy with your choice, Gloriana?"

"Yes, I am. I love Jeremiah. He is generous and kind

and loves me as well. Do not worry about me, Maggie. Look to your own happiness." I picked up my skirts and hurried away. I was not about to let Becks close to me. His reek could cling to my clothes and hair. That would never do. I rounded the front of the stage and bumped into a man who had obviously chosen to bathe in perfume.

"Your pardon, sir." I backed up quickly.

"Ah. It is the lovely lady I found in the street with the drunken Scot. I haven't forgotten that night." A gold tipped cane landed on my shoulder before I could get away. "You remember me, do you not, my dear?" He smiled and I could see he had no care for his teeth.

"Certainly, my lord." I dipped a curtsy. "I must thank you again for offering your aid. It was very kind of you, Lord Summers. Fortunately we made it home safely and had no further problems."

"I see your protector has found his purse. Very pretty." He traced my necklace with this cane until it landed right between my breasts. The gold top this night was a snarling tiger and the teeth snagged on one of the sapphires. "I find I am still interested in becoming your, hmm, friend. Say your name, girl." His eyes gleamed as he studied my figure.

"Gloriana, my lord." I smiled politely and attempted to move past him but his cane stopped me. I reached up to untangle my necklace then tried to step away again. When I backed into another hard male body, I wanted to scream.

"There you are, Gloriana. Campbell sent me to fetch you." Robert MacDonald kept his hand on my elbow. "Sir, are you quite through inspecting this filly?"

Lord Summers cackled with amusement. "Filly. Right you are." He thumped his cane on the floor. "She has got good lines, don't you agree?"

"Very good lines. But Campbell is the jealous sort. I wouldn't test his temper, if I were you." Robert's hand tightened on my elbow.

"Pah. Young men and their women. He'll soon tire of her. Then she'll be eager enough for a new handler. Eh,

Gloriana?" He reached out to stroke my chin. One of his heavy rings would have scratched my cheek if I hadn't jerked my face away. "Very pretty. I might even put her to stud. Never can have enough bastards, I say." He looked me over again. "Those hips look made for child bearing. I have many properties that can use good stewardship. Think on that, Gloriana. I take good care of those gels who bear me sons and their offspring."

I bit my tongue, sure the getting of those sons would involve some of his rough handling. I didn't dare say a word because his cold gaze promised he would make a bitter enemy if crossed. I merely stared down at my feet, as if too shy to speak after such a generous offer.

"You will have to wait your turn, my lord. I have already spoken to her about being next, should Campbell release her. A bidding war would be unseemly." Robert looked the older man up and down. "I don't think you want to measure your, um, purse against mine." He put himself in front of me.

"Grasping greedy Scots. London is overrun with them these days. I hear there is a group determined to cut down their number. Catholics? Or do they have other reasons for attacking a man of your type?" Lord Summers' eyes were hard. "It will be interesting to see how long this king lasts and how your purse fares betimes."

"That sounded like treason. My king will see you in the Tower if I whisper in his ear that you think his days are numbered here. If we look in your house, will we find a rosary? A seditious Catholic text perhaps? But then a searcher can find anything, if he is clever. Do I make myself clear?" Robert rested his hand on his sword hilt.

"Relax, dear boy. My own mother came from the Highlands. I may not wear the kilt, but I can trot out enough close connections to the king to keep my head out of a noose." Summers sneered and gazed around the room. "Keep the gel. There are willing women aplenty, though she was certainly to my taste." With that he turned on his heel and wound his way through the crowd.

"Thank you." I sagged against Robert's arm as soon as I was sure Lord Summers was far enough away not to hear me. "I despise that man."

"Who doesn't?" He touched my hand. "Will you have wine? You look upset."

"I will never drink wine here again. It tastes like river water and I should know." I did let him lead me to a chair against the wall and sat gratefully. "He spoke as if I weren't standing right in front of him. He holds women in such contempt it makes you wonder why he is so eager to bed one."

"Summers is a dangerous man with dark appetites. Few of the women who have served him were seen again. Though now I wonder if they are somewhere in the country with one of his brats." Robert sat beside me.

"Did Jeremiah really send you to look for me?" I didn't see Jeremiah when I scanned the room.

"Of course not. Our temporary truce is over. He is speaking with the captain of the King's Guard. Campbell is a former warrior. His knowledge of strategy and warfare is seen by some as valuable. The king asked him to advise the captain about how to proceed during this time of unrest."

"Then why did you come over?" I wondered if Robert had been a warrior as well. He certainly had the look of one. But he didn't seem jealous of Jeremiah's value to the king. I couldn't read minds, but he was focused on me, giving me his full attention.

"I didn't like to see Summers pawing you." Robert pulled out a small looking glass and studied my necklace more closely. "Well done, Campbell. At least he is finally taking better care of you, Gloriana."

"He says he loves me." I flushed. "Do I sound foolish? Is that something your kind says to make your mortal companion more eager to offer a vein?"

"It is not something I say readily." Robert put the glass away and gazed into my eyes. "You wish to ask me about

Campbell's past. I will not discuss it. Our families have a bloody history and part of it involves a woman, his woman. I am surprised he has laid his heart at your feet. He lost it once before and it brought him great pain. I'm sorry to say, my family was behind it." He glanced around the room. "It won't be long before the play will begin. I'm looking forward to it. Master Shakespeare and his company should be quite entertaining. King Jamie can speak of little else."

"Please don't change the subject just yet." I laid my hand on his sleeve. He looked very fine this night in his plaid with a claret velvet doublet trimmed in fine black silk needlework showing nightingales in flight. His black velvet jacket was adorned with rubies. He was very handsome, his light hair and blue eyes striking in those colors. If I didn't love Jeremiah, this man would tempt me. He stared at me and read the thought, leaning toward me.

"What is it you want, Gloriana?" His smile showed me straight white teeth with just a hint of fang that no one across the room would even notice.

"I want to become," I leaned closer, raising my fan to whisper in his ear, "vampire. What do you think?"

"I think you are mad." He reared back and stood. "Your value is in your mortality, woman. And if you think I will be the one to do the deed, think again. I assume Campbell has already turned you down."

"You would be right." Jeremiah appeared in front of me. "This cozy scene has gone on long enough. I can have my knife at your throat in but a moment, MacDonald, if you don't step away now." He frowned down at me. "Where the hell is Fergus?"

"He is close by." I stood and smoothed down my velvet skirt. "Robert rescued me from Lord Summers. You won't remember it since you were too far gone with blood loss, but the night you both almost killed each other, his lordship stopped his carriage and offered his help. Unfortunately, he took a fancy to me." I shuddered. "He has a taste for pain with his pleasure. I'd sooner go back to starving than serve the likes of him."

"There will be no need of that, Gloriana." Jeremiah's jaw was taut. He bowed toward Robert. "I suppose I must thank you. But Fergus should have been the one to keep her safe."

"I am here. I was behind her when MacDonald intervened." Fergus walked up, Maggie by his side. "I could not very well tell a lord of Summers' standing to leave Gloriana alone. MacDonald handled the matter without causing a scene."

"The play is about to start." Jeremiah sent Fergus a look that made him drop Maggie's arm. "Come, Gloriana, we have reserved seats." He took my arm and swept me away, never even asking about Fergus's lady.

"Jeremiah, you were rude. Fergus never forgets his duties, as you well know. It is time that you remembered he is a man with needs. You should have at least asked to be introduced to Maggie." I spoke low into his ear as he led me to our seats only three rows from the stage. We were to sit in a sea of plaid. Robert was on my other side. I smiled at him just to show Jeremiah I was not rude and had my own friends.

"Fergus has a job to do. This is not the place for his courting." Jeremiah nodded to some of the other men around us. "You look very well. Smile, if you please. And I do not like how familiar you are with MacDonald. You call him Robert? It is not seemly."

"I will smile when I am happy. Right now you are making me unhappy with your selfish attitude. Robert has been kind to me. I will call him what I please." I pulled out my fan and waved it slowly in front of my face, as if I was bored and merely enduring the company around me.

"Damn it, Gloriana, where did Fergus find that doxy?" Jeremiah had turned around and had spied Fergus and Maggie behind the seated crowd. "They are standing with the servants."

"That doxy is my friend from the theater." I closed my

fan with a snap. "If it wasn't for her and the loan of a certain green dress, you and I would never have met. She has a kind heart and a miserable life. So has Fergus, if you must know. You give him no time to seek his own pleasure. What kind of life is that?"

"Would you two quit quarreling? The play is about to start." Robert was grinning.

Of course he had heard us whispering with his vampire hearing. I was sure no one else had above the excited talk from the crowd. But he was right, Master Shakespeare stood in front of the curtains on the stage. The king took his place in a special chair in the front row and waved his hand as if giving permission to proceed.

Master Shakespeare spoke a few words about the play, then bowed and walked offstage. The crowd got quiet when a man with a staff hit the boards three times. There was an air of anticipation as the curtains parted. Candles were extinguished except for those on the stage and the play began.

The Moor of Venice was a rousing success but I had a damp handkerchief by the time it was over. Richard Burbage had delivered a masterful performance as Othello. By the time he died onstage, no lady and some of the men in the audience were able to hold back their tears. Even Becks had done a credible job as the villain Iago. I had to admit that the new actor who played Desdemona made a much better woman than Horace did as the hapless Emilia. Horace didn't look well, his costume was tight, and he frequently looked befuddled, losing his lines. This play was not kind to him, since he usually played for laughs.

There was much applause and the king himself took the stage to give prizes to those actors who had pleased him. Master Shakespeare was in his element and soon had two women clinging to him as he walked through the crowd, taking congratulations.

"Hello, if it isn't Gloriana St. Clair." He nodded to me when we came face to face. "You are looking very well."

I introduced him to Jeremiah. "We enjoyed your play very much. I daresay it will become a crowd favorite." I touched a handkerchief to my eyes. "Well-played by the cast. I hope you were pleased."

"Some players were better than others. Of course I can always see room for improvement." He looked me up and down. "I look forward to the day when there will be a real woman on stage to play those parts. Now wouldn't that be a treat?" He laughed then moved on through the crowd.

"He's dreaming. The king would never countenance such a thing. He is already hearing complaints from some of the very religious who want to outlaw plays again." Jeremiah looked after the playwright.

"You never know what the future holds. Maybe someday women will act and be given prizes for it. And you will live long enough to find out, will you not?" I saw Fergus talking to Maggie. "What would you say if Maggie came to stay with us? She could help clean the rooms and do my hair. I would dearly love to have a lady's maid." I smiled up at him.

"You know that won't work." He frowned. "And you know why."

"Come now, Jeremiah. If you don't feel you could trust her to keep your secrets, you could wipe away her memories. As you used to do mine." I clung to his arm.

"This would please you? Would it please you enough to forget this mad notion you have?" He pulled me away from the crowd. "You know what I mean."

"I am willing to wait a bit. But I won't forget it." I pressed against him. The play had made me melancholy. So much death, so much betrayal. Why hadn't Shakespeare presented a comedy? But I knew why. The king didn't care for light fare and he'd requested a tragedy. He had certainly gotten that. "I want to go home now. I want you to make love to me. Will you do it?"

"I am always ready to make love to you, Gloriana. But how will it be if Fergus brings another woman into the

221

place? There will be no privacy." He caught Fergus's eye and gestured for him to join us.

"Are you ready to leave? Shall I fetch the carriage?" He glanced back at Maggie.

"Gloriana seems to think you wish to have the woman with you, living with us. My love has been taking me to task for ignoring your needs as a man. Is she right?" Jeremiah locked eyes with Fergus. Of course, they could see into each other's minds.

"I have been happy to serve you for many years, Jeremiah. But things change." Fergus nodded at me. "I know I am just the hired help and have no real say in how we arrange things. But I cannot go on much longer watching you two and your happiness without some kind of…" He shook his head. "You know what I mean."

"I see." Jeremiah glanced at me. "Then we will need a bigger place. What do you think? Is the woman willing?"

"Her name is Maggie, Jeremiah. Which you would know if you had stopped to be introduced." Fergus was clearly angry. "I *am* a man, just as you are. I understand that I have a job to do, but it wears on me to always put my needs aside in favor of yours and now Gloriana's." He looked as if he wanted say more and seemed to come to a decision. "I am glad you are happy with her. But I have been lonely, Jeremiah. So has Maggie. I can see into her mind and heart. I believe she will be willing if I ask her to join us. She can work alongside me, share some of the chores, even if she is not ready to be more to me than a friend."

"Aye. I understand what you're saying and thinking." Jeremiah frowned. "We were planning to move anyway. So look for bigger lodgings. After you see if this Maggie wishes to join us. Then we'll have to be careful. You know we have our secrets. She will have to guard them well or be kept in ignorance."

"I know she can be trusted, Jeremiah." I grinned at Maggie when I caught her watching us. "It will mean a lot to me to have company during the day. I hate being alone when you are sleeping." I glanced up at him through my lashes. "I am not used to your schedule. Mayhap I never will be as long as I am mortal. Having another woman around will help keep me entertained."

"I thought I did that." Fergus growled. But I could see he was teasing.

"'Tis not the same and you know it." I hugged Jeremiah. "Thank you. I will stop bothering you about changing what I am. For now, at least."

"Then it is time for us to go home. You did say you were in a giving mood." He grinned at me. "Fergus, arrange things for later in the week. Tell your lady goodbye for now."

"I will that." He strode off into the crowd.

Jeremiah had to take his leave of the king. That took a while since there were many people eager to do the same and the king was in a fine mood, happy with the play and eager to discuss it and the coming Yuletide season. Because there were some Protestants who disapproved of the lavish Scottish festivities, he was thinking of leaving for Edinburgh soon. That meant his supporters from the Highlands would also be leaving London. Jeremiah seemed excited about the idea by the time we finally got to the door and he helped me with my cloak.

I was afraid to ask what a move to his home in the Highlands meant for me. Instead, I clung to his arm, enjoying his good humor.

"Now Fergus will have a woman of his own. I hope you noticed how willing I am to make you happy." He kissed the side of my neck. "It is no small matter to bring another mortal into our household."

"You will make Fergus happy. It is long overdue." I was not about to be persuaded to just forget what I really wanted.

"Tell me more about this woman. She was your friend at the Globe. Did she have a protector there?" Jeremiah waved for our coach but it was caught in a line of them. We could see Fergus up on the box next to the coachman.

"Of a sort. It was a sham marriage. She was tied to Horace, the man who played Emilia tonight."

Jeremiah laughed. "Oh, my. Sham indeed. The man was barely able to speak his lines. I can see him in a comedy, but he did poorly in this night's play. And I swear he split his dress when he raised his arms in the last act."

"Yes, I worry for Maggie's future if she has to rely on his standing in the company. Master Shakespeare will surely lay into him for the way he had to be thrown his lines several times." I was afraid Horace might be shown the door. Forgetting his lines in front of the king! Shakespeare would not soon forget that.

"Ah, here's the coach." Jeremiah helped me inside. "Now, you were going to be grateful I believe, that I am willing to have a woman to keep you company during the day. I will even pay her generously for that duty." He settled next to me, his hand under my skirt and sliding up my thigh. "You cannot say you are ever lonely at night, can you?"

"Of course not. You are good company then, Jeremiah." I sighed as he slipped a finger inside me, exciting me instantly. "You have proved that vampires are lusty. Are all of them so?"

"No. I have known men who were more priest-like. Whatever urges they had as mortals, they continue to have or not have as vampires." He leaned down to kiss the swells of my breasts. "I told you before. I was always eager for lovemaking. Now I will be that way forever." He looked up and met my gaze. "And there you have hit on one reason I might be tempted to turn you, my love. A Gloriana forever hot for sex. It is any man's dream." He ran a fang across my neck and the jugular vein that he loved so well. "But then I would miss the heat of this skin. The hot pulse of your vein when I bite into it and your blood fills my mouth."

I shoved him away. "I know I promised, but you brought up the subject. What if I want to live forever? What if I'm afraid I'll grow old and displease you as my hair grays and my skin wrinkles?" I pulled his hand from under my skirt. I could feel his hard stare in the dark coach. He didn't like my tone. Well, I didn't like his stubborn refusal to even consider my needs. "You say you love me. I love you enough to please you any way I can. Why won't you please me? Oh, yes. I get pretty baubles." I pulled off my earrings and dropped them in my lap. Next came the necklace and bracelet. "These might as well be coins."

Was I mad? A few love words and I was testing him. He could well push me out of the coach and leave me to the likes of Lord Summers. No, I needed to say this. I burned with the need. To live forever. Suddenly I wanted that so much I was willing to beg him for it.

"Stop it. You looked beautiful tonight. You glowed with health and life. A vampire doesn't glow at all. We are dead inside." He leaned back and stared out the other window.

"You don't look dead to me, Jeremiah. Nor do you feel dead." I had my ways. Of course I touched him where he pulsed with life. Yes, there, under his kilt. That got me a stony look. He lifted my hand and tossed it back into my own lap.

"Damn it, Gloriana. I had to die before I was reborn as what I am. It is a painful transformation, you have no idea how painful. You feel as if you are being ripped apart, burned with torches…" He shook his head. "It is beyond description. You also have no idea what you would lose as a vampire." He had never been so serious with me.

"No, I am just thinking of what I would gain." I faced him, ready to have this out. "Eternal life."

"Eternal night."

"Eternal youth."

"Blood drinking." His face could have been carved in granite.

"Mind reading."

"Fangs."

The coach jolted to a stop. We sat as far from each

225

other as the seat would allow.

When Fergus opened the door, he stared at us. "We still have a few blocks to walk. You know how it is." He gave me his hand and I took it. Jeremiah jumped out, landing a few feet away.

"Nice trick." I held my cloak around me in the chill night air. "You have quite a few of those. I have seen them. You can run faster than any human, jump higher than one as well. And don't forget shape-shifting."

Jeremiah had no answer to that. He nodded at Fergus who had paid the coachman. Once it rumbled away, he stood waiting for us to move.

"Are you two fighting now?" Fergus looked from me to Jeremiah. "Gloriana, I was hoping you would give up this mad notion."

"What is mad about it? I am in love and want to be with the man I love forever. But this stubborn Scot isn't interested. I can only think he can't imagine staying with me for eternity." I suddenly had to fight tears. Oh, foolish. Why couldn't I just leave this alone? He had told me his reasons. But I was as stubborn as a Scot it seemed. I walked toward home. I suddenly noticed that Jeremiah had disappeared. No, not disappeared. He was a big black bird, sitting on the stones in my path.

"Really? You changed? What now? Are you going to peck at me? Make me afraid of you?" I laughed. "Go ahead, blackbird. I can't wait to shift. What will I be? A pretty yellow canary?"

"You are making him angry, Gloriana." Fergus stayed by my side. "The first time a vampire shifts can be terrifying. I saw one try and then fail to go all the way. We had a devil of time getting him back to human form."

"Now you are trying to scare me." I took his arm. "Don't shift as well, Fergus. I need your strong arm to protect me from that fierce blackbird." I felt the wind from his wings as, with a screech, Jeremiah took off toward home. "Go, fly away. I would never make love with you in that form. Believe that."

"You are foolish, Gloriana. Remember your place." Fergus pulled out the keys to our hovel. Yes, Robert MacDonald had been right. It was little more than that. I hoped Fergus found a better place before he brought Maggie to live with us. I didn't doubt she'd agree that we lived poorly now, though it was bound to be better than the room she shared with Horace.

I walked inside and handed Fergus my cloak. "Wine. I need some of that fine wine you served me earlier." I was in a mood. I wasn't denying it. Jeremiah was nowhere in sight but I had a feeling he was in our bedchamber, probably already naked and waiting to take me. Of course, that was my purpose here. And I was supposed to be grateful that he was finally treating Fergus like a man. Damn him.

Fergus filled a goblet and silently handed it to me. "I have an idea for our lodgings. I am leaving now to see about it." He said that loud enough for Jeremiah to hear him on the other side of the hearth. "Gloriana, too much wine makes your blood taste different to Jeremiah. Do you really want to do that?" He had noticed that I had finished already and was pouring more.

"Why not? What care I if the taste is not to his liking? He cares little if he pleases me." I drank deeply.

"If you are the worse for wine, it may well make him the same if he drinks from you soon after you..." Fergus frowned when I slapped his hand away and picked up the bottle. I poured the rest of it into my goblet.

"Now that I would like to see. Jeremiah Campbell out of control. From wine. Not from a fight and blood loss." I laughed. "Go. We will be very busy, I believe, and you would not want to witness what happens here." I pushed him toward the door. "Find us a nice place." Did my words slur? I didn't care. I was relaxed, the wine warm in my belly. "Maggie is going to love being with you, Fergus. I bet you are a fine, lusty lover. Horace prefers men. Did you know that?"

"Hush, Gloriana. You cannot say such things." Fergus picked up his cloak. "No more wine, I beg you."

"Just go. We will need two bedchambers in our new place." I wagged my finger in his face. "Privacy. Very important. I wonder if Maggie is a screamer when pleased?" I drank the last of the wine. "Do we have another bottle, Fergus?" I showed him that my goblet was empty.

"No, that is all. Good night, Gloriana." He stepped outside and closed the door.

I heard the key turn in the lock.

"Are you proud of yourself? You embarrassed him." Jeremiah leaned against the doorway to our bedchamber. He wore his shirt and nothing else.

"Hah! So you were listening. And lying in our bed expecting me to come to you. Like a good little mistress would." I slammed the empty goblet onto the table. I reached up then remembered I'd already taken off my jewels. Where were they?

"I have your baubles. I put them in my waistcoat while we were in the coach. You were so busy railing at me, you would have dropped them when we got out to walk home." He stepped toward me.

I could see his bare legs beneath his shirt tails. Such fine legs. Not that they swayed me. I was furious with him. I pulled the pins from my hair and dropped them on the table. My locks flowed down my back and I deliberately reached up to run my hands through them, making my breasts almost fall out of my bodice. He was watching me, his eyes gleaming. He was so easy to excite.

I unlaced my dress. Not for him. No. It was so tight it pained me. I had to stop eating savory stews and lemon tarts. Everything he had bought for me, the clothes that were so pretty, felt too snug. And my hips. Lord Summers was right, they were good for child bearing but that was a kind way of saying they were now wide and well padded, thanks to the good food Jeremiah had made sure I had each day.

"Here is another reason why you don't want to be

turned vampire, Gloriana." Jeremiah was suddenly close against me. He stroked my hips. "Vampires cannot breed. Lose your mortality and you give up any chance of ever having a babe. Could you live with that decision? You are very young. Are you sure you can decide now that you would be happy never becoming a mother?"

Such a question. It was too weighty for a woman who had desires burning between her thighs. I was too full of wine, too relaxed and he looked too good to me to bother with thinking. I pulled his head down and kissed him, my tongue in his mouth. I sent him a message in my mind that had him lifting my skirt and clearing the table, my empty goblet and the wine bottle crashing to the floor. Hairpins flew everywhere.

Before I could do more than moan, he was on me and in me, taking me hard and fast. Yes! Decisions were for another night. For now, I needed him. Wanted him. And had him. It was enough.

SIXTEEN

Fergus had indeed found us fine lodgings. I ignored the fact that they weren't far from where Marin and Jean-Claude had also lived. It was a series of underground tunnels and was obvious that Jeremiah wasn't the first to make use of the space. There was a fine fireplace, separate rooms for sleeping and, most wonderful of all, pipes for running water.

My concern was how Maggie would react to living underground and without windows. I needn't have worried. She was so happy to be away from the theater and in the arms of a good man who appreciated her that she cared not where she slept.

Not that there was much sleeping with those two. Fergus was a new man with Maggie's adoring gaze following him around the rooms. He strutted, I swear it. Jeremiah was amused and I had all I could do to keep him from teasing the shifter.

Did Maggie know that Jeremiah and Fergus were not mortal? Not yet. But I was sure she was puzzled by our strange sleep schedule and the fact that my lover locked himself away each night near dawn in a room little better than a storeroom. She was easy to distract, though, with shopping trips and gossip about the theater. It seemed she had left at the right time. Horace had been sent away in disgrace after the performance for the king. He had packed up and abandoned her and their room without so much as a by-your-leave. If not for Fergus paying what was owed their landlord, Maggie would have been in terrible trouble.

"I tell you, Gloriana, Fergus is my hero. I know I haven't known him long, but he has changed my life!" She confided in me while the shifter was gone to fetch our luncheon. "I have never had a man take care of me before. It was always the other way around. Do you know what I mean?"

"Of course." I glanced at the door to Jeremiah's room. Though Michael had taken care of me at first, our roles had soon reversed. The actors wanted their women to be at their beck and call, taking care of their rooms, their laundry and, of course, their physical urges. If Michael had been sent from the theater, I had often wondered if he would have expected me to get a job as a server at the local inn to pay for our room while he looked for another acting position. He certainly had never considered doing any physical labor. "Any word on what became of Horace?"

"Becks said he thought Horace had a friend in a traveling show." She flushed. "You know what kind of friend. Anyway, he certainly didn't care if I landed in gaol for debts, did he? If he starves, I won't lose sleep over it."

"You're right. He owed you more for the years you gave him than to leave you like that. It is a disgrace!" I hoped I would have warning when Jeremiah decided he no longer loved me. My breath caught at the thought. No, he wouldn't be that cold, that unfeeling. Would he? I know it would break my heart to lose him. But I had to prepare myself. There was still talk at court of the Scots moving to the Highlands for Yuletide. Was I to go with him? I had not been invited. I knew it was one thing to parade your mistress before the king, far from home. Did you take her into the bosom of your family?

"You look worried. What is on your mind, Gloriana?" Maggie also looked toward Jeremiah's room. "I have already learned not to ask questions here. But I can't help but notice that your lover has strange hours."

"Yes." I faked a saucy grin. "Mayhap I wear him out when we are together."

"I don't doubt you keep him mighty busy." Maggie picked up some needlework. She was darning socks for Fergus. She seemed happy to keep her sewing habit. "Not that I am paying heed to what you do when I am fully occupied myself." Her smile was wide, her eyes bright. "Oh, Gloriana, I will never be able to repay you for this chance at making a new start. If you had not brought Fergus to the Globe…"

"You are just what he needed, Maggie, never doubt it. He has been lonely. Seeing Jeremiah and I so happy together made his own single state more painful to bear." I heard the key in the lock. "Here he is now. I vow I will not stuff myself, no matter what delicious food he brings. I can hardly fit into my clothes as it is."

"No worries, lovey. I will let out the seams. It is what I did time and time again for Horace. We will certainly not let those pretty clothes your lover has bought you go to waste." She put aside her mending and greeted Fergus at the door, taking a basket from him. "Oh, my! You won't be able to resist this, Gloriana. Steak and kidney pie." She kissed Fergus on the cheek. "How did you know it is my favorite?"

"Did I not tell you, my love? I can read your thoughts." He had another basket which he set on the table. "I brought sweets as well. Gloriana is partial to them." He winked at me. "I have reason enough to be grateful to her. She is the one who introduced us." He pulled Maggie to him and kissed her on the lips. Then he frowned and put his hand to her cheek. "You feel warm. Have you been sitting too close to the fire?"

Maggie laughed. "No, but you put me to the blush, sir. Lay out the food. I must visit the chamber pot." She hurried out of the room, her hand on her stomach.

Fergus stared after her. "Could she be ill? I heard talk in the inn there are signs of the plague near here. Then I saw them myself. I can't lose her, Gloriana. Not when I just found her." He walked toward the room where she'd closed the door. "Has she complained to you? How are you feeling, Gloriana?"

"No complaints. She seems well enough and I am fine. Hale, hearty and very interested in the pie you brought." I rested my hand on his arm. Fergus was in love. It was good to see the big man so concerned for Maggie. I loved them both. I patted him reassuringly then got busy setting out plates and forks. We would eat together as we had been doing since we arrived here. It had been more than a month since we'd moved in and we had settled into a comfortable routine. I had made the decision to stop bothering Jeremiah about becoming vampire after our fight. After all, he had agreed to have Maggie come stay and I enjoyed having a female companion. I was not about to risk pushing him away with constant nagging.

Not that I had forgotten my need to be turned, just that I had decided to bide my time. I loved Jeremiah and hoped I could find a way to change his mind. The last thing I wanted to do with Maggie in the house was start another fight. Or test his love when he was thinking about leaving London soon.

I was happy, most of the time. Jeremiah and I spent many of our nights together at court. It still amazed me that I had such a handsome man eager for my presence by his side. I knew I was a credit to him. I had learned how to talk to the fine folks there and even had a ruby necklace and earrings that looked wonderful with a new gold silk dress. I topped them with a new cloak trimmed in fur. Such riches!

I appreciated Jeremiah's generosity but worried. With each new bauble I tried to see my future. Was he giving me jewels so I could have them to sell once he was gone? It didn't bear thinking about. How would I go on without him?

I knew I would gladly dress in rags and throw every jewel in the river if it would guarantee he would stay by my side. Of course I didn't dare complain. Nor would I beg him to never let me go. What man wanted a woman who turned into a desperate nag?

I sat and ate sparingly, remembering the passionate night before. Jeremiah never seemed to tire of our lovemaking and I thanked the gods for that. Surely he would find it hard to leave me behind when he left for Scotland if for no other reason than the way we fit together when he held me. I knew I would never forget the smell of him on my pillow, the taste of his kisses or the feel of his arms around me. How could he even think of letting go of the special connection we had?

No court tonight. He had been called upon to lead soldiers for the king as unrest continued. This wasn't the first time Jeremiah and Fergus had left on such a mission. I stayed in, glad for Maggie's company. We would talk and play card games, safely locked in. I might go to bed when Maggie tired, well before dawn. If I did, I knew Jeremiah would wake me when he came home to make love to me. It was my duty and my pleasure. I sighed when I realized I had cleaned my plate. Oh, I would never fit into my clothes at this rate.

"Gloriana, would you see if Maggie is all right? She has been in the retiring room a while now." Fergus paced the floor in front of the fireplace. "Her food grows cold."

"Of course." I hurried to the small room we'd set aside for the chamber pot and the hip bath. Maggie had marveled at the fact that Jeremiah and I bathed so frequently. But she'd soon learned to enjoy bathing as well. I had heard her with Fergus in the room one afternoon with much laughter and the sound of splashing water. It had made me take to my bed for a nap with a pillow over my head.

"Maggie, are you well?" I hesitated at the door to the small room.

"Come in." Her voice was weak.

I pushed the door open and saw her sitting on the small stool next to the tub. Her head rested on her knees. "Maggie! Fergus is worried about you. What's wrong?"

She looked up and I was relieved to see her smiling. "I think--I hope I am with child, Gloriana. That is why I am so sick to my stomach. I have seen it often enough with the women in the theater." She pressed a wet rag to her pale cheeks. "It is a miracle. I am old. Nine and twenty. But Fergus is lusty. And we…" She flushed. "Well, I have not had my monthly since I've been here and it is usually to be counted on, if you know what I mean."

I didn't. But I couldn't tell her that. Since I had waked up on those stones, years ago with no memory, I had not had what the women behind the stage had complained about. Did it mean I had no means of making a child? Was I damaged in some way? I had no time to give it thought. Maggie was off her stool and crying into my shoulder.

"What do you think Fergus will say? Will he cast me out to raise this child on my own?" She sobbed. "I love him. He says he loves me. But what man wants this kind of burden? We are just learning about each other. Oh, I should have been smarter. Asked the others at the Globe how to keep from…" She sniffed and leaned back. "You have not been careless, have you?"

I had no answer to that so I just shook my head. Jeremiah had told me he couldn't father a child so that was that. But Fergus. Obviously he could. And now he was going to have to tell Maggie the truth. He would certainly not cast her out. He did love her. I saw that in the way he looked at her.

"Come now. Dry your eyes and let's go tell Fergus the happy news. Are you sure? Could it be an illness? Horace did not look well when we last saw him." I took her wet cloth and wiped her cheeks.

"He has the pox. Of course he looks poorly. It's what you get when you lie with the worst sort of…" She shook her head. "I love steak and kidney pie, but the smell just now sent me running to heave up everything I ever ate. If that's not a sign, I don't know what is." She ran a hand through her hair. "And my breasts are sore. Swellin' a bit. Another sign. It's early days yet, but I'm feelin'..." She grinned. "I just know it's true."

"Then I'm happy for you and I'm sure Fergus will be as well." Did I believe that? I had no idea what kind of family Fergus had in Scotland. He seemed like an honest man. But for all I knew he could have a wife waiting for him there. I was not about to bring that up when she wiped her wet cheeks again and straightened her hair.

"I'd best tell him right away. I hate secrets. It was horrible all those years with Horace. Having his secret hanging over me was..." She shook her head. "Well, no matter what Fergus says about the babe, I am happy. I have always wanted a child. But I was trapped, you see. Horace never touched me, not in that way. And no man would come near me at the theater." She smoothed down her skirt. Fergus had bought her several new dresses as soon as she'd moved in and she was very proud of them. This one was a dark blue that matched her eyes. "Where else would I have met someone?" She grabbed my arm. "Until you brought me Fergus. My dear, dear friend." She hugged me and sniffed. "I can never thank you enough."

"No need to thank me. Just be happy." I sighed and patted her back, praying Fergus would be as happy with this news as she was. What a shock it would be for her when she found out her dear Fergus was not what he seemed. And the babe. Would it be shape-shifter or mortal? Oh, what a coil. She might hate me when she learned the truth about the father of her child. I took her hand and led her to the table where Fergus sat. He jumped up when he saw us.

"How are you, dearling?" He helped her sit, frowning when she pushed the plate he'd fixed her away. "Don't you want to eat? Aren't you hungry?"

"Not right now. Give me a few minutes and I will probably be starving. That's the way this seems to work."

Maggie patted the bench next to her. "Sit, love. I have something to tell you."

"I am going outside. Was it a fair day, Fergus?" I grabbed my shawl.

"You are not supposed to go out by yourself, Gloriana." Fergus looked frustrated. "Jeremiah--"

"I won't go far. Just a few steps outside the passageway. For some fresh air and a bit of sun. Is the sun out today?" I saw he'd left the key in the lock.

"Yes, the sun is shining, but it's cold." He frowned when I turned the key. "Stay close. Promise me."

"I will. You two need to talk. Come and get me when things are settled." I smiled and left. It felt good to be alone for a change. I knew Maggie was puzzled that I was always guarded. We explained it away by telling her a lord who liked to hurt women had taken a fancy to me. I doubted Lord Summers would think to take me by force, but there was enough truth to the story that Maggie believed it. She had seen him accost another woman with his cane the night of the play and hadn't liked his looks.

I walked down the long tunnel to the second door and pushed it open after I took the key from where it hung beside it. Once outside, I paused to take a breath. Fresh air, it almost made me dizzy. I quickly locked the door again and slipped the key into my pocket, hugging my shawl around me. It *was* cold, but I wanted to walk a bit. The river was nearby, I could smell it, but had no desire to see it. I hated that foul place. I turned instead to a street where I could see tradesmen had set up booths. I was still hungry and had money to buy a treat. Despite my best intentions, I purchased a warm sweet bun and ate it as I strolled along, looking at the things for sale.

I lifted my face to the sun, though there was little warmth to be had from it. Could I really choose to never see it again? Become a night creature? For a month or more I'd seen little of the day. Winter coming meant there was not much of it, night falling early. Had I missed the daylight? As long as I had Jeremiah each night…

"Mistress Gloriana, how is it you are alone?" The voice near my elbow almost made me drop the last of my bun. I turned, relieved when I saw who stood behind me.

"Bran. Do you live nearby?" I glanced around me. Of course Robert MacDonald wouldn't be about. It was still an hour or more before sunset.

"Aye. I was the one who told Fergus about the lodgings you now share with Campbell. I hope they suit you." He had a basket over his arm.

"They are very fine. I hope we aren't too close to your master." I liked Robert, but knew Jeremiah was still eager to fight him.

"Closer than either of the men would like. Fergus and I are doing our best to keep them from knowing that." He selected a meat pie and paid, putting it in his basket. "You really shouldn't be here by yourself. Where is my cousin?"

"With Maggie. Have you met her?" I started to walk back toward our tunnel at his insistence. "Are you escorting me?"

"Yes. To both questions. There are some troublemakers hereabouts and you would be wise to stay inside these days." Bran looked around. "You are well-dressed and look like you might carry coin. I have seen women surrounded and robbed here. A pretty one could well disappear into a brothel and never be seen again."

"Now you are scaring me." I had to skip to keep up with his long strides. I looked around, finally paying attention to my surroundings. Some of the men did look menacing. I had never been bothered before because I had always had Fergus with me. With his size, he could give anyone a hard look and they scuttled away.

"You should be wary. As to Maggie, it is a fine thing that my cousin has a good woman to warm his bed." Bran pushed me into a doorway as a man approached us. "Stay here." He pulled out a knife. "You there, if you think to bother the lady, is it worth your life?" He waved the knife in front of him when a man stepped too close. "I will slit you from gut to gullet if you so much as take another step this way, do you hear me?"

"Stow your gab, mate. Can you take three of us?" With a gesture, the first was joined by two more burly men, all of them with knives or cudgels. They pushed in, making Bran draw blood as he leaped toward the leader.

"Shit, the man weren't bluffing. Take 'em, boys." The wounded ruffian clutched his bleeding arm and backed up while his friends moved in. Suddenly there was a growl and an enormous dark brown dog stood between me and the thieves. The creature snarled, his teeth longer than my fingers and gleaming in the sunlight.

"What the devil!" Screams filled the air as the huge animal lunged, tearing into the nearest thief's leg. Blood spurted then the man yelled and dropped his knife to grab the wound. Other people on the street panicked, screeching and running for their lives.

"Thieves!" I screamed. "Help! And a wild dog. Mercy!" I pressed against the door to stay well out of his way as Bran leaped again, his howls and snarls sounding as if he would tear the men limb from limb. When there was a gunshot, I shrieked too, terrified that someone had managed to hit Bran. Soldiers on horseback had entered the other end of the street and now rode toward us. How was Bran going to get out of this? He couldn't just change back in front of all these witnesses.

"Run, Bran, run! I'll be all right." I reached down and jerked on his tail, hoping no one noticed that I wasn't afraid of this wild creature. He turned and glanced at me, golden eyes shining. They were surrounded by tangled dark brown fur, but they were Bran's eyes. Then he looked back at the riders coming down the street toward us, the crowd parting before them. The one in front waved a pistol. His first shot had obviously missed. Did he have another one? "Go!"

Bran took off, around the corner and out of sight down a narrow alley. The soldiers couldn't follow on horseback and quickly dismounted. The would-be thieves had run away at the first sign of soldiers, taking their wounded with them.

"Mistress, are you all right?" The leader made his bow. "Captain Marcus Danforth, at your service. I cannot believe that creature was loose on the streets."

"Where could he have come from?" I covered my face and pretended to sob. When I finally looked up, the captain's hand was on my shoulder.

"Mistress. Are you hurt?"

I sniffled into my handkerchief. "I was terrified but am not hurt thanks to your timely arrival, sir."

"I supposed it could be someone's lost pet gone wild or escaped from a bear baiting. He seemed quite vicious." The captain gestured and his men ran down the alley. "We will kill it if we can catch it."

"There were thieves, trying to steal my purse. Did you see them?" I pointed at blood on the ground. Surely Bran would be able to change back before they would get a chance to shoot at him. "They were following me. The creature actually saved me from them. He might be someone's pet. A guardian, trained to attack. I've heard--"

"Unlikely." The captain dismissed such fanciful thoughts instantly. "You should not be out without an escort, mistress." He looked me over, then his eyes widened. "You did not come from inside that house, did you?"

"What?" I glanced behind me and gasped, jumping away from the door clearly marked with a red X. "Oh, no! Of course not. Does that mean…"

"Plague, mistress. It would be wise for you to stay inside your own home from now on. We have heard reports of illness reaching this part of town. Do you live near here?"

Just then Bran came running up. "There you are, mistress. I have been looking for you. Are you all right?"

"Are you her servant?" The leader looked him over disapprovingly. "This lady should not have been left unattended. She was almost mauled by a wild dog."

"What? While I was sent to fetch your cloak?" Bran

held out a dark cloak. "The mistress was chilled. She asked me to go home and get her warm cloak. I was gone but a moment."

"Long enough for her to be in danger from a dangerous beast and the plague." The man swept his hand toward the door behind me. "Take her home and lock the door. It is not safe to be abroad these days. She says thieves were stalking her as well. Do your job, man, or she should replace you."

I offered the soldier a shy smile and a flutter of my lashes. "You are very kind, Captain. A hero to come to my aid." I allowed Bran to lay the cloak over my shoulders then turned and pretended to berate him. "You took too long. What were you doing? Flirting with the housemaid again? The captain is right. When I tell the master how I was almost killed this day, it will be a wonder if you are not turned off without a reference." I flounced off toward home. "Are you coming?" I sniffed in Bran's direction. We were playing roles and I knew he was as eager to get away from the soldiers as I was.

"Yes, mistress." Bran hung his head, hurrying after me.

As soon as we were out of sight, I sagged against a wall. "What a day. Bran, you saved me." I plucked at the cloak. "Where did you get this?"

"Stole it. Shopkeepers need to look sharp." Bran grinned. "How did you like my mastiff, Mistress Gloriana?"

"Very handsome and fierce. You certainly scared those thieves away." I took a shaky breath. He hadn't hesitated to leap to my defense. I knew it was what shape-shifters were paid to do but it had still made my heart stop. "You risked your life for me. I won't forget it. You lost the dinner you were buying when you came to my aid. Can I pay you back?"

"No, indeed. It was fun. Though I'm sure you won't believe that." He gestured toward home. "I will walk you to your door now. Fergus should never have let you go out alone. We have proof of that. What Campbell will say when he finds out about this day, I would hate to hear."

"If he didn't read my thoughts like an open book, I wouldn't tell him." I sighed and pulled the key out of my pocket when we got to the door to our tunnel. "You can go now and thank you."

"No, I want to have a word with my cousin. I saw that red X on the door where we were standing. Plague. It is time to leave London. Past time. There's been talk when we're at court of going soon. I want to hear what Fergus knows." Bran took the key and opened the door, escorting me with a hand on my elbow.

"Surely I cannot fall ill with the plague just from standing in front of the door." No one who lived in London could take the threat of plague lightly though. "Can a shifter or vampire even catch it?"

"Not vampires. They are like dead things, as I'm sure you've been told. But shifters? We are living beings, mistress. So, yes, Fergus and I may fall ill, but it's a rare happening. Diseases are not likely to kill us, not like a sword or bullet can. It is how we live so long." Bran knocked on our door. When Fergus threw it open, he bowed. "I have brought your lady back to you safely. We had a near miss."

"Gloriana! What's this?" Fergus looked back at Maggie. She was eating her steak and kidney pie as if her stomach had finally settled.

"I'll tell you all about it. Later. Well?" I glanced at Maggie. "What do you have to tell me, Fergus?"

"I am going to be a father." Fergus's chest swelled. "What do you think about that, cousin?"

"I think we had best get you both out of London as soon as may be." Bran cast a worried look at Maggie. "But that's good news. Aye, fantastic news." He hugged Fergus, pounding him on the back, then walked around to kiss Maggie on the cheek. "Call the banns. You won't be making the child a bastard and that's that."

"I don't take orders from you, cousin. But that's what I think and Maggie has agreed to become my wife. Now why do we have to leave London?" Fergus glared at him.

"Plague. Mistress Gloriana and I were close enough to touch it just today." Bran glanced at me. "It's coming closer and you don't want your lady at risk. Nor your bairn."

Fergus sat down at the table and picked up Maggie's hand. "No, I do not."

"Fergus, I have never been out of London." Maggie looked pale again.

"I have a fine house in the Highlands, Maggie mine. And money put aside. The plague will not reach us there. Can you trust me to see to your health and that of the babe?" He put his arm around her.

"Everything will be strange there." Her eyes filled with tears. "Will Gloriana come with us?"

Fergus exchanged looks with Bran. "That will be up to Jeremiah, love. I have no say in his affairs. Nor do I have a say in exactly when we leave this blighted town. There is a rumor that the king wants to hie off to his castle in Edinburgh by the end of this week. That should get us moving."

"Aye. I heard the same and Master MacDonald already has me packing." Bran smiled at me, his eyes soft. "It was a pleasure to be of service to ye, Mistress Gloriana. Mayhap we'll meet again. Now I'd best be going. It's close to sunset and we both have masters to please." Bran bowed to me and to Maggie. "We have a big family, Mistress Margaret. You will make friends in Scotland, I guarantee it. I hope to be the first one." He nodded to me. "Mistress Gloriana, who knows what the future will bring? You were quite clever today. Tell Fergus how we outwitted the soldiers." And with a wink he left.

"Soldiers. I don't like the sound of that." Fergus got up and fixed me a plate with an apple tart on it. "You should eat one of these. As you see, Maggie has found her appetite. Please sit and tell your tale. How is it Bran brought you home when you were supposed to stand next to our own door?"

I sat and ate a few bites while I told him everything.

The mastiff appearing brought a gasp from Maggie, but she clearly didn't understand that it had been Bran in another form. Obviously her lover hadn't told her his secret yet. Of course he was reluctant. She was so happy to be carrying his child. As for Fergus? He wasn't happy with me. In his opinion I'd wandered off and could have been hurt or worse. The plague being nearby was his biggest worry. No one would be going out in a crowd from now on. Our shopping trips were over.

"Bran says you and he can also catch the plague, Fergus." I glanced at Maggie. She had more interest in reaching for one of the apple tarts for herself than in our conversation.

"Aye, it's true. I will be very careful who I buy our meals from as I go out." He frowned. "When Jeremiah wakes, we will need to talk. The sooner we get out of London, the better. If it was up to me, Gloriana, I would take you along." He shook his head. "But that is not my decision. If you have to stay behind…"

"Then I will be left with money for a safe place." I put on a brave face. "Jeremiah promised me that. Perhaps I can stay here. If you could find a strong man I could hire to help me, I wouldn't even have to go out for food until the danger of plague passes."

"I could make some inquiries." Fergus was clearly not happy. "You should really try to find a new protector, Gloriana. The next time you go to court, look around. Surely there is a kind man who would take care of you as you deserve." He stood. "A woman like you shouldn't be alone. It's not safe."

I knew he was right. A woman living alone would not last long in this town. I had seen how dangerous the streets were just today. When my money ran out that's where I would be. If I didn't die from the plague first. Find a new protector? I loved Jeremiah and he claimed to love me. If he truly did, could he just abandon me here? Pass me on to another man? The thought of him with another woman made me want to snatch one of the knives Fergus was so carefully cleaning for his master as we sat around the table. First I'd stick the wench who thought to take my place. Then—

"Gloriana. You look ready to do murder." Jeremiah's hand on my shoulder gave me a start. I'd been so lost in my gloomy thoughts I hadn't heard the creak of Jeremiah's door opening. Obviously the sun had set. Fergus jumped to his feet, determined it seemed to talk about the future. I was up just as fast and threw my arms around my lover.

"It's nothing." I glanced at Fergus, daring him to interrupt me. "Jeremiah, do you have to go out tonight?"

"Aye. It is the king's order." He smiled down at me and my heart turned over. "What is it? You look upset."

"Later. We can talk when you come home. Let me prepare a bath for you. Would you like that?" I tugged him toward the room with the tub. "Fergus, hot water, if you please." I issued the order with a raised eyebrow. "There will be time enough to discuss things later."

"Of course." Fergus took a kettle off the hob and brought it into the small bathing chamber. Soon Jeremiah was relaxing in the bath.

I shut the door and pulled off my dress. Fergus had found us a larger bathing tub and I climbed in with Jeremiah.

"I hope you don't mind if I join you." I sat across from him, letting my toes climb his stomach.

"Not at all." He frowned. "But I can see you are worried about something. Tell me or I'll read it in your mind."

"There is plague close by. I know you cannot catch it, but the rest of us here can." I sighed and reached for the soap, rubbing it over my breasts. "Of course I am worried about it."

"How do you know this?" He leaned closer.

"I saw a door marked with an X and almost fell into it. It is mere steps from our own tunnel." I used a cloth to wipe away the soap. "Fergus has commanded Maggie and me to stay inside for now. But I will go mad if I am trapped here." I looked at Jeremiah through my lashes. "Can you understand that?"

"Of course." He took the cloth from me. "Come here." He held me against him. "Fergus is right. You need to be kept safe."

"He wants to leave London." I said this against Jeremiah's neck. "I know the king is leaving soon. I expected you would go as well." I leaned back and looked up at him. "Where does that leave me, Jeremiah?" There, I had finally asked the question. "Am I to stay here and wait for the plague to take me?"

He looked at me for a long moment. What did he see? My true desire? I didn't try to hide it from him. I let him see my heart and my hope. He finally shook his head and put me away from him, rising from the tub, water streaming from his hard and, to me, beautiful body.

"There's no time now to talk about this, Gloriana. The decision is too important. Too permanent." He dried off with a cloth and wrapped another one around his lean hips. I just sat there, watching him and waiting.

"Are you saying..?"

"I'm saying nothing, woman. Leave it alone. We will talk later. I must dress and leave now. Stay inside. Lock the doors. Fergus and I will be back before dawn with time to spare." He strode from the room to our bedchamber to dress. He would put on his sword and knives and any other weapon he might need as he searched out the king's enemies. I wasn't supposed to worry about him. Of course not. He couldn't be killed and would return as promised. I hoped Fergus would return as well since he always fought at Jeremiah's side. I got out of the tub, wishing we had a fireplace in the small room. It was cold and I dried quickly, slipping back into my dress. By the time I got to the main room, the men were at the door, ready to leave. Maggie was so worried about Fergus, she was near tears.

"Lass, I will be fine. We will be surrounded by the

king's soldiers and Jeremiah is the finest swordsman you will ever hope to see." He kissed her and winked at me. "Gloriana, see to it she doesn't sit and fret. Play cards, then it's early to bed. She needs her sleep."

He turned to Jeremiah. "I'm to be a father, Jeremiah. What do you say to that?"

Jeremiah froze. It was almost as if he had been hit in the head by a rock. Then he seemed to shake it off and found a smile. "Well done, Fergus." He clapped the shifter on the back. "Maggie, you are blooming. Now I know why." He kissed her cheek and caused her to turn rosy. "Fergus, your family will be happy to hear you may have sired an heir."

"Aye. But I wouldn't mind a wee girl to spoil." Fergus nodded. "So, Maggie, get your rest. We'll be back and I expect to see you in bed tucked up and sleeping sound."

"All right, my love." Maggie smiled as they left.

"Jeremiah!" I ran to the door. "Take care." I pulled his head down to kiss him. "I know you do, but I needed to say that."

"We will talk later, I promise." He pulled me close and kissed me again, his heart in it this time. "There are things you don't know, Gloriana." He shook his head. "Fergus is right. Get some sleep. No need to wait up until dawn. I will wake you when I come back."

And then he was gone, the key turning in the lock once they were outside the door.

"I don't like that we are locked in. What if there was a fire? We would be trapped." Maggie pulled out her sewing basket.

"There is an extra key. Jeremiah showed it to me. It is here." I pulled a stone away from beside the hearth. "See? Under this stone. So don't worry. We aren't prisoners. At first I felt like one. But now Jeremiah trusts me to know that I can leave at any time." I sat across from her. I had a book that I could now read, thanks to days with Fergus helping me learn. "Would you like me to read to you?"

"Oh, please. It will certainly take my mind off the danger our men are in." Maggie pulled out a shirt with a tear in the sleeve.

I opened my copy of *The Merry Wives of Windsor*. It was one of Shakespeare's plays and Jeremiah had bought it for me. We were well into it. I began reading and Maggie was soon laughing, her sewing forgotten.

"I swear, Gloriana, you could be on the stage. You are so much better than Horace ever hoped to be." She wiped her eyes. "You read with so much feeling. I can see it just as it was at the Globe. There were so many women's parts. Horace would have made a better Falstaff but he was forced to play Mistress Ford. It was his lot in that company to always be the woman because of his pretty face and soft body. There was no persuading Master Shakespeare of any other type of role for him."

I knew it was true so I just kept reading until we were both yawning. I wasn't really sleepy but blew out candles and put on my nightgown when Maggie took herself off to bed. I thought to stay awake for Jeremiah, but my busy day took its toll and I drifted off to sleep.

I was running, being chased by a large snarling dog, no, a witch. She laughed as she shot lightning at me out of her fingertips. Fire hit me, burning my back and setting my hair aflame. Where could I hide? If only I could run faster, leap higher. But I was weak, losing strength. I saw nothing ahead but darkness and had no safe place to go. I fell, screaming when she grabbed me and held me down. She would take all my blood, drain me dry. I knew it.

"No! No! Let me go!" I hit her, desperate to get away. Why couldn't I move her? I was helpless and knew this was the end for me. I gasped my last breath.

"Gloriana, it's me, Jeremiah. Stop it. You're safe." He touched my cheek.

I finally realized where I was and opened my eyes. "Jeremiah." I threw myself against him and held on. "I had the most horrible nightmare. It was as if Marin had come back for me. I couldn't get away." I tried to calm my racing heart and took deep breaths. I realized he was naked and had crawled into our bed.

"A very bad dream." He leaned back and studied my face which I was sure was pale from my fright. "Did you know vampires don't dream?"

"You don't?" I hadn't given it any thought.

"No. That's another thing you would lose, Gloriana, if I turned you. We never sleep. I told you we die at sunrise. So we cannot dream." He let go of me and lay beside me.

"So you've been thinking about it. Turning me vampire." I leaned on one elbow, staring down at him with my hand on his chest. "I thought you wouldn't even consider it."

"That was before the plague came so near. I saw three doors marked with that red X near us when I was out tonight." He pulled me down so I was lying on his chest. "I love you. I don't want to lose you."

I sighed and kissed his firm skin. I did love him so. "I don't want to lose you either, Jeremiah. Make me vampire and we could be together forever."

"You say that so easily. You have no idea what you are asking me to do." He pushed me away and stared into my eyes. "No idea at all."

SEVENTEEN

"Explain it to me, Jeremiah. Why is making me vampire such a grave thing?" I leaned over him, catching his eye. He did look serious, as if I asked him to break a blood oath. "Is it forever you're worried about? You say you love me. Or are those just words? Said to make me give you my vein willingly?"

"I mean them, Gloriana. I do love you." He took my face between his hands and looked deep into my eyes. "I can see you think this is what you want. But there is no turning back from this decision."

"Of course. Once a vampire, always a vampire. Do you think I am a fool?" I tried to tease him. "It's not like choosing a hat. I have been considering this seriously for weeks, Jeremiah." I sighed. Teasing wasn't the right approach here. "Say what is on your mind. Do you fear you will tire of me?"

"At this moment? I can't imagine it. But, Gloriana, what you don't understand is that when a vampire turns a mortal, he becomes his or her sire. Some among us can do so and walk away. I am not like that. I see it as an obligation. A decent sire should guide his creation. Teach her, train her, keep her safe. Forever."

"Would that be so horrible? To do those things for me? You are already feeding me, clothing me and seeing to my safety. I see little difference than if I were to become one of your kind." I turned my face to kiss his rough fingertips. If we were married, we'd have that eternal tie. But Jeremiah had never mentioned marriage and I was not about to throw *that* into this discussion. "I like to imagine us as night creatures together. Yes, forever. But perhaps you would miss my mortal blood. I suppose you would seek out another mortal to drink from. A woman?" The thought of that made me pull back.

"Your blood would still be a heady drink to me, whether you were vampire or mortal. You are the only woman I desire." He smoothed my brows, ran his fingers over my cheekbones. "Please, listen to me. You say forever like it is nothing. Did you not see what a thousand years had done to Marin? She went mad from dealing with the challenges of the long life she'd led."

"She didn't have you to guide her." I sighed. "If you are reluctant to do this, why not just take me to the Highlands with you as your mortal mistress?"

"I cannot." He kissed me, then rolled us so that I was under him. "You do not understand how it is at the castle."

"Explain it to me. Are you ashamed of me?" I hated to say it. But that was the only explanation I could think of. He'd introduced me to his king. It seemed to me that his parents would be a simpler matter. But I was not his wife and there had been no talk of calling the banns, had there? Oh, I had to stop thinking of it. He would read it in my mind and... I didn't know why, but it was not how he saw me. As his wife. I shoved down the pain that caused and waited.

"Ashamed? No, of course not." He stared down at me. "You are beautiful and very clever. Any man would be proud to have you on his arm." He frowned. "But we are a family of vampires, Gloriana. Long ago we decided that bringing mortals to a family meeting is a bad idea. Mortals are nothing more than food, at least to the older ones among us. I could not be sure you would be safe there. And it would be breaking a long-held promise we all made."

"You sound as if some among your family cannot be trusted." I pictured wild Highlanders pouncing on me and tearing into my throat for a taste. It made me shudder.

"It's true, I'm sorry to say. Marin is not the only ancient vampire to go mad. She had no family that we know of. I suppose Jean-Claude was all she had to call hers. And she clearly ruled him. It is not the same in the Campbell Clan. We take care of our own. My father is the Laird. When one of ours falls prey to uncontrollable blood lust, we take him or her in and make sure they stay safe. We don't want a Campbell to find himself ashes at the end of a stake." He stared past me, blindly, as if recalling a bad time.

"So you won't take me with you as I am. Would it be better to leave me here? Leave me with the plague surrounding me? Men eager to prey on me? I was beset by thieves today when I dared walk a few steps away from our home. Bran said I could have been dragged off to serve in a brothel. Fergus surely told you about it while you were out tonight."

"Aye, he did." Jeremiah frowned. "I know I can't keep you under lock and key until I come back to London. It would be your right to seek a new protector while I am gone."

"And who would that be? Do you think I so easily give my heart and my," I drew in a breath, fearing I would break down and sob on his chest, "body to just anyone?" I flung him off and he let me or I couldn't have managed it. I crawled out of bed and stood beside it, shaking. "Of course you do. I had only to meet you in that alley and I was willing to lie with you. We had known each other for less than an hour and I was in your bed, naked and all yours." The shame of it. I wanted to look away, but couldn't. It was the ugly truth.

"That was not all willingly, Gloriana." Jeremiah stared at me, still very solemn. "I am not proud of using my skills on you. Mind control, my love. Vampires can make mortals follow us, whether they want to or not. I saw you, smelled your blood and knew I had to have it and you in my bed. It took very little to bring you home that night. I stared into your eyes and you were helpless. You would have followed me anywhere."

I stared at him, disbelieving. Was he truly saying that I'd had no control over choosing him? That I had been under his vampire spell? I had hoped Fergus was wrong. That I'd come willingly. But Jeremiah had just admitted it. I trembled, afraid to ask. Was I still under his control?

"No!" He was out of the bed and beside me before I could jerk open the door to our bedchamber. He held it closed. "It has been many weeks since I used any of my deceits on you, Gloriana. Please believe me."

"Believe you? A sorcerer who admits he can lure any mortal woman to his bed? I was easy prey, starving and desperate." I felt sick and gulped for air, the room spinning. No. I would not be that weak. I steadied myself by grasping the door frame then faced him.

"Mayhap that is why you are reluctant to turn me vampire. Heaven forbid I should have the skills that will let me see into *your* mind. Let me control *your* will." I balled up my fists when he tried to pull me against him. "You, you bastard!" I hit him, sobbing. To think that he'd controlled me, probably still controlled me. I hate, hate, hated him. I kept hitting him, furious and hurt to think he had professed to love me and yet treated me like I was nothing more than one of those pets Marin had claimed vampires were eager to own. Yes, own!

"Please, love, calm down. I am thinking of you when I say losing your mortality is not what you truly want." He grasped my fists and kissed them.

He was so strong. Manipulative swine. It was too easy for him to drag me back to the bed and sit me down to face him. He dropped to his knees in front of me, staring into my eyes. Was he using more of his power? Was he even now calming me with his mind tricks? I raised my chin and looked away.

"Don't do this. Don't try to soothe me with one of your stares and vampire wiles. I, I could not bear it." I flinched when he took my chin in his hand.

"I won't do it. I am being honest now. I love you. I love your strong spirit. You would make a fearsome vampire, a woman any man would want to have with him forever. A woman I would want with me forever." He kissed me, hungrily, and I hated myself for still wanting him. Tasting him and thinking he was the only man who had ever satisfied me.

I drew back, gasping. "Jeremiah, stop. Let me think. My own thoughts. Not some ideas you have planted in my head."

"I'm not doing that. I swear it." He pulled me up to stand in front of him. "If I turn you, you will be able to read my mind and my heart, but only if I let you. It is possible to block our thoughts and that is a skill I could teach you. You would have power then and could protect yourself. You would know I couldn't sway you with my mind tricks." He ran his hand down my body, as if every curve was one he desired and wanted to use again and again.

I swayed toward him. How could I love this man when he'd just confessed such a horrible thing? He'd wanted my blood and my body so he'd taken them. What about me? My mind, my thoughts and desires? I was a person. Would I still be one to him if I lost my mortality? I ran my own hands over his body, feeling the cool hardness and thinking of how that would be my eternal temperature if I did this thing.

Vampires were dead things. Dead. Every day at sunrise. And any mortal could take advantage of that with a stake of olive wood.

"If I turned you, I would see to it that you were safe during the day. I would have someone take care of you. Like

Fergus does for me. Even if for some reason we parted."
Jeremiah leaned down, pressing a kiss to my vein.

Oh, yes, he did love that vein. "Take care of me forever, Jeremiah? I am not a child, helpless and needy. There is no need for such a promise." Of course he thought of me that way. Hadn't I been starving when we'd met? I had to work to make him see me as more than that. But that would take time. Time I would have if I became vampire. I was sure, too, that the future would always be uncertain, vampire or not. "I cannot imagine why we would ever be parted. I love you." I felt the press of his desire against me. "Of course you might like variety or could tire of me." I dragged my mouth down his chest to his stomach. "Are you tiring of me, Jeremiah?"

"God, no." He groaned when I pleasured him, reminding him of things he had already taught me.

His hands were in my hair until I could tell he was about to spend. I stood and pulled him to the bed, lying back and inviting him inside my body. We still had this. When he took my vein, I held him close, whispering his name. He was mine, mine, and I was going to keep him. Giving up my mortality was a small price to pay. Later, we lay close, my cheek on his chest as I listened to his slowly beating heart.

"If you are still determined to do this, promise me something, Gloriana." He stroked my back.

"What is it?" I leaned up and looked into his eyes.

"Take tomorrow and go outside, into the sunlight. Take a good long look at it. Breathe the air and think about what you would be giving up. Eat all of your favorite foods. Think about how that might be for the last time." He smiled. "I saw you swallow just now. You will miss your sweet treats, will you not?"

"I admit it." I kissed his chin. "But look what I will be getting. Immortality. A forever lover. Mind reading. And I will be able to shape-shift, like you and Fergus do. That will be amazing."

"The change into vampire is painful, Gloriana. Like the

worst torture. I will not lie to you about that." He was back to being solemn again. "I have never done it myself to a mortal but have seen it done. I will have to drain you. Remember when I took too much of your blood? Fergus told me about it. After the fight with MacDonald."

"Yes, I was very weak." I had almost died. Now I fell back on the bed.

"Well, this will be worse. I will take your blood until your heart stops beating. You *will* die. Then I will force you to drink my blood. It will not be pleasant and you will fight against the drinking of it. It will feel as if it is burning you from the inside out. Once you finally come to life, you will be crazed. And starving for blood." He sighed. "We will send Fergus and Maggie out of here for the night. Or they will be in danger from you."

"Surely you exaggerate. Attack my friends? I cannot imagine…"

"Of course you cannot. It is beyond imagination. I remember parts of my own turning and wish I did not." He kissed me gently. "I hate to do this to you. But it is the only way I can take you with me to the castle. If you are vampire, you will be welcome as my guest. Do you understand?"

"It is what I want, Jeremiah." I pulled him down to kiss him hungrily. "Promise you won't kill me and then leave me dead?"

"Of course." He smiled into my eyes. "Promise me you will think hard about this tomorrow as you look into the sky and see the sun for what may be the last time."

"I will." I pulled his head to my breast and held him. He was worried. Which made me worry as well. "Does this turning ever go wrong, Jeremiah? Have you ever heard of someone not surviving it?"

"Aye." He sat up. "So keep that in mind tomorrow, my love. You could be ending your own life with this decision. I will do my best to make this go right, but there are no guarantees."

"I could catch the plague tomorrow as well. A falling

chamber pot could smash my head and end me like it did Michael." I sat up and faced him. "Or a gang of thieves could catch me and throw me into a brothel where I die of the pox. It is a cruel world, Jeremiah, I have reason to know that." I leaned down and kissed him, lingering over it. He could read my mind, of course. Did he bother? Not when I was running my hands down his body again. I smiled and brought his hand to my breast.

"Anything can happen, Jeremiah. I'll take my chances, with you."

* * *

"Gloriana, I don't like it." Fergus had been trying to talk me out of my decision all day. Now he was packing a sack with a few things so he and Maggie could spend the night at a different lodging. "Change your mind, girl." He had waited until Maggie had gone to fetch her sewing basket to try to persuade me one more time. It was almost sunset and he knew Jeremiah would wake at any moment.

"I had a wonderful day. Clear skies and the sun was shining, rare enough for London. Thank you for taking Maggie and me to the fair, Fergus." I kissed his cheek. "Don't worry. I will see you when you return."

"If all goes well." He frowned. "I have heard--"

"Maggie! Fergus told me he has found a nice place nearby. It is high time you two had a bit of privacy." I turned to my friend and handed her the surprise I had bought for her at a shop we'd passed during the day. "Open this when you are ready for bed."

"You bought me a gift?" Maggie flushed. "You shouldn't have."

"Why not? I am happy for you and Jeremiah is generous with his coin." I knew Fergus was going to have to tell Maggie about vampires this night. It would be hard. Would he also finally shift in front of her? Show her his bear or some other animal so she would truly understand what she had fallen in love with? I hugged her and whispered in her ear.

"Fergus is a good man. Remember that."

"Why, Gloriana, you don't have to tell me about my Fergus." Maggie drew back and wiped her eyes. She turned to Fergus. "He has made my dream of having a child come true. And promised to marry me once we get to his home. I cannot imagine a better man." She kissed his cheek.

"I wish I could take you to a fine inn, Maggie mine, but the threat of plague worries me. There is a set of rooms nearby that I know are cozy." He picked up their bags. "We'll be snug inside and no innkeeper to bother us." He looked around. "Are you sure you wish us to leave you, Gloriana? Jeremiah should be up any time now."

"Go." I pushed them toward the door. I knew Fergus was taking them to rooms next to Robert MacDonald's place. Bran had found them for him. Of course his cousin knew what was afoot. We had run into him at the market and he'd seen my concern on my face. It was impossible to hide anything from mind readers. I would be glad when I was vampire and had that skill of blocking my thoughts that Jeremiah had promised to teach me. Bran had pulled me aside and added his own urgings not to be hasty with such a big decision.

"Take care, Gloriana." Fergus pulled me in for a hug. This was not like him and Maggie laughed.

"Here now. We're only going away for a night." She shook her head. "I think the thought of becoming a father has made him a bit daft. See you tomorrow, Gloriana." She waved as she walked out the door.

I sat at the table. Did I want to eat one more thing? I admit I had stuffed myself all day. Mostly sweets. It had been a cold, crisp day and hot chocolate had been a delicious treat. Then there were those buns with fruit. And tarts. I did love lemon tarts. We had supped on roast beef as well. Wine with luncheon. In fact, I had eaten and drunk so much I was almost sick with it. I decided a hot bath would make me feel better and ended up soaking in the tub before I dressed in a silk night robe. I had bought a beautiful one for Maggie. I was sure she would be shocked and pleased when she opened her package later tonight. Fergus would certainly like it.

I lay back on the bed, fighting nerves when the door to Jeremiah's room creaked open. Fergus had installed a heavy bolt on our bedchamber door before he'd left. From now on there would be two vampires sleeping the day away in this bed. If there were no problems with my turning.

"You look terrified." Jeremiah sat on the side of the bed and picked up my hand. "And very beautiful." He leaned down and kissed my breast through the thin silk. "Perfect."

"I think I have gained a stone or more since you met me." The silk was taut over my breasts and my hips.

"In all the right places." He eased the straps down so he could see me. "You needed more flesh. The starving woman I met in that alley was much too thin. Now you are just right." He pulled the silk down until he could toss it aside. "No need for this."

"I spent the day in the sun as you asked me to do. I did not change my mind." I pulled his shirt off over his head. "Will you do as you promised, Jeremiah? Will you make me vampire?"

He fell onto the bed beside me. "You are determined."

"Yes." That came out more weakly that I expected. I cleared my throat. "Yes, I am. Of course I'm scared. You and Fergus, even Bran, have warned me of the dangers and the future I will be facing."

"Bran? Fergus's cousin who works for MacDonald? Why are you having anything to do with him?" Jeremiah sat up. "MacDonald is not to know my business."

"You remember. Bran helped me when I was attacked. We just happened to meet him today, in the market. He read my mind. Like all of you do." I looked away. "I cannot wait until I am able to block my thoughts from vampires and shape-shifters. It is humiliating that my every thought is there for all to see."

"That is not a good reason to lose your mortality,

Gloriana." He ran his hand through his hair. "I don't like this. Knowing MacDonald…" Someone pounded on the outside door. "Oh, yes. I wouldn't be surprised if that is the man himself. He wants you. If Bran let him know what we are planning tonight, he will try to interfere."

"You don't answer to him." I pulled the covers up to my neck.

Jeremiah got out of bed and arranged a plaid around his hips. "He won't go away. I might as well get this over with." He smiled. "With luck, this will give me an excuse to kill him."

"Stop!" I jumped out of bed and wrapped myself in a sheet. "Please, Jeremiah." I followed him to the door.

He stopped and leaned against it. "I smell him. It is MacDonald." He picked up a knife from the table behind him then unlocked the door. "Come in."

"What the devil are you doing, Campbell?" Robert strode in, his eyes blazing. He stopped when he saw me clad in nothing but a sheet. His nostrils flared. "Mistress Gloriana." He bowed. "I see I am in time."

"In time for a knife in the gut. What the devil are *you* doing, MacDonald?" Jeremiah took a warrior's stance in front of me. "You have no business here."

"My man Bran told me you are planning to turn Gloriana vampire this night. Is that true?" Robert drew himself up, his hand on his sword.

"What of it?" Jeremiah smiled. "She wants it. It will make her mine forever. Is that what has your plaid in a knot?"

"Greedy son of a bitch. Have you told her how it will go? Of the pain? The things she will lose?" Robert tried to move Jeremiah out of the way so he could look at me. "Gloriana, you cannot know--"

Jeremiah wasn't budging. "I told her. She seems determined. She loves me. Imagine that."

"You fool." Robert paced the floor. "You could kill her."

"He told me that, Robert." I was touched by his worry. I placed my hand on Jeremiah's back. "Let me talk to him."

"Why? Have you feelings for him? Do you wish for him to be your sire?" Jeremiah wheeled around. "I have told you how I feel about your familiarity with my enemy."

"He is not *my* enemy." I tugged my sheet higher when it began to slip. "Please, Jeremiah. Let us talk. He is only showing concern for my well-being."

"I don't trust him." His back was rigid.

"Well, I do. Now move out of the way." I pushed and he finally moved. "Robert, thank you for coming."

"Gloriana, this is unwise. You will be tied to Campbell for eternity. You have no idea what that means. The bastard will make you regret it. I have reason to know that." Robert tried to take my hand but Jeremiah made sure there was a knife between us.

"This is my decision, Robert. If you are so concerned, mayhap you can stay for the, um, change. See to it that it goes well." I looked at Jeremiah. "What do you think, love? Would it be all right if there was another vampire at hand? In case something goes wrong?"

"If it were anyone else I would say yes. I would like help. But MacDonald?" Jeremiah's face was as flushed as I had ever seen it. "I cannot say this often enough, Gloriana, I don't trust him. We have had dealings before, in the Highlands. This is not about you. Never think it. Our families are enemies for a reason. MacDonald knows it."

"Put that aside for now, Campbell. Think about Gloriana. Have you ever turned a mortal before?" Robert was clearly agitated. "Have you?"

"No." Jeremiah again ran his hands through his hair. Was he nervous? Scared of what was to come?

"Christ! What are you thinking? So many things can go wrong. You could fail to drain her completely. She could go mad when you give her your blood. I've seen it. The pain can make a mortal hurt those around him or her. If there is a weapon about they might even try to kill themselves and have done so."

"Have *you* turned a mortal? Where is your vampire? If you are a sire, where is the fledgling you made?" Jeremiah practically growled it. "Or are you one of those careless types who makes vampires whenever the mood strikes them and then leaves them to run wild with no supervision or guidance?"

"No, of course I haven't turned a mortal. Do you think I want some sniveling vampire trailing me around for eternity? Or worrying that I created a monster who is out there somewhere doing God knows what? I never wanted that responsibility weighing on me. I do have a conscience, though I'm sure you don't believe me, Campbell." Robert winked at me. "No offense, Gloriana. I'm sure you would be a delight to have on my coattails or in my bed forevermore."

"Then what makes you an expert?" Jeremiah put his arm around me. "This is madness. If I do it, I surely don't need you around as a witness."

"But I have been a witness. Many times. My da made me stand and help when he turned my younger brothers and sisters. You know that's how we do it in my family and in yours. We take care of our own. I am the oldest, as are you. I'm surprised you weren't forced to stand in at the transitions. It is another reason why I have no taste for making my own fledglings. It is a brutal business." Robert couldn't take his eyes off of me and I wondered if I could slip into the bedchamber and put on a modest dress. "Gloriana, think carefully. This is painful and there is no turning back."

"MacDonald is right about that. My father and mother took care of the transitions in our family. I was never privy to it. I just remember when I was turned." Jeremiah tightened his hold on me. "Yes, both my parents were there. It took two of them to keep me down when the blood lust took hold."

"You see? You will need me." Robert nodded. "I know it will be your blood alone going into her. I have no desire to bind myself to her, no matter how lovely she is." He smiled. "But if you are determined to go through with this, Gloriana, I am here to stand as witness and as a help if you should need me."

I couldn't get that image out of my mind. Jeremiah's parents had turned him and grappled with him because he'd been so crazed with blood lust. How could a mother or father do that to a child? I looked into his eyes. He wasn't even seeing me. He was obviously remembering his transition and the "torture" as he'd described it. The pain. His father was his sire. But he wasn't so strongly tied to his da, as he called him, that he wasn't allowed to roam free to London and go his own way. Was I really so determined that I could ignore these warnings? I took a deep and shuddering breath. To my surprise, I realized I was.

"I think I would like for Robert to be here, Jeremiah." I said this quietly, hopeful that this didn't seem disloyal. "I cannot imagine that I would be too strong for you to manage, but he does have experience that you don't have. He could be a help. I don't want to hurt you."

"Unfortunately, I understand. His experience could be valuable." Jeremiah nodded once. "This is your last chance, Gloriana. We don't have to do this. Keep your mortality. I will buy you a nice house here in London. Hire a sturdy guard to keep you safe. I'll come back in the summer and we can be together again."

"No. I am sure of what I want. I don't want to grow old or risk the plague while I wait here for your pleasure. I want to spend eternity with you." I touched his face. "Please."

Robert made a noise. "She is certainly besotted. I hope you are not going to regret this, Gloriana." He took off his sword and set it on the table. "I am sure you want to do this in the bedchamber, Campbell. She will be more comfortable there. As comfortable as she can be."

"Aye." Jeremiah looked resigned. "You will watch, nothing more, unless I ask for your assistance."

"As you wish." Robert smiled at me. "Thank you for your trust, my dear. We will be friends forever. Unless one of us meets a stake or a sunrise." He raised an eyebrow. "Pray God that never happens." He followed us into the bedchamber and sniffed. "The place reeks of love play. A lusty wench, aren't you, Gloriana? Well done, Campbell."

"If you wish to stay, you will show some respect, MacDonald." Jeremiah threw off his plaid and crawled into bed. "Gloriana, come here, love." He patted the bed beside him. Then he held up the coverlet. "Under the covers, if you please."

I climbed in, careful to keep Robert from seeing my naked body. I knew it was important to Jeremiah. I lay back with my head on the pillow. I was shaking and terrified, I couldn't deny that. They had both kept talking about the terrible pain and, first, I had to die.

"I keep hearing about Gloriana's wonderful blood. Would it be too much to ask for a taste before you drain her completely?" Robert pulled up a chair and sat at the side of the bed. "You know you shouldn't drink all of her blood yourself anyway. That could make her change difficult. She will need almost pure vampire blood when she takes her first drink."

"I'm sorry but that is true, Gloriana." Jeremiah reached for a glass on the table beside the bed. He leaned forward and licked the vein in my neck then sliced across it with his knife. I didn't feel it. Then he filled the glass with the blood that poured from it. "Here. It is truly something special." He handed the glass to Robert with something almost like pride before he leaned down to lap up the blood that kept sliding down my neck. "So warm. I will miss this heat."

"Aye." Robert drank. "By God! I have never had such a potent drink. More, if you please." He handed him the glass and Jeremiah let him fill it again. "Nectar of the gods, if I do say so myself. No wonder Marin raved about it." He stood beside the bed while Jeremiah continued to drink.

I drifted in and out of awareness. The room faded and

there was only Jeremiah at my throat. I touched his hair, then tried to hold onto his shoulder but my hand fell to the bed. The candles flickered and the room grew cold. Was I floating away? Why was it getting dark? I wanted to speak, to ask for more light, but the words wouldn't come.

"Stop what you are doing. She is getting very pale."

"Aye, the blood flow has slowed. How are you feeling, Gloriana?" Jeremiah touched my throat.

How was I feeling? The room was fading away. I tried to answer him but darkness closed in on me.

"One more glass, I think. Squeeze her vein. She must be truly empty, you know, before this can go further. Put your ear to her chest and see if you hear her heart beating. It must stop." Robert said something else but it was as if he spoke in a faraway tunnel.

I was cold, so cold. I wanted to raise my arm and pull up the coverlet but I couldn't manage it. Breathing became too difficult and Jeremiah's head against my breast was unbearably heavy. I tried to tell him to get off but words wouldn't form. My eyes closed, my lids dropping over them even though I wanted to see… I fell into a hole of nothingness, cold, dark nothingness where there was no sound or light.

Suddenly liquid splashed into my mouth, scalding it. No! It burned, hurting me. I tried to fight, but my arms were shackled, and I was weak, too weak. All I could do was shriek inside as the fluid scorched and seared its way down my throat and into my veins. My lungs flamed. I tried to choke, to gasp and take a breath, but couldn't. Scream. No sound but a squawk of pain and panic.

More of the molten drink flowed into me. Then I realized that the fiery fluid was giving me life again. Strength I desperately needed. I grasped the source and devoured it, holding on as I sucked the intoxicating life force into my starving body. I had to have it. To live.

"She'll kill you. We have to pull her off."

"I had no idea she'd be this strong. Help me."

They were trying to tear me away from what I craved. What I wanted most. I wouldn't let go. Steely arms wrapped around me. Rough fingers pushed into my mouth and tried to pry my teeth open. No! I needed more of that sweet nectar. It was making me whole again. I was finally coming alive. They couldn't take this away. Not yet!

"Hold her."

"I'm trying."

"Bastard. Don't touch her breast." Cursing, then I was shoved to the bed and wrapped tightly. I couldn't move. I tried, crying out and screaming curses when I could not get free.

"It's almost sunrise. I can feel it. Stay here. In my room. I'll lie beside her. We'll see what she's like when the sun sets and she wakes."

Noise, bed moving and arms around me, holding me. I smelled the sharp scent of a man. Jeremiah. I needed... Nothing.

EIGHTEEN

I woke with a start. Starving. Where was I? Why couldn't I move? Jeremiah lay next to me. His eyes were open and he stared at me.

"How do you feel?"

"Like I've been dragged through hell." It was the only way I could think to describe it. I looked down and saw I was wrapped in the sheet from chin to toes. "Help me get out of this."

"And if I do? What will you do first?" He touched my throat. "I forgot to heal you." He leaned down and slid his tongue over my vein. "That's better."

"Not to me." I inhaled. "I can smell you like I never have before. I'd like more of your blood but you need a bath." I sniffed. "So do I." I wiggled. "Please, Jeremiah. I hate being trapped like this."

"New vampires are always thirsty. You cannot have more of my blood. You took too much last night."

"Too much? Are you all right?"

"Of course." He smiled. "You couldn't help yourself. I understood." He cocked his head. "We still have company. I can hear MacDonald moving around in the other room." He reached for the edge of the sheet and began to unwind it. "I hate to admit it, but he was a help last night. It took both of us to pull you off of me."

"I'm sorry. I don't remember much of what happened after you cut my vein." I sighed. "Except pain."

"*I'm* sorry about the pain but I warned you." He rolled me away from him, pulling at the sheet until my arms came free.

I sat up and jerked at the sheet until I could move my legs as well. "Yes, you did. I do remember yelling. Did I curse?"

"You surprised me. I didn't know you knew such words." He smiled and lifted me into his lap. "You *will* need more blood soon and it can't come from me. I am already weak from the amount I gave you last night to get you started."

"Then where will it come from?" I smoothed a hand over his cheek. His beard was rough and he needed to shave.

"I would be happy to oblige the lady." Robert MacDonald had opened the door.

"Did I forget to bolt that last night?" Jeremiah frowned.

"Apparently." Robert strolled over to stand beside the bed. "You are still pale, Gloriana. Campbell is right. He has given as much as he can until he has fed." He bowed and held out his arm. "Let me be of service. I am willing to let you drink from me." He waved his hand. "Campbell, there can be nothing to bother you about Gloriana taking a sip from my wrist."

"It would bother me to have her drink a single drop of MacDonald blood, sir." Jeremiah set me aside, grabbed his plaid then got out of bed. "I can have a mortal in here in matter of moments."

"In here? From the streets? For her first feeding as a vampire? Are you serious?" Robert shook his head. "A filthy, perhaps pox-ridden mortal? Or mayhap they will carry the plague in here. What will that do to your shifter and his lovely bride, I wonder, when they return?" He sat in the chair he'd left next to the bed the night before. "Are you crazed from blood loss, Campbell?"

"Jeremiah, I don't want to try my first time with a stranger. If you cannot give me blood, let it be from Robert. Please?" I knew this was not what my lover wanted to hear but Robert's words had made me think. I would have to find my food, if vampires called it that, from mortals from now on. Or from other vampires. I could see that Jeremiah was unusually pale. I couldn't remember every detail but I must have required a lot of blood from him in order to be turned.

How did I feel? Strange. Light from the candles seemed brighter. Smells stronger. Which was an unexpected problem. Not all smells were pleasant. We needed clean bed linens for one thing. I remembered Robert's comment about the scent of our love play. Yes, the chamber reeked of sex and it had been two nights since that had last happened. I flushed with embarrassment. Except when I put my hands to my cheeks they weren't warm, merely cool.

"Are you hungry, Gloriana?" Jeremiah swayed next to the bed. "I told Fergus to stay away for two nights because I wasn't sure how this would go. I will have to leave you here alone with MacDonald. I must go outside to hunt for a mortal."

I refused to think about Jeremiah grabbing some poor person against his will and taking his vein. I wondered about hunger. *Was* I hungry? How did that feel now? I touched my stomach. No pains of hunger there. But something throbbed in my throat. A need. And when I looked at Robert I knew he was willing to provide what I craved.

"I don't know if I am hungry or not, Jeremiah. But go. I can see you are weak. Feed, that's what you called it. If Robert is willing, it is out of kindness. You know you can trust me and I trust him. You can read my mind when you come back if you are worried that we will do more than drink blood here." I glanced at Robert. "Would you leave us now, Robert, so I can dress? That will help ease Jeremiah's mind. I don't want to sit around in a sheet while we do this."

"The sheet suits you," Robert smiled when Jeremiah growled. "But get dressed, by all means. Campbell, I want to see this transition through. We made her vampire, by God. Well, *you* did. Now she's one of us. So I can offer a vein. I would do as much for any one of us in need. And you will owe me a favor, Campbell." He chuckled as he strode to the door. "Come into the next room when you are ready, Gloriana. We will do this at the table in front of the fire. See how appropriate we can be?" He shut the bedchamber door behind him.

"I don't like this or him, Gloriana. I could see the way he looked at you. He admires you and your body." Jeremiah pulled on his shirt. "Unfortunately I must go out. I am too weak to do much more than find the first healthy mortal who will be easy to take. I know that is hard for you to understand but it is how we live. Once I have my strength back, we can drink from each other. Last night was unusual. I will teach you the right amount to take for a normal feeding as we go on."

I cast off that ridiculous sheet then ran to put my arms around him. "I hate that I was too greedy. Thank you. I know it wasn't easy for you to give me my heart's desire. I won't ever forget it." I pulled his head down to kiss him. To my shock, my new fangs came down. "Oh! I'm sorry."

"Don't say that. I find they make me want you more. They can emerge when you are excited. Soon you will be able to control them, but when you smell fresh blood that will become more difficult." He kissed me, licking his way into my mouth. Then he put his thumb inside and looked closely. "Very pretty little fangs they are. The older you get, the longer they will become." He kissed me again. "When I return and you have used Robert to your satisfaction we will both bathe and make love as only two vampires can. I can't wait to show you."

"The vampire way." I sighed and leaned against him. "I can't wait either."

"Then let me go and take care of my needs while you take care of yours. Think of my drinking from a mortal and your drinking from Robert as no more than how you used to devour a meat pie. What do you or I care if you make it for me or if I buy it from someone else? What matters is that we are both strong and well fed when we come together." He smiled. "That is what I am telling myself so I won't put a knife to MacDonald's cock before I leave."

"Jeremiah! I have no interest in MacDonald's man part, believe me. His vein? I am starving for it." I shoved back from him. "But only because I can't have yours again yet. Now hurry. I will send him home as soon as I am satisfied that I have had enough to drink." I reached for a dress and donned it hastily, lacing it for modesty. I wasn't going to do anything to encourage Robert's interest in me.

"You do that." Jeremiah finished dressing and strode to the bedchamber door. He turned to look at me when he got there. "I won't read your mind when I get back, Gloriana. I trust you. Let him show you how to go on. MacDonald has proved to be surprisingly helpful. He may want you but he can't have you."

"No, he can't. But he can be a friend. Just as Maggie is my friend. I have made that clear to him before but will do so again." I kissed Jeremiah once more then walked him to the outer door before joining Robert.

"I am likened to your friend Maggie?" Robert dropped his head to the table and knocked it against the wood a few times. "You wound me."

"You heard?" I sat across from him.

"Test your new vampire hearing. Be quiet and listen." He raised his head. "Can you hear your lover's footsteps as he goes down the tunnel to the street?"

"Through the thick door?" I shook my head.

"Listen."

So I shut my mouth and concentrated. To my shock I could hear Jeremiah's boots hitting the stones, then the key turning in the lock before he stepped out into the street.

Other sounds also came to me. The steady dripping of the water from the faucet we never could get to stop leaking. The rustle of a mouse somewhere in the straw where Fergus stored his provisions.

"It is amazing!" I looked around the room. "And the smells. The scent of candles burning. The smoke from the fire. Why, I can even smell the roses in my soap from the bathing room."

"Yes, I saw that room with the tub. You are an unusual woman with your habit of bathing." He smiled and held out his hand. "I like it. I noticed your sweet smell right away."

"And I noticed that you are clean as well. It is uncommon at court." I picked up his wrist and sniffed his vein. Oh, but my new fangs were very interested. "Look, I have fangs!"

"I know, Gloriana. I watched Campbell give them to you." Robert laughed. "It was quite a spectacle. You latched onto him like he was a treat you wanted to devour until every drop was gone. We had to tear you off of him."

"I hardly remember that." I didn't know quite how to go about this. I wanted to bite his vein and taste the blood running through it. Yes, I could smell that too. Was it proper to just have at it? I had his permission. I remembered when Marin had taken my vein there. She had used her tongue first. Just as Jeremiah did to make the pain go away. The idea of doing that to Robert seemed somehow to invite more than a meal. I looked into his eyes and saw his amusement again.

"I'm glad last night isn't clear to you. Now go ahead and lick the spot where you see the blue vein in my wrist. Doing that is only to dull pain. You don't want to hurt me, do you?" He nodded when I pulled his wrist toward my mouth.

I dabbed it with my tongue.

"No, do it right. A long sweep. As if you love my skin and the taste of it." He sighed when I did just that. It was salty and delicious. Oh, I shouldn't think that. Was this really necessary or was he playing with me? "Now take those pretty little fangs and strike. Not gently. Fast, as if my wrist will run away if you don't get it now."

I wanted to, desperately. I scraped his skin but couldn't pierce it, only made faint red lines. "I can't."

He pulled a knife from his sporran. "Here, this will help you get going." He ran it across his wrist and blood welled. "Smell it. Go ahead, lean closer."

I did lean in and the smell was intoxicating. Like the finest wine. Before I could stop myself, I licked it clean. When blood continued to flow I kept licking.

"Woman, you are driving me mad. Keep that up and I will toss your skirt over your head and have Campbell's ire to deal with." Robert gripped my hair and shoved me closer. "Here."

Suddenly my fangs were in his vein. Oh. They soaked up his blood. I swallowed as it filled my mouth. The taste! Delicious. I could feel it giving me strength. I vaguely remembered that last night Jeremiah's blood had done the same. Was it always like this? So heady? So incredible? I gripped his arm drawing until he jerked on my hair to pull me away.

"What?" I looked up, indignant. "I was enjoying that."

"Too much, my little savage." He grinned. "Finish by using your tongue again to close the wound. You will see it disappear. Vampire magic. I'm sure Campbell has shown you that before."

"Of course. But what if I want more?" I looked down. His blood still welled from the two holes I'd made next to his cut. I leaned in again. He pulled my hair to keep me from connecting with it.

"You have had quite enough. Do you want me to be too weak to walk home or shift there? Are you trying to drain me dry?" He tugged on my hair until I looked up at him. "See how pale my face is? Check my eyes. I am fading from blood loss, Gloriana. Know these signs. They mean you must stop or you will kill your source."

"Robert! I am sorry." I pulled up his wrist and licked the wound closed. Yes, it was vampire magic and now I had it too. His wrist showed no signs now that I had ever been at it. Amazing!

"Of course perhaps Jeremiah whispered to you that killing me is his heart's desire. He is your sire now. It would be only natural that you would want to do his bidding." Robert leaned back. He did look very pale and tired.

"I won't kill for him." I felt energized. Full of life. If that was possible. I had a difficult time remembering that I had died last night. I felt strong, stronger than I could have imagined. I had to test it. I stood and picked up the end of the thick oak table, gasping when it lifted easily. "Look at me. I have vampire strength." I gave him a saucy grin. "Will you let me hit you? I would like to see if I can knock you down. Especially after that remark about lifting my skirt. As if I would have allowed it."

"Hit me? After you well-nigh drained me? No, thank you. But that extra strength is because of the blood you just drank. I am over a hundred years old so I can give you power just as Campbell can. When you drink from a mere mortal, you will be able to tell the difference. A mortal's blood is not nearly so heady. It keeps us alive and strengthens us, but has none of the great power that an ancient vampire's blood acquires." He picked up my wrist and held it to his nose.

"I swear you were never a mere mortal even before last night, Gloriana, no matter what you seemed. Your blood was never ordinary. As a vampire?" He smiled. "I won't test Campbell's temper by begging a sample now, but, if you ever part from him, please seek me out. Once you've aged a bit, what a treat you'll be."

"Jeremiah and I will be together forever, so you will just have to forget about sampling me." I took back my wrist and sniffed for myself. My own blood held no allure to me. What could he mean?

"Time for me to find my own mortal." He stood and

strapped on his sword.

"I'm sorry if I got carried away, Robert." I was almost sorry to see him go as well. Who knew when we would meet again? "You have been wonderful. A true friend to me." I hugged him. "If you ever need anything," I tapped his chest and playfully shoved him back when his hold on me tightened, "besides a bedmate, you have only to ask." I walked him to the door. "Will I see you in the Highlands?"

"I will be there, but I doubt we will cross paths. The Campbells and the MacDonalds are mortal enemies. I know Campbell has not told you the reason why and it is not my story to tell. If we see each other, you would do well to pretend not to know me. The Laird would be suspicious if you claimed a friendship with a MacDonald." Robert kissed my cheek. "Trust me, the Laird and his lady never forget or forgive."

"I am sorry to hear that." He *had* become a good friend to me. But I knew better than to ask questions. I looked into his eyes. Could I read his mind? Of course not. He wasn't about to let me see why the Campbells hated the MacDonalds. Jeremiah refused to discuss it.

"Take care, Gloriana. I hope you don't come to regret your decision to join us in eternal night." He bowed and opened the door.

"I won't." I turned the key in the lock once he'd left. I had much to think about. Heading for the Highlands might not be the pleasure trip I had hoped for. Jeremiah's parents seemed to be difficult, from the way they turned their own children vampire, to the grudges they held. I just prayed they didn't take me in dislike. Their son and heir would be bringing home his first fledgling vampire. Perhaps it would be a matter of pride that he'd made his own fledgling. I could only hope.

I filled the kettle and put it over the fire to heat for our bath. I was sure Jeremiah would be back soon and we would enjoy bathing together. Then lovemaking for the first time with both of us vampire. It was something to look forward to.

* * *

"Really, Jeremiah, I cannot believe my new vampire senses." I sat astride him, eager to get on with the next step in my vampire education. So far our lovemaking had been as it always was. Except… I savored the flavor of his skin as I kissed the familiar paths across his body. And everywhere he touched me seemed more sensitive, more eager to be explored. It was like I had been reborn. This Gloriana couldn't yet read his mind, but I somehow sensed what he wanted and moved quickly to bring him pleasure. Now I leaned down to inhale his throat where I knew his vein throbbed. I sat up again. I didn't want to do anything I shouldn't.

"You are very eager, aren't you?" He smiled up at me. "I ran into MacDonald outside our door and he said he had to pull you off his vein or you would have drained him. Still thirsty, my love?"

"Yes. And I'm waiting for this vampire lovemaking you promised me." I felt him throbbing inside me and moved, watching his eyes close with pleasure. "We have done all of this before. Not that I mind it. You always make me feel amazing, my love." I kissed him with all the love in my heart.

He flipped me over so I was staring up at him. "I am very fond of the way we make love. But if you want to know how two vampires may go about this in a special way, you will have it." He was suddenly beside me and we were no longer connected.

"What now?" I leaned up on one elbow. "Do I take your vein?" I touched the one in his neck.

"Remember how Jean-Claude took advantage of the one on your inner thigh?" Jeremiah lost his smile. "The idea that he had done so maddened me. It is the vein I used when we made love later. It should be reserved for lovers with a special bond."

"Even when I was still mortal, it was very exciting. Now…" I realized my heart was quickening at the thought.

"Jeremiah, we do have a special bond. And do you have a vein…" I looked to where his cock stood ready, "there?"

"I do indeed." He showed me the vein inside his thigh so very close to his sacs. "Come here, Gloriana. Lie on me and let me pleasure you, drink from you, while you drink from me. If you think you have felt completion before, my love, you have experienced nothing compared to this." He reached for me.

I crawled over him awkwardly, but of course Jeremiah knew just how to position me to make this work. I was still not sure how to make my tiny fangs strike, but the scent of his blood was strong when I got close to that vein. I stroked his cock as I leaned in and remembered to lick the place where his blood ran inside his thigh. Before I knew it my fangs were in and I was drinking. Gods, the taste. Jeremiah was mine and there was nothing like his blood.

Then he was touching me, his tongue on my own vein before he struck. With the first deep draw, I was lost, my body coming apart as we joined in a new way. Sensation after sensation made me tremble and my hands shook as I remembered to keep touching him. I drank and pushed against him. I'd never felt anything like it. I soared, losing my mind as I gripped Jeremiah's thigh and his cock. When I heard him shout my name, something broke inside me and I fell back, finally releasing him.

He lifted me into his arms and held me against his chest. I heard his heart rumble beneath my cheek as I tried to understand how we could be dead when we breathed, moved, and could give such incredible pleasure to each other. I stroked his stomach and kissed his chin.

"I love you, Jeremiah."

"Lass, you are a wonder. I will always love you." He sighed into my hair. "We are not done. You must always remember to close the wound. Whether you are with me, another vampire or a mortal. It is a courtesy and it is for your own safety that you leave no sign of your use." He gently steered me back to where I had taken him. Yes, blood still oozed from the two small holes. I looked up and saw he was a bit pale. Had I taken too much? He shook his head. Mind reader. When would he teach me how to do that? I gently kissed away the two spots then lay back with my head on his thigh.

"Did you close my wound as well?" I opened my legs. "I don't remember if you did or not. You distracted me."

"I should hope so." He lifted my legs and spent a good long time pleasuring me until I was calling his name.

"Oh, you make me wild," I murmured, my hips moving as he held me. "You are a demon."

He was grinning when he finally dropped me to the bed. "No, you are lucky you haven't met one of those yet." He lay beside me again. "There are many creatures roaming the earth that mere mortals have no idea exist."

"Really. Demons?" I shivered. "And we met a witch. If there are more strange things about, don't tell me yet. I have enough to get used to. I just hope Maggie will accept Fergus and his shape-shifting."

"It will be difficult. If that goes well, he may also try to explain that he works for vampires. It is a lot for a mortal to understand. You accepted it better than most would." Jeremiah traced my nipple with a fingertip. "We live in a secret world. That is why I always erase a mortal's memories when I send them away. The idea of creatures such as we are is too much for them."

"I guess Maggie and Fergus will be here when we wake at sunset tomorrow." I stretched and yawned. "I am beginning to feel tired. Is that what you mean when you say you feel the dawn?"

"It is. So we should get ready to die together, Gloriana." He got up and bolted the bedchamber door. "You are right, I feel the sunrise coming." He lay beside me and pulled up the coverlet. Then he turned and kissed me. "Good night, my love."

I started to say the same but all went dark.

* * *

I woke with a start and looked over to see Jeremiah's eyes open. Sunset. Would I ever get used to this? I would have eternity to do so. I heard sounds coming from the other room. Fergus and Maggie were back. I got up and washed using the basin and pitcher I'd set out the night before. My vampire senses meant I could smell our lovemaking. I wanted a bath but was too curious about Maggie's reaction to Fergus's revelations to wait.

"It's awfully quiet in the other room." Jeremiah watched me pull on a chemise, then a dress. "But I do smell Maggie there. I hope she isn't too upset with him."

"I must learn how to do that, identify mortals by their particular smell." I inhaled and my fangs were down. Mortal blood. My new instincts realized that much. "I sense that there are definitely two different two scents next door. One is very rich and I think it must be Fergus. The other has a hint of my rose-scented soap to it. It is also rich though."

"Fergus has a rich scent because of his shape-shifter blood. He is also fairly old. We don't drink from his kind without permission as a courtesy or unless we have no choice." Jeremiah was on his feet and his hand landed on my shoulder. "Maggie's blood is rich because she is with child. I would never drink from a mortal woman carrying a child."

"Oh, of course not." I turned to face him. "I wouldn't want to hurt the babe."

"But that blood is very tempting." He touched my lips where my fangs were thrusting against them. "Look at you. If you went into that room right now you would scare Maggie."

"Am I to lock myself in here forever?" I told my fangs to go away. I closed my eyes and willed them to retreat. But when I touched them with my tongue they were still there, sharp and, yes, terrifying to a woman like my friend.

"Concentrate, my love. You couldn't possibly be hungry. You fed twice last night. You don't *need* her blood. It is unreasonable to want more now." He pulled me close.

"I know." I leaned against his chest and fought tears.

"What's wrong with me, Jeremiah?"

"You are a fledgling. This wild thirst is normal. But you must control it."

"I'm trying!" I held onto him. He was so strong, so in control of himself. Gods, but I hoped I would find that strength of will. He ran his hand up and down my back and murmured love words, trying to soothe me.

"You can do it. You are very strong. I have seen it. Brave girl. Now think. You are not really needful of a mortal's blood and you want to check on your friend. She surely had a bad day and night yesterday."

"Yes. She will need my support if she saw Fergus shift for the first time. Her world has been turned upside down. I remember how I felt when I saw it for myself. And she is carrying his child." I straightened my back and stepped away from him. "I am not some mindless creature. I am Gloriana St. Clair. Strong." I breathed, in and out, telling myself that I could do this. But every breath brought a whiff of that seductive mortal blood to me. Oh, blast! I couldn't, wouldn't drink from Maggie. "Can I stop breathing while I am in the room with her?"

"Yes, you can. Stop. Right now." He smiled down at me. "Clever girl."

I tried. But I'd had a lifetime habit of it. Just shutting my mouth didn't work. I certainly couldn't hold my nose while I was with her. I shook my head. "Good idea but I am too new at this." I walked over to the door. "Get dressed. If I fail to keep my fangs hidden, you may have to come rescue me and erase Maggie's memories."

"I can do that." He reached for his plaid. "You did make your fangs disappear."

"For now." I was glad of that. "Do you think he told her that we are vampires?"

"I doubt it. It would be too much at once." He shook his head. "Try to think of other things while you are with her, Gloriana. I will tell the king we are leaving for the Highlands in a few days. He is leaving soon anyway. I'm sure he won't object."

"Then I am definitely going with you. I am so glad to have that to look forward to, it will fill my thoughts. Thank you, Jeremiah." I walked back to kiss him. "Robert says your parents are a challenge."

"He's right. But I expect them to welcome you. I will insist on it." He dipped a cloth in the basin. "Go, check on your friend. I will be out in a moment."

"Wish me luck." I checked one more time with a fingertip. No fangs.

"You don't need luck. You are amazing. I know you will be fine." He winked at me as he washed his chest. I stopped, as usual interested in watching him. "Go or we will never leave this bed."

"Not a bad idea." I had to face Maggie sometime so I opened the door and stepped into the other room.

The first smell to hit me was chocolate. Maggie sat at the table sipping a steaming cup of hot chocolate. I inhaled and had a fleeting thought of how much I would miss it. I had to be glad though that it masked the scent of her blood. I studied her face. She looked upset. No surprise there. Fergus was busy polishing Jeremiah's blades. Since they were already gleaming, I knew this was an excuse for them not to talk.

"Good evening." I stayed close to the fire, another smell that helped me keep my fangs at bay.

"Gloriana." Maggie jumped up and ran to me, throwing her arms around me. "Did you know? About Fergus and what he can do?"

"Maggie! Yes, I knew." I practically threw her at Fergus, who was behind her in an instant. Oh, Gods, but I could certainly smell her now. I turned to face the fire. No, no, no! This couldn't be happening. "Of course I knew. Tell me what he did." I said this to the flames while I fought my base urges. I was not hungry. Not.

"He showed me how he could change into the most fearsome beast or the sweetest lamb." She was trembling as she took his hand. He led her back to the table. "I couldn't believe my eyes."

"She was verra brave, Gloriana." Fergus stayed behind her, his hands on her shoulders as he forced her into a chair. He eyed me as if ready to fight if I made a move toward her. I turned to face her but kept a hand over my mouth. Fergus read my mind easily enough and nodded. "She has accepted me for what I am. It was all I was willing to burden her with yesterday."

"Fergus, you are not a burden." Maggie grasped his hand. "It is passing strange, but I understand you cannot help how you are born." She glanced at me. "Gloriana, are you ill? Come, sit at the table. I have more of this delicious chocolate if you want some."

"No, thank you. I have fed." I turned away again. "I am thinking about a warm bath." I reached for the kettle. "Fergus, would you fill the tub?"

"In a moment. I don't want to leave Maggie just now." He tilted his head, silently telling me he wouldn't leave her alone with me. I understood.

"Fergus, you shouldn't neglect your duties. I am fine." Maggie sighed. "Gloriana, did you know the babe I carry could have the same talents Fergus has? What if I end up with a child who could do such tricks?" She rubbed her eyes. "It is hard for me to understand."

"Of course it is." I sat across from her and took her hand. This was my friend and she needed me. "But it is a wonderful thing. Fergus saved me when he turned into a bear once. And his cousin Bran was that mastiff in the market that kept me from being taken by thieves and perhaps sold into a brothel." I wanted to convince her that shape-shifting could be a wondrous gift.

"Was he indeed?" Maggie's eyes widened. "Gloriana! What is wrong with your mouth?" She wrenched her hand from mine. "Your teeth! Fergus! What else aren't you telling me?"

"Nothing, my love. You are tired and it's making you

see things that aren't there. You got little sleep last night. You tossed and turned and kept crying out with bad dreams." Fergus pulled her up into his arms and pressed her face to his chest. "Gloriana, why not go into the bathing room and start filling the tub yourself? I will bring you hot water."

"I know what I saw." Maggie pulled out of his arms. "What is happening to you, Gloriana?" She stared at me but I had covered my face with my hands again.

"She has to be told, Fergus." Jeremiah stood next to the table.

I hadn't heard him come in. "No! She will think us monsters."

"Are you? Monsters?" Maggie was shaking. "Fergus, I will have the truth. I am having your child. Are you risking both of us by keeping us here?"

"It is my job to keep Jeremiah and now Gloriana safe during the day, Maggie mine. I am paid well for it." Fergus tried to pull her to his side again but she refused to let him touch her. "You have said more than once that you don't understand the hours they keep."

"No, I don't. Sleeping the day away, staying awake all night instead." Maggie stepped closer to me. "And now you look strange, Gloriana."

"Step back, Maggie. It's not safe to be so close to me." I hated to say it. But her blood. Gods, her blood. It throbbed through her veins, calling to me. I would never allow myself to drink from her. I reached for Jeremiah's hand and he held onto me, ready to hold me back if necessary.

"What are you saying?" She looked from me to Jeremiah. "Why would I not be safe with my best friend?"

"I am now like Jeremiah, Maggie. It was my choice. We are vampires. Night creatures. We, um, drink blood to survive." I pressed my hands over my eyes so I wouldn't have to see the horror in hers. "I can smell your blood, my friend, and am desperate for it. But I'll die before I touch a drop of it. I swear it." I sobbed and ran out of the room.

"Gloriana!" Maggie's voice followed me. Everything was so loud now. I heard Jeremiah talking to Fergus, urging him to take Maggie outside to explain more about us and his duties.

Jeremiah's footsteps were loud as he walked into the room where I had started filling the bathing tub. He carried the kettle of hot water.

"She will be all right."

"Will she?" I dumped the last bucket into the tub then stripped off my dress. I felt dirty, ashamed and out of control. Who was I now? I had wanted to dive for Maggie's vein and drink until she had nothing left to give. I climbed into the tub and sighed as the water reached my chest. If I put my head underwater, would I drown? Of course not. There was no way out of this misery.

"Fergus assured me that she loves you and wants to believe you would never hurt her. She has been here for more than a month and has seen nothing to alarm her." Jeremiah threw down his plaid and climbed in with me.

"Until now." I knew we were testing her friendship.

"Maggie is a very practical woman. You heard how she has accepted life with a shape-shifter. Even the idea of being mother to a babe who may well have the same talent, as she called it, hasn't sent her running."

"Yes, that surprised me." I reached for my rose-scented soap. I was also a practical woman. That thought went a long way toward making me decide that moping about, wondering if I had made a poor decision when I'd become vampire, was not only futile, but stupid. I inhaled the floral scent then ran it over my breasts before I grabbed Jeremiah's plainer soap and tossed it to him. "Maggie is so grateful for her new life, she may well decide that working for a pair of vampires is worth the security it brings her."

"Aye. Fergus is fairly sure those will be her thoughts exactly." Jeremiah rinsed and laid his soap on the table beside the tub. "Do we smell better now?"

"Yes." I rinsed and stood, reaching for a dry cloth. "I

have been thinking about shape-shifting. I think I will wait a while to try it. Fergus mentioned once that he knew of a vampire who had trouble with it." I reached for a dry cloth. "I won't risk being stuck half bird, half woman."

"I thought you were brave enough to try anything." Jeremiah watched me dry my body then grabbed his own cloth. "But I certainly like the shape you are in now."

"So do I and there is no reason to hurry. I have forever to explore my new powers, do I not?" I patted away the last of the water and let down my hair.

"Yes, you do." Jeremiah smiled. "So what would you like to learn first?"

"Mind reading." I pushed against him, skin to skin, then looked down. "Some things are too obvious. Clearly there is no need to read your mind to see that you want me yet again."

"You are right." He held me close. "So you want to just read *my* mind?"

"I want to be able to get into the mind of every person I meet."

"I doubt you will like what you find there, Gloriana. Most people are a dead bore, worrying about their next meal or whether their lover is seeing another. You could also come to regret knowing how they think of you. Take Lord Summers." Jeremiah traced a line up my arm to my neck.

"No, thank you. I'm sure his mind is a horrible place."

"You're right. I am still haunted by what that bastard wanted to do to you when I ran into him at court." Jeremiah looked thunderous. "He asked me if I'd tired of you yet. It was all I could do not to run him through. Too bad he has family the king holds dear."

"Promise me you won't kill to protect me, Jeremiah. It would upset me." I stepped back and wrapped a dry cloth around me, then pulled him toward our bedchamber.

"I cannot promise you that." He stopped in the doorway when I began stripping the bed. "What are you doing?"

"Putting on fresh bed linens. This new vampire sense of smell is turning out to be a nuisance." I took fresh ones from the chest at the foot of the bed. "Help me with this." I tossed a sheet to him. "Now why can't you promise not to kill to protect me?" I stood across from him, pulling the sheet and the coverlet straight. "Jeremiah?"

He looked across the bed, his face very solemn. "This I vow. As long as we live, and that should be forever, I will be your sire and your protector. To me that means I will do whatever it takes to keep you safe. If that requires a killing, so be it."

I just stared at him. I didn't like the sound of this. For him or for me. Had I really understood what I was asking when I'd made him turn me vampire? Perhaps not. But it was done now and could not be undone. I crawled across our made bed, glad that it now smelled sweet from the herbs Maggie had tucked into the chest.

"I love you, Jeremiah, and I pray you never regret this." I kissed him with all the passion in my heart and soul. When I finally drew back, I knew my fangs were down. Yes, I wanted him in every way.

"Here is my own vow. I will try not to become a burden to you. If it seems as if I have become one? Then I will let you go." I laid my hand over my heart to show I meant every word.

"Enough of this solemn talk." He tossed me onto the bed. "The only burden I see in this room is that cloth hiding your body." He jerked it away. "Now let me love you and I will show you how to read my mind. First, stare into my eyes…"

I looked up and saw love and a promise. Forever. Was it too much to ask? Time would tell.

What happens when
Gloriana gets to the Highlands?

Watch for
Real Vampires:
A Highland Christmas

Coming Fall, 2018.

If this is your first experience with the **Real Vampires** series, welcome! Here's a complete list of the series and thanks for reading! You can always come to my website at **http://gerrybartlett.com** for more information about the series or to sign up for my newsletter. My email address is also there. Hope to hear from you!

Gerry Bartlett

Real Vampires have Curves
Real Vampires Live Large
Real Vampires Get Lucky
Real Vampires Don't Diet
Real Vampires Hate Their Thighs
Real Vampires Have More to Love
Real Vampires Don't Wear Size Six
Real Vampires Hate Skinny Jeans
Real Vampires Know Hips Happen
Real Vampires Know Size Matters
Real Vampires Take a Bite Out of Christmas (Novella)
Real Vampires Say Read My Hips
Real Vampires and the Viking
Real Vampires: When Glory Met Jerry

Rafe and the Redhead—Spinoff about Rafael Valdez

ABOUT THE AUTHOR

Gerry Bartlett is the nationally bestselling author of the Real Vampires series, featuring Glory St.Clair, a curvy vampire who wishes she'd known she'd be stuck in that full-figured body when she was turned in 1604. Gerry is a native Texan and lives halfway between Houston and Galveston where she has an antiques business that lets her indulge her shopping addiction. You can see her purse collection on Pinterest.

Would she like to be a vampire? No way. She's too addicted to Mexican food and sunlight. You can reach her on http://gerrybartlett.com or follow her and her dog Jet on Facebook, twitter or Instagram. Her latest release is *Real Vampires: When Glory Met Jerry* (Real Vampires #13) available now.

Want to try something without fangs? Gerry also writes contemporaries and romantic suspense for Kensington's Lyrical Shine line. Look for the Texas Heat series: *Texas Heat*, *Texas Fire* and *Texas Pride*, available wherever e-books are sold. Coming November, 2018, *Texas Lightning*, a romantic suspense set in Austin.

Made in the USA
Lexington, KY
12 August 2019